A KISS IN THE DARK

Once on the terrace, he steered her toward the end where a large trellis supported a profusion of roses. She took one sip of wine before he set the glasses on the stone balustrade.

"Thea," he whispered as he caught her to him, his lips descending to hers. "I've wanted to do this all evening."

She wrapped her arms around his neck, pulling him closer and opening her mouth to his. Sliding her fingers to his face, she tilted her head, deepening their kiss as his palms and fingers elicited a spiraling heat that struck her to her core.

When he broke the kiss, she whispered, "Dom, I want more."

His tongue teased a sensitive spot near her ear. "More what?"

She rubbed her hands over his chest. "I am not sure. I thought you might know. . . ."

Books by Ella Quinn

Published by Kensington Publishing Corporation

When A
MARQUIS CHOOSES
A BRIDE

ELLA
QUINN

ZEBRA BOOKS
KENSINGTON PUBLISHING CORP.
http://www.kensingtonbooks.com

ZEBRA BOOKS are published by

Kensington Publishing Corp.
119 West 40th Street
New York, NY 10018

All Kensington titles, imprints, and distributed lines are available at special quantity discounts for bulk purchases for sales promotion, premiums, fund-raising, educational, or institutional use.

Special book excerpts or customized printings can also be created to fit specific needs. For details, write or phone the office of the Kensington Sales Manager: Attn.: Sales Department. Kensington Publishing Corp., 119 West 40th Street, New York, NY 10018. Phone: 1-800-221-2647.

Zebra and the Z logo Reg. U.S. Pat. & TM Off.

First Printing: September 2016
ISBN-13: 978-1-4201-3957-0
ISBN-10: 1-4201-3957-6

eISBN-13: 978-1-4201-3958-7
eISBN-10: 1-4201-3958-4

10 9 8 7 6 5 4 3 2 1

Printed in the United States of America

Chapter One

Early afternoon sun poured through the windows of the large airy schoolroom in Stern Manor. The space was filled with bookcases, four desks, two sofas, and sundry toys.

Miss Dorothea Stern sat on the larger of the much-used sofas, threading a strand of rose silk through her embroidery needle. She had one more Damask rose to complete before the slippers she was making for her mother were finished.

But no matter how hard she tried, she could not escape the fact that the neighborhood was sadly flat now that her best friend, Lady Charlotte Carpenter, was gone. For years, they had planned to come out together, just as they had done everything else since they were in leading strings.

In the meantime, there was a great deal to keep Dotty busy. Since her mother's accident, she had taken up Mama's duties. Dotty enjoyed visiting their tenants, talking to the children and their mothers, and finding ways to help them.

"Dotty," her six-year-old sister, Martha, whined, "Scruffy won't stay still."

Scruffy, a three-legged dog Dotty had saved from a hunter's trap, was resisting Martha's efforts to tie a ribbon on him. "Sweetie, boys don't like frills. Put it on your doll instead."

Fifteen-year-old Henrietta glanced up from the book she was reading. "She took it off the doll."

"Henny," Dotty asked, "aren't you supposed to be practicing your harp?"

Her sister stuck her tongue out. "No, I'm supposed to be reading *Ovid* in Greek."

Their father, Sir Henry, was a classical scholar and had been a rector before his older brother's death a few years ago. Much to Henny's dismay, he had decided to teach all the children Latin and Greek.

Dotty took in the book her sister held. The marble cover was a trademark of the Minerva Press novels. "*That* is not *Ovid*."

Puffing out a breath of air, Henny rolled her eyes. "Aren't ladies supposed to be fashionably stupid?"

"No, they are supposed to appear stupid," Dotty replied tartly. "Which is completely ridiculous. I refuse to marry a gentleman who thinks women should not have brains."

"If that's the case, you may become a spinster," Henny shot back.

"Lord Worthington likes that Grace is clever." Dotty resisted a smug smile. "I'm sure there must be other gentlemen who believe as he does."

Charlotte's older sister, Grace, was now the Countess of Worthington. She had taken all five of the younger children with her to London for Charlotte's come out. Shortly after arriving in Town, Grace had met and fallen in love with Mattheus, Earl of Worthington. They had wed three weeks later.

Not long ago, Grace and her new husband had returned to Stanwood Hall for a few days so that Lord Worthington, who was now guardian to her brothers and sisters, as well as his own sisters, could inspect the property.

Before Henny could retort, the door opened. "Miss"—

Dotty's maid, Polly, glanced around the room, her gaze settling on Dotty—"Her Ladyship asked me to come fetch you."

Dotty pulled the thread through, secured the needle, and set the slipper down. "Is she all right?"

"Oh yes, miss." Polly bounced from foot to foot. "She got a letter from London and sent for you straightaway."

Dotty hurried to the door. "I hope everything is all right." There was nothing wonderful in receiving a letter from London. Practically everyone they knew was in Town for the Season. Mama and Dotty should have been there as well, yet the day before their planned departure her mother had slipped and broken her leg.

"No, miss," the maid said as she hurried after her. "Her ladyship was smiling."

"Well, I suppose the sooner I get to her, the sooner I shall find out what she wants." A minute later, she knocked on the door to her mother's parlor and entered. "Mama, what is it?"

Waving a sheet of paper in her hand, her mother smiled broadly. "Unexpected and wonderful news. You shall have your Season after all!"

Dotty's jaw dropped. She snapped it shut and made her way over to a chair next to her mother. "I don't understand. I thought Grandmamma Bristol couldn't sponsor me because of Aunt Mary's confinement."

"This"—Mama waved the letter through the air again—"is from Grace."

Dotty's heart began to beat faster, and she clasped her hands together. "What—what does she say?"

"After dear Charlotte received your missive telling her you could not come to Town for your Season, she prevailed upon Grace to invite you. She says"—Mama adjusted her spectacles—"having you would be no bother at all. She is bringing out Charlotte and Lady Louisa Vivers, Worthington's sister, you know, and one more in a household of ten children will hardly be remarkable. She comments that your good sense will be very welcome." Mama glanced up. "Not that I disagree with her. You do have a great deal of sagacity, but I am sure Grace said that for Papa's benefit. You know how he does not like to be obliged to anyone." Mama went back to the letter. "And it would be a great shame for you not to come out with Charlotte as you girls have planned for years." Mama set the paper down with a flourish and grinned. "What do you think of *that?*"

For what seemed like a long time, Dotty could think of nothing. Her mind had never gone blank before. It was almost too good to be true. She shook her head, and finally managed to find an answer. "I never thought . . . Well, I mean I knew Charlotte was going to ask Grace, but I never even imagined that Lord Worthington would agree. Although her last letter said she missed me dreadfully. Lady Louisa, Worthington's sister, even wrote to me saying she had heard so much about me that she felt as if she already knew me and wished I was going to be in Town."

Suddenly, the fact that Dotty was actually going to Town hit her. "I really am going to have a Season!" She jumped up, rushed to her mother, and hugged her. "I wish you could be there as well."

Mama patted Dotty's back. "Yes, my dear. I wish I could go too, but Grace will take good care of you."

"When shall we tell Papa of Grace's offer?" What if her father refused to allow her to go? That would be horrible. "I'm not sure he will be as happy as we are."

Her mother glanced briefly at the ceiling and let out a sigh of long-suffering. "If he had his way, you would not come out until you were at least twenty. He has gone somewhere. I left a message to have him attend me as soon as he returns." She pushed herself up against the pillows. "We have no time to lose. There is so much to discuss. Polly," Mama said to Dotty's maid hovering in the door, "have the trunks brought down from the attic and start getting Miss Dotty's clothes together."

"Yes, your ladyship."

Once the door closed, Mama leaned forward a little and lowered her voice. "Papa will dislike the idea of you going to London without me at first, but don't worry, dear, I'll talk him round."

Dotty sat back down and folded her hands in her lap. They trembled a little with excitement. She was really going to be able to come out with her best friend in the whole world! "I should write to Charlotte and Grace to thank them."

"Yes, after it is all settled." Mama opened her pocket-book and wet the tip of the pencil with her tongue. "We must think of who will accompany you. Papa will not allow you to travel with only Polly to look after you. I believe Mrs. Parks said her sister was going to Town to visit a friend. I shall ask if she will look after you. After all, it will save her the trouble of booking and paying for another coach."

Dotty nodded. "Yes, Mama. I believe Miss Brownly is leaving in a few days. She planned to take the mail."

"Then she will be glad for a chance to ride in a private coach and break the journey at a good hostelry. Run along now and help Polly. I shall send for you after I have spoken with Papa."

Dotty kissed her mother before running in a very unlady-like fashion up the stairs to her room. Four trunks already stood open and her wardrobe cabinet was empty. She started folding the clothes she found on her bed. "Polly, I do hope Mama prevails."

The maid paused to think for a moment. "I don't think Sir Henry has a hope against her ladyship." She gave a decisive nod. "She'll get her way."

Dotty smiled. Her mother usually did. "Still . . . I'll feel much better when I know for sure that I'll be going."

* * *

Two hours later, Sir Henry Stern frowned at the letter in his hand as he ambled into his wife's parlor. "This is from Lord Worthington. I suppose you have one from Grace."

Lady Stern smiled. She loved her husband dearly, but there were times his self-sufficiency went too far. She had no intention of allowing him to spoil Dotty's Season. "I do indeed. I do not think I have ever been so pleased for Dorothea. She and Charlotte have dreamed of their come out for years, and all the new gowns we bought for her . . . Well, I would hate for them to go to waste."

Her husband appeared unconvinced. "Worthington promises to take care of Dotty as he would his sister Lady Louisa and Charlotte"—his scowl deepened—"but, Cordelia, we would be entrusting her to his care. *In London*. And we do not know him that well."

"Henry"—Cordelia used her most patient tone—"we know Grace, and Worthington was perfectly amiable when she invited us to Stanwood Hall to dine during the few days they were here. He has a good reputation. Nothing smoky about him at all, as Harry would say." Her husband's lips folded together, and Cordelia rushed on. "Besides, Grace would not have trusted him with *her* brothers and sisters if he were not a good man."

"But looking after three young ladies?"

She almost laughed at the look of horror on his face.

"You forget Jane Carpenter, Grace's cousin, is still with them, and the Dowager Lady Worthington as well. The girls will be well chaperoned, and Grace commented on Dotty's good sense."

"Yes, well." He glanced at the missive and drew his brows together so that they touched. "As the Season is well under way, Lord Worthington asks for an immediate reply. I suppose I should write to him."

Cordelia smiled again. "Does that mean you'll allow Dorothea to go?"

A bit of humor entered her husband's eyes. "I know you,

my love. If I say no, I will never hear the end of it. You are every bit as determined as your mother. How do you propose Dotty make the journey?"

"You cannot complain about that, my dear. If we were not strong-willed, you and I would never have been allowed to marry." Cordelia struggled to keep the triumph out of her voice. It was fortunate that the Sterns had been friends with the Carpenters for generations. "I shall make all the arrangements."

"Very well, then. I know you'll send Dotty off as soon as possible. I do want a word with her."

"Of course, my love." Cordelia tugged the bell pull and called for her daughter.

Dotty's steps faltered as she entered Papa's study. Her stomach lurched as she took in his grim countenance. He was not going to allow her to go to Town. She may as well make the best of it. Getting into a state would not help. She took a breath and readied herself for the bad news. "Yes?"

"Your father wishes to speak to you." She whipped her head around, seeing her mother lying on a sofa. This must be important if Mama had had herself moved.

Papa came around from behind his desk and took Dotty by her shoulders. "You may join Charlotte for your Season. However, you know my feelings about this. You are still young, and there is no reason you must marry anytime soon."

She kept her face as serious as her father's. "I know, Papa."

He cleared his throat. "If a young man is interested in you, have him apply to Lord Worthington first. He will know best if the gentleman is suitable."

Dotty nodded. Relief and excitement rushed through her. Yet her father wasn't done yet. She waited for him to continue.

"With the number of inhabitants already in Worthington's

household, and the dogs, you must promise me not to bring stray animals or people to Stanwood House. They won't appreciate it."

"I promise, Papa."

"Now, I must make sure the coach is ready."

As soon as her father closed the door, she gave a little shriek and hugged her mother. "Oh, Mama! Thank you so much. I shall never be able to repay you."

She patted Dotty's cheek. "Yes, you will, by having fun. Though mind what your father said. With all those children and *two* Great Danes, the Worthingtons do not need three-legged dogs or half-blind cats, not to mention homeless children."

"Yes, Mama. I'll do my best." Dotty grinned.

Everyone loved Scruffy. The cat was the best mouser they'd ever had, and Benjy was turning into a fine groom. People and animals only needed a chance in life. Nevertheless, her parents had a point. Bringing strays home to Stern Manor was one thing, taking them to someone else's house quite another matter altogether. Dotty said a quick prayer that she would not meet anyone in need of help.

Chapter Two

Dominic, Marquis of Merton, settled into his apartment at the Pulteney Hotel. His pride still stung at having been ejected from his cousin, Matt Worthington's, town house. Blowing a cloud was the latest thing. Not that Dom would attempt to smoke in White's, that was not allowed, but he outranked Worthington and should have been treated as an honored guest, not summarily told to leave. Still, it was probably convenient that Dom did not actually enjoy smoking, as he was sure the Pulteney would not allow it either.

He should have gone on his Grand Tour instead of taking a bolt to Town. But his mother had received a letter informing her of his cousin's plans to wed, and he decided starting his own nursery would be the most responsible course. After all, the succession would not look after itself, and he had a duty to his family and dependents. Perhaps he would travel after he married.

Not that Dom truly wished to leave England. He liked an ordered life and travel was sure to disrupt the structure with which he was comfortable. He did not wish to visit France at all. Any land where the inhabitants would murder their betters held little interest for him. It all came back to the proper order of things. Life was much better when everyone followed the rules and knew their places.

He reconsidered opening up Merton House for the Season, but there was really no point when his mother was not here as well. Without her to act as his hostess, he would not be able to plan any entertainments other than for his friends. The hotel would suit for the short time he planned to spend in Town. It should not take him that long to find a wife. He was a marquis. Even without his considerable fortune, he would have been a desirable *parti*.

"Kimbal," he called to his valet.

"Yes, my lord."

"I shall be dining at White's."

"Yes, my lord."

Dom scribbled a note to his friend Viscount Fotherby asking if he would like to join Dom for dinner. By the time he was dressed and had donned his hat, Fotherby's answer affirming the invitation had arrived.

A short while later, just as a light sprinkle turned into a persistent rain, Dom handed his hat and cane to the footman at White's and found his friend lounging in the room that held the club's famous betting book. William Alvanley, another of Dom's friends, was seated next to the window with another man staring intently at the rain.

He turned to Fotherby. "What are they doing?"

"Five thousand quid on which raindrop will reach the bottom of the sill first."

Despite being close with many of the Prince Regent's circle, Dom could not abide the excessive wagers his friends made. Alvanley would end up ruining himself and his estates at the rate he was going. "Are you ready to dine, or are you awaiting the outcome?"

"Famished." Fotherby tossed off his glass of wine. "Thought you weren't coming to Town this year."

"My plans changed." Dom and Fotherby entered the dining room. "I have decided to take a wife."

"Wife?" Fotherby choked. "Any idea who?"

"Not yet, but I have a list of qualifications. She must be well-bred, not given to fits of temper or strange starts, quiet, biddable, easy to look at—I must get an heir on her after all—know what is expected of a marchioness. And not prone to scandals. You know how my uncle hated them. I think that about covers it."

"A paragon, in other words."

Dom gave a curt nod. "Indeed. I could wed no one less."

Dotty arrived at Stanwood House in Berkeley Square, Mayfair, just after three o'clock in the afternoon. From the letters she'd received from Charlotte, it appeared that the Carpenters and Viverses were getting along well. Louisa's mother, the Dowager Countess of Worthington, was also living with them. Lord Worthington, however, was the sole guardian of his four sisters.

Royston, the Stanwood butler, opened the door, and Dotty was almost bowled over by a sea of children and the Carpenters' Great Dane, Daisy.

"We saw your coach arrive," one of the children shouted.

Daisy, tried to wrap herself around Dotty as Charlotte and a young lady with dark chestnut hair, Dotty guessed to be Louisa, hurried forward. Dotty laughed. "I didn't know I would receive such an ecstatic welcome."

A deep bark came from the side of the hall.

"That is Duke," Charlotte said over the roar.

"Enough." Lord Worthington's commanding tone had everyone except Charlotte and Louisa, backing away from the door. "Let her in the house."

Once the younger children had moved out of the way, his lordship, a tall, broad-shouldered gentleman with the same dark hair as his sister, came forward holding Grace's hand. They made a beautiful couple. Grace, with her gold hair, was a perfect foil for her husband.

"I did say we were looking forward to you joining us." Grace laughed as she hugged Dotty.

"Yes, you did." She grinned. It was wonderful to be with the Carpenters again. "That was quite a welcome."

Charlotte threw her arms around Dotty. "I'm so glad you're here. This is Louisa, Matt's sister and my new sister." Charlotte pulled a face. "Not technically, of course, but we had to call each other something."

Dotty held out her hand to Louisa but got kissed on the cheek instead.

"I am so happy to finally meet you." Louisa smiled. "The three of us are going to be the best of friends and have such a wonderful time."

Dotty remembered she had not yet greeted his lordship. He took the hand Dotty held out, yet when she would have curtseyed, he held her up. "There is no point in standing on ceremony here. Call me Matt. All the other children do."

"Thank you, sir. I can't tell you how happy I am to be here *and* that you wrote my father."

Before he could respond, Charlotte grabbed Dotty's hand. "We must show you to your room. It is next to mine. We'll let you clean up and change. Then we'll have tea before taking a stroll in the Park. Louisa and I have our own parlor, and now it will be yours as well."

Dotty followed her friend up the stairs. "After two days of sitting in a coach, I would love a walk."

"I completely understand." Louisa linked her arm with Dotty's. "I don't know how one can want to *rest,* when one has been cooped up in a carriage for more than a day."

Charlotte and Louisa showed Dotty where the small parlor was located and then escorted her to her chamber. Once there, she was left alone to splash her face and wash her hands.

Polly came in from a door to what must be a dressing

room. "Here you are, miss." She hung up a pink muslin walking gown and paisley spencer. "Let's get you changed."

A few minutes later Dotty entered the parlor and found Louisa and Charlotte looking over fashion plates.

"Come and tell me what you think of this." Charlotte patted the seat next to her.

She handed Dotty a picture of a lady in a cream ball gown decorated with lace. Charlotte had the same coloring as Grace, and Dotty thought it would look lovely on her friend. "Very pretty."

The tea arrived a few minutes later. Once they all had cups and a plate of biscuits, she was told about all the balls and other entertainments she could look forward to, including Louisa and Charlotte's come out ball.

"Grace and Mama agreed the ball will be in your honor as well." Louisa beamed, apparently not minding a bit that she would have to share her ball with yet another lady.

Dotty finished off a ratafia biscuit. "It will be so much fun. I can't wait to see everything. You two have such an advantage over me."

All her dreams had come true. Although she'd received letters from Louisa proclaiming her friendship, Dotty really had not believed it until now. It would have been difficult if Louisa had taken it into her head not to like Dotty.

Before long, they were walking out the door to the Park with three footmen following a discreet distance behind.

Strolling in between her two friends, she commented, "Mama said she always had a maid with her when she walked in Town."

"Matt says footmen are more practical," Louisa responded. "If one of us is injured he can carry us home, whereas a maid cannot."

"And," Charlotte added, "if we go shopping they can carry packages more easily."

They arrived at the path around Hyde Park, which Dotty was told was referred to as "the Park."

Charlotte made a funny face. "One is supposed to pretend that one always knows everything and play at *ennui,* but I think that's nonsense. Why act as if you are not having fun, when you are?"

"It does not make much sense to me either." Dotty sighed. "Here I thought I was ready, but instead I have such a lot to learn."

"It was the same for Louisa and me," Charlotte assured her. "You will catch on quickly."

A few moments later, they were hailed by two stylishly dressed gentlemen whom Charlotte and Louisa obviously knew. They stopped, allowing the men to approach.

"Miss Stern," Charlotte said primly. "May I present Lords Harrington and Bentley. My lords, a friend of mine from home, Miss Stern. She will be residing with us for the Season."

Both men bowed over the hand Dotty held out. Thank Heavens for all the lessons in deportment she and Charlotte had shared. Dotty curtseyed. "I am pleased to meet you, my lords."

The gentlemen accompanied the ladies for a short while, begging them for dances at tomorrow night's ball. Once they had gone, Dotty gave herself a small shake. "I cannot believe I am already engaged for two sets."

"They are very nice, aren't they?" Charlotte blushed.

Louisa glanced slyly at Charlotte. "I think Lord Harrington will ask to court Charlotte."

"Well, from the looks of it, Lord Bentley is quite smitten with you," she retorted.

"I wish he would not be." Louisa cast her eyes skyward. "He is a good man, but not one I wish to marry."

In the short time Dotty had known Louisa it was clear poor Lord Bentley was not up to her weight. She would need someone older and more sure of himself.

Dotty took Charlotte's hand and squeezed it. "How do you feel about Lord Harrington?"

Charlotte's face became even redder. "He is very charming, but Grace says to give it time."

They resumed ambling on the side of the path. Suddenly there was a commotion and a shout from behind. Dotty whirled around. A small dog had grabbed the tassel on a man's boot and was backing up growling with its tail wagging, trying to shake its prize loose. Foolishly, the man kept kicking out at the dog, making the animal think he was playing.

She put a hand over her mouth to keep from giggling, yet when he lifted his cane to strike the poor little thing, she rushed forward. "Here now, sir! What do you think you're doing?" She bent to the dog who turned out to be nothing more than a puppy. Turning to the man, she narrowed her eyes and scowled. "Shame on you."

Dotty worked on releasing the tassel from the puppy's grip, but each time the man shook his leg, trying to get the animal off, the puppy held on harder, growling and shaking his head. "Stop moving. Are you so stupid you cannot see the dog thinks you are trying to play?"

"Get him off me," the man shouted in a voice growing higher in fright. "Someone will pay for this. Is he your beast?"

Determined to ignore him, she counted to ten, took a breath, and finally managed to release the gold bobble from the puppy's sharp teeth. "There now." Picking up the dog, she stroked its wiry fur. "Where is your master?"

Just then, two school-aged boys came running up. "Oh, miss. Thank you so much. We've been looking for Bennie all over. He got away from us."

By this time Bennie was snapping at the ribbons of her bonnet. Dotty laughed as she tried to free them. "Here now, sir. Those are not for you either." She saved the ribbons and handed the puppy to one of the boys.

"We'll pay you for the damage, miss."

"It's no bother." She smiled at both of them. "Use the money to buy a lead. That will keep Bennie from running away."

"He's only twelve weeks old," the other boy said proudly. "We didn't think he could run so fast."

"Or so far," added the other.

"Thank you," they both said in unison.

Ah, well. Puppies would be puppies and boys would be boys. "Run along now, and keep Bennie out of trouble."

"Wait just a minute," the man with the tassels growled. "You owe me compensation. Your vicious beast ruined my boots."

"Stuff and nonsense." Dotty closed her eyes for a moment before fixing the man with a stern look. "It was entirely your fault. If you had acted like a sensible person and just picked the poor puppy up, your boots would not have suffered any damage."

By this time Charlotte and Louisa were ranged beside Dotty. The footmen were close behind.

"Dotty, are you all right?" Charlotte asked.

"I am fine." She glanced at Louisa who seemed to be glaring at the man's companion, whom Dotty had not previously noticed.

The contrast between that man and his friend with the tassels was remarkable.

She knew now what her father had meant when he had spoken disparagingly about "dandies." The man whose boots Bennie had attacked was obviously one of that set. His shirt points were so high he could barely turn his head. His waist was nipped in and his garishly striped waistcoat was covered by so many fobs and other ornaments, one could hardly see the cloth. Whereas his companion was dressed with elegant propriety in a dark blue coat and buff pantaloons. No gold tassels adorned his boots, which were so highly polished, the sun reflected off them. With stylish gold hair and deep blue eyes, he was very handsome indeed. Then his lips curved up in a mocking smile, ruining the favorable impression she'd had.

"Merton." Louisa infused her voice with a note of disgust. "A friend of *yours* I suppose."

Merton cleared his throat. "I dare say, Fotherby, that the lady is correct. You should have been able to stop the animal before any damage occurred."

Fotherby turned to Merton, staring at his companion as if betrayed. Merton's masked eyes were unreadable to Dotty, but something in them must have made an impression on Fotherby for he turned to her and bowed slightly.

"Ladies, my deepest apologies for not acting promptly to avoid an unnecessary scene."

Never one to hold a grudge, Dotty inclined her head, "Your apology is accepted, sir."

Merton lifted one brow and looked pointedly at Louisa.

"Very well," she said, in no good humor. "Miss Stern, may I present the Marquis of Merton, a cousin of mine. Merton, Miss Stern, a longtime friend of Lady Charlotte's family."

Dom bowed and watched with appreciation as Miss Stern gracefully curtseyed. He had not been paying much attention to her encounter with Fotherby, thinking her just another modern termagant, until she stood and faced him. Botticelli could not have painted such perfection. The glossy blue-black curls peeping out from her hat served as a perfect frame for her heart-shaped face. She gazed at Dom with bright moss green eyes. Surreptitiously, he sucked in a breath. He'd seen many beautiful women this Season, including Lady Charlotte, but none came close to equaling Miss Stern.

But *Dotty*, what a horrible name. It must be short for something. He prayed it was short for something. If not, the name would have to change.

Cousin Louisa had not given him an indication of Miss Stern's station, other than that she was a lady. However, a

Miss Stern could possibly be the daughter of a viscount. That wouldn't be bad. Anything lower in rank would not do. Unless her bloodlines were superior. If that was the case, he could make an exception. He had the consequence of the marquisate to consider.

Bowing over her hand, Dom grasped her fingers. "It is my greatest pleasure to meet you, Miss Stern. I pray you will allow me to call."

"Well," his cousin said in a voice intended to dampen his spirits, "only if you care to come to Stanwood House. Miss Stern is residing with us for the Season."

He repressed a shudder at the thought of having to face that brood again, especially Theodora, Worthington's youngest sister. He kept a smile pasted on his face. "Perhaps I shall."

The animosity between the two families was such that Worthington had told Dom in no uncertain terms that he was not welcome to court any ladies under his guardianship. Of course, at the time, only Ladies Charlotte and Louisa were at issue. He wondered if that prohibition applied to Miss Stern as well.

After the ladies said their adieus and continued on their way, Fotherby turned to Dom. "How could you make me out to be an object of sport? That Miss Stern had no right to say what she did. Pert is what she was, and I didn't like it."

Dom took out his quizzing glass and leveled it on his friend. "I did it in an attempt to save you from continuing to look like a fool. Really, Fotherby, it was a *puppy*. A rather small one at that."

Fotherby stared down at his boot.

The mangled tassel hung damply against the moderate shine of the boot. Why Fotherby kept a valet who could not get a decent finish on his boots, Dom didn't know.

"Yes, well." Fotherby frowned. "I suppose you're right. I just don't like dogs."

"Not liking dogs"—Dom barely repressed his disdain—"is akin to treason. It is un-English. Everyone has them. How else would we hunt?"

Fotherby remained silent for several moments before turning the subject. "Yes, of course you are correct. Silly of me really. Do you intend to dine at White's this evening?"

"Where else? Shall I look forward to seeing you there?"

"Yes, wouldn't miss it. Half past eight?"

Dom inclined his head. "I shall see you then."

A short while later he took his leave, making his way back to his hotel. However, upon entering and ordering tea to be sent to his rooms, Dom was informed he no longer had a chamber. "I beg your pardon?" He looked down his nose at the clerk. "I believe I would have remembered if I had given up my rooms."

The man bowed and handed him a note. "My lord, I was told to give you this."

He opened it and immediately recognized his mother's hand. She was in London and expected him to relocate to Merton House. She had planned to spend the Season at home; what could have brought her to Town? "Thank you."

Turning on his heel, he strode back out the door and hurried to his house. It would be nice to have his staff. They knew his routine and the proper deference to show him. As long as nothing was amiss with his mother, her arrival was a welcome surprise.

Chapter Three

Eunice, Marchioness of Merton, paced her elegantly appointed parlor decorated in various shades of blue. Dominic should be home at any time now. She turned to her cousin and companion of many years, Miss Matilda Bradford. "Do you think I was too highhanded in removing Dominic's belongings from the hotel?"

Matilda gave Eunice a quizzical look. "It is not whether *I* think you were managing, but whether *he* thinks it."

Eunice sat perched on the sofa under a bank of windows overlooking the back garden. "Well, I suppose it does not matter. He is going about this wife business all wrong. When he sent me the list of ladies he was considering, I could have screamed with frustration. Not one of them has the will or desire to stand up to him. They will all nod and simper, happy to be the Marchioness of Merton. Worse, they will assist him in becoming more set in his ways than he already is. A stodgier twenty-seven-year-old man I have never known. His poor papa must be rolling in his grave."

Matilda pulled a face. "I agree, but it is not entirely Dominic's fault."

"No, you're right. My brother, Alasdair, never should have been named Dominic's guardian. One could not doubt his sincerity, but he was determined to make Dominic aware of his duty and consequence. The result has been a disaster. Did you know that Worthington's sisters call Dominic "His Marquisship?"

Matilda gave a dry chuckle. "I had heard something to that effect."

"It is embarrassing to have such animosity in the family." Eunice stood again. "Now that Louisa is making her come out, it cannot be hidden. I am determined he shall not remain the butt of fun to most of Polite Society. We must find Dominic a young lady who will have enough influence over him to make him rethink his views. We live in modern times. As the Marquis of Merton, he should be leading the way, not hanging behind with the older generation."

Matilda gave Eunice a dubious look. "How do you propose to do that, pray tell?"

"It is simple. He must fall in love with a woman who will challenge his beliefs."

"But, Eunice, you know how difficult that will be. Most girls and their parents would give their eyeteeth to marry a marquis. They will agree with everything he says just to be a marchioness."

Her cousin was right. Trusting that Dominic would accidentally find the right lady was fool's work. "Make a list of the most liberal families in Town and tomorrow we shall begin visits. Dominic always escorts me to my entertainments. He may not like it, but I shall insist we attend those events first. I am determined to find someone suitable."

"He will, assuredly, not like it." Matilda went over to the small writing desk. Taking out a sheet of paper she started to write. "However, this will, at least, point us in the right direction."

An hour later, Eunice called for tea, and Dominic entered the room coming straight to her. Concern coupled with irritation etched his handsome face. "Mama, is everything all right? When did you arrive?"

She laughed and offered her cheek for him to kiss. "Everything is fine. We arrived shortly after noon. I called at your hotel, but you had gone out. Since you always stay at home when I am in Town, I saw no reason not to assist you, by having your belongings brought here." She raised a questioning brow. "Was I in error?"

Relenting, he smiled at her. "No, not at all. I'm happy to be here."

She took his hand and led him to a small sofa. "Come, let us be comfortable."

Dominic gave her a quizzical look. "Why *are* you here, Mama? I thought you'd decided to eschew the Season this year."

She regarded him, careful to give nothing away. "It seemed as if everyone in the neighborhood was gone, and life became very dull. Matilda and I decided we needed more diversion than the country was going to give us."

He searched her face for a moment. "Is that the only reason?"

"Of course it is." She held his gaze and lied. "What other cause could I possibly have?"

"I sent you the list," he said. "It did cross my mind that you might be taking an interest in the subject of my marriage."

Eunice gave him a wide-eyed look. "My dear son, that is a matter for you to decide. I would not dream of interfering."

After sending a note to Fotherby, canceling his plans to dine at White's, Dom dined with his mother and her companion before taking himself off to his club where he joined a party of his friends.

Alvanley, a young baron the same age as Dom, strolled up. "Thought we'd see you in the dining room."

He took the glass of wine a waiter handed him. "No. My mother decided to come to Town. I dined with her."

"I see." Alvanley lifted his glass of brandy, and after taking a sip, he asked, "Are you serious about trying to find a wife this Season? I would have thought you've time yet."

Dom returned the salute. "The men in my family have a habit of dying young. I must ensure the succession."

"Have you considered Lady Mary Linley?" His friend took a sip of port.

"Lovely girl, but I don't think we would suit." Dom had considered and rejected Lady Mary. He neither wished nor expected to love his wife. His uncle had been exceedingly clear that strong passion and emotions were to be avoided in a marriage. They led to disaster. Liking and companionship were sufficient in those of rank. Still, he wanted to have some desire for a wife. Though pretty enough, she reminded him strongly of a pond of ice. The surface was hard and the underneath would be just as cold. His thoughts drifted to Miss Stern. She had a great deal of passion, albeit misdirected. Would it translate to the bedchamber?

Alvanley took another drink. "Too bad. Her brother's trying to get rid of her this year."

"Tired of having his wife play gooseberry? Her portion is large enough," Dom replied. "He shouldn't have a problem."

"What about Miss Turley?" his friend asked.

Dom hesitated. "Very lovely, yet I do not care for some of her personality traits. However, I am sure she will be fine for someone else."

Alvanley frowned. "You're being deuced hard to please for a man who just needs to get a child on the chit. Don't tell me you want a love match?"

Dom raised his quizzing glass. "Of course not. Anything but. However, she must represent the family properly, and I *will* have to bed her."

He wandered over to the betting book and placed a wager on a curricle race to take place the next day. After which he spent the next couple of hours playing whist. At the end of the evening, even though he had a tidy sum stacked up in front of him, he couldn't say he had enjoyed himself. For some reason, spending evenings at his club was beginning to pall, as were the endless rounds of entertainments required to find a wife.

This year's batch of young ladies was no better than the previous year's. Possibly worse. With the sole exception of Miss Stern, not one of them had caught his attention. Dom had never seen a young lady as lovely as she. Simply beautiful, despite her outburst this morning. Still, he could forgive her that. Many young ladies had a fondness for puppies and did not wish to see them hurt. At least she liked dogs.

Dom regarded Fotherby, sitting at a card table across the room. He was in his cups and excited about something. Not a good combination. The man had all the discretion of a bull. It occurred to Dom he had better ensure his friend didn't mention Miss Stern.

"Merton, Merton, I say," Fotherby called. "Tell them what happened to my boots today."

Dom pulled out his snuff box. With a flick of one finger—just as Brummell had shown him—he opened it and took a pinch of snuff, raising it languidly to one nostril. "Fotherby, surely you do not wish me to repeat that you were afraid to stop a puppy from harming your boots. A very small puppy."

Fotherby's countenance turned a purplish red hue, and he sputtered. "No, the girl, Merton. The girl. She ought not be allowed to accost a gentleman like that. Shows poor breeding."

Dom linked his arm with Fotherby's, practically dragging his friend out of his chair. "I would be extremely displeased if you were to bandy the lady's name about."

Huffing a bit, Fotherby sputtered, "What's it matter to you?"

"She is residing with my cousin. As head of the family, it is my responsibility to protect its members."

After a moment, Fotherby touched a finger to his nose and tapped. "Oh yes, I see. Quiet. Not a word then."

Dom smiled thinly. "You have my deepest appreciation."

"I say, Merton, a game of piquet?"

"No, I'm for home. M'mother arrived today."

Fotherby glanced around as if expecting his mother to appear as well. "Understand. Dreadful thing, mothers. Always in one's business. There's no pleasing them."

Dom could almost sympathize with Fotherby. His mother was one of the gorgons of the *ton*. Nothing her second-born son did measured up to her expectations. Though to be fair to the lady, she might have reason on her side. He had come into the title and, thus far, Fotherby's main interest seemed to be clothing, brandy, and cards.

Dom retrieved his hat and cane from the doorman then walked down the steps to St. James Street. What had changed that he was suddenly so dissatisfied with his life? Good Lord, he was only seven and twenty. He mentally reviewed the list of prospective wives he had been so optimistic about only a few days ago. All of them were well-looking, some Diamonds of the First Water. But if Lady Mary was cold, Lady Jane was too solicitous. Miss Farnham laughed like a horse, and Miss Turley, hung on his every word, agreeing with whatever he said. Despite what he had said to Alvanley, until Dom had seen Miss Stern, Miss Turley had been at the head of the list. Yet how to approach Miss Stern when she was residing with Worthington, with whom Dom did not particularly get along?

He walked to his home. As expected, the door opened before he reached the top step. He had everything a man could want: a well-run house, wealth, position. He should not be so discontented. Perhaps he'd take another stroll in the Park tomorrow. This time without Fotherby.

Dinner in the Worthington household had been a raucous affair. Dotty had dined many times with the Carpenters, yet the addition of Matt's four sisters added considerably to the noise level. She could not have enjoyed it better. She had grown up with Charlotte's family and was extremely pleased to see everyone getting along as if they had always lived together.

Dotty was even a little wistful her own sisters and brothers were not here as well, but perhaps in the summer the families could all visit. After dinner, the younger children were sent to the schoolroom and the adults, along with her, Charlotte, and Louisa sat in the spacious drawing room. Heavy sage green velvet curtains were drawn across the windows overlooking the front of the house. The side windows had a view to a narrow garden and a brick wall decorated by rose trellises.

"Dotty," Matt's stepmother, the Dowager Lady Worthington said, "how did you like your stroll in the Park today?"

"It was very nice, except for my encounter with a certain gentleman. My father had told me about dandies, yet I did not have a good appreciation of what he meant until I saw one today."

"My dear"—the Dowager Lady Worthington's smooth forehead wrinkled—"you make it sound like something from a freak show. Are you sure you are being kind?"

Louisa glanced at them. "Mama, it was Mr. Fotherby."

Matt coughed. "Then it must have seemed more like something from the Royal Menagerie." His eyes danced with mirth. "But, Dotty, you cannot call Fotherby a dandy. That is to be unfair to those who truly are. He is a macaroni."

She furrowed her brow. "What is the difference?"

"A dandy might be extreme in his shirt points, but he takes

care to always be subtle in his costume and is an adherent of Brummell's philosophy that one should do nothing to draw attention to one's dress."

"Are you a dandy?"

Matt grimaced. "If I must claim a group, it would be the corinthians. We are a more sporting bunch."

"Do not listen to him, my dear." Lady Worthington shook her head at Matt. "He'll make fun of any of the macaroni set. You will see a lot of them, though perhaps, none quite so . . . stunning as Lord Fotherby."

Louisa told them about Dotty saving the puppy then added, "*Merton* was with him."

"Louisa, remember." Grace's calm tone held a note of warning. "We have all agreed to treat him with courtesy."

"He was actually helpful today," Charlotte reminded Louisa. "When he agreed with Dotty, that is."

"Yes, I suppose he was," Louisa grudgingly agreed. "But I shall wager there was some benefit to him."

The comments that Louisa had made before and during the current conversation sparked Dotty's curiosity. "Louisa, why don't you like him?"

"He's a pompous bore," Louisa replied roundly. "A few years ago, he came to Worthington Hall and went on and on about how he, as the head of the family, needed to look after us. Matt reminded him that his title has nothing to do with Merton as the title descended through a female ancestor, but he wouldn't give it up. Matt finally told him to leave before he threw Merton out on his ear. Even Theodora remembered it, and she was only three at the time."

Dotty tried to reconcile that with the short, albeit favorable, impression she'd had of him when he had taken her side. Then remembered the way he had dealt with his friend. "I see. High in the instep?"

"I would say rather insufferably aware of his own consequence," Louisa remarked. "Someone needs to bring him down a peg or two, but if he marries Miss Turley, *that* won't happen."

Charlotte nodded. "Very true. She hangs on him like gold coins come out of his mouth. Which is ridiculous. He has not an original thought in his head, and what he has, all spring from half a century ago." She turned to her sister. "Grace, do we attend the Featherington ball on Friday?"

"Yes, we must also make some morning visits so that Dotty can be introduced. Lady Thornhill is having a drawing room on Thursday, and I received Dotty's vouchers for Almack's from Lady Jersey yesterday."

Charlotte turned to Dotty. "You will love Lady Thornhill. She has the most interesting guests."

"I'll look forward to it." Dotty pressed her fingers to her lips and tried to hide her yawn. "I am sorry."

"Not at all." Grace smiled. "It has been a long day for you. Get a good night's sleep and we'll see you in the morning."

Once in bed, Dotty's mind cast back to Lord Merton. It was a shame his family disliked him so much. Even Charlotte, who was the most loving of creatures, seemed to accept that Merton was not worth even trying to improve. Perhaps he was insecure, yet he didn't seem as if that were a problem, though one never knew what a person hid deep inside.

She hoped he would pick a lady he could love. That might be exactly what he needed. With the right encouragement, anyone could reach their full potential. But would he?

The next morning, Dotty was awakened by what sounded like a herd of horses. Considering she was in a new place, she had slept surprisingly well. After ringing for Polly, Dotty rose. Warm water was already in the pitcher and the fire had been stoked. Polly arrived only a few minutes later. "That was fast."

"I've been up and about for a couple of hours, miss. Lady Charlotte's maid, May, is teaching me new ways to do your hair and the like. On our day off, we've been promised a trip to see some of the sights."

Polly and May had grown up together. It must seem like a reunion for them. "That sounds like fun. I hope I get to see something of London as well."

"Oh, you will. I'm sure of it. The younger children are downstairs breaking their fast. I'm to tell you tea and hot chocolate will be served in the Young Ladies' Parlor."

Dotty grinned. "So that was what I heard coming down the stairs."

"They make quite a racket, don't they?"

When Dotty entered the parlor, Charlotte handed her a cup of hot chocolate. "We thought you would sleep longer. Did the children wake you?"

Dotty took the cup. "Yes, but I slept well and long enough. What are the plans for today?"

"We'll start out with a trip to Bond Street. You will want to subscribe to the circulating library. After that Louisa and I will take you to Phaeton's Bazaar. We like to replenish our stockings and gloves from there. It is much less expensive than other places. They also have a number of other interesting things to see. Then we have morning visits. After that . . ."

Charlotte rattled off a list including another walk in the Park and concluding with this evening's ball. As much as Dotty had anticipated this Season, she truly had not had a good appreciation of what was involved. Yet, she felt prepared. Thank goodness Mama had insisted Dotty attend the local assemblies and perform on the pianoforte when they had company.

She looked forward to strolling in the Park again and wondered if Lord Merton would be there.

After breakfasting alone, Dom spent the rest of the morning on his correspondence and accounts. Although his steward, Mr. Jacobs, was a competent man, Dom's uncle and guardian until he'd attained his majority, Lord Alasdair, had always said it was Dom's duty to review everything. Which Alasdair had done since Dom's father's death when he'd been six years old.

During the rare times he had chafed at not being allowed to attend school, instead of having an array of tutors, his uncle reminded him it was his duty to learn more than was taught at Eton. One must jealously guard his estates, show to advantage in all the gentlemanly sports, be loyal to the Crown whether one agreed or not, and ensure the succession. One must also marry a suitable lady.

Before Merton attended Oxford, his uncle introduced him to five young men whose ideas were to have been compatible with Merton's duties. However, Reggie had been sent down after impregnating the daughter of a don. Joss and William went into the army, and now there was only Alvanley and Fotherby left. The first was increasingly being drawn into the Prince Regent's debauched circle, and Fotherby cared for nothing but fashion. It was not easy for Dom to make new friends and lately he had felt very much alone.

He tugged the bell pull and the door opened immediately.

"My lord?" the footman bowed.

"Tell Mr. Jacobs I would like to see him."

The servant bowed. "Yes, my lord."

A few minutes later, Jacobs knocked on the open door and entered. "You wanted me, my lord?"

Dom rubbed his forehead. "Yes, please have a seat. I've been reviewing your request to attend a seminar at Holkham Hall. You do know that the family supported the Americans in their war against us?"

Jacobs squirmed in his seat for a moment. "I'd heard something about that, but the reason I want to go is to learn more about the agricultural innovations being made there."

Merton drew his brows together. He didn't like the idea that his house could be associated with a Whig family. "Is there not another place you could go to study?"

"No, my lord. All the most modern methods are being used at Holkham."

Duty to his land or duty to his king?

"Everyone goes there now, my lord. No politics are discussed, only farming."

Merton was unconvinced about new ideas. His uncle had always told him the old ways were the best. Still, Jacobs had never asked to do anything like this before. "What is the reason for this sudden interest?"

"Our yields have not kept up with others in the areas, on all the estates. When I talked to one of the other stewards, he mentioned the new ways being tried in Norfolk and how they helped him."

It was a sound idea and good for his lands and tenants. "Very well. Make your plans."

Jacobs stood. "Thank you, my lord. You won't regret it."

Still not entirely convinced, Dom lifted a brow. "It is your duty to see I shall not."

After bowing, Jacobs closed the door behind him, and Dom was left alone with his thoughts. New innovations. There seemed to be a deuced lot of them lately. That steam engine they had on display had blown up, but there were rumors the inventor hadn't given up. Talk of canals being cut to move coal and tin. What would his uncle think of it all? Unfortunately, his uncle was no longer alive to ask. Until recently, it had not occurred to Dom how much he'd relied upon his former guardian. He would have to start making his own decisions as he just had with Jacobs.

After finishing his reviews, Merton put his pencil down and left his study. Perhaps a stroll would help clear his head. He might meet Miss Stern again. The thought made him smile. He must discover if she was even an eligible candidate for the position of his wife.

Chapter Four

"The Marchioness of Merton," Royston intoned from the door to the morning room.

"Oh, ma'am." Grace rose from her desk to greet Eunice. "I am so happy to see you. It has been an age."

"Grace, my child." Eunice took the outstretched hands and kissed Grace's cheek. She had grown into such a beautiful woman. "Yes, indeed. Much too long. How have you been doing?"

"I am well, as are the children." Her lips pursed. "I didn't know you were in Town, or I would have called on you. Merton said . . ."

"I arrived just yesterday." Eunice gave a small cough. "It was rather a surprise to him." She held Grace out, studying her. "I am sorry I was unable to attend your wedding. However, allow me to congratulate you on your marriage. You look exceedingly happy."

Grace smiled gently. "I am. We all are. Truly, I could not have picked a better man. Worthington is at the Park with the whole group now to give me a few moments to catch up on my correspondence."

Eunice could not have been prouder of Grace if she'd been her own daughter. She had defied everyone's expectations when she'd won custody of her brothers and sisters. Then to have married so well. It was a miracle she had met a man who was up to it all. "Your mother would have been very happy to see you so well settled."

"I think so." Grace tugged the bell pull and ordered tea. "Come sit and tell me how you've been."

Eunice sank into the offered chair. After settling her skirts, she took a breath. "I have come for your help."

If Grace was surprised, she did not show it. "Anything I can do, of course I will. Besides being my mama's closest friend, you are now my cousin."

"Thank you." Eunice let out the breath she had been holding. She had spent hours last night thinking of how to approach Grace, and had come up with nothing. "It is not very difficult; at least I hope not." Eunice paused, still trying to find a way of putting it. And, nothing came. "I have decided that I would like to be introduced to the more forward thinking members of Polite Society. It is something I should have done years ago, but while Alasdair was alive, I let him influence me. Too much." Grace shook her head as if not understanding. Eunice continued. "By doing so, I allowed him to lead Dominic astray."

Grace pressed her lips together and choked, but her eyes danced with merriment. "I do not think you need to worry that Merton is spending time in bad company. Quite the contrary I would imagine. I could ask Worthington, yet I seriously doubt he will have heard your son has been rambling around the gaming halls and flesh houses."

And that was exactly the problem. "No, no, my dear, you mistake me. I would feel *better* if Dominic was behaving like a normal young man. Instead"—Eunice frowned—"he has never given me a day of worry."

Grace chuckled, but quickly sobered. "Yes, I quite see your point. He would have been better off being allowed to get into some scrapes. Or rebelling and having to find his own way of viewing the world."

"I'm so glad you understand." Yet the question was would Grace help her? "When my brother was alive he instilled a fanatical notion of duty and self-consequence in Merton. I know Alasdair was only trying to be respectful of the family's heritage, but I do not think it has done Dominic any good at all. Rather, it has done him a great deal of bad." Eunice balanced the cup of tea Grace handed her on her lap then took a sip. "He is not yet out of his twenties and a dead bore. Which would not have made his father at all happy. When I think of the larks David kicked up before we were married, well . . . Dominic should be having the same type of fun. I did have great expectations when he came on the Town that he would do *something* to create a stir, but my hopes were dashed." Eunice could not stop herself from sighing. "Even his mistresses are dull."

Another burble of laughter escaped Grace.

"Go ahead and laugh, my dear, but I saw one of them. You cannot imagine what a depressing sight it was. She was dressed like a governess."

"But, ma'am, perhaps it wasn't his mistress. It might *have* been a governess or some other poor relation."

Eunice shook her head. "*Dominic* in a sporting carriage with a *governess?* No matter how gently bred she was, he's much too high in the instep for that. Aside from that, he had no reason to be with either a governess or a poor relation. He would have handed her immediately over to me."

Grace went into whoops. At least someone could see the humor in Dominic's behavior. To the best of Eunice's knowledge, he had never even been in his altitudes.

Finally Grace brought herself under control, though her voice was a bit shaky. "Naturally, I am glad to be of assistance. But how will my introducing you to the more liberal set influence Merton?"

Eunice waved her fingers in the air. "He escorts me to all my entertainments, no matter how tedious. Therefore, if I attend a party or musical, he will as well. I just hope it is not too late to save him."

Grace was quiet for a few moments, then said, "Lady Thornhill's drawing room."

"Ah, yes." Eunice had heard that name before and tried to place it. "Is she the bluestocking who has poets, painters, and other artists at her home?"

"The very one." Grace nodded and leaned forward, obviously warming to the scheme. "If you think that might be too much of a shock for Merton, I am sure any of my friends would be happy to send you cards to their balls. Truth be told, despite how Worthington and his sisters feel, Merton *is* extremely eligible and can be trusted to behave. All the entertainments I am attending with the girls will have a number of young people present. I can send round a note or two if you would like. Once the hostesses know you are interested, you should begin receiving invitations."

"That would be the perfect place to start." Rising, Eunice held her hands out to Grace. "Thank you so much. I knew I could depend on you."

"For your sake, I hope it works. I shall have to remember to tell Worthington not to make fun of Merton." Grace had a doubtful look on her face as if she would have difficulty with the task.

There was nothing for it. Eunice might as well let Grace know that she knew how bad the situation between their families was. "I heard what his sisters call Dominic."

"Indeed." She looked as if she had eaten a particularly sour lemon. "I do not know that we will ever be able to convince Theo to stop, but the others know I expect better behavior. Unfortunately, he did an excellent job of aggravating Worthington's stepmother."

"Obviously, it is past time I stepped in." Eunice blamed herself. She should never have allowed her grief over her husband to separate her from her son.

* * *

Later that afternoon, her butler held out a silver salver. She picked up the envelope and opened it. As she had expected, Grace had been prompt. It was the promised invitation to Lady Featherington's ball on Friday evening. Next was a small packet, which Eunice recognized as her vouchers for Almack's. "Thank you, Paken."

She briefly wondered what Dominic would think of attending an entertainment not filled with Tories, and shrugged. He would simply have to get used to it. She refused to allow him to marry a milksop, or a toad-eater, or a woman who would never love him.

Merton had walked around Rotten Row twice. He had seen many of his acquaintances, but not the young lady he sought. Just as he started his third circuit, he caught sight of Miss Stern and his cousins. She was delightfully lovely in a pale yellow muslin walking gown. The well-cut spencer showed off the outline of her breasts, causing his blood to race. A parasol shaded her porcelain complexion. She smiled when he hailed her. Then Louisa said something, and Miss Stern nodded, the wide smile fading from her lips.

He was damned if he would allow his cousin to intimidate him. "Good afternoon, Miss Stern."

She curtseyed so gracefully, he thought his heart would stop.

"Good afternoon, my lord."

When she glanced at him her eyes were the color of the new leaves in spring. He bowed and lightly kissed her gloved hand, all the while wanting to touch her bare skin. "How fortuitous to see you again."

A light blush painted her cheeks. She inclined her head only slightly. Such dignity of manner. She must be the daughter of a viscount.

"It is my pleasure as well, my lord," she replied.

She had a low, pleasing voice. One he could listen to for hours, definitely over the breakfast or dinner table, and at night, especially at night. He swallowed. In bed, when her inky curls caressed her shoulders, and her lips, those deep rosy lips . . . More than anything he would love to kiss them and feel them on his . . . Oh Lord, was he really having *those* thoughts about an innocent young lady? Gentlemen were supposed to take their pleasure with mistresses and not burden their wives with such primitive urges.

He must be going mad. This had to stop. "May I accompany you ladies on your walk?"

He waited, expecting Louisa to say something cutting; instead, Miss Stern smiled again. "Thank you, my lord. We would be honored."

Since he couldn't take the arms of all three ladies, he stayed on the outside and offered his escort to Miss Stern. She very properly placed her small hand on his arm, and they resumed the promenade. "How do you like London so far, Miss Stern?"

"I barely know, my lord. I arrived only yesterday. Thus far, I am having a wonderful time. I shall not bore you with all the details, but today we went shopping. . . ."

Bore him? Never. Not with the way her hand heated his arm and her voice sounded like music.

"This evening we shall be at Almack's. It is my first time there. On Friday, we will attend Lady Featherington's ball."

For a minute he was struck dumb. Lord Featherington was a *Whig*. Then he remembered; so was Worthington. Of course Miss Stern would attend *those* entertainments. Dom would never see her except in the Park. A few years ago, after he had made it clear to any hostess with Whigish leanings that *he* would not attend, the cards had ceased arriving. Yet now, the only lady he was interested in resided in a house of *liberals*. He repressed a shudder.

There was Almack's, of course, but that was only on

Wednesdays. Perhaps he had been too hasty in considering Miss Stern as a marital prospect. Yet what was he to do when every other lady paled in comparison to her?

Dotty was surprised at how her hand seemed to warm on Lord Merton's strong arm. Perhaps he had a fever and was unaware of it. He made small talk about the weather, and she responded easily. Despite what Louisa and Charlotte thought, he was really very pleasant to be around and so handsome. His hat was set at a stylish angle and his golden locks glinted in the sun.

He took her elbow, helping her over a small rut in the path. "I would not want you to trip."

As if she was a fragile maiden instead of a lady who frequently tramped for miles in the countryside. "Thank you, my lord. Without your help, I am sure I would have stumbled."

Louisa gave a light snort. What else was Dotty to have said? Really, Louisa was much too hard on Merton. He was a perfect gentleman. He did not know she climbed over stiles and marched through deep uneven ground at home.

"Miss Stern," he said, bringing her attention back to him. "Do you enjoy the opera?"

"I have never had the pleasure of seeing one, but I have heard arias. I am positive I would love it."

"I have a box." His chest looked as if it had grown larger. "Perhaps if I made up a party, you would be willing to join it."

He glanced down at her as she looked up at him. He seemed so nervous. "I would have to ask Grace."

"Yes, of course." He sounded flustered. "Shall I send the proposed details to Stanwood House?"

Merton's behavior became stiffer. Perhaps he *was* a little shy. She nodded. "Please do."

They had reached the point at which she and her friends had entered the Park. Charlotte and Louisa, walking a couple of steps away, stopped and waited.

Dotty gazed up at Merton's deep blue eyes. "I must go home now."

"Yes, of course," he said, but he did not let go of her hand. "Perhaps I'll see you tomorrow, Miss Stern?"

Dotty wanted to sigh when he kissed her fingers. "I shall look forward to it, my lord."

He bowed again. She joined her friends, refusing to look back to see if he was still there.

"I wouldn't have believed it." Louisa stared at Merton as he made his way down Rotten Row.

"Believed what?" Dotty asked.

Louisa grinned wickedly. "I think Merton is taken with you. What a surprise he is going to have."

Dotty shook her head. She was very attracted to him, yet it was much too soon to think of anything between them. Nevertheless, her heart gave a little flutter. "I do not understand you. We barely know each other. And what if he is? Even if he did propose, I would not accept him solely because he is a peer. Any man I marry must have principles and believe in the same values I do, and we must be in love."

Charlotte chimed in. "Dotty and I have discussed the type of marriages we both wanted for years now. I can assure you, she is quite set in her beliefs."

Louisa's grin widened. "Exactly."

As Merton strolled off, he resisted the urge to glance back at Miss Stern. He congratulated himself that their conversation had gone extremely well. He would invite her and his mother and . . . his mind blanked. Who else could he ask? If he had only Miss Stern and his mother in the party, it would be too singular. If he included Louisa and Lady Charlotte, he would have to invite two other gentlemen to keep the numbers even. Yet the only two he knew well were Alvanley and Fotherby. That would be a disaster of major proportions even if Worthington could be convinced to allow his sisters to attend. Alvanley spouted all the nonsense the Prince Regent did, and Fotherby thought of nothing but trying to distinguish himself in the most outlandish costumes. Charlotte was well behaved enough to put up with Fotherby, but Louisa would argue with Alvanley the entire evening. Dom considered every mix of people he knew, but couldn't come up with either the right numbers or the right persons to make up his party.

He entered his house, giving his hat and cane to Paken. "Is her ladyship in?"

"Yes, my lord. I believe she is drinking tea in her parlor."

Merton took the stairs two at a time, something he had not done since his youth when he'd been reprimanded for it by his uncle. A moment later, he burst into the parlor without knocking. "Mama."

She turned, a shocked expression appeared on her face. "Dominic?"

Of course, he'd been too precipitant. "I'm terribly sorry, but I have a dilemma I cannot seem to solve."

"My dear boy." She patted the seat next to her. "Pray, what has got you so upset?"

"A lady. Well, rather a situation with a lady. I am trying to make up a party to the opera, and I can't seem to find the appropriate mix."

"Indeed." She seemed a little let down. "Perhaps I can help. You would not want to bring too much notice to her."

"Exactly what I thought." He did not like bothering his mother and made a habit not to do so, still the tension he'd been experiencing lessened.

"Have I heard of this lady?" Mama smoothed her skirts. "I mean, is she one of the ladies on your list?"

"No. I found none of them actually suit me. Her name is Miss Stern. She is residing with Worthington for the Season."

"Oh, I see." His mother blinked. "Or rather I shall."

"What do you mean?" Dom shook his head trying to clear it. His mother wasn't usually so obtuse.

"I shall meet her on the night of the opera, of course, if not before. You must ask her to dine with us. In the meantime, I will put my mind to who else should be invited."

He felt as if a weight had been removed from his shoulders. There was nothing to worry about after all, and he had been right in asking his mother. "Thank you. Do you plan to attend Almack's this evening?"

"Why, yes, if you would like to escort me. Shall we leave at nine?"

Dom smiled as his mother handed him a cup of tea. "If you wish."

Almack's would give him the opportunity to see Miss Stern in a neutral setting. He would quite like to dance with her, perhaps even a waltz. His uncle hadn't approved of the German dance, but Dom enjoyed it; at least he would with Miss Stern.

Chapter Five

As Dotty clasped the single strand of pearls around her neck she looked to Grace for approval.

"Very nice," she said. "Just the thing for Almack's. Remember, you may not waltz until one of the Patronesses approves you."

"How will I know who they are?" Her mother had impressed upon Dotty how important it was to make a good impression at the exclusive assembly. The ladies in charge made exceptions for no one. Even the Duke of Wellington had been denied entrance when he failed to wear knee breeches. Normally, Dotty did not have a nervous disposition, but the name *Almack's* made her tremble in her beaded satin slippers.

Grace smiled. "There is no reason to be concerned. You will be with either Louisa's mama or me until a gentleman is recommended to you as a partner."

A man had to *want* to dance with her? Dotty paled in earnest. "But, aside from Matt, I have only met three gentlemen."

"Goose." Grace laughed. "You have never been at a loss for partners. When it comes to the male sex, the ones in London are really no different than at home. Oh, to be sure, they have a bit of Town bronze, but a beautiful girl is a beautiful girl whether in the country or in London."

That made Dotty feel better. She forced her lips into a smile. "Thank you."

Grace put her arm around Dotty's shoulders. "Come. We must be leaving soon. Let's see how Charlotte and Louisa are faring."

They joined the others in the Young Ladies' Parlor.

"Oh, Dotty, you are so beautiful," Charlotte said. "I wish I could wear white."

"Me, too," Louisa agreed. "I think it is so elegant."

"But I could never wear that shade of pink," Dotty said to Louisa before addressing Charlotte. "Or green at all."

"You girls look lovely indeed." The Dowager Lady Worthington grinned as she made shooing motions with her hands. "Now come along. It wouldn't do to arrive after all the gentlemen have made other dance commitments."

Matt was in the hall when they descended the stairs. Yet his eyes were only for Grace. "Don't you look enchanting?"

Giving her hand to him, Grace gazed up at him. "I think the girls look very pretty."

He glanced at them and groaned. "I'll be beating them off all evening."

Dotty frowned. "Why would you want to fight anyone?"

"He's referring to the gentlemen." Louisa laughed. "I, for one, would like to have more offers than dances available."

Charlotte nodded. "Grace, you must make him behave and not scare off any of our potential suitors."

Taking Matt's arm, Grace's lips tilted up. "I shall do my best. Fortunately, Almack's is quite strict in who it will allow to attend."

They arrived about twenty minutes later. Once at the assembly rooms the doorman looked at their vouchers. Matt accompanied the ladies into the large rectangular room with long windows. A small balcony jutting out over the dance floor held the musicians. A few of the chairs arranged along the walls were filled with older ladies in colorful turbans decorated with feathers and birds. Though it was still early by *ton* standards, the rooms were filling quickly as any latecomers were turned away. Grace touched Dotty's elbow, guiding her to a group of chairs.

Charlotte and Louisa were claimed for the country dance beginning to form and Dotty prepared to take a seat next to Grace, when a gentleman came up and addressed Matt. "Worthington, may I be introduced?"

Matt grinned, clearly amused. "Miss Stern, may I introduce a friend, Mr. Featherington. Featherington, Miss Stern is a close neighbor of my wife's in the country."

Mr. Featherington bowed and took the hand Dotty held out as she curtseyed. "My pleasure, Miss Stern. Will you join me for this dance?"

Dotty smiled. Grace was right; that had not been hard at all. "It would be my pleasure, Mr. Featherington."

He led her to where the other couples were forming the set. She glanced around and wondered if she'd see Lord Merton here this evening and if he would ask her to stand up with him. Perhaps she could even waltz with him.

Dom escorted his mother and cousin to Almack's. After showing them to a group of chairs, he scanned the room. Worthington and his wife were present but Dom did not see any of the young ladies. Then a flash of shimmering white caught his eye. There she was, Miss Stern. He sucked in a breath as if he'd been hit by Gentleman Jackson himself and couldn't help but stare.

God, she was lovely. Dressed all in white with a simple strand of pearls, she was easily the most elegant woman in the room. When the pattern of the dance brought her closer he could make out the silver thread embroidered on her gown. That's where the shimmer came from.

"Dominic?"

He turned to his mother. "Yes?"

"Who is that young lady you're looking at so intently?"

"I am not doing any such thing."

She raised a brow.

A flush rose in his neck. Thank God for cravats. "It is Miss Stern. The lady I told you about. I met her the other day at the Park. Nevertheless, I am not watching her. That would be unseemly."

His mother's lips twitched slightly. "What do you know of her?"

That was a question he hadn't even asked himself. Somehow it had not been important. "As I said before, she is residing with Worthington for the Season. Some friend of Lady Charlotte's."

"Well, she ought to be unexceptional then. I shall be pleased to make her acquaintance."

Much to his annoyance, he found himself shuffling his feet. What the devil was wrong with him? "Mama, you don't expect me to introduce her?"

Why had he said that when he had asked his mother to form the opera party? Naturally, she would expect to have Miss Stern presented to her. He wasn't making any sense, even to himself.

Mama's eyes started to sparkle in a way he'd never noticed before. "Could you procure Matilda and me glasses of lemonade, my dear?"

"My pleasure." He was glad to have something to do, besides stare at Miss Stern. As he made his way to the refreshment table, he wondered if she had been approved for the waltz and strode toward Countess Esterhazy.

"My lady." He bowed over her hand. They made small talk for a few minutes, before he judged it safe to ask his question. "There is a young lady, a Miss Stern who has arrived with Lord and Lady Worthington. Can you tell me if she is allowed to waltz?"

Lady Esterhazy gave Dom a curious look. "Not yet."

He resisted a strange urge to run a finger between his neck and cravat and wondered how it would be taken if he requested Miss Stern be given permission. It might look too singular. He bowed again. "I see. Thank you."

He was about to turn away when she placed her hand on his arm. "I am happy to perform the introduction, if you would like."

Well, as long as the countess offered, it would be rude to refuse. He would not wish to harm Miss Stern's reputation by not dancing with her. "You are very kind."

Countess Esterhazy raised a brow. "I am rarely accused of that, but I will forgive you. Meet me at the end of this set."

He bowed for the third time. "Thank you, my lady."

Resuming his way to the refreshment table, his steps were lighter. Dom shook off any thoughts that he was singling Miss Stern out. He was simply going to be the first gentleman to waltz with her. Someone had to be. Why not him? He hadn't been this pleased since he'd popped his first hit against Jackson.

Dotty curtseyed to Mr. Featherington when the dance ended, and he escorted her back to Grace.

"Miss Stern, may I fetch you a glass of lemonade or orgeat?"

She smiled. This was all going so well. "Lemonade, please."

Charlotte and Louisa returned and their escorts also offered to fetch drinks.

"How do you like it so far?" Charlotte asked.

Dotty tamped down her excitement. "Very much."

"Most of the gentlemen complain that it's dull."

That was surprising. "But why?"

"Because they cannot play cards or drink wine or other

spirits," Louisa replied. "I am glad. It makes them dance more often."

Dotty drew her brows together slightly. "Speaking of dancing, I wonder when I shall be allowed to waltz."

As she spoke, Charlotte's lips formed an "O." "I don't think you'll have to wait long at all."

Dotty turned in the direction her friend was gazing. Merton and a young matron with an elaborate headdress were coming toward them. "Who is the lady?"

Charlotte answered. "Countess Esterhazy, one of the Patronesses. Her husband is the Russian ambassador."

"Oh." Dotty glanced at Grace, who smiled and nodded encouragingly. By the time Dotty looked again, Charlotte and Louisa were curtseying. Hastily, Dotty did the same.

"Miss Stern?" the countess asked.

"Yes, my lady."

"May I recommend to you the Marquis of Merton as an acceptable partner." It was phrased as a question, but was not.

"Thank you, my lady."

Merton bowed. His hair seemed to turn gold under the many candles in crystal chandeliers.

The violins started the prelude to the set, and he offered his arm. "Miss Stern, if I may?"

Dotty let out the breath she'd been holding. "Thank you, my lord."

The touch of his hand, even through their gloves, was electric. When she glanced up, his deep blue eyes, the color of twilight, sparkled, as if he had just accomplished a difficult task.

He smiled as they took their places. Merton really was very handsome.

"Miss Stern, may I say you are the loveliest lady here this evening."

And charming. Was it proper to compliment a gentleman as well? "Thank you. You are extremely elegant."

His eyes seemed to warm. "Thank you."

He twirled her around the room as if she was on air. Despite everything she had been told, to her Merton was a very kind man. Louisa and Charlotte had to be wrong about him.

Dom didn't think he had ever danced with a lady of such poise. She fitted perfectly in his arms. As if he was holding a feather. Her laugh was like a tinkling of bells, and he did not think she found him amusing solely because he was a marquis. "May I take you for a ride in my curricle tomorrow?"

She glanced down shyly for a moment before raising her gaze to his. "If Grace has no objections, I accept."

He hid his groan. Worthington would make him suffer for this. Yet it couldn't be helped. He had to see her again. "Then I shall apply to her."

"No." Miss Stern lifted her chin. "I shall do it."

She was not at all like Miss Turley or any of the other ladies he'd been thinking of marrying. They had preferred that he talk to their parents. Yet, perhaps it was because Miss Stern knew about the estrangement with his cousin, and was trying to save him from having to approach Worthington.

By the end of the set, when he returned her to his cousin, Merton would have done almost anything for another waltz. Yet he knew very well what a catch he was and that would bring too much attention to her.

She took Grace aside and spoke in a voice too low for him to hear, then turned back to him. "Please come for me at five tomorrow."

He slowly let out a breath he had not realized he was holding. "Until then."

As he was strolling toward his mother, Alvanley stopped him. "How is the wife hunting going?"

Merton struggled not to glance back at Miss Stern. "Slowly."

"Well if you plan to get married this Season, you should stop wasting waltzes on squires' daughters." His friend stopped to take a pinch of snuff from his enameled box. "Care to try my new sort?"

Dom took the box and inhaled. "Too much Macouba."

Miss Stern was a baronet's daughter? He never thought to even ask, though who he could have gotten the information from he did not know. What else did his friend know?

"Though I suppose," Alvanley continued, "you were forced to dance with her due to your relationship with your cousin."

Merton raised a brow indicating his friend should continue.

"Old family. Had the property for centuries."

The hairs on his neck prickled. Surely Alvanley was not interested in . . . "Indeed, why did you think to inquire?"

"Good-looking chit. Thought if her dowry made it worth the while I'd give it a go."

"And does it?"

"No, just barely respectable. Not enough to tempt me to put on a leg shackle."

God, Dom was holding his breath a lot tonight. He needed to find someone else to dance with so as not to make his dance with Miss Stern appear remarkable. "I see Lady Mary. I think I'll ask her to join me in this set."

Alvanley bowed. "Good hunting."

He did ask Lady Mary to dance and Lady Jane. He avoided Miss Turley, even though her stare bore holes into him. Finally he decided it would be churlish not to stand up with her. He bowed. "May I have the honor of this dance?"

She smiled politely, but her blue eyes were hard as ice. "Of course, my lord. Such a good thing you waited until the evening was almost over, I would have had to refuse you earlier."

"Then it is my good fortune to find you free." He returned her smile. It was a dashed good thing he'd already decided not to marry her, else he'd probably not have discovered what a cat she was until it was too late.

After the set he returned her to her cousin. "I must go to my mother. She will wish to depart soon. I bid you a good evening."

"I wish you the same, my lord."

Elizabeth Turley watched Merton weave his way through the crowded room. "What am I to do, Lavvie? Papa has his heart set on Merton."

Her cousin, Lavinia, Lady Manners, sighed. "He does seem to have cooled. You may have to think of something drastic."

"Such as?"

"Hmm." She tapped her fan against her cheek. "Perhaps something that would require him to marry you."

Elizabeth closed her eyes for a moment. Lavvie's idea would never work. "You do know his reputation? He is so stuffy, he made his mistress dress in high-necked gowns and would only buy her subdued jewels."

"How on earth do you know about that?" her cousin squealed. "You are not supposed to know anything about mis—that sort of female."

"Hush, you'll draw attention to us. How do you think I heard? My brother told me. Gavin was at Oxford with Merton."

Lavvie fluttered her fan. "Gavin should not speak to you of such things."

Elizabeth shrugged. "He only told me because he has seen my interest in Merton." She lowered her voice to a whisper. "Someone has to pull us out of River Tick."

"Would Gavin help you with Merton?"

"No." Elizabeth shook her head. "My brother doesn't like him. Gavin says he's a dry stick and would make me unhappy."

"'Unhappy' is not having enough money to live on. At least your portion is safe."

"Yes, it is a good thing my grandfather had the sense not to allow my father to handle it. I wish I could marry for love." Elizabeth blinked, keeping the tears at bay. "Still, I have an obligation to my family. We need to think of something and fast."

"You aren't the only one who has had to sacrifice."

Elizabeth nodded. Lavvie had been made to marry a man that ignored her for the most part then blamed her for not giving him an heir.

"Enough of that," she said bracingly. "What's done is done." She moved to rap her feathered fan against one hand. "Let me think about it. I am sure to come up with a scheme."

Elizabeth pressed her lips into a thin line. Sometimes her cousin's plans were not the best, yet what choice did she have? "As long as it does not ruin my reputation in the process."

After Lord Merton left, Dotty danced every set. Finally footsore, she rejoined Grace and the others. "What a wonderful evening this has been."

Louisa smiled and Charlotte said, "You are a success. I wonder if the gentlemen will think of a silly name for us."

Louisa cocked her head to the side. "What do you mean?"

Dotty laughed. "Last year in our home county, Charlotte and I were dubbed Sun and Moon."

"Ah"—Louisa's eyes brimmed with laughter—"I understand. Well, I would love it if they thought of something for the three of us."

Behind them Matt made a growling sound. Charlotte and Louisa started to giggle. He was so protective. It really was very funny.

"He's never going to make it through the Season at this rate." Grace took his arm. "Come, my love. There is a brandy waiting for you in the drawing room."

In fact, wine, biscuits, fruit, cheese, and brandy awaited when they returned home.

Louisa took a glass of wine and fell on the biscuits. "I am famished. There is nothing but bread and butter at Almack's."

"It has always been that way." Grace dipped her spoon into a roll of Stilton. "Which is the reason for this. I do not know how one can expect to dance all evening without nourishment."

Dotty ate a few strawberries and a soft white cheese. "I agree. I am ravenous."

"We may have to add some bread and meat," Matt said, getting up.

After their hunger was assuaged, Dotty, Louisa, and Charlotte went upstairs to their parlor. Tears of joy suddenly pricked the back of Dotty's lids. Being here with Charlotte was everything she'd hoped it would be. It did not even matter that Merton had ignored her the rest of the evening. "I am so happy I'm here."

Charlotte hugged her. "I'm glad, too. The Season would not have been the same without you."

"I agree." Louisa opened the door. "The three of us will have so much fun."

Dotty took a seat on the sofa as she reviewed the evening. Lord Harrington had stood up twice with Charlotte. Lord Bentley asked Louisa several times, but her dance card had been full. She confided in Dotty that even if it had not been, she would not stand up with him more than once.

Still, Dotty was impressed. "It looks as if the two of you have already made conquests."

Louisa plopped down on a chair. "Please do not say that. Lord Bentley is very kind, but I feel nothing for him other than friendship."

"Poor Bentley." Always softhearted, Charlotte pulled a face. "You will break his heart."

"I don't want to do that. If only he would take my hints." Louisa sighed. "Being too direct with him would be like kicking a puppy."

"Perhaps we can come up with something," Dotty said. "Charlotte, what about you? Do you wish Lord Harrington would take himself off?"

"No." She smiled softly. "As I said before, it is early days yet, but I think I may have found my match."

A few moments later, Dotty yawned. "I am for my bed. I shall see you in the morning."

Entering her chamber, she found her maid curled up in a chair. "Wake up, drowsy-head. I'm back."

Polly jerked her head up. "Oh, miss. I'm so sorry. I must have fallen asleep."

"Next time lie down on the sofa. It will be much more comfortable." Dotty wished she could tell her maid not to wait up, but there was no one else to help her. "Unfortunately, I'll never get out of this gown without your help."

"It don't matter." Polly yawned. "May told me all about the late nights."

Dotty pressed her lips together. "Be that as it may, you need rest as well. Try to find time to take a nap during the day, or if that is not possible, do so after I leave. I promise, I shall understand."

Once she was in her nightgown, she dismissed her maid and sat on the window seat. Tonight everything had been perfect. All the gentlemen were polite and danced well, but Merton stood out as the most handsome, most graceful, and kindest. He was the one who had enabled her to dance her first London waltz. Although he had not asked her again, she had caught him glancing at her throughout the evening, and he never danced with another lady more than once.

She sighed. It was probably much too soon to form an

attachment. Then she remembered her mother saying that the first time she saw Papa, she knew he was the one. Perhaps it would be the same for her. But would the gentleman feel the same? Perhaps, she should have gotten her father's side of the story as well.

Chapter Six

Dom handed his mother into the town coach waiting for them outside of Almack's and closed the door. "I have decided to walk."

"Good night then, dear. I won't wait up for you."

He tapped the side of the vehicle and it started forward. Alvanley's comments concerning Miss Stern stuck in Dom's mind and wouldn't let go. A baronet's daughter. Of course many peers wouldn't think anything of it. She was after all a lady. But the Marquis of Merton, his uncle had said, never married out of the peerage. Even if the family was old and respected.

The problem was she was everything he had ever dreamed of. Not that he had actually dreamed of a lady, but when he saw her he knew she was what he wanted. And he had dreamed of her last night.

Lush pink lips, hair blacker than midnight with fine curls that danced around her slim shoulders. Her green eyes put emeralds to shame. Her gown had given him tantalizing glimpses as to what lay beneath. Her bodice cut just low enough so as to give him a hint of the lovely milk-white mounds. He had never liked the low necklines many gentlemen admired, but damn if he didn't wish her gown had been the slightest bit lower. But then, other gentlemen would see her charms as well. He didn't want that. She incited him with a desire he'd never had for a woman. Yet perhaps that was the very reason he should look elsewhere. Passion, or rather love in a marriage, was to be avoided.

Uncle Alasdair said it always ended badly. It was that which caused the untimely deaths of Dom's father and his grandfather before him. His uncle told him how his father was showing off for Mama when he died, and his grandfather had tried to make it through a storm to get to his grandmother's side when she was sick. Grandmamma had lived, but his grandfather never recovered from the chill he had caught. What ill would befall Dom and thus his family if he married for love rather than duty?

Turning the corner into Grosvenor Square, he shrugged, attempting to dislodge the weight that had descended. He had invited Miss Stern to the opera, but after that he should probably put her out of his mind. The door opened as he climbed the steps. He handed the servant his hat and cane. "Good evening, Paken."

Bowing, his butler replied, "I trust you had a pleasant evening, my lord?"

"As expected." Dom turned toward the left and started down the corridor to his study. He didn't drink much, but right now he desperately needed a brandy.

Eunice turned her head in the direction of the door to the corridor. "Well?"

"He's home, my lady," her maid said. "Don't look too happy about it either. Went to his study and called for brandy."

"That may be a good sign. He doesn't normally drink spirits and never alone." Yet, due to all the nonsense Alasdair had filled Dominic's head with, she never actually knew. A mother should know her child better than she did.

"Matilda, do you think he could be smitten with Miss Stern?"

Matilda's lips formed a moue. "He certainly had trouble keeping his eyes off her tonight. On the other hand, he did not single her out."

"No." Eunice frowned. "Although, even if he is interested, one could not expect him to indicate it at Almack's. It would cause too much talk. He did manage to be the first to waltz with her."

Her cousin fell quiet for a moment, then said, "Perhaps at the Featherington ball he will make more of a push. He is just so cautious."

"So unlike his father." Eunice sighed. "Why, when David saw me for the first time, he finagled an introduction and barely left my side until the accident."

She blinked back the tears.

Matilda reached over and patted Eunice's hand. "There, there. You didn't have him for long, but you know he loved you."

She took out a handkerchief and dabbed at her cheeks. "Yes. I never for a moment doubted his love. Now, if only Dominic could find the same type of love, I wouldn't worry about him so much." She sniffed one last time and took a sip of wine. "What do we know about the girl?"

"According to your cousin, Grace, she is the daughter of the local squire. Sir Henry Stern . . ." Matilda told Eunice all the information she'd been able to glean over the course of the evening. It was not much as Grace had been busy with her charges and stepmother-in-law as well as friends who had stopped by. Still it was enough for Eunice to form an opinion.

She took another swallow of wine. "Miss Stern sounds perfect. Someone who will challenge Dominic rather than be cowed by him."

"I agree, yet how to bring it about?"

Drumming her fingers on the round side table, she

turned the problem over in her mind. "First we must ensure Miss Stern is interested in my son, and he feels the same. Once we know that, I am sure something will come to me. David always said I was the most imaginative person he knew."

Dom woke the next day still bothered by Miss Stern. Somehow he must manage to avoid her. He groaned. *The carriage ride!* He'd engaged to take her for a drive today. A sense of guilt nagged at him, and he could hear his uncle's stern voice berating his decision. Yet he had rarely been happier and was looking forward to spending more time with her. To pay homage to his duty, he resolved to remain at home and work on estate matters until it was time to leave.

Midway through the morning, he was interrupted by his cousin Worthington striding into the study. Dom glanced up, fighting the urge to scowl. "Is there a reason my butler did not announce you?"

"Because I told him not to." Uninvited, Worthington dropped into a chair as if he were in his own home.

"See here, Worthington. I don't like being disturbed without notice."

He raised a brow. "Neither do I. Yet you had no compunction about running roughshod over my butler."

There was that, but it was different. "I am the head of the family."

"You are not the head of my family," Worthington growled.

Dom decided to ignore his cousin's ill humor. "My uncle said—"

"I don't give a damn what that old windbag said." Worthington leaned forward in the chair, his hands clutching the arms. "I'll show you the charter if you don't believe me."

Dom knew of the charter, of course. And despite what his uncle had said, the titles were different. But Uncle Alasdair insisted that as a marquis outranked an earl, Dom was still the head of Worthington's house. Now that his uncle was dead, Dom didn't know what prompted him to needle Worthington every time they met, but he just couldn't seem to help himself. "I'm busy. Why are you here?"

Worthington leaned back in the chair. "To speak to you about Miss Stern before anything can take root."

Dom had never before had the desire to reach out and grab a man by the throat, but now seemed like an excellent time to start. "What are you talking about?"

"You. Dotty deserves better than to be courted by a cold fish like you."

Sweat broke out on Dom's hands as he tapped his pencil. Was his cousin going to forbid him from seeing her? Even the name, Dotty, that he'd hated, didn't seem so bad anymore. "Who said I was courting her?"

Leaning forward again, Worthington's brows drew together. "That is exactly what I am talking about. You care for no one but yourself and your blasted consequence."

His hands curled into fists. "You know nothing about me."

"I know how you vote," Worthington snarled. "I know you supported the Corn Laws that will end up causing men, women, and children to starve."

Of course Dom had voted for the Acts. His uncle had explained how it would help the country. "Supporting the government is the right thing to do."

"Only if you are a large landowner who doesn't give a damn about anything or anyone else." Worthington's jaw clenched. "But I didn't come to talk politics to you. How can you say you're not courting her when you made an engagement to attend the opera with her, had Countess Esterhazy, of all the busy gossips, introduce you to Dotty to waltz, and asked her for a drive in the Park today? Do you honestly think the rest of the *ton* will be as sanguine as you are being? *You* will have brought her into their sights, and if you cast her aside, where will she be? Or do you even care? After all, she's only the daughter of a country baronet."

The pencil Dom held snapped in two. Rage coursed through his veins, and he wanted to strike out. He forced himself to calm down. Fighting with his cousin would not help him. "Just what do you suggest I do?"

"Cancel your plans. Say you have an emergency at Merton or one of your other estates, and leave Town."

He breathed through his nose to keep from leaping over the desk and pummeling Worthington. All his life he had done what others told him to do. No longer. Damn. Baronet's daughter or not, he wanted her. "No. If necessary I will see her father and ask his permission, but you are not going to stop me from *courting* her."

Worthington rose from his chair, his hands fisted.

Dom stood as well, keeping his eyes on his cousin's. He took a step to move out from behind his desk.

And the door opened.

"There you are, Worthington." Eunice smiled as she strolled into the room. "Grace has come to see me, and she said you might be in here. Oh no, please do not stand on my account. I came to invite you to join us for a cup of tea."

Eunice glanced from her son to Worthington. Grace had been correct. The two idiots were about to kill each other. Eunice took Worthington's arm in both her hands. "I shall not accept a refusal, so come along now. We do not see near enough of you and your family. You too, Dominic. You spend far too much time on estate business." She turned back to Worthington. "You do not know how happy I am that you and Grace have married. I am a distant cousin of hers, and her mother was my dearest friend. I longed for her happiness."

She made sure to keep up a string of worthless chatter,

not allowing them to get a word in edgewise while almost dragging the man with her. Thank Heaven she had been in time to stop a brawl. Men! What would they think of next? Although she had no problem with Dominic hitting some-one, it could not be his cousin. She and Grace must find a way to reconcile the families. This animosity had gone on long enough.

Good Lord, the distance to the morning room had never seemed so great before. Eunice was very glad for the infor-mation Grace had given her about Dotty. In fact, Eunice could hardly wait to officially meet the young lady. Though there still remained much work to be done to convince Dominic to start thinking for himself. Perhaps today was a beginning.

Grace glanced up sharply when Eunice entered the morn-ing room. She gave an imperceptible nod, and Grace seemed to start breathing again. Men made things so much more difficult than they needed to be. However in this case, a little of the right sort of opposition might be just what Dominic needed to push him closer to Miss Stern.

That afternoon, Dotty, Louisa, and Charlotte were drink-ing tea in the morning room on the first floor in the back of Stanwood House. They had been discussing the changes being made to Worthington House, where they would reside after this Season.

Dotty swallowed another bite of the excellent ginger bis-cuits. "When will the renovations be far enough along for us to see them?"

"I think in about a month," Charlotte said, placing her cup down. "They will not be finished until later in the summer."

Apparently, the whole of the schoolroom floor and sev-eral other rooms had to be refurbished. "Will you still come to Stanwood Hall this summer?"

Charlotte's smile was a little sad. "Yes, for at least most of the summer. Matt insists that Charlie remain conversant with his estate. We shall spend the rest of the year at Worthington Hall. She paused for a moment. "Even in this short time, Matt has made many things so much easier for us."

Since their father's death, Charlie, Charlotte's brother, was the Earl of Stanwood, but he was just sixteen and still in school. Grace had been in charge of everything concerning the estate.

"We do not actually know when we'll be at Worthington," Louisa added. "With Grace increasing, and all the children, Matt is renovating the Hall as well. Perhaps we shall be at Stanwood for a much longer time."

This was news. "Grace is having a baby?"

"Yes." Charlotte laughed lightly. "Apparently our wedding wishes were answered. She is due in December."

"Your wedding wishes?"

"I so wish you had been there." Her eyes sparkled. "We made Charlie read a letter we had all written. It ended with the hope that there would be more children."

"As if eleven were not enough!" Dotty couldn't help but chuckle. "He may have to add a whole new wing."

They talked of the changes being made to the estate and the parties they were due to attend that evening. Then Louisa directed her gaze at Dotty. "Are you really going driving with Merton this afternoon?"

She smiled and hoped the idea that Merton might court her did not drive a wedge between them. "I am. I have listened to all you have said, but until he shows himself to be someone I do not wish to know, I will allow him to squire me. He was truly very helpful last evening."

Louisa frowned. "Only because he wanted to dance with you."

"I won't deny he benefited, but so did I, and then he did his duty by standing up with other young ladies."

Charlotte sighed. "He is very handsome."

"Charlotte," Louisa and Dotty said at the same time. Dotty laughed. "Yes, but as Papa says, handsome is as handsome does. We shall see."

"I don't want to see you hurt," Louisa said softly.

Dotty took her new friend's hands. "Neither do I. Yet risk is part of life."

A knock came on the door and a footman entered. "Miss, Lord Merton is waiting for you."

"Please tell him I shall be down directly."

"Yes, miss."

Donning the bonnet and gloves she'd brought to the parlor, she glanced at her friends. "Perhaps I'll see you at the Park?"

"You shall. After all, we would not desert you." Louisa hugged Dotty. "We shall be along shortly. Charlotte is driving the carriage. If you need to be rescued, we can whisk you away."

Dotty descended the stairs, surprised to find Merton gazing up at her. She had thought the butler would have put him in a parlor. His eyes were so warm, heat rose in her cheeks. Charlotte was right; he was very good-looking.

When Dotty got to the bottom tread, he took her hand. "You look charming."

"Thank you, my lord."

She started to curtsey, but he held her up, tucking her hand in his arm. "I did not know what you liked, so I brought a less spirited team."

"I appreciate your consideration, but it wasn't necessary." As they stepped to the pavement, she saw the perfectly matched pair waited patiently. "Oh! Grays are my favorite."

He smiled and handed her into a dark green curricle with yellow detailing. The seats were gray leather, two shades darker than the horses. "I'm glad you like them. Do you know a lot about horses?"

"Yes, my father is the squire. I was taught to ride almost

before I could walk, and was driving when I was just ten years old. At home, I have my own gig, but nothing nearly as lovely as this."

Though he was still put out about Worthington's visit earlier, apparently Miss Stern knew nothing about it. Dom went around to the other side of the carriage. She should have a vehicle every bit as beautiful as she was. She was quiet while he navigated the busy streets, but he sensed that she noticed everything around them. "Is this the first time you've visited the Park in a carriage?"

What a stupid thing to have asked. He knew it was. Yet, when she peeped up at him with those green eyes, he suddenly didn't feel like an idiot anymore.

"You handle the horses very well."

Dom's chest puffed out. Since when did a woman's compliment mean so much? "Thank you. I'm a member of the Four Horse Club."

Good God, now he was bragging, and by the confused expression on her face she didn't even know what he was talking about. "Never mind. It is not important. Did you have fun last evening at Almack's?"

She smiled and made a tinkling sound. "Yes, indeed. I danced every set. It was very kind of you to ensure I could waltz."

"You're welcome. It was the least I could do." Dom wanted to groan. From stupid to callow. What was happening to him?

"Today, all three of us received so many poesies and other small gifts, I was amazed."

That's what he'd forgotten to do. Damn Worthington for putting him out of temper. "It was only to be expected. You were the three loveliest young ladies in attendance."

She blushed slightly and turned her face from him so that only her profile showed.

"Charlotte and Louisa said it might happen, but truly I didn't expect it."

As they were nearing the Serpentine, the waterway that snaked through part of the Park, Miss Stern's attention was drawn away from him toward the water. The only thing he could see was a couple of boys with a sack.

"Oh no. Not here, too!" She glanced quickly at him. "My lord, please, you must stop!"

The second he slowed, she jumped from the carriage before he had a chance to hand her down. Skirts flapping around her ankles, she raced toward the youths. "Cease. Immediately!"

To Dom's amazement they did. He applied the carriage brake and strode after her. Although he couldn't hear what she was saying, having heard her chastise a man before, he had a deuced good idea. She was as imperious as a duchess when her ire was up. Nothing at all like he would have expected a baronet's daughter to act. Who knew how those ruffians would react.

As Miss Stern reached for the bag, the young men's faces became surly. They were both taller than her and, from their ragged garb, used to low society.

The one holding the sack scowled. "What ye 'bout? This here's none of yer concern."

She narrowed her eyes and the fierceness in her tone shocked Dom. "It is if what's in that bag is what I think it is."

The bag wiggled and emitted a small chirping cry.

"Aha." She held out her hand. Making it clear she expected to be obeyed. "Give it to me at once."

"Dotty"—Lady Charlotte appeared next to Miss Stern— "what is it?"

Dom glanced around; his cousin Louisa was here as well. Not only that, but a small crowd was gathering.

"Kittens," Miss Stern replied. The boy started to leave and she reached out to stop him. "Oh no you don't. Give them to me."

"We's just doing our dooty," the other lad said.

Duty. Did it excuse everything, even such cruelty? If

they were not going to listen to her, they would damn well listen to him. He took hold of the boy holding the sack, gripping the skinny wrist until the lad winced. "Miss Stern, you may take the bag now."

She grabbed it as the youth let go. The other lad advanced menacingly toward her. "We was promised a yellow bob if we brung them cats back dead."

Someone in the group surrounding them gasped, but Dom was focused on the threat to Miss Stern. "One yellow bob for the two of you?"

Not taking his eyes off the wiggling bag, the youth nodded.

Dom dug into his waistcoat pocket and flipped one coin at the boy as he made a grab for the bag. It landed at his feet. He glanced at the lad whose arm he was still gripping. "Here's one for each of you. Now leave."

The boy who'd been holding the kittens appeared as if he wanted to argue but his friend, seeing the frowning faces all around them, pulled him away. After a few short words, the lads left.

Dom addressed the crowd that had gathered around them, "This is no concern of yours."

He heard a couple of low sniggers made by a few of his acquaintances from White's. Damnation, this was going to be all around Town by this evening.

"Saving animals now, Merton?" a snide voice remarked. "What will you do next?"

Raising his quizzing glass, Dom slowly surveyed the portly gentleman. His red face clashed with his purple coat, nipped in so tightly at the waist, he must be wearing a corset. "Perhaps I should save you from your tailor, Seymour."

The man raised his chin. "This is the very latest fashion."

Dom raised a brow. "Lavender pantaloons with yellow stripes?"

"I'm setting a trend."

He gave an exaggerated shudder. "Lord save us from your sense of fashion."

Finally insulted, Lord Seymour huffed off. Dom looked around to see if anyone else required assistance leaving, but the crowd was drifting away. Miss Stern, Louisa, and Charlotte huddled around the bag.

"What are you going to do with them?" Louisa asked.

For the first time Miss Stern seemed a little lost. "I don't know."

"We shall take them home with us," Lady Charlotte offered. "You know how everyone fell in love with Whiskers after you saved her."

Miss Stern shook her head. "I cannot. I promised Papa I would not bring any stray animals to your house."

With what Dom could only describe as an evil grin, Louisa glanced at him. "Ask Merton to take them."

Miss Stern looked up at him, her beautiful green eyes pleading. "I know I am asking a great deal, but would you, my lord? Give them a home?"

At that moment, he would have done anything for her; getting the better of Cousin Louisa was only an added benefit. "Of course. I'm sure they will come in handy."

The smile Miss Stern gave him was more than the sun, moon, and stars all together. "Thank you. We should get them there quickly. I cannot let them out of this bag until we do."

"Of course." Just as he was wondering how he was going to keep them on the curricle after he took her home, Lady Charlotte solved his problem.

"We will all go and make sure they are safe and comfortable."

As they walked back to the carriages, a barouche was stopped on the verge. Lady Bellamny, one of the Gorgons of the *ton,* nodded. What the devil did that mean?

He inclined his head. "My lady."

"Glad to see you finally doing something useful, Merton."

Before he could respond, she signaled for her driver to move on.

A groom standing by the phaeton his cousins arrived in helped the ladies up.

Dom took the squirming bag from Dotty and, once she was settled, gave it back to her. "How many are there?"

"The best we can figure is three, but I won't know until it's opened."

He started his horses. "Cats are thought to be useful. I wonder why the boys were being paid to kill them."

Miss Stern bit her lower lip. "It is possible they were going to be used for fur."

"Fur?" Disgusting. He remembered being allowed to hold the kitchen cat when he was young, before his father died. "Who would buy anything made of cat fur?"

"Sometimes it can pass for rabbit or another animal." She pulled her full lower lip between her teeth. "Thank you for agreeing to take them." Her tone, almost a whisper, was infused with emotion. "I know Louisa made it difficult to refuse."

He was pleased that Louisa had very little to do with his decision. It was his regard for Miss Stern that made him do it. "Not at all. I would have offered even if my cousin hadn't said anything."

Miss Stern turned to him and there was that smile again. "I know you would have. You are not nearly as black as you are painted."

What the hell was he to say to that? Did people really think he was heartless? He nodded curtly. "Thank you."

In a few minutes Dom brought his curricle to a halt outside of his house. The door opened and two footmen came running out to help the ladies. Dom almost laughed at the look on the face of one of the servants when Miss Stern handed him the sack while she prepared to alight from the carriage. He came around to help her. Now he would have to figure out what he was supposed to do with a bunch of cats.

"My lord?" She shook out her skirts. "Could you have some cream brought to a parlor while we take a look at them? Afterward, I suppose they will have to start earning their keep in the kitchen."

He hadn't expected her to be so practical and it pleased him immensely. "Of course. I'll send for my mother as well."

Miss Stern nodded. "That is a good idea."

"Paken," Dom said. "I need a large bowl of cream and probably some scraps of meat. We shall be in the morning room. Please ask my mother to attend me."

His butler bowed. "I believe her ladyship is already present, my lord."

Miss Stern turned to Dom; her wide green gaze made him want to kiss her. "Thank you so much."

"It was nothing. I daresay they will be a beneficial addition to my household."

He shoved the idea that he might be starting to fall in love with her far back into his brain. That he must not do. Love had no place in his life, only duty.

Chapter Seven

Dotty placed her hand on Merton's arm as he escorted her down a corridor, to a room at the back of the house. Louisa and Charlotte followed behind. He opened the door and sunlight flooded the light yellow chamber. Two middle-aged ladies sat on either side of the fireplace. One had dark brown hair, with just a few strands of silver. The other one's hair was the same color as Merton's but a bit faded.

The blond-haired woman set aside her novel, stood, then came forward. Her pale blue eyes sparkled with curiosity. "Dominic?"

Merton took the woman's hand. "Mama, allow me to introduce Lady Charlotte Carpenter, Lady Louisa Vivers, and Miss Stern. Ladies, my mother."

Dotty, Louisa, and Charlotte curtseyed.

Lady Merton smiled broadly. "I am very pleased you've come to visit. Miss Stern, may I know your first name?"

"Yes, my lady. It is Dorothea."

"Lovely." Lady Merton glanced at the wiggling bag. "What have we here?"

"Kittens," Dotty replied. "We rescued them today, and Lord Merton very kindly offered them a home."

Her ladyship's smile grew broader. "Did he indeed? Well, then, let us see how they look."

"I think it would be better if I sat on the floor." She glanced at her ladyship, hoping neither Merton nor his mother thought she was being ill-bred. Yet one could scarcely keep track of kittens otherwise.

"Yes, indeed," Lady Merton responded. "The kittens are likely to fall off the sofa. I would join you on the floor, but I am afraid that a low stool will suit me better."

Lord Merton quickly placed a stool covered by an embroidered cushion next to his mother. Dotty, Louisa, and Charlotte, took places on the floor in front of her ladyship. Merton sat in a chair near his mother.

Dotty opened the sack, expecting the animals to crawl out on their own. Instead, the first one gazed up at her with round yellow eyes. She reached in and, one by one, pulled out four small gray cats.

"Oh, aren't they beautiful!" Charlotte reached for one and handed Louisa another.

Lady Merton motioned for a kitten to be given to her as well. It chirped. "My, my, how unusual. Ladies, I believe you have rescued a litter of Chartreux. See their yellow eyes, and feel how thick and soft the fur is? When I was a girl, we visited cousins in France. The daughter had a cat like this. It followed her everywhere." She addressed the kitten. "I do not know how you ended up here, but I suspect you have quite the pedigree."

Dotty glanced at Merton who warily watched one of the kittens scramble over his boot. "I thought they could make their living in the kitchen and storage rooms."

Lady Merton placed the kitten on the floor next to the bowl of cream that had arrived. "Hmm, they are known to be great hunters. However they also bond with one person, much like a dog does."

"I'm going to ask Grace if I can have one." Charlotte held the kitten close to her.

"I shall as well," Louisa said. "Dotty, it is too bad you made that promise to your papa not to bring animals to Stanwood House."

"Yes." She would have loved to have a kitten. "But one must keep one's word."

Charlotte and Louisa rose, each holding a kitten. "We will see you back at Stanwood House," Charlotte said.

Lady Merton smiled kindly. "Miss Stern, you may visit the remaining two anytime you wish. Simply send a note around."

"Thank you, my lady." It was a lovely offer, but Dotty knew her ladyship was just being kind. She glanced at Merton whose brow was furrowed as he watched the cats eat the bits of meat. Did he regret his decision?

When he stood, his face was a mask. "We must not keep the horses standing. Miss Stern, I shall take you home now."

"Yes, of course." Dotty took the hand he held out and rose. Once she was back in his curricle, she settled her skirts. "I'm sorry if I caused you a problem."

He glanced at her, the mask was gone, and his eyes twinkled with humor. "It's no difficulty for me at all. My mother and staff will care for the remaining animals."

"Of course." How silly of her to think *he* would actually take care of them. Yet, what had made him appear so pensive?

One of the footmen held the door open as she entered the hall. Childish screeches of delight emanated from the back of the house, then a command for them to be quiet stopped the noise. After giving her hat, parasol, and gloves to the footman, she strolled to the morning room and stood next to the wall. All the children were present as well as their governess and tutor. Daisy, the younger Great Dane, was stretched out on the floor gently nosing one kitten.

Charlotte held the other one up to Grace. "Isn't she precious?"

Grace took the kitten. "She is. We have never had house cats before; I suppose it's time."

"I knew you would say yes." Charlotte clapped her hands.

Dotty gave a small sigh of relief. She had managed to rescue the kittens and keep her promise to her father.

Stroking the small bundle of fur, Grace grinned. "Where did you find them?"

"Dotty and Merton saved them from being killed."

"Merton?" Matt strode to Grace. "That's hard to believe."

"I know, but it's true." Louisa took her kitten from Daisy and gave it to Mary, at age five, the youngest of Grace's sisters. "Be gentle with her." Mary nodded. Louisa glanced at Matt. "Dotty saw some boys with a sack, and Merton made them give her the cats. We brought home two, he and his mother kept the other two."

"Harrumph." Matt rubbed his chin. "He may have been helpful today, but a man doesn't change overnight." He glanced at Dotty, but Grace laid her hand on his arm and shook her head.

As much as she was beginning to like Merton, she knew that he must have done more than lord it over Matt for him to dislike his cousin so much. Maybe Grace would tell Dotty the whole story.

After Dom had returned from taking Miss Stern to Stanwood House, he made his way to his study, across the corridor from the morning room. As he was about to close the door, a gray streak flew by him, stopped, and stared up with wide eyes.

"What are you doing here?"

The kitten blinked and made a chirping noise, before sauntering to Dom, then stretching up on his boot.

"If you claw those," he said sternly, "my valet will make you into a muff."

He strolled over to his desk and the cat followed. "I believe, sir, you are under a misapprehension. I do not like cats."

Completely ignoring him, the animal laid down next to Dom's foot.

A knock sounded on the door, and it opened to admit one of his footmen. "Sorry to bother you, my lord. One of the kittens is missing." He looked down. "There you are, you little beastie. Come with me now."

As the servant bent down to take the cat, it scooted behind Dom.

The footman gave an exasperated sigh. "I'm sorry, my lord. Cyrille here keeps escaping."

Dom raised a brow. Named so soon? "Where are the rest of them?"

"The young ladies took two, and her ladyship has the other one." The footman indicated the cat. "But this little devil won't stay with his sister."

Dom twisted and stared down at the kitten. "Escaping the ladies already?" The cat rubbed against his boot. "Very well, as long as you don't make a habit of it, you may hide here for a little while."

After the footman bowed himself out, Dom addressed the animal again. "Do not become used to staying with me. As I told you before, I am not at all fond of cats and would not have lifted a finger to help you. Unfortunately, your benefactress is unable to house you."

And the look on Miss Stern's face when he had agreed to take in the kittens was worth even his boots being scratched.

Cyrille followed Dom when he went to a chair next to the fireplace and picked up a book. "You may lie at my feet. My valet won't like cat hair on my pantaloons or coat."

As if the kitten understood, he curled up on one of Dom's boots and fell asleep. His mother had said they were like dogs, which put him in mind of Poodle Byng. His French poodle accompanied him on carriage drives. Merton glanced down at Cyrille. "Before you get any more ideas, you may not go driving with me."

The kitten stretched out a sleepy paw and yawned.

"Good. I am pleased we have an understanding."

He thought back to Miss Stern's fierceness in rescuing the kittens. How far did her desire to help others go? Was she one of those reformers who tried to assist anyone she perceived to be in need, even when they'd made the decision to live less than honorable lives?

Despite what he had said to Worthington, her birth alone made her unsuitable to be his bride. Alvanley had been right; Dom was making wife hunting harder than it needed to be and all because of a pair of clear green eyes and black hair. Since he had met Miss Stern, the more popular blond-haired ladies seemed to fade into the background. He couldn't even bring himself to make another list.

He reached down to stroke Cyrille. His mother was correct; the fur was very soft. The kitten rolled over, offering its stomach just like a dog. There was one fortunate thing about having the cats. At least now he would have an excuse to visit Miss Stern. She would wish to know how her protégés were faring.

The next day, Dom made himself stay away from Miss Stern, attending to the estate business he had neglected the day before. Instead of remaining at home, he had luncheon at his club with Fotherby, then eschewed the Park. But he could not seem to expunge her from his mind, and by late afternoon he was even looking forward to attending the Featherington ball solely so he could see her.

That evening when Dom entered Lord and Lady Featherington's town house with his mother and Matilda, he caught himself searching the ballroom for Miss Stern, Dorothea. If he had his way, she would be called Thea or Doro. Though perhaps the second was too close to Wellington's nickname. Thea it was, even if he did not yet have permission to use her first name.

He found her as a gentleman claimed her for a country

dance that was forming. Dom's chest tightened when she placed her hand on the other man's arm. What was it about Thea that made him want to keep other gentlemen away from her? That gave him the sense she was his alone?

She glanced up. When their eyes met, she smiled. Damn. If he didn't find something to distract him, he was liable to lean against the wall making a cake of himself watching her. Glancing around the room, he noticed Miss Turley still didn't have a partner, and he walked over to her. "Miss Turley, may I have this dance?"

She smiled and curtseyed politely as she always did. "Of course, my lord."

Perhaps he had misjudged her. Still the fact remained that he felt nothing as he bowed and kissed her fingers. None of the warmth or excitement he experienced with Thea.

While taking their places on the dance floor, his gaze strayed to Thea again. He really should focus on a more suitable lady to wed. Someone who didn't cause scenes in the Park or, come to think of it, have radical ideas about estate management, and saddle him with kittens. His mind boggled at what else she might be capable of, given time. If she felt called to rescue animals, why couldn't it have been a good hunting hound?

He grinned, then realized Miss Turley thought he was responding to something she'd said. The corners of her lips turned up. She was considered one of the Diamonds of the Season. Perhaps he should have paid more attention to her, but her golden hair and pale beauty didn't appeal to him. He caught sight of Thea again and could barely keep his mind on his dance partner while Thea smiled, talked and, apparently, enjoyed herself with another gentleman. The desire to snatch her away from the man rose up in him and he let out a low growl.

"My lord, are you all right?" the young matron next to him asked.

"Perfectly. Just something in my throat." Jupiter, he had to get a hold of himself before he created a scene.

What possessed his mother wanting to come here when there was Aliesbury's ball? At least there he would be around his own friends, and he would not be subjected to the sight of Thea dancing with others. Dom forced his attention back to Miss Turley. What was her first name? He had been considering her as a wife and hadn't even bothered to find out.

After returning her to her cousin, Dom pushed his way through the crowded ballroom to Thea, interrupting another gentleman about to request a dance. "Miss Stern?" She glanced at him from beneath her long black lashes and smiled. He sucked in a breath.

To hell with duty.

"Are you still free for the supper dance?"

"I am, my lord."

"See here, Merton," Mr. Garvey said, "I was about to request the same set."

Dom wanted to cheer, as if he'd won a battle. Instead he raised his quizzing glass. "Next time you will have to be faster."

Garvey's scowl made Dom want to laugh. He and the man had been friends when they were young, but after Dom's father had died, Garvey never came around anymore.

Thea's eyes sparkled with pleasure, and Dom's heart buoyed as if he'd won some sort of prize. Never in his life had he felt like this. Tomorrow he would deal with finding an appropriate woman to wed. For now, he was going to enjoy having Thea in his arms.

Dotty glanced only for a moment at Merton's retreating back, before she realized Miss Meadows was speaking to her. "I'm sorry, what did you say?"

The young lady placed her hand consolingly on Dotty's

arm. "You poor dear. It is such a shame Mr. Garvey spent so much time greeting you rather than asking you to dance."

She almost gaped at the young woman. "I am sorry, I do not understand you."

Her eyes widened at Dotty's confusion. "Why, having to stand up with Lord Merton of course."

"Indeed." Miss Featherington nodded. "He is a very good dancer, but has no conversation at all."

"As far as I am concerned"—Miss Smyth raised a brow—"one is allowed to be dull when one is a marquis, and he is very good-looking."

How could they say such mean things about Merton? Anger burbled up inside Dotty, but she maintained her calm mien. "I do not find him dull or without conversation in the least." All three ladies stared at Dotty as if she'd gone mad. "I think he is very charming," she said, warming to her topic. "In fact, just yesterday, he helped me rescue kittens from some boys who would have drowned them."

This time Miss Meadows's jaw dropped. "If anyone else would have told me that story, I would not have credited it."

"Admirable indeed, but what pray do you discuss?" Miss Smyth asked.

"All manner of things." Or rather, now that Dotty thought of it, she had spoken of a wide variety of issues, Merton merely nodded at the appropriate times, except for the once or twice he had paled slightly. "And he's a very good listener."

Now *that* was the absolute truth.

"I think he is taken with you, Miss Stern," Miss Featherington said. "For he rarely says a word to me when we dance."

"Perhaps he *is* shy," Miss Smyth added. "I suppose even a marquis can be uneasy around others."

Whatever it was about Merton, he fascinated Dotty. She enjoyed speaking and dancing with other gentlemen, but when Merton's gaze met hers, his eyes warmed and there was nothing boring about him. Her next partner arrived to claim his dance. The evening seemed to drag on forever before Merton finally was bowing to her to claim his waltz.

"Miss Stern?"

She relaxed into his arms, never fearing he would miss his step or trod on her toes. This time she decided to allow him to speak first.

The silence stretched for several minutes until he finally asked, "Are you interested in how the kittens are doing?"

"Yes. I would love to hear about them." How happy she was he had brought up the subject. By the end of yesterday afternoon, she'd convinced herself he had been trapped into taking them.

His expression was stern, but his eyes twinkled. "My mother took it upon herself to name them. The female is Camille, which means of unblemished character. I'm certain that is currently the case, yet one wonders for how long. The male is Cyrille, which means lordly. I think Mama could have used a little more discretion in naming him. He seems to have taken it to heart and has already cowed my footmen and entranced the maids. Although my butler still seems to have the upper hand with him, for the moment at least."

Dotty was unable to hold back a giggle. "Oh dear, I hope he is not causing too much disruption?"

"Only to me it appears."

She stopped smiling. "I'm so sorry. What has he done?"

This time he grinned. "He attached himself to me the first day and nothing I do will convince him I am better off without his company. This evening, he tried to accompany me."

Thea laughed again, a light tinkling sound that caused Dom to puff his chest out, just a little. He wasn't sure any lady had ever been truly amused by him before.

"I take it your butler was able to stop Cyrille?"

"Only by the expedient of grabbing him by the neck." Her eyes flew wide and he hastened to explain. "I assure you, it did no injury to the kitten. I am told that is what their mothers do."

Her face fell for a moment. "I wonder what happened to her. The kittens are only a few weeks old."

"I doubt we'll find out, unless those boys come with another bag of cats." If they'd not been in the middle of a crowded dance floor, Dom would have pulled her into his arms to comfort her. He gave himself a shake for thinking such thoughts.

"Perhaps they will and then we could have one of the servants follow the lads."

He did not know another lady who had as much compassion as she had. "Do you try to save everything?"

"When I'm able to, yes." She worried her bottom lip, obviously thinking of the kittens. "I believe it is our duty to help others, including animals."

Duty. There was that word again. Was he ignoring his obligations by dancing with Thea, knowing he should not consider marrying her? His uncle would be appalled, yet Dom had never had so much fun or been so drawn to a woman.

Thea lit corners of his soul he had thought permanently darkened. All he wanted to do was crush her to him and kiss her, run his hands over her body and make her his.

After tonight, he could not see her again. He would find some excuse to return to his estate. Worthington was right. If he remained in Town, he'd not be able to stay away from her, and that was not fair to her. Her father had probably spent a great deal to bring her out with hopes she'd find a proper match. And it could not be him.

Dom's stomach twisted at the idea of her in another man's bed, but she was everything his uncle had warned him against. No fortune, not of the peerage, and a reformer. Why did he want her so badly?

"After all," she said, "most people do not choose to be in a bad position."

Her beliefs were the exact opposite of those his uncle

had taught him. Yet, rather than debating her, he nodded. When the dance ended, he escorted her to the supper room, bracing himself as they joined his cousin.

Worthington had insisted Merton and Thea sit with them for supper. Other than their political differences, he had no idea why Worthington was so upset about Dom accompanying her. After he'd had time to give it some thought, his attention to Thea could be passed off as doing his cousin a favor. Therefore Worthington had no reason to berate Dom. He didn't like his cousin's attitude one bit. *Confound it.* He was one of the most eligible gentlemen on the Marriage Mart. Worthington had no right to treat him as if he was a penniless rogue.

At the end of the evening, Dom retrieved his mother and cousin, bid his hostess good-bye, went home to his well-appointed library, and poured a brandy with the intention of sorting out his muddled thoughts. Still smarting from Worthington's Turkish treatment, Dom scowled into his glass. Perhaps it was for the best. He had a duty to marry well, despite how much he was coming to like Thea.

A pair of laughing green eyes hovered in his mind.

Hell.

He tossed off the tumbler of brandy and slammed the glass on the table.

A footman adding wood to the fire, jumped. "You all right, my lord?"

Merton clenched his teeth. "Never better."

Rising, he left the room, resisting the urge to slam the door. Taking his temper out on servants would not do, but hitting someone would help. Tomorrow, he'd go to Jackson's Boxing Parlor.

The next morning, carrying through on his promise to himself, Dom sparred with one of Jackson's most promising young fighters. Stripped to the waist and barefooted,

Dom exchanged blow for blow. Sweat poured down his face and into his eyes. When he and his opponent were both winded, but refused to quit, Jackson himself called a halt to the bout.

"That's enough for today, my lord." The former champion removed Dom's gloves. "Don't know what's happened, but I've never seen you display more to the advantage. Pity you're a gentleman."

He nodded to Jackson and took a towel one of the boys handed him. Despite how well he'd done, it hadn't helped. All the frustration he had experienced last night was still present. After he changed, he made his way back home.

As he handed Paken his hat and cane, Dom turned to go to his study and almost tripped over Cyrille. "What do you want now?"

The cat stared up at him with a knowing look on his face. "Yes, well, perhaps you're right. Paken?"

"My lord?"

"Have my curricle brought around. I want the bays this time."

"Right away, my lord."

Not more than fifteen minutes later, Dom climbed into his carriage and threaded the ribbons through his fingers. A gray streak landed beside him followed by a footman clutching his wig. "I'm sorry, my lord. The little devil got away from me."

Dom glanced down at the cat. "So you think you're coming too, do you?"

Cyrille sat up as if he belonged there and was prepared to enjoy the sights.

"Well, don't forget it was your idea," Dom muttered to the kitten, before addressing his footman. "He may remain."

This was how far he had descended, talking to a cat and allowing the damned thing to accompany him. If anyone saw Cyrille, Dom would be a laughingstock. Fortunately, the kitten was small and blended into the seat. Hopefully,

Thea would like seeing the animal. After all, he needed some excuse to see her, or he'd look like a regular coxcomb chasing after a mere baronet's daughter. And that was a blasted lie. She was perfectly eligible—a prickle started on his back as if someone was staring at him, and he almost turned around to see if his uncle was there—eligible for anyone but him.

Dotty was descending the front steps of Stanwood House accompanied by Charlotte and Louisa when Merton's curricle drew up. She didn't dare glance at her friends. Louisa would not approve, and Charlotte saw romance around every corner.

Merton greeted them before turning to Dotty. "Miss Stern, I understand from some of the things you've said that you are experienced in training animals."

She was, but did not recall ever actually mentioning it to him. What was he about? The corner of her lip twitched as she tried not to grin. "I do have some knowledge."

He held out his arm. "In that case, would you please give me the pleasure of your company and your assistance on a rather urgent matter?"

She raised her brows a little, indicating her interest. "Of course." Glancing at her friends, Dotty said, "I shall see you later."

Louisa narrowed her eyes, but Charlotte opened hers wide and said with false sweetness, "Naturally, if Merton requires your help . . ."

Dotty wanted to roll her eyes. No doubt, she and Louisa would be laying in wait for her to tell them about the "emergency."

"You see"—he led her away and lowered his voice—"I am having a problem with Cyrille."

"Indeed, my lord?" She tried to keep her tone serious. "What might that be?"

Merton cleared his throat and indicated the carriage. "I do not think he realizes he is a cat."

She looked in the direction he indicated. There was the kitten. Sitting as nicely as you please, surveying the area. She put her hand over her lips to keep from laughing, but her voice shook with it. "Oh my."

"You see what I mean?" His voice was grim. Yet when she glanced at him, his eyes danced with amusement.

She glanced over her shoulder at Louisa and Charlotte who were staring at Dotty and Merton. "You go on without me. I think this will take a while."

Louisa furrowed her brow, and Dotty hastened to reassure her friend. "I shall be fine. It is just a small matter."

Her friend nodded. Dotty was thankful they had not seen the cat. It would only make Merton the butt of some cutting comments. He handed her up and Cyrille moved to sit between them. She still did not quite know what to make of Merton. He seemed to arouse strong feelings in so many people who were dear to her.

Matt, who'd known Merton most of his life, described him as a cold fish, a man with no personality or heart. She could not agree; in many ways he was very good company, possessing a laconic sense of humor as evidenced by the cat. He was definitely a conundrum, and Dotty loved a good mystery, yet where would that lead her?

He started the horses and once in the Park, Dotty turned back to the problem at hand. "Cyrille appears to be exceedingly well-behaved. What seems to be the difficulty?"

"He doesn't talk."

"I beg your pardon?" She tried and failed to hide her grin. "Surely you do not intend to hold a conversation with him."

The corners of Lord Merton's lips turned up. "No, but you see, he doesn't make the usual sounds a cat should make. I do have some acquaintance with the race."

Dotty folded her hands in her lap as her governess used to do when setting out to explain a difficult matter. "We, my friends and I, noticed the same mannerisms in the kittens they have. It appears, when all is well, the cats are silent. Yet if they are in need, they make a small chirping sound. Have you heard that?"

He glanced at the now-sleeping Cyrille. "No. I cannot say I have."

"Then perhaps"—Dotty was hard-pressed not to laugh when Merton had looked at the cat—"he has no complaints."

"I don't see how he could; he's got the entire staff kowtowing to him," Merton stated baldly.

"You did say he'd taken his name to heart."

He slid a warm glance her way and her heart took the opportunity to flutter. She truly did enjoy being with him.

"That must be it. Still he follows me everywhere."

"I believe that is a characteristic of the breed as your mother said."

A man hailed them from the walking path. She glanced around to see Lord Fotherby. Dotty bit her lip. She didn't like the man. Her feelings went beyond his kicking the puppy that day. Somehow she knew he was not to be trusted.

As she suspected, Merton's countenance shuttered, showing only the well-bred, bored expression so common among the *ton*. Was he afraid to allow even those he called friends to see who he really was?

He pulled up alongside the verge. "Fotherby, good day."

Lord Fotherby glanced sharply at Dotty and inclined his head. "Merton. Miss Stern, a pleasure."

From his snide tone, he was anything but happy to see her. She smiled politely. "Good afternoon, my lord. Such fine weather we're having."

"Yes, as you say." He looked past her to Merton. "I expect I'll see you at Lady Wilton's ball?"

His lips tightened slightly. "I am not sure what my mother has planned."

Lord Fotherby speared Dotty with a look of distaste

before returning his attention to Merton. "Then at the club later?"

Merton gave the other man a slight noncommittal nod, and started the horses again. How different he was around other people.

"I shall take you home now."

"Yes, that would be best." The encounter with Lord Fotherby had cast a pall over their easy banter. "I have a great many things to do before this evening."

When they arrived at Stanwood House, Merton escorted her to the door then took her hand. Though rather than bow over it, he stared at her for a few moments. His eyes suddenly desperate, almost pleading. She wanted nothing more than to reach out and comfort him. "Thank you for the drive. I had a lovely time."

His mask slid into place as he recalled himself. "As did I. Your advice was much appreciated."

She couldn't help but watch as he regained his curricle and left. For a moment, he had seemed so sad. She desperately wanted to help him, but how?

Chapter Eight

Dotty found Louisa and Charlotte in the parlor they all shared.

"What did Merton want?" Louisa asked.

Dotty hesitated. Her friend was so prone to finding something wrong with all Merton's actions that she didn't want to give her an opportunity to make a game of him. "He had some questions regarding the cat. I do not think he has ever had one before and was concerned over some of its behaviors."

"Is that all?" Louisa's shoulders relaxed. "For a moment, I was afraid it was an excuse to spend time with you."

Tea had been served and Dotty reached for a biscuit. "Would that be so bad?"

"Are you seriously considering him as a husband?"

"It is too soon to think about that," she lied. "And I am in no hurry to wed."

Charlotte stuck a finger in her book and glanced at Dotty. "Do you plan on making him one of your projects?"

She poured a cup of tea, taking her time adding the sugar and the sweet milk they preferred to cream. "Perhaps. Do you have any objections?"

Louisa harrumphed. "You are in Town to look for a husband, not fix Merton's life."

"That might," Charlotte said softly, "be too large an undertaking even for you."

"Matt says Merton has no heart," Louisa stated firmly.

Yet Merton did not seem uncaring. He'd been nice to her and even let Cyrille drive with him. "How did Matt come to that conclusion?"

"Merton's votes in the Lords." Louisa took a drink from the glass of water on the table next to her. "He supports bills that harm those less fortunate than we are."

Charlotte nodded. "Actions speak louder than words."

Dotty pulled her lower lip between her teeth. She knew what legislation that was. Harsh laws had been passed allowing death or transportation for even relatively minor offences of the law. She could not even think of marrying a man who was so blind to the suffering of others. Yet she was not convinced he was so hard-hearted. There really was much more to Lord Merton than met the eye. He seemed to show one side to her and another to everyone else. Almost as if he was two different people. Or was she simply being naïve? After all, Matt would not lie about Merton's votes. Perhaps he was not for her after all.

Unfortunately, she could not discuss him with her friends. "Well, until I meet a gentleman I am interested in, I can still help Merton."

Charlotte returned to her book.

"If that's the way you wish to spend your time, so be it." Louisa shrugged. "It cannot hurt anyone and may actually be of benefit to him. You could help him find a wife other than the ladies he has been looking at."

"What an excellent idea." Dotty could help him find a lady who was not as vehement in her ideas as she was. "I shall begin casting around tonight. There must be someone who would be good for him."

After all, he was so handsome with his strong features and aquiline nose. And when he gazed at her, his eyes reminded her of the deep blue of the ocean she had seen in a painting. If only she had someone to confide in about him.

Dom returned to Grosvenor Square intending to barricade himself in his study. Thea—he really should not have started thinking of her by that name—was interfering with his work and his search for a wife. This afternoon when he'd stared down at her, all he wanted to do was cover her deep pink lips with his own. He had tried to ignore the voice of his uncle telling him duty came before all else and that strong emotion interfered with one's obligations. Why the devil couldn't what he wanted and what he should do march together? They always had before. Yet, despite all his uncle's warnings, he desired nothing more than to make Thea his.

Uncle Alasdair wasn't the only problem. Given an opportunity, Worthington would try to queer Dom's suit. If he wasn't so far under her spell, he'd let his cousin do his worst. He'd already had a glimpse of what life would be like with her. His house would be full of strays, charity meetings, and who knew what else. She would be after him to support the Whig causes, possibly even Radical ones as well. His ordered life would be total chaos.

Blast it to hell. He needed to remember that Miss Stern was not, *not* eligible to be his bride. But no matter how often he repeated that to himself, it didn't change the fact he wanted her. Badly.

He raked his fingers through his hair and reached for a bottle of brandy, only to find it wasn't there. If only all that misplaced compassion wasn't packaged in such a perfect form. Breasts that begged him to touch and explore. Eyes that shamed emeralds. Curls he wanted to wrap around his fingers as he drew her to him. His groin jerked. He tugged hard on the bell pull.

The door opened immediately. "My lord?"

"Bring me a bottle of brandy."

The footman's jaw dropped. Dom almost never partook of strong drink before evening. But damn it, this is what she was driving him to. "You heard me."

"Y-yes, my lord. Right away."

What seemed like an inordinate amount of time later the door finally opened. He had never known his servants to be so slow in carrying out his wishes.

He let out a low growl. "What kept you?"

"Dominic, since when have you begun drinking brandy during the day?"

He whirled around. His mother followed by a footman entered the study.

"I—um." This was his house and he was an adult. Why was he searching for excuses to make to his mother, and who the hell called her down? "I felt like it."

She smiled gently and signaled for the servant to place the tray on a low table next to a sofa. "I thought I would join you. It is almost time for tea in any event."

The tray held tarts, biscuits, sherry, and brandy.

Mama never came to the study. Dom kept his jaw from dropping, but couldn't stop staring at her. Had everyone gone mad this Season?

She sat on the sofa and after pouring a glass of sherry for herself and brandy for him, smiled again. "You look out of sorts. Is there anything I can do to help?"

Taking the tumbler she handed him, he took a drink. He did want to talk with someone, but his uncle's voice came back to him.

Don't bother your mother, Merton. You're the master now and must be strong for her. In fact, it might be better if she visited your aunt in Bath for a while.

"No. I'll sort it out."

She frowned slightly, then took a sip of sherry. "It has occurred to me that, perhaps, I left you too much to your uncle."

His fingers tightened on the tumbler. "Why would you say that?"

"I do not think you and I are as close as we should be. Alasdair always seemed to know what was best, and after your father died, I was ill for a long time. Although lately, I have come to the conclusion that I should have taken more of an active role in your upbringing."

"He *was* my guardian." And his uncle had been a force to be reckoned with. It would not have been easy for her to oppose him. In fact, Dom didn't want to think about the problems that would have caused. "What are your plans this evening?"

"The Countess of Watford, an old friend of mine, is having a ball."

Watford? Another Whig. What the devil was his mother up to? "Very well, nine o'clock?"

She rose. "Yes. Will you join me for dinner?"

He reviewed his alternatives. For some reason, his club didn't hold the interest it once had. "It would be my pleasure."

"I shall leave you to your work, but, Dominic, if you ever do need someone to speak with, I would be happy to lend an ear."

He went to her and kissed her cheek. "Thank you, Mama."

Once in the main hall, Eunice gave the order for a more regular tea to be served in her parlor.

As she opened the door, Matilda glanced up. "Well?"

Eunice felt like dancing a jig, but instead grinned. "He is definitely suffering. He ordered brandy to be brought to him. And he drank it, too."

"Did he tell you what is bothering him?"

"No, unfortunately. Though I have a feeling it is Miss Stern. He took her driving again today."

Matilda widened her eyes. "Did he? Well, that is good news indeed. Does that not make twice now?"

Eunice nodded. "Yes, and he will attend the Watford ball with us this evening." Her skirts moved causing her to look down. The kitten, Camille, pawed the hem of Eunice's gown. "Come, and I'll hold you for a while."

Crossing to her favorite chair, one in the French style with a wide seat and bolstered arms, she sat and patted her lap for the kitten to come up. "Grace assured me she will bring the girls, which means Miss Stern will be there as well."

"If only Lord Worthington did not dislike Merton so much."

"There is that." Eunice stroked the cat. "Yet, to be fair, from Worthington's point of view there is not much *to* like about Dominic."

"Do you think Worthington will attempt to influence Miss Stern?"

"I am quite sure of it." Eunice frowned. She must think of a way to counter his influence with the young lady if necessary. "Though in my opinion, if she decides she wants something, she will get it. I only pray she will want Dominic."

After dinner with the children, Dotty and her friends repaired to their chambers to dress for the ball. Her gown for this evening was an ice pink trimmed with small flowers embroidered with seed pearls. She added the brightly painted fan she had bought that day and a reticule in the same color pink.

When she entered the parlor, Louisa, Charlotte, as well as their younger sisters, were present. The children, warned not to touch their sisters, exclaimed over the three of them.

"You look too pretty." Theodora, Louisa's eight-year-old sister stared at them in awe.

Mary, the youngest Carpenter, vigorously nodded her head. "I want a gown like that someday."

"We shall all have gowns like that when we come out," Alice, one of the Carpenter twins, was no doubt counting the years until she would emerge from the schoolroom.

Dotty wished her sisters were there as well. This was the first time she had been apart from her family, and she missed them.

Grace shooed the girls out and up the stairs to the school-room. "Shall we go?"

Matt waited in the hall for them and, as he did every evening, complimented them on their looks.

As Watford House was only two doors down, they walked and had just joined the receiving line when Lord Merton and his mother arrived. He was resplendent in a black coat and breaches. His linen was ivory in color instead of the standard white. Nestled in his perfectly arranged cravat was a sapphire tie pin, the same shade as his eyes.

When it came to his looks, he was everything a lady could want. If only his views were not so old-fashioned. Dotty renewed her resolution to find him a wife. Despite his votes in the Lords, he deserved to be happy.

"My dear Miss Stern"—Lady Merton held out her hand—"how pleased I am to see you again."

Dotty rose from her curtsey and took the offered hand. "Thank you, my lady. How is Camille?"

"Doing nicely." The older woman smiled. "I am indebted to you for bringing her to me. I have never enjoyed an animal more."

"I'm so glad you feel that way." At least that had turned out well.

Hearing talk of the cats, Charlotte and Louisa were drawn into the conversation. As the line moved forward, Merton's palm settled on the small of Dotty's back. Warm tingles spread from where he touched her up to her neck.

She expected him to be behind her, but when she glanced up, he was by her side.

"You look particularly lovely this evening," he murmured.

Heat rose to her face and she knew she was blushing. "Thank you, my lord."

He continued to guide her and after a while, although the tingles didn't stop, his hand felt as if it belonged.

By the time their group was finally through the line and had entered the ballroom, Dotty had promised a waltz to Lord Merton. Since her goal was to find him a wife, she probably should not have, but when she looked into his eyes and saw the warmth, she could not resist.

The first set was a quadrille, which she danced with the son of the house. Merton stood up with Lady Mary Pierce. Though she was beautiful, in a cool sort of way, she was not as graceful as he, and they appeared oddly matched. Dotty dismissed the lady as a potential wife for him. What gentleman who was so graceful would want a wife with two left feet? She immediately berated herself for being petty. If a man loved a lady, he would not care about her ability to dance.

The next set was a country dance and although his partner was graceful enough, she just did not seem right for Merton, and so it went on for the rest of the evening. By the time he claimed his waltz, Dotty had run out of prospects for him. None of the ladies would be good for him.

"Miss Stern." His warm voice flowed through her

"My lord." He lightly brushed his lips against her gloved hand before leading her out. "Are your toes not hurting?"

He tilted his head quizzically.

Oh dear, now she would have to admit she'd been watching him. "I mean I saw the one lady tread upon your foot."

"Ah, yes." His lips tilted up at the corners. "I'm fine. Though I thank you for your concern. I think the same happened to you, and your slippers are not as sturdy as my shoes."

"Yes, but I'm used to it. I taught my older brother to dance."

He smiled down at her, and her insides unaccountably tumbled about.

"That must have been a trial. I hope you wore thick shoes."

"Yes, I did." He held her closer as they made the turn and she wanted to lean against him.

"Do you have only the one brother?"

"No, I have two brothers and two sisters." Dotty grinned. "It is quite a lively household when everyone is home."

He was quiet for a moment. "I used to wish for other children in the house."

The music came to a stop and so did her heart. "You are an only child?"

"Yes, my father died when I was very young." He placed her hand on his arm, but when he glanced at her, his eyes had a bleakness she'd not seen before. "Do you miss your family?"

She searched for something to say to lighten his mood. "I did not until this evening when the younger girls came down to look at Charlotte, Louisa, and me before we went out. I wished my sisters were there as well. Mama, too."

"Perhaps your mother can come to Town."

"She broke her leg. That is the reason I am staying with Charlotte. I suppose she could come after it has healed, but Stanwood House is so full of people as it is, and Papa let the house we were going to lease go."

Finally he smiled again. "I think that is probably a vast understatement. I do not know where Worthington and Grace put them."

When she looked up, their eyes met. Dom's hand on her waist tightened. Suddenly, she did not want to find another lady to marry him, but did he feel the same way? And what was she to do about his views? Not to mention what her friends thought of him. She stifled a sigh. She had not even been in Town a month and already things were in a muddle. Could one retrain a marquis and if so, how would one go about it?

"Fortunately, most of them are in the schoolroom."

"There is that."

Dom inhaled sharply as Thea's warm gaze captured him. A rush of longing came over him as he held her. If he didn't stop, he'd do something stupid and likely to cause a scene. Not for the first time he considered Worthington's advice. Dom should leave Town and let Thea get on with finding a husband. Then he would be free of her spell. But for now, he'd savor the feel of her lush curves and inhale her light lemony scent.

He tried to ignore the part of him urging him to carry her away and make her his forever. He could not allow desire to override his duty to his family and dependents. After the set ended and he escorted her back to Grace, Dom vowed to stay away from Thea, no matter what it took. As soon as he was able, he left the ball. If only he didn't care for her so much.

Rising early the next morning, he determined to get his life back on course and went to White's for breakfast. He sat in one of the club's large leather chairs with the *Gazette* opened, ostensibly reading it, even though he hadn't turned the page, when someone tapped his shoulder. Putting the paper down, he glanced up.

"Thought I had your schedule down to the minute," Fotherby said tightly. "But I haven't seen you around here much. Wouldn't have to do with that Miss Stern, would it?"

Dom's blood began to rise at the way Fotherby spat her name. Lately, he'd been more of an irritant than a friend. Who Dom kept company with was none of Fotherby's business, and, furthermore, even if Dom could not marry her, he didn't like the way the man treated Thea.

Carefully folding the newssheet, he bit back the retort he was about to make. "My mother's in Town. When she is here, I must spend time with her."

"Yes, of course, I'd forgotten." Fotherby's tone was contrite, and he paused for a moment, contemplating one of his many fobs. "Didn't see you at Lady Aliesbury's ball last night either."

Where the devil was the man headed with this? Dom kept a rein on his rapidly fraying temper. "I allow my mother to select the entertainments she wishes to attend. She only chooses one each evening."

Fotherby let out a huff of air. "That explains why you were at Featherington's ball. I told Alvanley it had nothing to do with that young woman."

In a cold tone, calculated to suppress further discussion, Dom asked, "Do you have a point to make, Fotherby?"

Apparently taking the question as permission to continue, Fotherby nodded. "Alvanley, Petersham, and me, we're your friends, Merton, and we don't want you to make a mistake. That female." He paused. "Well, she was seen at Lady Thornhill's house."

He'd been focused on a spot over Dom's left shoulder, but now glanced at him. He carefully schooled his countenance. If his friend was hoping to see a reaction, he'd be disappointed.

"It's just that"—Fotherby swallowed—"Lady Thornhill, you know."

Dom did know about the Thornhills, a Radical couple interested in promoting liberal ideas and the arts. It came as no surprise to him Grace would have taken her charges there. "Miss Stern *is* residing with Worthington."

"Of course, that must be the reason." Fotherby nodded, but didn't move away.

He knew Dom hated to be interrupted reading the paper. Trying not to grit his teeth, he asked, "What is it?"

"You marrying her wouldn't do. There are plenty of young ladies—"

"Enough!" He slammed his hand on the arm of the chair. "I am perfectly capable of choosing my own wife, without assistance from you or anyone else."

Fotherby stiffened, and gave a slight bow. "As you say. I shall leave you to your reading."

"Thank you." Dom shook out the paper and buried his nose back in the newssheet. Lines of words faded to be replaced by the image of a raven-haired temptress with green eyes. He wondered what Thea would say about how he saw her? She would probably be shocked. Except for that one time last night when he couldn't break his gaze from hers, she most likely did not even realize the torment he was going through.

Other ladies offered themselves up to him on a silver platter. Any one of them would be flattered to receive a proposal of marriage from him, but would Thea? Did she even care that much about him?

A half hour later, after forcing down a cup of the club's normally excellent coffee, he was walking down the front steps and ran into Alvanley. "Good morning."

Alvanley stopped. "Hiding yourself away lately?"

Since when was Dom answerable to his friends? He kept from scowling. "No. My mother's in Town." Was he going to have to go through this with everyone? Attempting to forestall more questions, he continued. "She has a desire to visit old friends."

Alvanley took out his snuff box and with a flick of one finger opened it before taking a pinch. "You have my deepest sympathies."

At least he wasn't going to ask about Miss Stern. "Indeed."

Taking the opportunity to make his escape, Dom stepped

onto the pavement. He strode down St. James Street toward Piccadilly and then on to Bond Street. The nerve of Fotherby. Even if Dom hadn't already decided Miss Stern wasn't eligible, his friend had no business sticking his nose into it. He knew his duty, and he would do it even if he hated every minute of it. He'd find an excuse to make to his mother and leave for his estate in Devon tomorrow. First he would pick up the books his mother had asked him to fetch.

"What ye think you're doin', miss? Let go of the lad; he's mine." A man's rough shout disturbed Dom's cogitations.

A group of people huddled in a circle. Standing taller than the rest, a footman in Worthington's livery was near the middle of the small crowd.

A furious female voice Dom knew well rose above the rabble. "He is only a small, hungry child. You *will not* arrest him."

Thea. He should have known. Quickening his stride, he swiftly arrived at the gathering of street cleaners, vendors, and the merely curious. The small crowd of onlookers parted for him. At the middle of the scene was Thea squaring off with a sturdy-looking farmer. An underfed, filthy child of perhaps six or seven years clutched an apple in one grubby hand and her skirt in the other, clearly recognizing her as his savior.

"How much for the apple?" she demanded of the farmer.

"That ain't the point, miss," the man said belligerently, spittle flying from his mouth. "He's a thief and deserves to be punished." The child ducked behind Thea as the farmer leaned to one side. "Hanged or transported."

Thea's chin rose as she stood her ground. "I am not saying he was right, but you might steal too if you were starving. The law in this case is too harsh."

Dom's cravat threatened to choke him. The law she referred to was one he had supported.

"Looky here, miss. Don't you go sayin' I'm a thief. Look't him. He's got bad blood."

The boy huddled closer to Thea and whimpered. Somehow, when Dom had voted for the bill, he hadn't envisioned small children, even though in theory he knew it applied to them.

She opened her mouth, then clamped her lips together and shook her head. "I am not casting aspersions on you." She dug around in her reticule. "Oh dear. I spent the last of my money on a pair of gloves." She glanced at the footman, apparently hoping he'd have a few coins, but he gave an imperceptible shake of his head. "Very well, then I shall remain here while you return the fan for me."

"No, miss, I can't. My orders were not to leave you."

Thea passed a hand over her brow. "I suppose the only thing to do is . . ."

Just then it dawned on Merton that she was perfectly capable of leading this motley crowd down Bond Street to the shop so that she could return the gloves and give the farmer his money. Just the thought of the resulting scandal made him cringe. "Miss Stern, may I be of assistance?"

She turned quickly toward him and the worry lines etched on her face cleared. "Oh, my lord. Yes, thank you. Will you please pay this man for his apple? I seem to have spent all the money I brought with me."

At the mention of "my lord," the farmer took a step back. This time when he spoke, his voice was not as loud and considerably more polite. "That boy stole from me. I'm calling the constable."

Holding his quizzing glass to his eye, Dom took his time surveying the man from the battered felt hat on the farmer's head to his hobnail boots. Someone tittered. He needed to get Thea out of this mess in a hurry before she became the latest *on dit*. "How much for the apple?"

The farmer glowered, but finally grumbled, "Two pennies."

Raising his brow, Merton replied, "Indeed. Perhaps we should have the constable on you. I'll give you two farthings and nothing more."

He dropped the coins into the man's outstretched palm before piercing the rest of the group with a stern look. "There is nothing for you to see. Be about your business."

The group scattered, and the footman heaved a sigh of relief.

Thea turned to the boy. "You may eat the apple now."

The child watched warily as the farmer left. "Wot if he comes after me agin?"

"He will not," she said soothingly "Lord Merton and I shall protect you."

The child gazed worshipfully from Thea to Merton. "Are ye really a lord?"

"Of course he is," the footman said. "That's the Marquis of Merton."

"Gor," the lad breathed. "I ain't never met a lordship before."

Merton stifled a sigh. It was too much to hope for that Thea would allow the child to return to his life of crime. "Miss Stern, what do you plan to do with the boy?"

She drew her brows together, wrinkling her forehead. "I shall try to find his family. If he is an orphan, there must be some way I could send him home. I am sure my parents could find a family to foster him until he was old enough to train for some sort of profession."

She glanced at Dom hopefully. Her leaf green eyes wide and anxious, and he knew he would regret what he was about to say. "I shall take him with me for the time being."

Thea smiled as if he'd offered her the most expensive and exquisite jewels in existence. "Perhaps he could be your Tiger until we find a permanent solution?"

He glanced at the lad. Despite the current fashion, there was no way in perdition he would allow a small child to handle his cattle. "I'm sure we'll think of something." It was not until then that it occurred to him that neither Cousin Louisa nor Lady Charlotte accompanied Thea. Was she alone? He'd kill Worthington for not taking better care of her. "What are you doing here by yourself?"

"I am not." She waved her hand at the footman. "I have Fred here, and Grace is at the shoemaker's. I came to get a book. That was when I saw the farmer grab Tom."

"Yes, yer lordship." The boy nodded and turned his reverent gaze back to Thea. "That's how it was all right. Miss saved me."

Apparently, no matter what Dom thought, Fate was determined to throw Thea in his path for the sole purpose of rescuing her from her follies. It would be Divine intervention if this turned out well. He glanced at the footman. "Take the boy to Merton House. Tell my butler that the child is to be bathed and fed. I shall remain with Miss Stern."

As the footman bowed, the corners of his lips seemed to twitch. "Yes, my lord."

Tom's clutch on Thea's skirts tightened, and she calmly removed his hand. "You will be fine with Fred. He'll take you to his lordship's house where they shall take care of you, but you must do as you're told."

Tears filled the lad's eyes. "Will—will I see you again?"

She smiled gently. "Of course you shall. I shall come see how you are doing as soon as I am able. Run along now. Everything will be fine."

He glanced over his shoulder, and a fine tremor shook him. "Yes, miss. I'll be good. I promise."

"I know you will." She leaned down and kissed the boy's filthy cheek. "I shall see you soon."

Grace arrived as Fred took Tom by the hand and led him off with the boy looking over his shoulder at Thea.

Glancing from Thea to Dom and back again, Grace raised a brow. "Would you care to tell me what exactly is going on?"

"Oh, Grace"—Thea grabbed her friend's hands—"Lord Merton was kind enough to take in poor Tom. . . ."

At the end of Thea's telling of the story, Grace gave Dom a queer look and remarked cryptically, "To be sure." After a moment, she brought her attention back to Thea. "Well, we had better finish our shopping."

Thea turned to him and her smile blinded him. "Thank you for your help. If you have no objection, I shall visit tomorrow to see how Tom is getting on. I would come today, but . . ."

He was an idiot to care so much about her approbation, to crave her smiles, to want to hold her. "Tomorrow is fine. I daresay he'll need an opportunity to settle in." He took her hand, bringing it to his lips. "Perhaps I'll see you later."

She gazed at him for a moment, her green eyes serious in their appraisal. "I shall look forward to it."

As Thea followed Grace into the circulating library, Dom stood where he was for a few moments watching until Thea disappeared through the door. What was it about her that made him act so strangely? More importantly, how was he to stop it? Then, feeling like a boy escaping his lessons, he grinned to himself. With his new responsibility, he couldn't very well leave Town now.

Chapter Nine

As Dom entered his front door a bloodcurdling scream reverberated from below stairs. "What the devil is that?"

Paken cleared his throat. "I believe that is young Tom."

What in the hell could the boy have got in to? "Is he being whipped already?"

"No, my lord. He is being given a bath. Something for which he apparently has a mortal fear."

Dom ran a hand over his face. "Afraid of bathing?"

"Yes, my lord. From what we have been able to understand his mother died taking one."

She probably drowned after drinking too much.

Fred, Thea's footman, burst through the green baize door and skidded to a halt. "My lord, thank God you're here. You must come immediately."

Dom shook his head. This situation seemed to be completely out of control. "I thought you'd be gone by now."

"Every time I tried to leave, the poor bantling grabbed on to me and started to cry. If you can just explain to him the water won't kill him, I think he'll be fine."

First a recalcitrant cat, now a badly behaved child. What else was he destined to be burdened with? "I'll come."

Dom arrived in the kitchen for the first time since his

father had died to find his housekeeper, Mrs. Sorley, standing with her hands on her hips staring down at a dirty mass of rags huddled in a corner. "You won't eat, until you're clean, and that's all there is to it."

Although the child's bones stuck out, even the threat of starvation wasn't doing the trick. "I'll take it from here."

She glanced at him, and instead of expressing consternation that he was personally involving himself in a servant matter, said, "Well, it's about time you got here . . . my lord."

He raked his hand through his hair and the thought that he was losing control of his carefully ordered life once again entered his mind. "Get the boy a mug of milk and a piece of buttered bread."

She bustled away muttering something Dom couldn't make out.

Holding his hand out, Dom used his firmest tone. "Come."

Tom lifted his tearstained face. Streaks of grime ran down it and great shudders wracked his emaciated body. He had never seen a child so terrified. Clearly, this was not going to be a simple matter.

"I'll die if I go in that tub."

Dom lowered himself onto a nearby stool. "Tell me why you think that is."

"That is what happened to my mother. She went into a tub and started to scream. Then blood came out of her, and she went to sleep and never woke up."

"Were you alone?"

Tom nodded. "After she died, old Mrs. White said I had to leave and some men came and took me away."

Mrs. White, whoever she was, would be hearing from Dom in short order. Fighting the urge to hit something, one by one he unclenched his fingers. How could anyone just throw a child out? "How long ago was that?"

Tom's large tired eyes gazed up at Dom as if he were a god. "I don't know."

Well, then, he would have to discover that detail later. First the child needed to bathe and eat. "I promise you, you will not die in the tub. I shall remain here to ensure nothing threatens you. Will that do?"

For several moments it appeared that Tom would refuse Dom as well, then the child nodded. "Do you promise I won't die?"

"Word of a Bradford." He was responsible for the lives of hundreds of people on his estates. Yet it was strangely humbling having this little boy think he had the power over life and death.

Still shaking, Tom stood and started to remove the rest of his clothing. Mrs. Sorley returned with the food and a maid took the soiled garments.

Dom was shocked at the bruises and other signs of brutality that covered most of the lad's body. "Who did this to you?"

Tom's mouth formed a thin line, and he shook his head back and forth. "I dare not say. He will kill me."

It appeared that Mrs. White was not the only person whom Dom was going to have to deal with. He lifted the boy into the tub. One of the maids soaped up a piece of linen and began scrubbing Tom's thin body. Once the dirt was gone, the child wasn't too bad of a specimen. His hair was dark blond, and his nose was a little too large for his face, but other than that, all his features were regular. There was something oddly familiar about him, but for the life of him Dom couldn't place it.

The maid slipped a nightshirt over the boy's head, and Mrs. Sorley inspected behind Tom's ears and the back of his neck. "There, that's a good lad. You can eat now. We need to get some meat on your bones."

"Yes, ma'am." Tom polished off the first helping of milk and bread. Then he was given some cheese and a piece of chicken before having his face and hands wiped. One of the maids took him to a bedchamber.

Mrs. Sorley stood at the door with her arms crossed over her massive chest. "A little bit of a mystery you've got there, my lord."

"What do you mean?" Dom had been watching the child go up the stairs, but now turned to his housekeeper.

"Did you not pay attention to the way he started to talk?"

Dom thought back to their conversation about bathing. Of course, he had lost his Cockney speech. "It was almost refined."

She nodded as if he had passed a test. Maybe he had. "What else did I fail to notice?"

"His hands have long fingers, well made, and he looks just like any other little boy in Mayfair."

"Someone's by-blow?"

"Could be." She shrugged. "Something for you to figure out."

"I could hire someone."

"You could, but it wouldn't take much time and you might learn something from it." It was clear from her tone that she wanted him to investigate the matter himself.

He frowned.

"Your father would have done it himself."

He just stopped his jaw from dropping. Hardly anyone mentioned his father, but he had never thought to ask why. Perhaps it was time for things to change. "Why bring up my father now?"

She shrugged again. "The senior staff knew your father all his life. But when Lord Alasdair moved in, he gave orders that we weren't to talk about him. Well, Lord Alasdair's not with us anymore. Now I've got work to do, and her ladyship says she'll join you for luncheon."

Dom walked slowly up the stairs. His first priority was to find out what he could about young Tom, right after he arranged to stand up with Thea tonight. He should not dance with her. He told himself it was his duty to ensure she had someone to dance with other than him, but trying to justify that reasoning became too convoluted even for Dom. The unadorned truth was he wanted to hold her and be with her in the only socially acceptable manner possible.

It was hard to believe he had only known her for a week, yet she'd taken over his thoughts—a small chirp made him look down and he patted the cat—and his life as well.

When Dom entered Rutherford's ballroom that evening, he took stock of the crowd and was pleased to find not many young gentlemen were present. Two seconds later he glimpsed Thea with some other young ladies.

Heedless of the others in the room, he strode straight to her. "Miss Stern?"

She glanced up and smiled. "Good evening, my lord. It's a pleasure to see you here."

"The pleasure is all mine." Unable to resist, he raised her fingers to his lips. "Do you still have the supper dance available?"

"I do." A light blush colored her cheeks.

None of the other young ladies were talking. Instead they appeared to be focused on Thea and him.

His chest tightened, making breathing more difficult than it should be. "Will you save the set for me?"

She looked directly into his eyes before answering firmly. "Yes. I will."

"Thank you." As he grazed her hand with the pad of his thumb, he wondered what she had seen that had decided her.

She drew a sharp breath, and her fingers trembled slightly at his touch. If only he could drag her into his arms, he'd nibble her creamy neck and . . . This was not helping.

He had absolutely no desire to dance with any other lady than Thea. Perhaps he could hide in the card room until it was time to claim her. Yet if he did that, he wouldn't be able to see her. But did he really want to watch as she stood up with another man? He had to be going mad.

Devil take it. From the corner of his eye, he saw Worthington coming his way. Two dances. Dom wanted two, but he had to hurry. "Will you stand up with me for the first waltz as well?"

Thea tilted her head, regarding him for a moment. "Yes."

"Thank you." He kissed her fingers again. "I should see about my mother."

Over the heads of the other guests, he met Worthington's gaze and grinned. Even he couldn't stop Thea from standing up with Dom. Although to avoid any awkwardness for her, Dom made his way to the other side of the room to wait. When a footman came by with champagne, he snagged a glass.

Before he could take a sip, a lady said, "Good evening, Lord Merton."

Shutting his eyes briefly, he turned, smiled politely, and gave a shallow bow. "Good evening, Miss Turley."

She sank into a curtsey. Strange, how he never before had noticed that she was not as graceful as Thea.

Miss Turley said nothing, obviously waiting to be asked to dance. He didn't want to, but if not her, his hostess would find another young lady in need of a partner. "Will you stand up with me for the first country dance?"

She inclined her head, a small smile on her lips. "My pleasure, my lord."

"Thank you." Not knowing what else to say and reluctant to get into another conversation where she agreed with everything he said, he bowed again. "If you will excuse me? There is someone I must see."

She curtseyed once more, and he made his escape. Not for the first time, the idea of marrying her, or anyone else on his list, turned his stomach sour.

* * *

Miss Elizabeth Turley let out a sigh as Lord Merton strode away. "That did not go as I had planned."

"No." Lavvie gazed after his lordship. "I was sure he would ask you to waltz."

"As was I." Elizabeth sighed. "On the other hand, he has not made any attempt to visit me. Before last week, I had hopes he would invite me out driving. I was so sure he was close to a proposal. Papa said the betting at White's was narrowing."

"Elizabeth!" Lavvie hissed in shocked tones, "Your father ought not to discuss such things with you."

That wasn't the only thing he discussed with Elizabeth. "You are right, of course, but it would be equally wrong for me to chastise him." She searched for Merton. Fortunately, his height and golden blond hair made him easy to find. "I wonder who he will waltz with."

"Perhaps no one. Or maybe he only asked the lady to dance because you were not yet here."

"Well, I couldn't have very well got here any sooner." Elizabeth was unable to keep the irritation out of her voice. "We didn't know where he would be this evening until a half an hour ago."

Lavvie slowly waved her plumed fan. "It was a very good idea your father had of getting one of the parlor maids to make friends with that stable-boy of Merton's."

"I just wish the information would be a little more timely." Elizabeth was careful to keep her countenance from showing her frustration. "Merton has not been acting like himself lately. My father said he is almost never at White's these days."

"I heard he and Fotherby had a slight falling-out." Lavvie tapped Elizabeth's shoulder with her fan. "I am sure it is nothing."

The violins started the prelude to a waltz, and Elizabeth

watched to see who would partner with Merton. "It's Miss Stern. He waltzed with her the other evening as well."

"I thought he only danced with her due to his relations with Worthington."

"Apparently not," Elizabeth snapped. He was slipping through her fingers, and she did not know how to get him back.

Lavvie's eyes grew wide. "Excuse me?"

"I'm sorry." The throbbing in Elizabeth's temple that had begun earlier in the evening grew worse. She rubbed the side of her head. It is just that this marriage is so important to my family. Have you come up with any way to . . ."

She could not even finish the sentence. The idea of resorting to trickery appalled her, but if Lord Merton had lost interest in her, there did not seem to be much choice in the matter.

"Not yet. But something is bound to come to me." Lavvie lowered her voice. "Here comes Viscount Wively to ask you to dance. He would make a good match as well."

"Except it will be years before he inherits, and I doubt his father would agree to my father's terms. Papa is sure he can talk Merton around."

A few minutes later, Elizabeth was twirling down the floor with Viscount Wively. She tried and failed to get a good look at Miss Stern and Lord Merton. If they were falling in love it would make what she had to do that much worse. Could she even live with herself if she destroyed a love match? Would he ever forgive her?

Dotty smiled up at Merton as he held her closer than he should have through a turn. This afternoon, when he had agreed to take Tom, she'd abandoned her search for a wife for him. Something was going on between them, and it behooved her to follow it through to the end.

Candlelight glinted off his hair, making it shine. She was close enough to breathe in his scent, soap and light cologne mixed with his own musk. Little tingles of pleasure passed through her fingers as he held them. His palm, heavy and hot on her waist, seemed to burn through her muslin evening gown to her flesh. When he smiled at her, his face and eyes lit up, as if he wanted to be nowhere other than with her.

"A penny." He grinned.

A bit of heat rose in her cheeks. If he only knew her thoughts were worth far more than that. "I so enjoy dancing with you."

He looked a little surprised, but his hands tightened. "Thank you."

She gazed into his warm blue eyes wishing they could remain here forever. Then she remembered her protégé. "How is little Tom?"

His countenance suddenly became serious. "He is well now. When I left the house he was still asleep. There is some sort of mystery surrounding him."

This was unexpected. "What do you mean?"

"I don't know if this is the place to discuss it. It is a rather long story." He twirled her down the floor.

"I shall ask your mother if I may visit him tomorrow, if you don't mind, that is."

"Not at all. You may have better luck convincing him to tell his story. I have little experience with children."

How sad that he was an only child. "Tell me about Cyrille. How was he after his carriage ride?"

Merton gave a bark of laughter, and the couple next to them stared. "He barely made it home before he had to use the facilities."

"Oh dear. You should probably have a harness made for him. It wouldn't do for him to jump down from the carriage."

His mien was still stern, but his eyes twinkled with mirth. "If you think I am going to stop my carriage so that he can get down and—"

"Oh stop." If she started to giggle she wouldn't be able to cease. "I shall embarrass us both if you do not. I doubt if going into whoops during a ball is acceptable behavior."

"Do you never try to hide your feelings?" he asked quietly.

"Sometimes." He probably wasn't used to a lady who didn't pretend to be bored. "If I do not want to hurt someone else. I would never, for example, tell Mrs. Jacobs, one of our tenants, that her biscuits taste like straw dust, even though they do."

His eyes rounded in shock. "You mean to tell me you actually eat them?"

Well, of all the silly questions. "Of course I do. Pray, how am I to avoid it?"

Merton shook his head slightly. "I suppose you cannot." He was quiet for a moment. "What I had meant by the question was do you never pretend you're not having fun when you are?"

"No, why should I? I think that is vastly ridiculous behavior especially in a lady just out."

"They do it to follow the fashion."

How to answer that? Dotty knew Merton was friends with Lord Alvanley, a good friend of Beau Brummell's. "I prefer to make my own fashion. One not based on deceit."

He stared at her intently for a moment, his deep blue eyes flickering with interest before saying, "You are an unusual woman, Dorothea Stern."

She didn't know if he was complimenting her or not, so she decided to take it as an accolade. "Thank you."

When the set ended, he escorted her to Grace, who was sitting with Lady Merton. Louisa and Charlotte arrived at the same time. "Where is Matt?"

Grace glanced up at the ceiling, which was the closest she ever came to rolling her eyes. "I sent him to the card room."

"Whatever for?" Louisa asked.

"To save his life," Grace replied grimly. "His brilliant plan to chaperone you girls this evening was to have me dance every set with him so he could keep track of you."

Charlotte frowned slightly. "But you like dancing with Matt."

"Under normal circumstances I adore dancing with him. Yet not when he is trying to stand guard over any of you. I live in trepidation of what he would decide was a reasonable recourse if a gentleman was too close to you or held your gaze a moment too long. It quite spoilt my enjoyment." Grace had been speaking to all of them, but now she turned to Dotty. "I understand you are engaged to Merton for the supper dance?"

She nodded, hoping it wasn't a problem. She liked dancing with Merton every bit as much as Grace seemed to enjoy dancing with her husband. "Yes, I am."

"Lady Merton has asked you to join her for supper."

That was good thinking on someone's part. If Dotty had to sit through another supper with Matt glaring at Merton, she would not be responsible for her actions. She also wished to hear about the other kitten and more about Tom. Although she knew they would be treated well, she liked to keep track of her charges.

She glanced at the older woman. "Thank you, my lady."

The supper dance was another waltz, and she wanted nothing more than to sink into Merton's arms.

When the dance concluded, he escorted her to his mother and they went down to supper. After seating them as far away from the Worthington table as possible, Merton commandeered a footman and returned with lobster patties, salmon poached in champagne, truffled guinea-fowl, stuffed pigeon's eggs, a salad, creams, tarts, and a small trifle.

His hand touched hers as he handed her a glass of champagne, causing the tingling to start again.

"I tried to procure all the foods you seemed to like the last time."

Amazed that he had remembered, she grinned, then took a small sip of wine. "Thank you, my lord."

Carriage drives, two waltzes, now this. Was it possible Merton was courting her? If he was, she would need to decide what her feelings for him were.

He had other dishes placed before his mother.

"Thank you, my dear. I am sure I shall like all of it." Lady Merton looked over at Dotty. "How are you enjoying your Season so far, Dorothea?"

"Very much, my lady. It is everything I'd hoped it would be." Dotty paused for a moment. "Could you please tell me how Camille is doing?"

Lady Merton's expressive light blue eyes sparkled. "She is the light of my life. She always seems to know when I want her and is there with me."

Dom took the seat on the other side of Dotty at the small round table. Under the guise of taking a bite of food, she slipped a glance in his direction and found him doing the same. His lips tilted up as he lifted the champagne glass to his mouth.

At that exact moment, when she'd been paying no attention at all to the conversation, Lady Merton asked, "Do you not agree, Miss Stern?"

Warmth rose in her cheeks. "I'm sorry—"

"Mama," Merton interpolated, "is that Lady Bellamny who just walked in?"

Dotty breathed a sigh of relief and flashed him a quick smile as his mother turned toward the door.

"Yes, I believe it is. I shall have to find her later. We used to be close friends at school."

"I thought I remembered something of the sort," he murmured.

Lady Merton looked at Dotty and Merton. "Dominic, I understand we have a new addition to the household."

"We do indeed. His name is Tom. Miss Stern saved him today."

Warmth crept back into Dotty's face as Merton told his mother how it came about and what happened later with the bath. "I hope you do not mind, my lady?"

"Of course not. It is a very large house. I doubt one little boy will be much trouble."

Dotty prayed Tom would settle in quickly. "I may know where we can find some of the information about him. At least who he has been with recently. Two of Grace's friends, Lady Evesham and Lady Rutherford, have opened an orphanage and have learned a great deal about children on the street."

"I don't think he's been alone," Merton said. "He mentioned someone else to me. I shall tell you when you come over tomorrow."

Lady Merton raised a brow and Dotty remembered that she had not asked if she could visit. "If I may, my lady."

"Naturally, I would welcome a call from you. Perhaps you can join me for luncheon?"

"Thank you. I would love to."

At the end of supper, Dotty excused herself to go to the ladies' retiring room. She was still behind the screen when two women, who obviously thought they were alone as they barely lowered their voices, began to speak.

"Merton standing up twice with Miss Stern and having his mother join them for supper is not a good sign," the first lady said in low desperate tones.

"We shall have to act quickly. Fortunately, I have an idea," a second lady responded. "You'll give a footman a note for Merton asking him to meet you by the fountain at one o'clock."

"I can't sign my name to a message like that. What if it landed in the wrong hands? I would be ruined."

"No, no, my dear," the other lady said soothingly. "It will be anonymous. Better yet, I shall write it."

There was silence for a few moments, then, "Very well.

Though we must hurry, we've only got about twenty minutes before the hour. What will you be doing?"

"I shall ask two or three of the ladies to stroll in the garden with me, for some air. When you hear me laugh, throw your arms around him."

Dotty put her hand over her mouth, stifling a gasp. What a wicked thing to do. Papa had warned her about men doing something of the sort, but that a lady would attempt to compromise herself was nothing short of shocking.

The first lady sounded worried. "Are you sure this will work?"

"Oh yes." The other one chuckled. "Merton detests scandals of any type. His being a prig will finally work in your favor."

There was that word again. He'd never acted stodgy around her. Really, where did people get these ideas?

"It's as good a plan as any, I suppose," the first lady said dubiously.

Dotty considered leaping out and declaring her intention to find Merton and reveal the plot, but that smacked of something a heroine in a novel would do, right before she was tied up. Besides, if she spoilt the scheme now, she might not be around when they tried again. Both women seemed determined Merton should marry the one lady.

"Good," the second lady said. "I have some paper and a pencil."

The soft scratching of the lead on paper was the only sound for several moments, then finally the door opened and closed. When Dotty peeked around the screen; the room was empty. She must find Merton and warn him. With any luck, he would have left the ball by now. She strode back to the ballroom as quickly as she could, without attracting attention. Why was it still so crowded? Across the room, Lady Merton sat with Grace and another lady. Drat, that meant he was still here. Skirting the edge of the room,

Dotty made her way toward the doors to the terrace just in time to see him stride out.

She caught up to Merton as he reached the meeting place. "My lord—"

"Miss Stern, what is the meaning of this?" Holding up the note he frowned.

"I've come to warn you." Her heart was beating so fast, she could barely speak, and she'd never before been alone with a gentleman. "You must go back inside now. Please!"

He shook his head. "I don't understand. You asked me to meet you here."

Of all times for him to pick to be difficult. Keeping her voice low, she infused it with urgency. "No, the note is a trap." She grabbed his hand and tried to pull him toward the doors. Unfortunately, the dratted man stood stock-still.

"A trap?" He frowned. "What do you mean?"

She resisted the urge to rail at him. It must be almost one. They had no time to waste. "I'll explain it to you on the way in."

He stared down at her. "You'll explain it to me now."

Of all times for him to act like a . . . Grrr. Didn't he read novels? As calmly as she could she said, "I overheard a conversation. There is a lady trying to force you to marry her." Dotty took his other hand and tugged. "Please, you cannot be caught out here."

Finally he moved, but the force of her pulling and him stepping forward brought them up against each other. Before she could move away someone gasped.

"Well, well, well, what have we here?"

Dotty recognized the voice as one of the ladies she had overheard earlier, but Merton's broad chest blocked her view.

He was so close, her breasts practically touched his waistcoat, and his arms were around her waist.

Dear God. This cannot be happening. We must look like lovers!

"Obviously we are interrupting a tryst," another woman twittered.

"Such goings-on in the garden," a third one said.

The fourth lady's laugh sounded like a cackle. "It's been a few weeks since we've had a good scandal."

It probably wouldn't help, but Dotty would try to talk Dom and herself out of this predicament. She raised up on her toes, barely able to see over Merton's shoulder. A tall blond lady's jaw dropped open, and her face flushed with anger.

"I—I was delivering a note." Unfortunately, her voice was anything but firm.

So much for being convincing. By the shocked looks on the faces of all four ladies, none of them believed her.

Merton placed his arms around Dotty's shoulders. "What you see, ladies"—his voice was so cold and wintery, she shivered—"is a proposal." He glanced at her. "I believe Miss Stern was about to give me an answer when you interrupted."

She couldn't breathe. Wed Merton? She liked him well enough, at times even more than that, yet she wanted to be sure the man she married loved her and she loved him, and there were the other considerations as well. She could not wed a man who did not feel as she did about social issues and politics.

He whispered in her ear, "You made a good effort, but it didn't work. There is only one way forward."

If only she knew what she should do. Did she have any options or was he correct?

Placing one finger under her chin, he tilted it up. His soft breath caressed her ear. "Would marrying me be such a tragedy?"

She searched his face, but could see little in the dark. Her heart beat so fast, her voice was breathless. "I don't know."

He looked at her as if he hadn't expected her answer. "We can become betrothed, and if you find you cannot stand to be my wife, you may cry off. At least we will have avoided a scandal."

Avoiding a scandal was imperative. It sounded like a good plan. Perhaps it could work. "Very well, I will become betrothed."

He was about to step back, when Matt pushed his way through the crowd, pulled Dotty away, and swung at Merton.

He ducked. "Worthington, it is not what you think."

Lord Rutherford seized Matt's arm and in a firm, low voice said, "Not here."

Matt shook off the other man, straightened his coat, and glared at Merton. "I shall see you at Stanwood House immediately."

"You will indeed." Merton took Dotty's hand, placing it on his arm. "Miss Stern has just agreed to be my wife."

What in God's name was wrong with him? Why goad Matt now? She wanted to stamp her foot on Merton's. Never would she understand why men felt it necessary to behave like children at times. "Enough. We shall discuss this when we get home. Merton, you may escort me to the hall." Lowering her voice, she added, "Remember to smile. We've just become engaged. We need to look the part."

He gave her a queer little grin, but did as he was told. Remembering her grandmother's advice, Dotty held her head high as they made their way slowly through the onlookers. She smiled at her friends, confusion and curiosity writ on their faces.

Time enough when they got to Stanwood House to tell Louisa and Charlotte it was a sham betrothal. The sad thing was that when she jilted Merton, for they would never see eye-to-eye, the blame would attach to him, not her. Everyone had already decided he was unlovable, but was he truly?

* * *

Elizabeth had almost made it to the ballroom door when a large hand grabbed her arm, She snapped her head around to see her brother, Gavin's stern face, then tried to break his hold, hissing, "Let go of me."

"Why?" He scowled. "So you can make a fool of your-self?"

"Who told you?"

Though his fingers relaxed, he didn't let go. "Our dar-ling cousin, Lavinia." He sneered. "This was her idea, wasn't it?"

When Elizabeth refused to answer, he went on. "Of course it was. You'd never think of anything so devious, or put your reputation at risk without her urging."

Drat, Lavvie. Why couldn't she have kept her mouth shut? "I'm doing this for you as well."

"No, you are doing it because Papa convinced you we are rolled up."

Elizabeth's eyes widened as the implication of what her brother said sank in. "You mean we're not?"

"No. It was Papa's way of ensuring you would accept Merton if he made an offer."

She stopped struggling, and her brother released her. Anger and hurt rose, threatening to choke her. She had always trusted her father. A sob broke loose. "How could he do this? I thought he cared about me."

"In his way he does." Her brother's tone softened. "He wanted to see you well settled. Merton's rich as Golden Ball, and he'd be kind to you. Unlike that rascal Lavinia married."

Elizabeth's throat tightened. She blinked to keep tears from falling. "But what if I had loved another?"

Gavin's gaze sharpened as he searched her face. "Do you? Do you love Merton?"

She shook her head slowly. "No. There is no one. Al-though I've always thought I would like to marry for love."

He seemed to relax. "Then it's a good thing you didn't go out there. Who could ever love a cold fish like Merton?"

She thought Miss Stern might, but held her tongue. A disturbance near the door caused her to glance over. Miss Stern, Merton, Lord and Lady Worthington, and Lord Rutherford entered the room from the garden. Merton and Miss Stern were smiling, nodding, and greeting the other guests. Lavvie, her lips forming a thin line, and three other ladies scurried behind them.

"What the devil?" her brother said.

"Do not use that language in front of me." Elizabeth frowned at him. "I suppose it is a good thing you stopped me. Imagine how awkward it would have been if both Miss Stern and I had arrived."

"Looks like Merton's going to get leg shackled without your help." Gavin grinned but almost immediately sobered. Listen here, Aunt Agatha is in Town, and I have arranged for her to sponsor you."

Their aunt, the Countess of Shirring, had married off all four of her daughters with good matches. Still, despite knowing that Elizabeth had no one, Aunt Agatha had not offered. "How did you talk her into it?"

He gave her a smug smile. "When I told her Lavvie had you in hand, she ordered her trunks packed and the town house opened. She doesn't have any better opinion of our cousin than I do. If you ask me, she was waiting for Papa to ask her to take you on."

Lavvie must have seen Elizabeth and her brother because her cousin had her polite smile on her face as she walked purposefully in their direction.

"Where were you?" Lavvie hissed.

"I stopped her." Gavin's voice was cold and scathing. "Have you lost what little brains you have?"

Almost breathing fire, Lavvie stood toe-to-toe with Elizabeth's much larger brother and whispered fiercely, "No,

Gavin. I am trying to help save my family from certain ruin."

The two of them had always been at odds, and Elizabeth prayed they wouldn't start a row in public.

He raised a brow. "I shall take care of that and my sister." Piercing Elizabeth with a stern look, he said, "I'll call for the coach now. Try to stay out of trouble until I get back."

After he'd gone, Elizabeth breathed a sigh of relief. "What happened?"

"When we got there, he was proposing to Miss Stern, but he'll not want her for long."

Elizabeth closed her eyes for a moment. She wasn't sure she even wanted to know what her cousin had done. "What do you mean?"

Lavvie shrugged one shoulder. "I merely told Lady Brownfield they looked as if they were about to anticipate their vows on the spot."

Glancing around to make sure no one was near, Elizabeth pulled her cousin farther behind the palm. "How could you do such a mean, spiteful thing?"

Unabashed, Lavvie responded, "She hurt you, my dear."

"You should not have—"

Suddenly a peevish male voice intruded. "What are you doing behind this"—Viscount Manners took out his quizzing glass and studied the plant—"bush? My wife ought to know better. Have you no care at all for what people think?"

The corners of Lavvie's lips trembled as she attempted a smile. "I was just getting a bit of air. The room seemed terribly close for a moment. I did not think to see you again this evening."

"You wouldn't have if Merton hadn't caused such an uproar. The ball is ending. No one can bear to be the last to relay the happy tidings to anyone not present. I am off to my club."

After Lord Manners left, her cousin gave Elizabeth a slow, wicked smile. Dear heavens. That was the same expression Lavvie had when coming up with the plan to trap Merton. What was she thinking of now, and how was Elizabeth to talk her out of it? Even if she told Lavvie the truth, she would be hard to stop.

Chapter Ten

By the time Dom reached the hall with Thea and his mother, the town coaches were waiting. He had been shocked then pleased when she'd taken control of the situation by ordering both him and his cousin to cease. She had determination and command that was rare in a woman her age and station.

He and Thea rode with his mother, telling her what had happened as they traveled the short distance to Berkeley Square.

"That was very brave of you, my dear." His mother nodded approvingly. "Not many ladies would follow their conscience as you did."

In a very few minutes they were all gathered in the Stanwood House drawing room where wine and brandy were served. No champagne, he noted. In fact, the only person who seemed willing to accept the possible marriage, other than Thea, was his mother. She'd had a wistful look on her face since she learned of the betrothal.

Once again, Thea had to explain what had occurred. Even after hearing her explanation Worthington still scowled. "I'll kill him."

"No. You. Will. Not." Grace frowned heavily at him.

"Merton must be betrothed to Dotty. It was not his fault, or hers."

"If anyone is to blame," Thea said, "it is the ladies who planned to trap him. Maybe I should not have tried to warn him, but what they wanted to do was wicked."

A low growling sound emanated from Worthington but other than that, he remained silent.

Grace glanced at Dom. "Do you have any idea who it could have been?"

"Possibly Miss Turley." He had known she wanted to marry him. Obviously, he had underestimated her determination. "Her cousin, Lady Manners, was with the group that came upon us. She was clearly surprised when she saw Miss Stern with me."

"Then what happened to Miss Turley?" Thea asked.

"I saw her arguing with her brother," Charlotte replied.

Dom's mother leaned over and patted Thea's hand. "It is a good thing Miss Stern intervened. I do not want Miss Turley for a daughter-in-law."

He'd never in his life heard his mother say anything like that before. "Mama!"

"It is the truth." She gave him an unrepentant look. "If the young lady is this deceitful now, what would she be like as a wife?"

"I do not want to believe Miss Turley could behave so badly." Charlotte took a sip of wine. "Unless she was forced into it. She *is* very biddable."

"I do not think we have anything to worry about." Louisa set her glass down. "After the Season is over, Dotty may call it off. By the time the Little Season comes around, the incident will be forgotten."

Worthington rose and poured another brandy. "And that is exactly what will happen."

Holding himself on a tight rein, Dom clenched his hands. *Not if I have anything to say about it.*

His betrothal to Thea might not have been planned. He

had been so conflicted over her, he did not even know if he would have asked her to marry him. Yet now that it was done, he knew to his bones she was exactly the woman he wanted to take as his wife.

To hell with his cousins and his uncle. All Dom had to do was convince Thea that he was the husband she wanted.

"I am afraid jilting Lord Merton will not be a possibility."

They turned to the door where the Dowager Lady Worthington stood with Lady Bellamny. Age had clearly not lessened the older woman's power in the *ton*.

Lady Worthington focused on him and Thea before continuing. "I did not see what occurred between the two of you, and I doubt the story circling is true; nevertheless, there must be a wedding. We must avoid a scandal at all costs."

"A month should do it." Lady Bellamny nodded, her chins jiggling. "Don't want it to appear rushed. Good thing you kept your wits about you, Merton. And you too, Miss Stern."

If Worthington hadn't been glaring at Dom, he would have sighed with relief. This was a much better result. Dom would have his marriage with the woman he wanted and without all the dangerous emotions that would have attended a real courtship.

Unfortunately, the next thing he knew, Thea erupted. "I don't understand. We did not *do* anything. Our hands were clasped because I was trying to pull him back inside, but that was all." She glanced at him. "Tell them."

He did his best to give her a comforting look, but thankfully, Lady Bellamny spoke again.

"It doesn't matter what *actually* occurred. We must deal with the perception." Her countenance took on a stern demeanor. "I shall tell you, young lady. If Merton had not kept his head when those gossips came upon you, you would be facing ruin."

Thea pulled part of her lower lip between her teeth,

making him want to kiss her. "What—what are people saying?"

Lady Worthington came to Thea, taking her hands. "My dear, suffice it to say, it was more than what actually happened. We will make it right. Merton's statement that he was proposing is also circling. Still, the betrothal must be announced, a ball planned, and a wedding date set."

More reluctantly than Dom liked, Thea nodded. "I understand."

Lady Bellamny lowered her bulk onto the chair next to his betrothed. "Notice has been taken of Merton's interest in you and yours in return. Many a successful marriage has begun with less."

Thea glanced at him, uncertainly, but resolved. "Very well. I agree we shall marry in one month's time."

He sucked in a slow breath and realized how frightened he had been she would refuse. "I shall make immediate plans to visit your father."

Matt lounged back on the sofa next to Grace, a slow smile forming on his lips. "No need for that, Merton," he drawled. "Sir Henry has given me his power of attorney to negotiate the settlement agreements."

By Jove's beard! Worthington would put Dom through hell just for the fun of it. He could have easily taken a swing at his cousin, but this was no time to lose his temper. After all, he was getting Thea, and there wasn't anything his cousin could do about it. He inclined his head. "Very well. Send me a draft when you have it ready."

"You'll have it in a day or two. I will notify you when we have been told where Sir Henry wants the ceremony held."

It seemed Worthington was going to make everything as difficult as possible. Dom's jaw clenched. "I would prefer it to be either St. George's or the chapel at Merton."

Thea rose, placing her fingers on Dom's arm. "I don't know if my mother will be ready to travel. You do remember she has a broken leg."

It wasn't what he wanted, but he covered her hand with his. "I'm sorry, my dear, I'd forgotten. We shall marry wherever your father wishes."

Lady Bellamny frowned. "If your mother can make the trip to Town, St. George's would be the best site."

"I shall write Lady Stern." Grace's lips pursed in thought. "We shall send one of our traveling coaches. The seats make into beds and it is well sprung. She'll have a comfortable ride."

Dom gave a slight bow. "I shall leave the arrangements to you ladies. At the moment, I would like to speak with Miss Stern alone."

He almost grinned when Worthington scowled again.

Despite everything, her lips curved in a tentative smile, and his heart seemed to stop.

He closed his fingers possessively around hers. "We shall be back in a few minutes."

Relative silence greeted Merton's words. Matt, Charlotte, and Louisa frowned. Lady Merton, who had been very quiet, nodded encouragingly. The Dowager Lady Worthington and Lady Bellamny, who were speaking quietly with Grace, didn't even glance up.

Dotty led Merton to a front parlor, and a footman hurried in to light the candles.

Once she and Merton were alone and the door had been closed, she turned to face her betrothed. His arms went around her and his throat worked as if he was having trouble swallowing. Finally, he said, "I shall do my best to make you a good husband."

"I'm so sorry." Tears pricked Dotty's eyes, and she blinked them back. "If only I had let well enough alone you would not be in this mess."

He stroked her cheek with the pad of his thumb. She was surprised to find it slightly calloused.

"And I would be marrying Miss Turley instead of you." Which is what he probably wanted. He had already been

considering Miss Turley. Why had she involved herself?
"But—"

"No." He stopped her before she could continue. "I am
glad it is you, Thea."

"What did you call me?" The heat of his body warmed
her, and his lips touched the corner of her mouth.

"Thea. Everyone calls you Dotty, but I wanted my own
special name for you. Do you mind?"

A blush rose in her cheeks. It seemed as if she was
always blushing around him. Her grandmother called her
Thea as well. And as uncertain as she was over their betrothal, she was inordinately pleased at his request. "No, I
like it. What shall I call you?"

"Dom. Only one other person called me that"—the mus-
cles in his throat worked as he swallowed—"and he is dead.
May I kiss you?"

Myriad thoughts and feelings had been rushing around
in her head, but his question brought her up short. Goodness, wasn't he already kissing her? Apparently, she had a
lot to learn. "Yes."

He feathered his lips lightly over hers. When she puckered her lips to kiss him back, he grinned and touched his
mouth to hers. His tongue ran along the seam.

"Open for me."

Dotty didn't understand what he planned to do, but did
as he asked, surprised at the feel of his tongue against hers.
She copied his movement, returning his strokes.

When he groaned, she jerked back. "Did I hurt you?"

"Never. You feel so good." He held her tighter.

Sliding her hands from his chest to circle his neck, she
pulled herself flush against his body. For some reason, until
this evening, she had not realized he was so tall. He tilted
his head and there was no more thinking. Only him, his taste
of brandy and musk. A deep thrumming started inside her.
No wonder ladies were not supposed to kiss gentlemen

unless they were betrothed. She didn't even know how she felt about Merton, Dom, but what he was doing to her felt wonderful.

His hands seemed to touch everywhere as if he couldn't stop. Her breasts ached, and when he ran his fingers over them sparks flew through her. She gasped, surprised at what she was feeling.

Suddenly he stopped. His palms moved to her waist, and his lips left hers. His tone was stiff. "I'm sorry. I should not have touched you so intimately."

Did he think she had not liked it? She placed two fingers over his lips to stop him from speaking again. "Please don't apologize. I enjoyed it."

Dom stared at her for several moments before smiling and placing a kiss on her palm. "I am exceedingly happy we are marrying."

"Yes, I think I am, too." Especially when he lost his formal manners.

Even though she had no experience with men, the way he'd touched her felt right. After those kisses, Dotty didn't know how anyone could think Dom was emotionless. *Reserved* was a better description.

He did have good points. He had saved her from ruin this evening, and he had helped her rescue the kittens and Tom. On the other hand, she would be miserable wedded to Dom if he did not change. Perhaps no one else had offered him the challenge of helping others, both personally and in the Lords. Could she be the right wife for him after all?

If only Charlotte and her family didn't dislike him so much. As soon as she could, Dotty would speak with Grace. Dotty didn't want to be estranged from her friends; as an only child, Dom would benefit from knowing his cousins better. There must be a way to bring about a reconciliation.

Dom gazed at her, his deep blue eyes warm, his face all hard, lean planes, reflecting his Norman ancestry. If they were not living in modern times, she could envision him throwing her up onto his horse and riding off. Suddenly, she knew she would love him and once he loved her, nothing would come between them.

She would have everything she had ever dreamed of.

Chapter Eleven

Dom covered Thea's mouth once more with his, intending to wipe away any doubts she had. Claim her as his. All of her. Forever.

She tasted of tea, and wine, and woman with a hint of lavender. From the moment he touched his lips to hers, she couldn't get enough. Although she was clearly an innocent, she hadn't been shocked when he stroked her. He had, quite frankly, never expected such warmth in a wife. Now that he had a sample of what could be, he could scarcely believe his good fortune. Suddenly, it was very important that she want their wedding as much as he did. She was his.

Her hard nipples pressed into his chest and she moaned. He slid his palms over her back and down to her bottom. He wanted to feel her silken skin beneath him, be in her, filling her with his seed. A month seemed like a very long time.

He slid his fingers over Thea's breasts again. She gave him a low breathy cry and kissed him with a naïve fervor that undid him.

He had always been able to please women, yet this was so much more important than simply giving pleasure. He should slow down, but he needed to bind her to him, make her his in a way he'd never thought important before. If only he could take her home now. . . . Perhaps that was the answer. As a country squire's daughter Thea had much to learn in order to fulfill the role of his marchioness. She should move to Merton House so his mother could show her how to go on. His mother being in residence would make it all proper. Surely her parents wouldn't mind. They would be ecstatic with this marriage. After all, it wasn't every day that the daughter of an unknown baronet married a marquis.

He broke the kiss. "We should go back before Worthington comes looking for you."

She sighed. "He is not at all happy, is he?"

"I would say that is an understatement. At the very least, he'd like to murder me." Though Worthington would probably consider castration as well.

Thea gazed up at Dom, looking like a thoroughly kissed woman. If his cousin saw her now, it would definitely be castration.

"Our betrothal was not your fault," she said. "It might even have been mine for not finding someone to go with me. It's just that there was so little time to warn you."

He kissed her lightly. He would not allow her to blame herself. If she had been more prudent, he wouldn't be engaged to her. Yet, when was she ever prudent? "Perhaps fate played a role. And, as I told you, I am pleased we are marrying. My only wish is that you are happy as well."

"It has all been so sudden, but I am sure I will be fine." She lowered her thick dusky lashes. "I like kissing you."

It was then he knew. When Thea looked at him, she did not see a marquis or a wealthy landowner, she saw only the man. Had that ever happened to him before? When was the last time he'd forgotten, even for a few minutes, who he was?

"Merton," his uncle said, grabbing him by the hand and dragging him away. "You have no business playing with the town boys. You have duties. You employ their fathers. Never forget who you are."

He had been ten years old, and he had never disobeyed Uncle Alasdair until then. Dom blocked out the criticism he knew his uncle would have heaped upon him. Still, even his uncle would understand he had to marry Thea.

Then again, he had gone outside hoping to meet her. He had stubbornly refused to listen to her warning. Had he wanted them to be compromised? No one had mentioned that part of this whole situation.

"Is everything all right?" He glanced down and concern lurked in her wide green eyes as she stared up at him.

"I beg pardon?"

"It's just that you looked far away for a moment."

He lowered his head, brushing his lips across hers once more. "Yes, I'm fine. Everything is fine."

It would be torture having her in his house. He could barely keep his hands off her now. No matter, they were marrying in any event. Nothing could stop that. Over half the *ton* had seven or eight-month babies. Why should he wait? Damnation, what was he thinking? Worthington would never allow her to move into Merton House, and Dom could not ravish her under his own roof. His uncle had been right. Too much passion made a man reckless. He had to keep himself under control around her.

Forcing himself to drop his arms, he quickly took her hand. "We had better go back."

They strolled slowly to the drawing room. When they entered the room, the ladies were still in deep discussions. But Worthington was gone, as were Charlotte and Louisa.

Dom didn't want to wait a month. He leaned down and whispered in her ear, "Three weeks."

Thea glanced up at him, confused. "Three weeks for what?"

"I do not wish to wait so long before we wed." He blew on her ear, pleased when she shivered. He slowly toyed with the curls at the nape of her neck. "Do you?"

She searched his face for a moment before answering, "No."

It was already close to the end of April. "We can marry in the middle of May. As soon as I receive confirmation that your father has been informed of our betrothal, I shall place the announcement in the *Morning Post*."

Thea nodded and glanced toward the others in the room. "Excuse me." She walked to where Grace, his mother, the Dowager Lady Worthington, and Lady Bellamny were talking. "Excuse me, but Lord Merton and I have decided we would like to marry in three weeks. There is no reason to wait longer."

Grace and her mother-in-law each raised one brow. Dom's mother smiled, and a knowing look appeared in Lady Bellamny's black eyes.

She chuckled. "Merton, it's about time you stopped being such a slow top."

He inclined his head and grinned. "Yes, ma'am."

"There may be hope for you yet."

As his uncle's voice battered him, Dom's hand slid to Thea's waist and tightened.

Duty, Merton. Remember your duty.

Somehow he'd figure out how to make her happy. Was that not a duty as well?

The next day, Elizabeth paced the morning room, waiting for her cousin to call. Finally, at noon, her maid brought a note from Lavvie, stating she had been detained. Elizabeth pondered warning Miss Stern, but they were not close, and Elizabeth might be able to talk her cousin out of whatever it was she was planning. If only Papa hadn't lied to her. That was what started this whole problem. Well, at least she would not have to speak with him about it. Gavin said he'd talk to their father.

As she was about to leave, the door opened, and Aunt Agatha entered in a flurry of scarves and feathers. "My dear Elizabeth, how fortunate to find you at home. Come give me a kiss. I have already ordered tea. You shall catch me up on all the latest *crim cons,* then I will take a look at your invitations. Don't worry, my love. I'll find you a husband in no time."

Elizabeth felt a little faint as Aunt Agatha embraced her. A floppy feather from her turban tickled Elizabeth's nose, making her want to sneeze. "I did not expect you so soon. Gavin told me only last night he had made arrangements for you to come."

"Well." Aunt Agatha sniffed. "Once your brother told me your father had put you in Lavinia's charge with orders to bring Merton up to scratch, I knew immediately it would not do. One does not go into a Season with only one marital prospect in mind."

It was no use trying to defend either her father or her cousin, and after what had happened, Elizabeth saw no reason to do so in any event. "Yes, ma'am."

"And"—her aunt shook her finger—"I don't like Manners. The man's a loose fish if I ever saw one. A marriage-able lady cannot be too careful of her reputation."

Elizabeth repressed a shudder at what she had almost done. Thank God Gavin had stopped her. When the tea arrived, she poured a cup for her aunt.

"I have already sent a note around to Lavinia explaining that she need not concern herself with you any longer."

"Thank you." With any luck, Lavvie would give up the scheme she was hatching to separate Miss Stern and Lord Merton.

Her aunt nodded. "You shall move to my house. Before that, however, we must call on Miss Stern."

Elizabeth choked on her tea and began to cough. "I—I beg your pardon. I barely know her."

"Unfortunately, there is a suspicion going around that

Lavinia started some nasty rumors about Miss Stern and Merton. We must distance you from any talk. Therefore, as soon as we've had luncheon, we will go round to Stanwood House. In any event, I am connected to the Dowager Lady Worthington, and it would be considered odd if I did not call on her. You may take the opportunity to wish Miss Stern happy."

Elizabeth wished she was a turtle and could hide in her shell, but Aunt Agatha was right. If anyone connected her with her cousin's gossip, it would destroy any chance she had of making a good match. And there was that note. She prayed no one would connect her with the message to Merton.

When she and her aunt arrived at Stanwood House the sound of feminine voices could be heard down the corridor. Once they were announced the room fell silent. She plastered a polite smile on her face as her aunt took her arm and swept regally into the room.

"Patience," Aunt Agatha said to a woman with blond hair seated with Lady Louisa.

"Agatha." The lady came forward and bussed Aunt Agatha on the cheek then glanced at Elizabeth. "What a lovely surprise."

"Allow me to introduce my niece, Miss Turley. Elizabeth, the Dowager Lady Worthington."

Elizabeth made her curtsey. "A pleasure to meet you, my lady."

The dowager smiled. "I am delighted you are here."

Elizabeth focused on Miss Stern. "It is nice to see you. I—I would like to wish you happy. I am truly pleased you are marrying Lord Merton."

Although she appeared a little surprised at first, when she smiled, it lit her eyes. "Thank you. I'm glad you came to visit."

"I have not paid many morning calls—"

"Unfortunately, I was late coming to Town," Aunt Agatha said. "I am sponsoring my niece, you know. A cousin of hers had been chaperoning poor Elizabeth, but I shall say nothing more about *that*." Leaving no one in doubt of her disapproval. "I believe my niece could benefit from a wider acquaintance. It is her first Season after all, and she must make the most of it." She smiled beatifically at Miss Stern. "I shall wish you happy as well. Make no mistake about it, though, you must take Merton in hand."

Miss Stern gave Aunt Agatha a rueful grin. "So I have been told, my lady." Miss Stern turned back to Elizabeth with another warm smile. "Please call me Dotty. All my friends do. Come, I shall introduce you to some of the other ladies. I think you already know Lady Charlotte Carpenter and Lady Louisa Vivers."

"Yes, we met before the Season began. I would like it very much if you called me Elizabeth."

Elizabeth let out a small sigh of relief as Dotty linked arms with her and set off toward a group of young ladies. If the future Marchioness of Merton accepted her, everyone else would as well. It was now even more imperative that Elizabeth stop whatever Lavvie was planning.

Cordelia, having tired of her parlor on the first floor of Stern Manor, now felt well enough to remove to the morning room, which overlooked the back garden currently resplendent with roses, dianthus, and nigella. Her butler handed a silver salver with three letters on it to her.

Taking up her letter opener, she popped the seal to Dorothea's letter first. "Thank you. Please have tea brought to me."

He bowed. "Of course, my lady."

She read the second line twice before her heart started

to pound. When she was finally able to give voice to her excitement, her tone sounded shrill to her ears. "Hudson!"

Without batting an eye, he replied in a sonorous tone, "My lady?"

"Fetch Sir Henry. Miss Dotty is getting married!"

This proved too much for even Hudson. His eyes widened. "Our Miss Dotty?"

Cordelia fanned herself with the letter. "Do you know another?"

"No, my lady. I shall find him straightaway. Our Miss Dotty getting married! Excellent, excellent."

She glanced down at the missive again.

Dearest Mama,
    You will no doubt hear the whole story from Grace. Try not to be too worried about how my betrothal came about. It has all turned out for the best. Even if we are not yet in love with each other. I am marrying a man I can love. Lord Merton has been everything that is kind. You will remember him as the gentleman who helped me rescue . . .

                    Yr Devoted Daughter,
                    Dotty

Tears came to Cordelia's eyes as she opened the note from Grace, who did indeed explain the whole situation and gave her opinion that, although Merton could be very high in the instep, he seemed to dote on Dorothea.

The third letter was from the Dowager, Marchioness of Merton. Marchioness? Dotty was going to be a *marchioness,* and she hadn't even mentioned his title. Cordelia shook her head, smiling. How like her daughter to be more concerned that he took in her strays. Not that with her birth and connections she couldn't look as high as she wanted. It was merely that Cordelia never thought that her daughter would make such an advantageous match.

Not too many minutes later, her husband strode into the room holding two letters and frowning.

"What is it, my dear?" she asked.

"I don't know if I like how Dotty is conducting herself in Town. I've half a mind to bring her home."

Cordelia glanced at the ceiling and took a breath. "You do not need to take such drastic measures. We have been invited by Lady Merton to come to London and stay with her as soon as I can travel. Grace has offered the use of one of her traveling coaches, which will arrive in the next day or two and remain until we are ready to leave."

Her husband heaved a sigh. "What about our other two daughters, my dear?"

"I wish Tilly was back with us, but unfortunately, her mother has taken a turn for the worse. I only hope we will not be required to find another governess. Until then, Nurse is perfectly able to take care of the girls for a week or so. We will, of course, bring them to Town for the wedding."

He still looked undecided.

Poor Henry; he hated to have his family away from him. "Or we can take them with us. We must also bring Harry down from Oxford and Stephen from Rugby for Dotty's marriage." She passed a hand over her forehead. "Perhaps it would be best if Harry fetches Stephen and escorts the girls."

"*Are* you able to travel?" he asked dubiously.

"I shall call for the doctor immediately." She set the letter on her lap. "Good gracious. There is no reason for such a long face, Henry." She handed him the letters she'd received and reached for the bell pull. "I am sure everything will be fine."

He glanced up from one of the missives. "If not, that young man will answer to me."

She resisted the urge to roll her eyes and wondered how her forward-thinking husband would take to the old-fashioned-thinking marquis and vice versa. Then she smiled. Dorothea thought they would fall in love. That was all Cordelia could hope for any of her children. "Won't Mama be surprised to hear this news?"

"You seem very happy about his title." Henry came to her and kneeled down. "Do you ever wish—"

"Never." She kissed him lightly. "I am even more in love with you now than I was twenty-two years ago. Although, I won't deny that I'm very pleased Dorothea is making a good match, I would not want it if she didn't think they would come to love one another."

Henry finally smiled. "Is that what she told you?"

"Yes, and even you must admit Dorothea is a sensible young woman."

"That she is." He sighed. "I suppose I shouldn't worry. I'll probably feel better after I've met the young man."

"I must write Mama immediately. I'm sure this news will wrest her out of the country and back to Town as soon as my sister is safely delivered."

The butler entered the room. "My lady, the regular post has just arrived. You have another letter."

Opening the missive, Cordelia quickly perused the lines. "My sister has finally had a boy. Mama says he is the picture of health, but looks like his father."

Henry gave a bark of laughter. "Poor lad."

Cordelia wrinkled her nose at him. "That is not kind."

"Yes, but accurate." He dropped a kiss on her forehead. "I'll admit he makes up for it in other ways, but Leonard was never a handsome man."

She ignored him and continued reading the letter. "Mama says she will be back at her house within the week." Cordelia put the letter down. "She never stays after the baby is born."

"Of course not. That's when all the work begins."

"It is just as well. Dorothea needs her in Town."

"Exactly." Her husband chuckled. "A duchess to give our girl a bit of cachet."

Not willing to concede the point, Cordelia retorted, "Our daughter is going to be a marchioness. Mama can show her how to go on."

"We *are* talking about the same woman?" Henry grinned. "The one the Prince Regent won't acknowledge because she told him to stop quacking himself?"

"That was a long time ago. I am sure he has got over it."

"I wonder if Merton will survive your mother. You might not want them to meet until after the wedding."

"Henry." How exasperating her husband could be. "You should not be so disrespectful. If it was not for her we would not be married."

"Now, now, my love. You know I'm only teasing. I esteem your mother greatly. Though even you must admit that after a few days it's a relief to see her leave."

"It is just that she likes things just so."

A wicked look suddenly appeared on his face. "Tell me she's staying with Bristol."

Cordelia shook her head. Henry would never forgive her brother and his one-time friend for not supporting their marriage. "No, he is still in the country."

Her husband planted a kiss on her lips. "I'm off to write Harry and Stephen. I want to be well out of hearing distance when you tell the girls. My eardrums would shatter with their screeches."

"Send for the doctor as well."

"I shall. The more I think about it, the more I want to be in Town. I'd like to get to know my future son-in-law better before the wedding."

Cordelia's good humor faded. "Henry Stern, I shall not be responsible for my actions if you attempt to scare him off."

"If Dotty wants him, she shall have him, but he'll soon

learn he'll have me to deal with if he mistreats my daughter."
He paused for a moment. "Besides, if he allows me to scare
him off, he is not the man for Dotty."

The door closed and Cordelia sank back against the
cushions. Perhaps she would ask Grace to have Worthington warn Merton about her husband's more radical ideas.
On the other hand, it might be better to wait and see where
the cards fell. This could be vastly entertaining.

Chapter Twelve

Two days after the betrothal, Dom received a terse letter from Sir Henry approving the marriage. No congratulations, no surprise or gratitude that his daughter would marry a marquis. Just a simple statement that Sir Henry Stern gave Lord Merton permission to wed his daughter, Miss Dorothea Stern.

Dom wasted no time sending the announcement to the *Morning Post* by one of his running footmen. For some reason, seeing it in the newspaper would make it less likely anything could stop the marriage.

Later that morning, Worthington sent over the first proposal of the marriage settlements. As Dom broke open the seal, he was surprised to find he was actually looking forward to finalizing the agreements and getting on with his wedding, even if his uncle would have considered it ill-bred haste. Most couples did not wait long to marry. Worthington hadn't.

However, the more he read of the draft, the angrier he became. Preposterous! No. It was worse. The damned thing was an insult.

What the hell was Worthington about suggesting that Thea keep all her property in a trust for her use only in addition to receiving an allowance? Thea would be Dom's marchioness. Of course, he planned to be extremely generous. She would have no need for her own money. What woman did? And stating that she would have her own coaches and horses. It was unthinkable that she would **not** have her own phaeton or whatever type of sporting carriage she wanted as well as a team and a hack, with his approval naturally. Or did Worthington expect her to set up her own stable? No woman was capable of choosing good horseflesh.

He snatched the offending document from his desk and strode out the door. Walking should calm him down. A few minutes later, the door to Worthington House, where his cousin still kept his office, opened as Dom stalked up the steps.

The butler bowed. "Good morning, my lord. I believe his lordship is expecting you."

Dom reined in his rage and inclined his head. "No doubt."

Expecting him indeed. A footman opened the study door, depriving him of the satisfaction of slamming it back against the wall.

He waved the document in front of his cousin. "What the devil is the meaning of this?"

Worthington leaned back in his chair and slid a file from the side of his desk to the space in front of him. "Good morning to you as well." He motioned with his hand to a chair. "Take a seat."

Dom gritted his teeth, but remained standing. "I will not agree to this."

His cousin smiled humorously. "Are you planning to jilt Dotty?"

Jilt her? *Never*. She was his. "No."

Worthington shrugged. "Then you'll sign it."

Dom clenched and unclenched his hands. His desire to punch his cousin was almost overwhelming. "Has she seen this?"

Worthington raised a supercilious brow. "No. I've told her what's in it, but she, of course, has no experience dealing with marriage settlements. What is important is that Sir Henry has approved it." Worthington tapped the folder. "Dotty is merely happy that you are being so generous. In fact, even my stepmother is inclined to look more favorably upon you."

Dom couldn't keep the scowl off his face. "You did this to embarrass me and for no other reason."

His cousin leaned forward, putting his elbows on the desk. "On the contrary. I did it to protect Dotty. As a matter of fact, my agreements with Grace are almost identical."

Suddenly, he felt like one of the hot-air balloons that crashed down in the trees. He was so startled, he could only croak out, "Yours?"

Worthington reached over to a small table with a decanter and two glasses on it. After pouring some of the amber liquid into both tumblers, he offered one to Dom. "Brandy?"

"Yes, thank you," he said, taking it gratefully.

"Grace and I aren't the only ones to change the way we look at agreements and what a woman might need. Several of my friends have as well. It is a modern age, Merton. You might want to try entering the nineteenth century."

He took a drink, savoring the smoky flavor and the burn as he swallowed. He did not need a lecture from his cousin, but he also didn't need a fight. "I'll sign it."

Worthington smiled, and this time it was genuine. "I thought you might. By the way, I understand your mother wrote to Lady Stern, inviting her and Sir Henry to stay at Merton House until after the wedding."

Dom nodded. Mama had told him of her idea, but he didn't know if she'd received a response yet.

"They will arrive at the end of next week. That is the soonest the doctor will allow Lady Stern to travel."

Of course they would come as soon as they were able. "I'd expected nothing less."

Worthington raised a brow. "Do not make the mistake of thinking Sir Henry and Lady Stern care about your rank. All they are concerned with is Dotty's happiness."

Had the whole world gone mad? Sir Henry was a baronet. He should be strutting around like a bantam cock.

Something of what Dom had been thinking must have shown on his face, because Worthington added, "Sir Henry is almost of the opinion that the peerage should be abolished."

For a moment, Dom was speechless. "But why? Doesn't he benefit from our system of order at all?"

His cousin nodded. "Yes, but what is more important to him is that a few have so much and still enact laws to make life harder for those with very little. If I were you, I would try to avoid a political debate with him."

Dom's mind quit working. He had always assumed that only supporters of the French rebellion and the former American colonies held those beliefs. "Does he disparage you?"

"No." Worthington grinned. "Then again, I vote the way he would."

Hound's teeth. That must be where Thea got her ideas from. What else did she believe? Dom set his glass down. "I would like to see Miss Stern now."

His cousin waved his hand in the direction of Stanwood House. "Be my guest. I have no idea if they are home."

That was too much. A man should keep track of his women. "I'd think you would make it a point to know."

"If you imagine," Worthington said dryly, "I am going to drive myself to Bedlam trying to keep up with their schedules during the Season, you've gone mad. I go where I'm told and try to make myself useful the rest of the time. Or have you forgotten that Grace and I still have ten at home and her brother, Stanwood, at school." He paused for a moment and took a sip of brandy. "Come to think of it, I believe I said good morning to your mother and her companion before I left the other house today."

How was that possible? Dom had seen his mother earlier at breakfast. She hadn't mentioned going out. "I shall stop by just in case."

"Do as you please." Worthington picked up his pen. "As soon as you sign the settlements, that is."

Dom took the pen, scribbling his signature before leaving the room.

What was his mother doing? Not that he minded her spending time with Thea. In fact he should have suggested it. Still, Mama ought to have at least told him she was going out. What if he had needed her? He strode across the square and knocked on the door of Stanwood House, where Worthington's family resided this year.

The door opened and the butler bowed.

"I would like to see Miss Stern."

"I'm sorry, my lord. The ladies are not at home at present. Shall I tell her you called?"

He shook his head. "No. I'll come by later."

The butler bowed again. "As you wish, my lord."

He glanced at his watch. It was too early for morning calls. Where the devil could they be? And why had no one informed him?

"Oh, Madame Lisette, it is lovely." Dotty stared at her reflection in the mirrors surrounding the platform on which she stood being fitted. The pale blue silk ball gown covered with silver netting had a lower neckline than what was considered appropriate for ladies just coming out. The puffed sleeves and flounce near the hem were trimmed with tulle. She'd never had anything like it. The gown was the first outward indication that her whole life was about to change. Even after Dom's kiss, their betrothal hadn't seemed real.

"*Oui, d'accord,*" Madame said. "*Moi,* I think it will do nicely."

"May I show the others?"

"*Naturellement.* I shall call them in."

A minute later, Grace, Charlotte, Louisa, and Lady Merton entered the small room.

"Dotty, you look wonderful." Charlotte practically breathed it out.

Grace smiled approvingly. "It's perfect."

"Splendid, my dear," Lady Merton agreed. "If you do not have any appropriate jewels, I believe I have just the thing to wear with it."

For a moment, Dotty was stunned by the offer. "I don't know if I should."

"Nonsense. You will be the Marchioness of Merton in a few weeks and all the family jewels will be yours."

Dotty rubbed her brow, earning a rebuke from the seamstress making adjustments to the garment.

"If you like," Lady Merton continued, "you may return them after the ball."

Turning only her head, Dotty glanced at Grace. "When is the ball to be?"

"I received a letter from your mother this morning. She will be in Town by next Friday." Grace laughed. "She had to promise the doctor she would not dance, and that she would stay off her leg as much as possible."

Dotty could see her mother convincing the doctor to allow the journey. "It sounds as if Mama browbeat him into giving his permission."

"You are probably right. Now that we have their arrival date, Lady Merton will hold the ball the Saturday prior to the wedding."

Now that was a surprise. "Not at Stanwood House?"

"It only makes sense," her future mother-in-law said. "Your mother accepted my invitation to stay with me. We thought you might like to move to Merton House as well. It will give you time to learn the staff and go over the house."

Dotty was beginning to suspect she'd be well advised to take better notice of the plans being made. "With no disrespect to Mama, I would have thought she'd write to me as well."

"Oh!" Grace gave a look of consternation. "You probably do have a letter mixed in with the rest of the post. I did not think to tell our butler to deliver it to you when he brought mine up."

"Yes, of course" was all Dotty could think of to say.

She had been having so much fun with her friends that she hadn't actually thought of living elsewhere. Which was silly. She would be married in less than three weeks, and she was happy about it. Ever since he had taken Tom in, she and Merton had become even closer, and he appeared to be abandoning his stiff ways. This would turn out very well indeed.

Chapter Thirteen

It was close to noon by the time Dom found his betrothed and his mother, accompanied by his cousin, Grace, and Lady Charlotte. They'd just regained the pavement and turned right on Bruton Street, heading toward him as he left Bond Street.

Thea's countenance lit when she saw him. "Good morning. Did you have business here?"

Yes. Hunting down her and his mother. He greeted the other ladies, then took Thea's hand, brushing his fingers over her knuckles. He hid his smile as she breathed in sharply. "No, just out for a stroll. You look lovely as usual." Her face and neck were once more a charming shade of pink, and he had a sudden wish to always be able to make her blush. He liked how natural she always was. "Are you finished shopping?"

"No, we are on our way to the shoemaker."

Tucking her hand in his arm, he turned to stroll with her back toward Bond Street. Dom lowered his voice so that only she could hear. "I believe I am jealous."

Thea's eyes widened. "Of what, pray?"

"Of the shopkeeper who will be allowed to touch your foot, when I cannot."

She slid him a sidelong glance. "Are you flirting with me, my lord?"

"I'm certainly trying to." He had never felt the need to flatter a lady before. He hoped she liked it. "Am I succeeding?"

"Immensely." Her complexion was even rosier now, but her tone was light and teasing. "I had no idea you were such a rogue."

What was he to say to that? Here she was newly on the Town, and already she knew more about the art of flirtation than he did. It must come more naturally to women. "Only with you, my love."

Thea promptly responded, "Yet, what about after we are wed? I thought the *ton* disparaged a married man flirting with his wife."

Hoisted on his own petard. The thought of another gentleman paying attention to her made his blood boil. He gave her back her own words. "I prefer to make my own fashion. One not based on deceit."

A burble of laughter escaped her lips before she put her hand over her mouth. "I'd forgotten I shouldn't laugh too loudly."

Damn the person who prescribed that everyone in the *ton* should appear permanently bored. He would not have her delight stifled. Particularly when her laughter sounded like the tinkling of bells and it was him she was pleased with. "As the Marchioness of Merton, you may do much as you please. You will be looked at to set fashion."

"That may very well be true, but as Miss Dorothea Stern, I may not willy-nilly break the rules." She gave him a sly look. "I shall wait until later."

She was so comfortable with herself, confidence that had nothing to do with her rank. Was it courage or an innate sense of belonging? She never behaved as if she had to prove herself to anyone or disparaged another to build herself up.

Pure lust surged through him. If only they were alone and he could kiss her again.

"Dotty." Ahead of them, Grace had stopped. "We are here."

The sign for a cobbler hung overhead. He would either have to let Thea go now and allow the blasted clerk to touch her foot, or remain and shoot the man black looks. Blast it all, he *was* jealous. "Shall I come by at five o'clock to take you for a drive?"

She grimaced. "I cannot promise we'll be home. I am not the only one we are shopping for."

Grace shooed the others into the shop, leaving him alone with Thea.

He would most likely have to put up with this orgy of shopping until their marriage. "Send a message round when you return."

Thea's face brightened. "I will. If we are too late for the Promenade, I'll see you this evening."

"You shall and this time I can remain at your side the entire night."

She gave a light laugh, and he released her to join the others. Tonight, he'd ensure that no gentleman would be under the impression theirs was a marriage of convenience. He walked back up to Piccadilly, then to St. James Street and White's to enjoy a beefsteak.

Fotherby accosted Dom as he stepped onto the shallow stair leading to the door of his club. "You are actually going through with it?"

Dom raised a brow. "I take it you saw the notice."

"How else would I know?" Fotherby replied peevishly. "You're never at your usual haunts these days. I just don't see how you could marry that chit."

Once again, anger at the way Fotherby referred to Thea speared through Dom. Yet he wasn't about to allow the man to ruin his mood. He made himself shrug noncommittally. "What would you have me do?" Fate had handed him the perfect opportunity to have what he wanted. But he was not about to discuss his desire to marry Thea with Fotherby or anyone else.

The man was rapidly becoming a dead bore. "The fact remains that I am."

"I suppose I should wish you happy," Fotherby huffed. "I'd feel a deemed sight better about it if I thought she wouldn't lead you on a merry dance."

Dom struggled to keep his lips from tilting up. She would indeed keep him busy, yet he would always know where he stood with her. "If she does, it won't be for long."

"I suppose there is nothing left to say. I saw what happened to my brother just before his wedding. You'll be as busy as a three-legged dog."

"There is that." Dom wondered if he'd be called on for an opinion of the ceremony or wedding breakfast at all. The ladies seemed to have it all in hand. "I still have a great deal of work to attend to. Duty does not stop because of a wedding. Unless you'd like to dine with me, I shall bid you good day."

"Wish I could. M'mother's in Town and made it clear she expects me at the house." Fotherby inclined his head and walked off.

Dom couldn't believe how relieved he was that his friend had other obligations. Two hours later, he climbed the steps to his home and was met by Cyrille, who gazed up at him, clearly expecting attention, and Tom waving a piece of paper in his hand.

"My lord, see what I've done. Mrs. Sorley says I'm a prodigy."

The boy's cultured accents became more pronounced with each passing day. Thea had noticed it when she visited the other afternoon. Dom took the paper, a drawing of Cyrille asleep in Dom's chair in his study. Although it was done in pencil, the child had captured the detail of the cat's shimmery coat against the slick leather of the chair.

Someone had taught the child how to draw. Who the devil were Tom's parents and how was Dom to find out when the lad refused to speak of it?

"That is excellent. We must find you a drawing master."

The boy's whole face shone with pride. "Thank you, my lord."

What would have happened to Tom if Thea hadn't rescued him? Most likely, he would have been taken to the local gaol, then possibly a workhouse, if not worse. Dom must do whatever it took to find the child's family. "Can you tell me where you lived when you were with your mother?"

The boy's countenance shuttered. "I'm not supposed to tell, or I'll get what for."

He signaled for tea to be served in his study and took the child by his hand. "I am confident I can assure you that as long as you are under my protection, no one will harm you."

The boy was silent for several moments. "You kept me from dying."

"Er, yes. Not only the first time but subsequently as well." Bath time was still difficult. Fortunately, once assured he had given one of the footmen his power to keep Tom safe, Dom had not had to attend the lad's ablutions again.

Tom hopped up onto the sofa, and stared at Dom. Finally, he nodded his head. "I don't know the address, but I'd recognize it if I saw it again."

He wanted to groan. This was liable to be a long and painful process. "Outstanding. Perhaps we'll take a drive in my curricle. You'll like that."

Tom nodded his head up and down so hard, Dom thought the boy would rattle his brain.

Tea arrived. Mrs. Sorley poured a cup and gave it to him. She handed a mug of milk along with a jam tart to Tom. "You eat that all up, mind. You're still too skinny."

"I will." Tom nodded. "It's very good. Even Cook's wasn't this good."

Mrs. Sorley glanced at Dom and raised her brows.

Clearly, he was supposed to make the inquiry. "Ah, did Cook live with you?"

The boy shook his head, munching on his sweet. "No. She used to bring us food. Mama said Cook was her most favorite person after Papa and me."

Papa? Had his parents been married? Dom ran a hand through his hair. Where was the scoundrel now?

Lord Fotherby was swinging his new gold-headed cane in time with the tassels on his boots as he strolled down the pedestrian walk of the Park when a lady called out.

"Lord Fotherby, how delightful to run into you again."

"Lady Manners." He bowed and lifted his hat. "The pleasure is all mine, I am sure."

She signaled to the footman to drop back. "Such sad news."

What the devil was she talking about? Did someone die? He would not wish her to think he was not up on all the *crim cons.* "Indeed. It took us all by surprise."

The lady's eyes rounded. "You as well? I would have thought he would confide in *you* of all people. Although he is very reserved."

Fotherby blinked. Who the devil was it she was talking about? Perhaps if she just kept up the conversation, he'd get an inkling. "No, no. He does, as you say, keep his own counsel."

Lady Manners nodded sadly. "He must be very embarrassed to have to marry so far beneath him."

Understanding crept into the recesses of his mind. He wasn't as bright as most of his friends, but he was well up to snuff. She must be talking about Merton and was obviously upset. "I daresay. Though I expect he'll make the best of it. Nothing else to do after all."

"Well." She blew out a breath that lifted one of the curls on her forehead. "I, for one, am in despair. The sly minx trapping him like that. He was to have married my cousin, Miss Turley. you know."

Trapped? Fotherby didn't like Miss Stern, but he never thought she'd do anything scurrilous. Still, Merton was a marquis. No wonder he had not wanted to discuss his betrothal. Not that he really had a choice. It had been all around Town before the announcement was in the *Morning Post*. A fellow was out of luck at this stage of the game. In fact, he should not have given Merton a hard time about it. "Bad business that, but what can one do?"

He'd meant his question to be rhetorical, but a gleam came in to Lady Manners's eyes and she took his arm, leaning in confidingly.

"Perhaps, if I had a gentleman to assist me, I could discover a way to stop the marriage from happening."

"I don't take your meaning. Merton would never call it off. He values his reputation too much. And the chit is residing with his cousin."

She fluttered her lashes, as if she had a speck in her eye. "But what if Miss Stern failed to appear at the wedding?"

Fotherby tried to take a step back, but Lady Manners latched on tightly to his arm. "Merton would not take well to being made a fool of."

"Precisely my point. He wouldn't give her another chance."

Fotherby wasn't at all sure he wanted to be a part of Lady Manners's plans. If it got out, he'd never hear the end of it from his mother. "I won't be involved in anything criminal."

"Not anything truly illegal, but if we were to ensure she was . . . elsewhere for a day or so . . ."

Lavvie petted Fotherby's arm in a soothing way. If she had known he was so hen-witted, she'd have picked someone else to assist her, but she had to help Elizabeth. If she couldn't marry for love, at least Lavvie could ensure her cousin married a man who'd be good to her. Unlike Manners, who never failed to blame her for everything.

The arm she held tightened as he sputtered, "See here, no matter what she did, I'll have no part in ruining Miss Stern."

The man was being more stubborn than she expected. If there was anyone else Lavvie could use, she would. Unfortunately, Merton did not have a large circle of friends, and Fotherby was the only one with a house near Richmond. Just far enough away to keep Miss Stern from being able to make her way back to London and close enough that no one would notice Fotherby's absence.

She swallowed her exasperation. "No, no, indeed. That would never do. We shall put it about that she went home. I've heard Lady Stern is unable to travel. What could be more natural than for the girl to realize that she is not prepared for the position as Merton's wife and run away to her mama?" When Fotherby didn't respond, Lavvie continued in her most coaxing tone. "We shall only keep Miss Stern for a day or so, then return her to the bosom of her family unharmed, and Merton will be free to select a suitable bride."

Fotherby glanced at her with his brows drawn together. "Your cousin, Miss Turley, for example?"

"Why, yes, if he still wishes to ask her."

Lavvie resisted the urge to roll her eyes while he considered her idea.

"Where will you take her?" he asked.

She leaned against his side a little more and glanced up at him, trying to portray a helpless look. "I had not gotten that far in my plan." She smoothed the cloth of his sleeve. "Do you know of a place near enough to Town for the purpose?"

"I have a cottage in Richmond my grandmother left me. It hasn't been used in a few years, but a couple takes care of it. I don't know that they'd agree to keep Miss Stern against her will."

"We could tell them she is a relative of mine who has tried to elope and must be kept safe until her brother comes to fetch her."

"I suppose that would work," Fotherby mumbled.

"Then the only thing to do is set a date." Lavvie acted as if the deal was done. She couldn't afford for Fotherby to back out. Who knew what kind of man her uncle would force upon Elizabeth if Lavvie failed?

"I'll only do this to help Merton, mind," Fotherby said in a whiny voice. "I've no wish to see him marry against his will."

"Naturally," Lavvie said, using her most innocent tone. "That is my desire as well."

She signaled for her footman to approach with the message she had given him. "My lady, you'll be late for your appointment."

"Thank you, Edwards. Mr. Fotherby, I am so pleased we could have this discussion."

He took her outstretched hand. "I as well. When will we—you know?"

She smiled. "I shall send you a note."

He nodded before mincing off toward St. James Street. Once he was out of hearing, she strolled toward the Park exit nearest Green Street. "Edwards, I want you to keep an eye on a young lady. I need to know her schedule."

"Yes, my lady. I'll find someone to do the job." He walked behind her, closer than he should have. Lavvie felt his breath on the back of her neck before she heard him. "I didn't like you leaning against that man." His tone was insolent, and she glanced at him in time to see his hot gaze raked over her bodice. "Don't let me see it again."

A shiver of delight speared through her. She couldn't wait to see him naked again and feel his hard body sink into hers. So much different than her soft, pudgy husband who could barely do his part, then blamed her for not conceiving. "Stop that. You mustn't let anyone guess."

One black brow rose. "You don't think his lordship would like me tupping his wife?"

That was the only fear she had for herself. If Manners knew, he'd divorce her. She would never survive the scandal. "He can't ever know."

"I want you . . . soon."

God, she was panting like a bitch in heat. "The old governess's room."

They entered the hall of her home. Under the guise of removing her cloak, he squeezed and kneaded her derrière. His low voice caressed her ear. "Don't keep me waiting."

She licked her lips. "I won't."

A knock sounded on the door. Edwards opened it.

"Lavvie, I did not know if I would find you home." Elizabeth did not even seem to notice the footman. "We need to discuss something."

Lavvie allowed her cousin to kiss her cheek. "I'm sorry, my dear, but I cannot visit right now. I have the most vicious headache."

"Not another migraine?"

"Indeed it is. Can your news wait?" She tried to look ill, when the only thing wrong with her was the dampness between her legs.

"Yes. I'm so sorry you are feeling badly. I have to get back now."

"I understand. Your aunt Agatha is here."

Elizabeth gave a small smile. "I hope you feel better soon."

Lavvie straightened her shoulders. "I am sure we shall see each other soon."

Chapter Fourteen

Dom had arrived home from White's and called for Tom to be brought to him. He now sat on Dom's lap. Obviously, the boy had lived with both parents at some point, and the time had come to find out as much about them as he could. No one had been successful before, but there was nothing for it, he hoped that the child felt safe enough now to give him the information. "Tom, what's your full name?"

"James Thomas Hubert." He frowned at Dom. "Are you angry with me?"

"No, of course not." Why would he think that? "Why?"

"Because my mama used to call me that when she was angry."

He ruffled the boy's hair. "You've done nothing wrong." He grinned. "But at least now I know what to call you when you do something wrong. So, ah, Mr. Hubert was your papa?"

"No, that's my third name after Mama's uncle who died."

Dom might be getting the first headache of his life. "What was your father's last name?"

Once again, the child's lips formed a mulish line.

Dom pressed his fingers to his temple and rubbed. "Let me guess, you're not supposed to tell."

Tom nodded his head emphatically. What or who the hell had scared the child so thoroughly?

Light feminine voices floated down the hall. Mama was home, and she had someone with her. Perhaps it was Thea. He tugged the bell pull and a footman popped his head in the door.

"My lord?"

"If Miss Stern is here, please ask her to attend me."

"Yes, my lord."

It was the correct response, but Dom had never heard it given with so much enthusiasm.

A few minutes later, his mother and Thea entered the room. Tom jumped up and wrapped his arms around her legs.

Thea laughed. "You are getting so big. You'll soon knock me over."

Dom glanced at the lad. In just a few days, Tom had put on enough weight that he'd started to look healthy. "Isn't it time for your lessons?"

"Yes, sir. I'll go find Sally." Tom ran to the door, closing it behind him.

Thea raised a brow. "Lessons?"

"With one of the maids until I have time to hire a tutor. We need to discuss the child. He's not what he first seemed."

"Yes, that's what you said."

Thea and his mother took seats on the sofa by the windows overlooking the garden and Dom rang for tea.

They discussed Thea's shopping until tea arrived. His mother motioned for Thea to pour.

Dom took his cup. It was nice having her here. He was impatient for the time when he would share every meal with her. "My housekeeper brought it to my attention. The child appears to be gently bred." He told them about his conversations with Tom. "After what he's been through, I don't want to threaten him."

"I agree." Thea poured milk into her cup and stirred. "Perhaps I can talk to him and find out more. Though I believe

I know why he is afraid to talk. From what you said, it appears he was taken in by a group of thieves that train children to rob."

He set his cup down with a snap. "You cannot be serious."

She gave a light shrug. "If one lives in London, it is fairly common knowledge."

Yet she did not live in Town and she knew of it. He looked at his tea and wished it was a brandy. "But why use children? I would think there'd be more risk in getting caught."

"Children are generally transported rather than hanged."

He spewed his tea. Fortunately, he got his serviette up in time before much damage was done. "*Transported?* I thought he'd be sent to a workhouse."

How she sat there so calmly, he didn't know.

"Not after being tried for theft. He would have been taken to Newgate."

Suddenly, the pounding in his head grew louder. "Newgate?"

Thea nodded. "Yes, which is the reason Lady Evesham and Lady Rutherford now have an orphan asylum and are working to change the laws. It is cruel to blame a child for something he has been taught to do in order to eat. He was probably told there would be dire consequences if he told anyone about either the criminal gang or himself."

Thea poured Dom another cup of tea as he tried to untangle what he had always believed with what appeared to be the facts. Had his uncle known of this when he counseled Dom to vote for harsh punishments for criminals of all ages? What if he would have just listened to Worthington and his set?

"Dominic?" his mother asked.

"Yes, Mama?"

"Dorothea has an appointment with Mrs. Sorley to go over the house. We shall leave you for now."

"Of course." He rose when they did and took Thea's hand. "I'll see you this evening if not before."

She searched his eyes and smiled. "One or the other, perhaps both."

At some point he had to get to the bottom of what had happened to Tom, but tonight all he wanted was to be with Thea at the ball. He could find a quiet parlor or a secluded place in the garden or on the terrace so he could kiss her as he wanted to do now. She was his and it was time he showed her.

Dotty left Dom mulling over his newfound knowledge. It had astonished her that he was so insulated from real life. She wondered if he would ever get Tom to tell the truth and thought she might give it a try. After all, she did have younger sisters and one younger brother.

"My lady?"

"You wish to see little Tom, do you not?"

She grinned. In just a few short days, she'd come to like and admire her future mother-in-law's perspicacity. "I would, after I meet with your housekeeper, of course."

"I think that is a good idea. He might confide in you more willingly than in Dominic." They continued to her ladyship's parlor where the housekeeper would meet them. "If you'd like a little hint regarding getting on with Mrs. Sorley, encourage her to tell you about the family. She was born at Merton and her mother was the housekeeper before her. There is not a family secret she does not know."

Dotty widened her eyes. "Are there secrets?"

"More than I knew." Lady Merton sighed.

They'd reached the parlor and found the housekeeper waiting. Mrs. Sorley appeared to be in her forties. She was of medium height with light brown hair and gray eyes. Her mien was pleasant but sober. Woe to the child who muddied her floors. Still, Dotty liked her instantly.

Mrs. Sorley curtseyed. "Miss, I'm pleased to meet you."

Dotty held out her hand. "As I am you, Mrs. Sorley. Shall we begin?"

The housekeeper took two of Dotty's fingers and released them. A grin split her long narrow face. "We'll start with the upper floors and work our way down if that suits you."

"It does indeed." It appeared Mrs. Sorley thought as Dotty did. "Most particularly the nursery?"

"Yes, miss. Precisely what I was thinking." She handed Dotty a pocketbook and pencil. "I'll take notes, but you might want to do so as well."

Dotty followed the housekeeper to the main hall then up three levels of stairs before they reached the nursery. As she expected, the house was clean and neat, but could use some redecoration in areas. Lady Merton hadn't spent a great deal of time here. After having seen the Stanwood House schoolroom floor and the plans for the one at Worthington House, Dotty was full of ideas for remodeling. Although she hoped never to have eleven children. Twelve, if one counted Grace.

In the schoolroom, Tom was busy reading with Sally, the temporary tutor, and asking her questions. "But, Sally, I don't understand this part."

The girl glanced over and scratched her cheek. "I'm not sure I know the answer myself."

Dotty moved behind Tom, reading the passage over his shoulder. It was an old book on farm management. "Sally, please do not take this the wrong way, but was there nothing else?"

The girl pulled a face. "No, miss. I can teach him letters from this, but . . ."

Dotty glanced at Mrs. Sorley. "Might there be something in the library?"

"No, miss. After his lordship's father died, Lord Alasdair had all the children's books thrown out."

What ailed the man to do something like that? "You mean

to tell me Lord Merton learned with books like this?" She picked up the offending tome.

Mrs. Sorley sucked in her cheeks, her disapproval evident. "Yes, miss."

No wonder Matt disliked Lord Alasdair so much. She bit her lip. She was not yet Dom's wife and had no right to criticize a member of his family. "Can a list be sent to a bookstore for more appropriate books?"

"If you make a list, miss, I'll send a footman." Mrs. Sorley had an almost defiant look in her eyes, her lips curved up enough for Dotty to know the woman agreed with her.

She sat at the small table, took out her notepad, and made a list of the types of books Tom should have.

"Miss?"

"Yes, Mrs. Sorley?"

"The boy's awful good at drawing."

Sally nodded and handed Dotty a piece of paper. "See here. He did that of me."

The picture was an amazingly good representation of the maid, even catching the twinkle in her eyes. "Drawing materials as well." She glanced at Tom who was occupied with another sketch. "Tom, how old are you?"

"Six." Suddenly he slapped his hand over his mouth. "I'm not supposed to tell, 'cause I look younger."

Dotty motioned for Mrs. Sorley and Sally to leave the room. After the door closed, Dotty picked him up and put him on her lap. "I know you were mistreated before coming to Merton House. But I promise no one will do so again. Do you believe me?"

Tom nodded. "His lordship said the same thing. But the men said . . ."

It was past time to slay dragons. She turned him so that she could look into his eyes. "Listen to me. Anyone wanting to get at you will have to go through both his lordship and me as well as Paken and *all* his footmen."

The child's eyes grew wide. "Even Mr. Paken?"

Dom's lofty and unflappable butler had made the impression she'd hoped for. "Do you think the people who had you could do that?"

Slowly, Tom shook his head.

"But in order for Paken to protect you to the best of his ability, you must help."

"How can I do that?"

"By telling me as much as you know about who your parents are and where you lived before being cast out on to the streets."

Tom stared at her for what seemed like a very long time before he sank back against her shoulder and began to recite. "My mama's maiden name is Sophia Cummings. Her father is James Cummings, Esquire of Bude, Cornwall. My father is Robert Cavanaugh. His father is the Earl of Stratton. Papa is a major in the 95th Rifles on his way to Brazil." Tom's voice started to tremble. "My name is James Thomas Hubert Cavanaugh. I was born April 6, 1809. I live at Number 14 St. George Street."

Dotty held him as sobs wracked his slender body. She blinked back the tears stinging her eyes. "Hush, now. It's all right. Everything will be fine. I promise."

When he'd calmed, Mrs. Sorley came back in the room with a cup she pressed into Tom's hands. "Some warm milk might help."

"Yes. Have Sally come stay with him. She should not leave his side. I'll put him to bed."

"Yes, miss. Shall I ask his lordship to come up here?"

"No, please ask Lady Merton to join me in the morning room, if you will."

"Thank you, miss. May I say I'm glad you're going to be joining the family?" The housekeeper bobbed a curtsey and left.

There was no lack of projects here. Dotty dropped a kiss

on Tom's head and took the empty cup, placing it on the table, then carried him into his bedchamber, and tucked him under the sheets. Cyrille jumped up on the bed and curled himself next to the sleeping boy.

The first thing to do was take care of Tom. Thank the Lord his mother had made him memorize his family information. How terrifying it must have been for her to be alone with a small child when she died. Dotty brushed away the tear traveling down her cheek.

Rage at the people who had mistreated Tom coursed through her. That landlady had much to answer for. Dotty didn't know if she could even be civil when she met her, but meet her she would. Mrs. Cavanaugh must have left some personal items behind and they belonged to Tom and his father.

Returning to the table, she occupied herself, until the maid returned, by reducing to writing everything Tom had told her. Before this day was out, she would confront the woman who had abandoned a small child to the streets, or more likely, sold him to thieves.

Dom raised his eyes from the documents he'd been reviewing when Thea entered his study, his mother following her. He rose until they had taken their seats on the two chairs facing his desk. He was glad to see them getting along so well.

He smiled, then noticed they both had their lips pressed tightly together, their eyes were narrowed, and tension seemed to crackle around them. Could it be the house, or God forbid, Mrs. Sorley? "Is anything wrong?"

Thea slid a small piece of paper across the desk. "Tom finally told me who he is. I had planned to go directly to his family's rooms on St. George Street, but your mother convinced me to discuss it with you first." Her voice hitched in anger. "I shall confront Mrs. White."

Dom put down his pen. "The landlady?"

"The very one. I surmise she sold Tom to the blackguards who were teaching him to steal."

Leaning back in the tufted leather chair, Dom tried to catch up with her. Whatever the boy had said obviously had overwrought Thea's sensibilities. "Start from the beginning and tell me what you know."

"It's all on the paper," his mother said. "Mrs. Sorley was correct. He is gently bred."

"If that is the case, we must find his family."

Thea rubbed her temples as if they ached. "What I do not understand is why the stupid woman did not contact the Earl of Stratton."

Glancing back and forth between his mother and Thea, Dom interpolated, "Stratton?"

As if he hadn't spoken, she continued. "Surely he would have paid her more than those blackguards."

"I'm not sure, my dear," Mama responded. "The earl is a hard man. What if his son had married a woman of whom he did not approve?"

"But to take it out on a child?" Thea clenched her small hands into fists. "That is criminal!"

Dom ran a hand over his face. What the devil were they talking about? "Would one of you please tell me what the Earl of Stratton has to do with Tom?"

Thea glanced at him, her wide eyes expectant as if Dom should know. "He is Tom's grandfather, of course."

"Damnation!"

"Dominic!" his mother said sternly. "You will not use that language in front of either me or Dorothea."

He growled and grabbed the slip of paper from his desk. "Yes, ma'am."

James Cavanaugh and Sophia Cummings Cavanaugh.

He shook his head. Tom's father was likely a few years older than Dom, and the only person he could think of to ask about it was Worthington. *Confound it.*

"We could approach the earl first," Thea said.

"I don't know, my dear," his mother responded. "Better to discover if there is any bad blood between father and son first. Oh, why have I spent so much time immured in the country and at Bath?" She stood. "First let us see this Mrs. White. Although I shall own myself surprised if that is her real name."

Thea rose as well. Dom stood out of habit. What did they think they were doing? Hadn't they come to him for advice?

"Dominic, I shall take Dorothea to Stanwood House after we visit St. George Street."

Apparently not. Had all the women in his life gone mad? He probably should have known Thea would go and confront the woman, but Mama?

His mother smiled as if she was doing nothing more than paying a social call. Devil a bit. He'd sort them out later.

"Wait a minute. I'm going with you." He jerked on the bell pull and a footman's head popped in. "Get the town coach, immediately."

"Yes, my lord." He closed the door. Dom could hear him running down the corridor. Damn. Tom must be distraught after revealing what he had to Thea. "Where is the child?"

Thea shoved a long pin in her hat. "He is asleep for now. Sally is with him with orders not to leave him."

He opened the door and stood to the side. "Shall we go?"

When Thea reached him, she stopped. "I am glad you decided to come with us. A marquis is just what is needed if the job requires intimidation."

He almost dropped his jaw. Then he wanted to laugh. She had finally found a good use for his rank. His uncle would have had apoplexy by now, yet Dom had never felt so alive in his life.

"That's what we marquises do best." He dropped a quick kiss on her lips. "I shall meet you in the hall."

As she hurried out, he returned to his desk and removed a small, but accurate pistol from the top drawer. One never knew when rank might not be enough.

Chapter Fifteen

Twenty minutes later Dom's coach came to a stop in front of a modest house on St. George Street. The façade looked innocuous enough. Pale gray, from the London grime, there were a few steps up to a door whose knocker needed polishing. Still, the house gave the appearance of being respectable.

Roger, one of the two footmen Dom had accompany them, opened the carriage door, then walked up the shallow steps and pounded the knocker. A slight girl with mousy brown hair and an apron covering her drab blue gown opened it.

Not looking at the maid, Roger announced, "The Marquis of Merton wishes to speak to Mrs. White."

The small bit of color in the young woman's face drained. "Don't know that she's here to visitors."

The girl was obviously more afraid of her mistress than some random marquis. Dom stepped around his footman. "Perhaps you should inquire."

When the maid tried to close the door, his servant stopped it with his foot, and said affably, "Here now, you don't mean to leave their lordship and ladyship out here, do you?"

The maid glanced at Roger, then Dom. "I guess not," she

grumbled. "Come in if you must, but I'll tell ye, she don't like seeing company."

"Right old screw is she?" the footman asked.

The girl seemed to soften a bit. "Ye could say that. As soon as I find another position, I'm gone."

Thea, now standing next to Roger, smiled. "Thank you very much for allowing us to come inside."

The maid stared wide-eyed and bobbed a quick curtsey. "Yes, my lady. I'll fetch my mistress, right away."

Thea glanced around the hall, swiped her finger on the newel post, and looked at her gloved finger. "This place could use a good cleaning."

A few moments later, a young matron came down the stairs holding the hand of a child about the same age as Tom. When she reached the bottom tread, she looked up. "Oh, I am sorry. I did not see you there. Have you come to look at the empty rooms?"

Dom was about to deny any such thing, when Thea shot him a warning look. "Why, yes we are. Have you lived here long?"

The woman smiled. "Only a couple of months. I had planned to return to live with my mother while my husband is arranging our home in Canada."

Thea wrinkled her forehead.

"Oh." The woman gave a small laugh and put her hand to her mouth. "I must sound like such a pea-goose. My husband is in the army and will be stationed in Canada for the next few years. We shall join him after he has arranged housing. I was going to stay with my mother, but Mrs. White has been so kind that my husband and I decided I would remain here until he sends for me. If he pays the rent in advance, she will even give us a reduced rate for the time I am here with my daughter."

Thea glanced down at the child. "Such a lovely little girl."

The young woman got a sort of misty smile. "Thank you. She is so good and will be rewarded with a little brother or sister in a few months, which is the reason my husband does not wish me to travel with him."

Thea's body seemed to stiffen, but her countenance remained calm and relaxed. She touched her stomach briefly. "How does Mrs. White like children?"

"She loves them. Why she even gave Susan here some toys that had been left by a previous tenant. So kind."

Thea stilled and Dom could see the effort it took for her to continue smiling.

He'd give odds the toys were Tom's. Something was very wrong here. "Madam, has your husband already departed?"

"Not yet. We still have another two weeks together." She held out her hand to Thea. "I'm terribly sorry, so rude of me. "I'm Mrs. Horton."

Thea responded in kind. "I am . . . Mrs. Merton and this is my husband and mother-in-law. What happened to the people in the empty apartment?"

The woman looked slightly confused. "I'm not sure. They left very suddenly about a month ago. She had been very kind to me. Her child was due sometime in the autumn . . ."

"Mama, can we go now?" the child asked. "Bessie will be waiting."

"Yes, my love, of course." Mrs. Horton smiled at Thea again. "Perhaps we shall be neighbors."

Thea's lips tilted up. "Wouldn't that be nice?"

No sooner had the door to the street closed, when the maid came back in. "She'll see you now. She *says* she ain't feelin' well, so you can't stay long."

Dom placed his hand at the back of Thea's waist as they followed the girl down a narrow corridor. The whole atmosphere of the house bothered him, and he needed to touch her, keep her safe.

They entered a parlor decorated in some tawdry flowered material. An assortment of vials and small boxes on the table next to a chaise, upon which a plump middle-aged woman, with improbable blond curls covered by a lacy cap, lay. A brightly colored shawl with a long fringe covered her ample proportions and a piece of wet linen was on her forehead. Unfortunately, it caused her heavy face powder to run. She reminded him of a Drury Lane actress.

"My lord, my ladies, forgive me," she said in a loud whisper. "I have been laid low and am unable to arise." She made a sweeping motion with her arm. "As you see I am almost at death's door, but I am honored by your presence in my humble house."

Thea made a choking sound and his mother a soft harrumph.

Dom stepped forward, inclining his head slightly. "Mrs. White, we have come to collect Mrs. Cavanaugh's effects."

For a moment, the woman turned a light shade of green under the powder and really did look sick, but she recovered quickly. "Poor unfortunate lady, I have nothing of hers left. I had to pawn the lot to pay her rent."

Clenching his jaw, he stepped forward again. "And her son?"

She gave a dramatic sigh. "The poor little mite ran away. I searched for days—"

"Enough." He took another step and stood right over her. "I will not be lied to."

Her hand went to her throat. "My lord, please. My heart."

"I don't believe you either." Thea stepped out from behind him.

"No, neither do I." His mother glanced around the room. "In fact, I would not be a bit surprised if most of these gewgaws belonged to the families of your victims."

Mrs. White narrowed her eyes and snarled, "You just try to prove it."

Thea had come around to stand at the head of the chaise. She picked up a silver box and stepped back. "I believe this is part of the proof. It is engraved with SC. Tom's mother's initials. Perhaps he will recognize it."

Mrs. White moved, but Thea was faster, dancing away from the woman's claw like fingers. "She gave it to me. As a present."

"Just like Tom gave you his toys?" Dom gritted his teeth. "I don't think so, Mrs. White."

The woman's terrified gaze went from Thea to Dom and then to Mama. "I told you he left. Ain't seen him since. Distraught he was."

Dom had never in his life wanted to throttle a person like he did now. Not even Worthington filled him with such rage. "So distraught that he remembers you sending him away with two men?"

Thea stood off to Dom's side, while his mother inspected the other objects in the overcrowded room. "That is what he said, is it not, my dear?"

She nodded. "Yes, that is exactly what he said."

"Said?" Mrs. White's tone was faint and for the first time she looked as if she'd swoon.

He reached toward her, but Thea put her hand on his arm. "Let the Runners handle it."

The minute the Runners were mentioned Mrs. White jumped up from the chaise and dashed to the door. Dom grabbed her shoulder. She swung around and tried to hit him, but her arms were too short; then she started to wail.

"What the devil is that sound?" a man in the uniform of the 95th Rifles demanded. "Oh, sorry, ladies, I didn't see you. What's wrong with Mrs. White?"

Dom loosened his grip, and the woman fell to the floor. "If I were you, I'd get my wife and child out of here."

"Major Horton?" Thea asked.

"Yes."

"I am Miss Stern. This"—she pointed at Dom—"is my betrothed, Lord Merton, and here is his mother, Lady Merton."

Thea put a hand on the major's arm. "This is not a safe place for your family."

He took in the scene and frowned. "Where are they now?"

"Safe, at the park they were going to," Dom's mother responded.

He nodded. "It's good they are not here for this. It would distress my wife." He paused, and seemed to study Dom. "Merton? Not Worthington's cousin?"

Dom stifled a groan. This incident would probably be all over Town by dinnertime. What had he been thinking of allowing his mother and betrothed to take part in something like this? Why was he there? What would Uncle Alasdair say?

"Didn't think you had it in you."

He stopped berating himself and stared at the major. "What?"

The man grinned. "From what Worthington said, you were too much of a dry stick to involve yourself in anything like this."

"That is not true." Dotty came to stand beside Dom. "He is as compassionate a man as there can be. He has helped me rescue kittens—"

"My love. Thank you, but it's not necessary."

A twinkle entered Major Horton's eyes. "Kittens?"

She raised her chin. "Yes, and a child. Which is the reason we are here." She glanced down. Mrs. White was taking the opportunity to crawl away. "Stop her!"

The major stepped in front of the door.

She rose to her knees, clasping her hands in front of her chest. "Oh, Major," she cried in a theatrical voice, "you must help me."

"I would like to know what is going on, if I may."

A knock sounded. "My lord"—Roger appeared in the doorway—"is everything all right in there?"

"Yes, if you'll call the constable to send to Bow Street, I think that will do."

"Major, if you will assist us, we would be happy to tell you what we know." Lady Merton handed Dotty the drapery cords. "I really think we should tie her up. She is liable to try to escape again."

Dom took one set and the major the other, making quick work of securing Mrs. White's hands and feet. Dotty pulled up a footstool and sat next to the landlady. "Tell me the whole story and do not leave anything out."

Mrs. White turned her head away. "I ain't talking to you. You got no proof I did anything. No one's going to believe a boy."

Thea raised a brow and in the calm commanding voice she used the night they were betrothed, said, "We need to question the maid. My lord, you might offer her employment if she gives an accurate accounting of everything she knows."

"She ain't that stupid." Mrs. White sniggered. "She says anything, and they'll come for her."

Taking out his quizzing glass, Dom fixed it on the landlady. "Not if she's under my protection."

Pressing her lips firmly together, she fell silent.

Dotty stood. "Since there is nothing to be gained here, I'm going to talk to the girl."

A tick formed in Dom's jaw. "Alone?"

She nodded. "I'll be fine. Roger will be with me. You need to remain here for the Runners. My lady?"

Her future-mother-in-law glanced at her. "Yes, my dear."

"Could you search through all this stuff and find anything with initials or an engraving?"

Lady Merton grinned. "What a wonderful idea, I'd be happy to."

Mrs. White started screaming and the major pulled out his handkerchief. "My lord, if you'll give me yours, I'll stop this caterwauling."

When Dotty got to the hall, the maid was sitting on the steps with Roger hovering over her. She sat on the stair next to the girl. "Tell me your name."

"Sukey." A tremor ran through her.

"Well, Sukey. It seems as if there have been some goings-on here."

The girl nodded. "Roger here says his lordship will take care of me if I talk to you."

"Roger is correct."

"What if they come after me?"

"Lord Merton will offer you employment in the country if you like. He has several estates. You will be perfectly safe."

Roger took her hand. "That's what you said you'd like. His lordship protects his own."

She glanced up at the footman and nodded. "I've been here 'bout a year. The first couple of times I believed my mistress when she said the folk had just up and left. But then there was the time a lady drank the tea Mrs. White gave her and she died."

Dotty bit down on her lip. "A lady?"

"Yes, ma'am. She was down on her luck, and Mrs. White took her in. I think she was breeding, but she had no ring." Sukey looked at Dotty. "Like she weren't married."

Or the ring no longer fit. She signaled the girl to continue.

"About a week later a man came to the kitchen door. Mrs. White shooed me upstairs, but I hid behind the curve. "He'd come for the lady."

Dotty shook her head a little. "What do you mean?"

"He was to take her to a place called Miss Betsy's."

Roger sucked in a breath.

Dotty turned to him. "Do you know what that is?"

"Yes, miss, but it's not fit for your ears."

Sukey continued her story about other ladies being carted off while they were asleep and children disappearing. Dotty didn't have the experience to understand what all of it meant, but she was sure the Runners would know. At the end of Sukey's tale, Dotty took the girl's hands. "Thank you for your help. We will stand by you. I promise."

Sukey glanced at Roger.

"You can believe the lady," he assured her. "His lordship don't go back on his word."

The front knocker sounded and Roger went to answer it.

A tall, slender man in a red coat entered the hall. "I'm Mr. Hatchet from Bow Street."

Dotty rose. "I am Miss Stern. You will find Lord and Lady Merton as well as Major Horton of the Life Guards in the parlor. I believe you will require help."

"My associate, Mr. Bonner, will be here soon."

"I shall leave you to it then."

Though she would have rather helped go through the items in the landlady's parlor, she decided to wait for Mrs. Horton. It wouldn't do to have her walking in on the scene unawares. What they had to tell her would be distressing enough. Even Dotty felt as if a lead weight had lodged in her stomach, and she knew a great deal about how cruel people could be to one another from the visits around the parish she had been making. Still, something told her that the worst was yet to come, and she would need all the strength and compassion she could muster.

Before long, the other Runner arrived and Dotty directed him to the parlor. Sukey, accompanied by Roger, went to the kitchen to make tea. Dotty sat on the stairs again. It seemed to take forever before Dom and his mother reentered the hall.

He held out his hand to her, helping her rise, then drew her into his arms. "Do I have a new servant?"

She loved how his dry remarks always made her feel better, and grinned against his coat. "Yes, you do. She cannot remain here at all. It is too dangerous."

"Roger will escort her to Merton House."

Remembering his mother was present, she jerked back. "My lady, I forgot myself. I shouldn't have—"

"You have had a hard day, my dear." She smiled gently.

"There is nothing wrong with allowing your future husband to comfort you."

Dom pulled her back to him. "Nothing at all inappropriate."

Though when Major Horton walked into the hall, Dom's arms dropped to his sides. "Major, where will you go?"

His face settled into grim lines. "I don't know. The Runners assured us that we could remain here for the next few weeks, but I will not leave my wife alone after I've gone."

"Is there no way you can take her with you?" Dotty asked.

The major ran a hand through his hair. "No. I may be able to get out of the mission, but it won't do my career any good. With the war over, it's getting harder to stay on active duty."

Dom's profile was grim. "What about your parents or hers?"

The major gave a bark of humorless laughter. "We talked of her staying with her mother, but it would be war. Our families hate each other. They haven't cut us off, but if my wife and child were to live with one over the other, it would drive poor Rebecca out of her mind."

Dotty exchanged a look with Lady Merton and an idea started to take root. "What if you had safe housing for your family?"

"What are you thinking, dear?" Lady Merton asked.

"I do not know the legalities or even if it could be done." Dotty glanced around the hall. "But what if this house, or one like it, could be purchased and made into a safe place?" Ideas flooded her mind as she spoke. "The apartments could be rented by families such as Major Horton's or widows with no place to go, or"—her next suggestion was so outrageous, she didn't know if even her ladyship would agree—"ladies in need."

Holding her breath, she waited to see if her future mother-in-law understood.

A glow of comprehension lit Lady Merton's face. "Yes, of course. There are so many gently bred ladies of limited means and—and others who need assistance."

Dotty breathed again. "My lord, will you buy this house and one or two others?"

Lady Merton glanced at Dom and raised a brow. "If he does not, I shall."

He regarded his mother for a few moments, then took Dotty's hand and brought it to his lips. "Probably not this one. It is too well-known to the criminal element. However, if it will make you happy, I shall have my steward look into others."

His gaze caught hers, warming her. She had been right. Dom was a kind and generous man, and he was hers. Hers to love. And she had never been happier. "Thank you."

"Gor, ain't he a fine gentleman," Sukey said from the corridor to the kitchen.

Major Horton gave a shout of laughter, but stopped when the door opened and his wife and child entered from one side of the hall at the same time one of the Bow Street Runners walked in from the side corridor, gripping Mrs. White's chubby arm. Tears had made tracks down her powdered face and the blacking she used on her eyelashes ran, giving her a ghoulish appearance.

"My goodness." Mrs. Horton opened her eyes wide and focused on her husband. "Lion, what is going on?"

Major Horton picked up his daughter and took his wife aside, speaking to her in a low voice. At one point, the lady gasped and cut a look first at the landlady, then at Dotty and Dom.

"Ladies, my lord, Major," the Runner said, "we'll need your statements as soon as possible."

Dom inclined his head. "Of course, if there is a desk, we shall make them immediately."

Once the Runner and Mrs. White left, Sukey cleared her

throat. "I'll take you to Mrs. White's office. You can have your tea there."

They all followed the maid to a small room at the back of the house. It was furnished with an old oak desk and several chairs. On one side of the desk stood a bookshelf filled with ledgers. While Dom sat and took several pieces of foolscap from the maid, Dotty searched the ledgers. Whatever else the landlady was, she kept meticulous records. They were filled with the household expenditures, names of the lodgers, and income. Mrs. White had kept records of her criminal dealings as well, including the amounts she received from her accomplices and either their initials or nom de guerre. At least that was what Dotty thought a name like "Snake" must be.

"Sukey, call Mr. Hatchet"

Dom raised his head. "Thea, what did you find?"

She held up the ledger. "She wrote everything down. If her victims are still alive, we might be able to save them."

He narrowed his eyes slightly. "You mean the Runners will be able to find them. You cannot go to Whitecastle or wherever the criminal gangs are. It's far too dangerous."

"Yes, of course." He was right about that part, but this Miss Betsy's was only a few streets away and the sooner she found the women, the better.

Chapter Sixteen

Dom sprinkled sand over his statement and relinquished the desk to his mother. The major and his wife were seated on the other side of the desk writing their accounts. Thea, on the other hand, was busy inscribing information from one of the ledgers into her pocketbook. Her green eyes sparkled with daring.

Dash it all, she was up to something. He truly did not think she would be reckless enough to try to approach the thieves alone, but what else could it be?

His uncle's voice had been railing in Dom's head for the past half hour, telling him that consorting with lower ranking members of society and the Runners was below his status as a Merton.

Remember who you are, Merton.

Shaking his head, he tried to clear it. The Runner, who was now collecting the ledgers, had told him that the selling of women and children, although rare in areas such as Mayfair, was common elsewhere in London. The man told him stories of young women who had come seeking respectable jobs, being kidnapped, and forced into brothels. Young children forced to steal to live, and those as young as five transported for crimes or simply because no one knew what to do with them. Lately, due to the war being over and so many military men out of work, the problem had grown. How had he not known about any of this?

The ugly thought came to him that this was part of what Worthington was so angry with Dom about. Had his votes and positions worsened England's problems? If caring for one's country was a duty, then it followed that doing something to help those in need was also a duty.

His uncle may have coddled Dom, protecting him from the harsher elements, but he had willingly remained swaddled. Perhaps now was the time to enter the real world. The one in which his cousin, betrothed, and even his mother, seemed firmly ensconced.

"My lord?"

Thea's voice brought him out of his thoughts.

"Yes?"

"Lady Merton and I have decided to go to this Miss Betsy's and fetch the women taken there."

Major Horton suddenly began coughing.

The Runner turned bright red. "Miss, my lady, you really should leave well enough alone. It's probably too late for those women."

"What do you mean?" Thea frowned, her brow furrowing. "Are they dead?"

"Er, no, not exactly." The man ran his finger under his neckcloth. "But they may as well be."

Mama's unbelieving expression matched his betrothed's. Apparently, she had been converted to the reformist cause as well.

"If they are ill," Mama said stiffly, "that is even more reason Miss Stern and I must find them."

Dom watched the Runner shuffle his feet. Could it be that the place was a bawdy house? He slid a glance at the major who mouthed, "Whorehouse."

Hell. All it needed was this. Somehow Dom would have to stop them. He could not allow his mother and Thea to consort with ladybirds or worse, and he couldn't take his coach, which was emblazoned with his coat of arms, to a place like that. He raked his hand through his hair. The real question was could he stop them? He had not been successful at thwarting their activities thus far.

"If the major will accompany me, I shall go. First I want to take Miss Stern back to Stanwood House." He addressed her. "You are going to be late for dinner, and you wouldn't want to worry Grace."

Thea shook her head thoughtfully. "You might scare the ladies. It will be better if your mother and I go alone."

The major cleared his throat. "My lord, Worthington might be more useful to you, and I would prefer not to leave my family at the moment."

"No, no, my love." Mrs. Horton laid a hand on her husband's arm. "I'm sure we will be fine. You must help save those poor women. While you are gone I shall make the other rooms ready, unless you think the ladies should go to a hospital."

He looked at his wife as if she'd lost her mind. "I still think we need Worthington's advice."

Thea glanced at the watch pinned to her bodice. "We have at least an hour until dinner. Surely we can accomplish our task before then."

"I agree. Come, Dominic." His mother turned to the door. "If we are to take Worthington with us, there is no time to lose."

Good God. None of the ladies seemed to have the faintest clue what Miss Betsy's was and how bad it could be. Somehow he'd have to stop them. His cousin might have an idea how to accomplish what was turning into a Sisyphean task.

"Roger, stay here until we return." Dom took Thea's arm and, followed by his mother and the major, strode to the coach.

The short ride to Berkeley Square was made in silence.

Dom assumed it was due to the events of the day being too horrific to discuss.

Until, that was, Thea glanced at him quizzically. "I do not understand why someone would pay for sick women."

Lord help him. He had to keep her from discovering the truth. She might know more about some of the horrible things that happened to people, but he was damn sure she didn't know much about brothels.

The carriage drew up in front of Stanwood House, and the door was open before he'd assisted Thea and his mother down from the coach.

Grace met them on the steps. "I was beginning to worry." Her gaze searched their faces. "What is wrong?"

Dom's mother bussed Grace's cheek. "Is Worthington at home?"

"Not to anyone else, but he will be for you. He is in my study."

They followed her into the hall and down a corridor. He stood when they entered the room. "Horton! I haven't seen you in a month of Sundays. What brings you here?"

Grace rang for tea and once it arrived Thea told them what they had discovered about Tom, Mrs. White, and Thea and Dom's mother's plan to find the missing women.

Worthington leaned back in his chair, regarding Thea. "Do you know what kind of establishment Miss Betsy's is?"

She shook her head.

Blast it all to hell! "She doesn't need to know. There is no reason you, Major Horton, and I cannot see to it."

Grace's lips firmed. "Merton, you cannot keep Dotty or your mother in ignorance. She will learn about those types of establishments soon enough after you are married."

Was Grace implying he would visit a bawdy house?

"Dominic, do not scowl," his mother said. "What Grace means is that once you are married, Dorothea will hear the kinds of things not discussed around innocents."

He swallowed and almost choked. "*Ladies* discuss . . ."

Grace grinned. "You would be surprised what we talk about. You will need at least one female with you, otherwise your help might be taken the wrong way." She turned to her husband. "I shall go."

Thea's jaw took on a mulish cast. "If Grace is going, I will as well."

Worthington closed his eyes for a moment, before uttering, "Dotty, it's a brothel."

His words seemed to take some of the wind out of her sails, though not for long. "But if Merton and Grace are with me, I do not see the problem."

His mother patted Thea's hand. "I shall accompany Grace. It really would not do for you to go. It could cause a problem if anyone sees you."

"I must say I agree," Grace added.

Thea took a sip of tea and puckered her brow. "What if I remain in the coach with the shades down?"

Worthington rubbed his cheek. "Someone would have to stay with you. One never knows who will be in the area."

Had everyone gone mad? "Worthington, may I speak with you alone?"

Grace rose from her perch on her chair. "I'll call for the coach. Ladies, will you come with me?"

Thea glanced at Dom before following Grace and his mother out of the room. Once the door was shut, he turned on his cousin. "What the devil are you about even thinking of allowing her to come with us?"

Worthington narrowed his eyes. "Did you see the look on her face? She is coming whether we want her to or not. Do you want her to show up with just a footman in tow?"

Dom slumped back in his chair. This wasn't supposed to be happening. He was the head of the family. Thea and his mother should do what he wanted them to. "There must be some way to stop her?"

"Short of locking her in her bedchamber, I doubt it."

He straightened. "That might work."

His cousin shook his head. "Someone would let her out in very short order. You'll soon learn that when you marry a woman with her own mind, your chances of getting your way greatly decrease."

Dom wanted to groan. If only he had settled for a suitable bride, but the idea of another man touching Thea ended that line of thinking. Worthington had to be wrong. He had merely given in too easily. Once they were married, Dom would have more control over Thea. After all, a woman had to listen to her husband.

With the days getting longer, it was still light when the two black coaches pulled up in front of a large house on the outskirts of Mayfair. Dotty fiddled with the veil Grace had loaned her. The lacework was made in such a way that she could see out of it, but no one would be able to make out her face. That had settled Dom somewhat, but he still wasn't happy. Well, as Grace said, sooner or later, he would have to get used to Dotty taking actions needed to save others.

The three gentlemen and the four large footmen carried pistols. Matt also brought a purse of coins to give to Miss Betsy in case that was the only way to get the women back.

Dotty had known about girls from the country being taken up to work as prostitutes. It had happened to one of the girls from their small town. Unfortunately, the young woman had died before anyone could rescue her.

A man who seemed familiar loitered on the street near the next building. When he faced her, she recognized Hatchet, one of the Runners from today.

As she settled back against the soft squabs to wait, Dom took her hand. "It goes against my grain, but Worthington is right. You are safer with me and the veil is heavy enough that no one will recognize you."

Her heart thudded, making her a little breathless. He would be her husband in a few weeks, and she did not wish to fight with him. Yet she had a feeling that it was important to Dom to think he was in charge. "You mean I may come?"

"Yes." His stern tone matched the grim look on his face. "But you must remain by my side. Clutch my coattails if you need to." His voice softened. "This will be a shock for you, I'm sure."

She wanted to kiss his cheek, but the veil would have gotten in the way. "I have little doubt you are right."

One of Matt's larger footmen knocked on the door, then stood aside. A man dressed as a butler, but brawny with a nose that had been broken, opened it and stood in the entrance.

Matt edged himself in the doorway. "We're here to see Miss Betsy."

The man bowed. "I'll bet you are. We cater to all here."

Dotty's hand was tucked in Dom's arm as they followed the servant into a large hall decorated in pale blue and gold. Small Roman statues stood on pedestals. She glanced at the ceiling that was covered with naked couples twined together.

She had never seen anything like that before. A tug on her arm brought her attention back to her betrothed. Then she made the mistake of looking at the servant.

The butler's gaze raked Dotty's cloaked form. "Let me know if you want it a bit rougher, and I'm happy to oblige."

Dom's arm turned to stone, trapping her hand next to his body. "Miss Betsy," he snarled. "Now."

"Brutus, what have I told you about that?" A woman dressed in a white Grecian-style gown trimmed with gold ribbon moved toward them. Bits of red showed through the barely opaque costume. As she walked, the skirts separated showing scandalous glimpses of her bare legs. Her toes were painted gold to match her sandals.

"Sorry, Miss Betsy."

Ignoring him, she focused on their little group. "Welcome to my house of pleasure." As the woman's gaze roamed over

Dom, she purred. "We shall go into my parlor where you will tell me your desires."

Dotty tugged him possessively closer. Never mind her staying close to Dom. He was obviously in as much danger as she. If that woman tried to touch him, she would not be answerable for her actions.

Miss Betsy glanced dismissively at Dotty. Before remembering the woman couldn't see it through the veil, she raised a brow, giving the female her haughtiest look.

The parlor Miss Betsy led them to was decorated in the popular Egyptian style of white and gold. They sat on the low chaises, and she called for wine.

Once they had been served, Matt took a scrap of paper from his pocket. "We are here for two young women whom you bought from Mrs. White."

Under her rouge, Miss Betsy paled, then she raised her chin. "I don't know what you're talking about. My girls come to me of their own accord."

Liar! Dotty wanted to scream at the woman. Instead she stared steadily at the brothel owner.

Next to her, Dom shifted. "Mrs. White has been arrested, and her ledgers are with Bow Street. We know the amounts you paid and the dates."

The woman's eyes became wary as she clearly tried to think of another story. "They weren't appropriate for my house. I had to let them go."

Dotty prayed it wasn't true. As bad as this place must be, somewhere else could be much worse.

Miss Betsy cut a sharp glance toward a door that was designed to look like part of the wall.

Dotty squeezed Dom's arm. "In that case, you won't mind if we look around and talk to the women. After all, it is early for customers."

The woman raised one shoulder in a shrug. "As you will. You'll find nothing."

Dotty rose and strode directly to the door.

"Here now, that's my private quarters. You can't go in there!"

Matt grabbed the woman's wrist. "You said we could look around."

She opened the door, which led to a flight of stairs, but Dom held her back. "I'll go first."

He took the stairs two by two. She hitched her skirts up following as quickly as she could. At the top of the stairs there was a short corridor with doors on either side. A sickly smell permeated the air.

Oh God, no! She took out her handkerchief, placing it over her nose. "Opium. Cover your nose."

He did as she asked, tying a piece of linen over his face. "How do you know?"

"We had to use it for one of our tenants." She tried to open the window at the end of the corridor. "It's stuck."

He managed to open it a couple of inches, but no more. "Probably nailed. Stand back." He kicked at the window, his boot shattering the glass. Then he grabbed a chair by one of the doors and smashed out the rest of the wood.

An outraged scream came from below.

"What's he doin' to me house?"

Dotty opened the door next to her. A pot stood on a small brazier in a corner of the room. A dark-haired female, wearing only a soiled chemise, was curled up on a small cot. "I think I found one of the women, but we need to get air in here and throw out the opium."

Dom pulled on the sash. Once again it opened only a few inches. "They're probably all nailed shut." He broke that window as well. "There now, you can toss the pot out."

Dotty grabbed a thin blanket and wrapped it around the brazier to keep her hands from burning, and tossed it out the window. She glanced at him and grinned, but he was already on his way to the next room.

They entered each chamber, breaking the glass to allow fresh air inside, and ridding the rooms of the braziers. Once done, she took stock of the women. There were six in all. None of them wore more than a grimy chemise. One looked to be hardly more than a girl. Had they all come from Mrs. White's house?

Chest heaving, Dom stood in the center of the last chamber. "We need more carriages."

"Where are we going to take them?"

"Someplace where they can recover from the drug." Lady Merton stood in the doorway covering her nose and mouth.

The energy that had driven Dotty began to fade, and the terror of what they had found struck her. Tears of rage stung her eyes. "I have never seen anything so evil."

Heedless of his mother's presence, Dom wrapped his arms around her. "You are distressed. Perhaps you should confine yourself to rescuing animals."

Although the words were pompous, and condescending, she thought she heard a hopeful note in his voice. He had probably never even imagined places like this existed. And as hard as this was to see, once she was Lady Merton, she would have the resources to do even more good than she'd done before. "No. This is just the beginning. I shall request a meeting with Lady Evesham and some of the other ladies. We shall find where the need is most pressing." Dotty leaned back, peering into Dom's face. "You won't try to stop me, will you?"

He pulled her back against his chest, and in a resigned voice, answered, "I wonder if I have a choice."

Yet he did. He would have the ability to attempt to curtail her actions. She had known he'd never been involved with charitable causes before, but surely he must now see the need. Yet what if he did not? How would that affect their future and their hope of finding love?

Chapter Seventeen

Suddenly, the sounds of groans, fisticuffs, furniture breaking, and a few feminine shrieks echoed up from downstairs. What the devil were Worthington and Horton doing down there?

Dom set Thea aside and pulled out his pistol as boots pounded up the stairs. Worthington erupted into the corridor.

Putting the gun back in his coat, Dom took stock of his cousin. Worthington's normally neatly tied cravat was crumpled and askew. The knuckles of one hand were bruised, and a red mark, which was certain to change color, marred his jawline. "Been having fun?"

A gleam entered Worthington's eyes. "You could say that. Miss Betsy's men are subdued, and we have the other women in the drawing room." He bowed to Dom's mother. "Grace asks you join her there to speak to the women."

"I would be delighted." Despite everything, Mama smiled. "Although the circumstances here are horrific, I have not felt so alive and useful in years."

Dom stifled a groan. His life was never going to be the same. "We need to figure out what to do with the females up here. They've all been drugged."

Worthington's grin grew larger. "I wondered why you were kicking out all the windows. Not your usual pastime."

Dom tried and failed to achieve a level of haughtiness necessary to depress his cousin's good humor. Truth be told, he hadn't had such a good time since he was a young boy.

"They were nailed shut." Dotty smiled up at him, emerald eyes glittering with pride. "He was magnificent."

The urge to puff his chest out came over him. He hadn't expected praise for acting like a bruiser. The way Thea was looking at him warmed his heart and other regions of his body as well. He held her against him. "Thank you." He glanced at his cousin again. "Does Major Horton look any better than you?"

"No, slightly worse. He got a vase smashed over his head."

"Oh no." Dotty's hand flew to her lips. "The poor major. I hope he had enough fun that it will make up for the lump that's sure to be on his head."

What an appalling thing to say. "Thea!"

She turned a wide gaze on him. "Papa says men like to get into a tussle every once in a while. Do you not?"

Dom was about to deny he enjoyed any such thing, but it would be a lie. Why else did he go to Jackson's Salon? Still, it could not continue. He'd so far forgotten himself as to bring his mother and his innocent Thea to a brothel. This could never happen again. He had to remember his duty.

"I completely agree with Thea," his mother said. "Your behavior here reminds me of your father."

He stared at her for a moment and was about to ask what she meant, but a low moan made him glance at the pitiful female huddled on the cot. "We need to find a place for these women."

Thea pressed her lips together. "First we must find them something to wear. They cannot leave dressed only in a chemise."

This room, like the others, was bare, except for a cot, chair, and chamber pot. "Not even a wardrobe."

"We should get them something to eat as well. Let's find the kitchen. The women will be safe enough here until we return. Matt, please make sure none of the Runners comes up here."

He saluted her and she followed Dom down the stairs. The parlor they'd been in before was in chaos. Miss Betsy's hands were tied behind her back and her thin gown torn in places. A shawl hung over her shoulders hiding her breasts from view. The maid who had served them wine huddled in a corner, cringing.

Thea went straight to the girl. "Don't be afraid, we're not going to hurt you. Can you help me take some broth and a bit of bread to the women upstairs?"

The girl nodded. "Yes, my lady. Cook should still be in the kitchen. Don't think anyone's thought to look down there."

Much to his surprise, the kitchen was well appointed and clean. Several pots were on one of the new closed stoves and a large, rotund female was giving orders to two maids.

The cook finished stirring one pot, before glancing up, then spearing the poor maid with a fierce look. "Lucy, what do you mean by bringing Quality down here?"

Thea stepped in front of the girl. "I told her I needed to speak with you."

The cook's hands went to her ample hips. "And just who are you?"

Thea stiffened and raised a brow. "I am Miss Stern. My betrothed, Lord Merton, and I found the women who were drugged. As soon as they are awake, they should be fed. Is there a housekeeper in residence?"

The cook eyed Thea suspiciously. "Where's the mistress?"

"The Bow Street Runners have restrained her."

The cook made a sign of the cross. "Thank the Lord."

Dom put a hand on his forehead, unable to believe what he was hearing. His uncle had always told him people picked their lives. Yet the women above clearly had not and now the cook seemed happy to be rescued as well. None of this made any sense.

One of the scullery maids peeped up at him. She couldn't have been more than fourteen or fifteen and very pretty. "Am I safe now, Mrs. Oyler?"

The cook smiled at the girl. "Mayhap ye are, sweetie." Mrs. Oyler's gaze switched to Thea. "I'll get the soup ready, but I don't like my girls going through the house. It's too dangerous."

"It's all right now, ma'am," Lucy said. "Ain't no one in the parlor, and I'll help."

"Here, miss, sit ye down." the cook said to Thea. "I'll get you and his lordship a cup of scandal broth. I'm Mrs. Oyler."

Thea took the chair offered, as did he. Once they were given tea and fresh bread with butter, Thea indicated Mrs. Oyler should sit as well. "Tell me why you are here."

"After my man died, it was hard for a Papist to find a job. Mrs. Spencer took me in and gave me a position. This was a respectable lady's house before that Miss Betsy got her hands on it. Acted like a fine lady, she did, and bought it from my old mistress's heirs. I thought about leaving, but without a reference it's hard to find work. Then I found my calling. Some of the girls brought in were young. Younger than May over there." She pointed to the pretty girl. "I started finding them apprenticeships and helping them escape. I think Miss Betsy caught on, because that's when she started with the opium."

It didn't take much imagination to figure out the rest. Once the women were dependent on the drug, they'd do anything to have it again. After that, they would have nowhere to go.

"Miss," Mrs. Oyler asked, "what do you mean to do?"

"Rescue the women who wish to leave." Thea sipped her tea. A small crease appeared between her brows. "First of all, we must have clothes and clean chemises for the women

Lord Merton and I found. I'll discuss where they will live with Lady Merton and Lord and Lady Worthington. I am sure we'll think of something."

The cook folded her hands on the table. "I'd be glad to help."

Thea nodded thoughtfully. "I have a feeling we'll need all the assistance we can get. This turned into a much larger undertaking than I had imagined."

That was the understatement of the Season. Dom stifled his groan. If he didn't get control of her soon, his lot in life would consist of following her around on her missions of mercy just to keep her out of scrapes. His uncle would have apoplexy if he could see Dom now. He was just amazed she hadn't suggested that he buy *this* house. However, the day wasn't done. She had plenty of time yet.

Mrs. Oyler heaved her bulk up and set about giving orders for bowls of soup and bread to be prepared and taken upstairs.

Thea rose. "Thank you, Mrs. Oyler. I'll come back down before we leave."

He'd stood as soon as Thea had, then followed her back up the stairs. "Why do you need to see the cook again?"

"Why, to reassure her she has a position. We can't leave her without a job. After all, there is no point in saving people from one bad situation only to put them in another."

Two more servants at least and a few houses; he should never have let Worthington talk him into allowing Thea to keep her own money. It would all be spent on charity. "You have a point."

She stopped one step up from him, cupped his cheek, and lightly put her lips to his. "Thank you. I didn't mean to make so much trouble for you."

Slipping his arm around her, he teased her mouth open. Her tongue tangled with his as he tried to keep his desire under control. He must be going mad. All he could think was that this was worth every penny. "No trouble at all. We had better see how everyone else is doing."

When they arrived back in the parlor, his mother, the Worthingtons, Major Horton, and five women were talking quietly. Miss Betsy was gone, presumably with the Runners.

His mother patted the seat next to her on a settee. "Bow Street will keep a man here and we will send one as well to stop anyone from entering the house. These *ladies* wish to leave." She placed an emphasis on the word. "The rest wish work elsewhere. Apparently, this place was like a gaol to everyone here."

Everyone except the ones the cook helped to escape. Dom had a new respect for the women who had survived such mistreatment. "Where will they go?"

"That is what we've been discussing," Grace said. "These ladies as well as the ones upstairs were kidnapped. Almost all of them have military husbands on assignments out of the country." She paused for a moment. "They need a home until their men return and may still require a home afterward."

It took Dom a few moments to understand her meaning. Then he wondered how he could have been so slow. After what they had been through, their husbands might not want them back.

Grace continued. "They can stay here for a few days, but we need to find a more permanent place."

"I am not sure that is a good idea," his mother said. "They all wore heavy makeup in an attempt to disguise themselves. If they are seen here we will have no hope of salvaging their reputations. Everyone would know what they've been forced to do."

Dom didn't think they had a chance in hell of saving the women's reputations, but he knew now that he, all of them, would do whatever they could. Thea chewed her lip. He hoped she'd stop before she masticated it completely.

"A widows' house," she finally said.

Everyone else's eyes lit up. Only he was left in the dark. "A widows' house?"

Thea nodded in that excited way she had when she'd come up with an idea. "Yes. A home for the widows of military men and wives of those deployed. That will also allow us to give jobs to the maids and the cook."

"We can raise funds for them," Grace added. "Perhaps even obtain money from the government."

Glancing at Dom, Worthington rubbed his jaw. "Would you support a bill?"

Thea gazed up at him lovingly. No matter what he had to do, he wanted her to always look at him like that. "Yes. The way we've treated our soldiers and their families is disgraceful."

One of the women near Grace began to sob. Grace bent down and rubbed the woman's back. "There, there, it will be all right. You'll see."

Another of the ladies put her arm around the woman crying. "It's dinnertime. She'll be better after she eats."

"Major Horton," Thea said, "would you object if we moved them into the house you are in until we can find a more permanent solution?"

He was silent for a few moments. "I don't think I have the right to deny them shelter. After all, if you had not discovered Mrs. White's doings, my wife might have been one of the women upstairs. I don't know how many beds there are. We'll probably have to take some bedding from here."

"Once it is dark," Grace said, "we can ferry them from the mews at the back of the house." She glanced at Worthington. "Can the footmen handle it on their own?"

"I'm sure they can."

Most of the women were at Miss Betsy's because of Mrs. White and, although none wanted to return, it was better than remaining where they were. The cook and maids decided to accompany the other women to St. George Street.

"Well"—Dom's mother rose and shook out her skirts—

"now that it is settled for the time being, we should take our leave."

Worthington, Thea, and Major Horton rode in one coach. Grace and Mama rode with Dom. With Thea gone, his mother and Grace were more forthright about the women's stories.

"The young lady that started to cry . . ." Grace said.

He nodded.

"She had only been married a few months when her husband was called away. Mrs. White gave her a drink and that night she lost her baby. Less than a week later, she was brought here. The madam tried to give her the opium, but she became deathly ill. She'd resisted being used, but was told that they'd tie her down and let several gentlemen have her."

Dom's stomach turned sour, and a rage blacker than he'd ever felt before speared him. Things like this had been going on all around him, and he had not even known about it. Worse, he had refused to listen to those who tried to tell him.

His mother's countenance flushed with anger. "They all have stories like that. Even the girls who had chosen to be prostitutes before they came to the house were not allowed to leave and were made to do unspeakable things."

He leaned back against the squabs. "Thank you for not discussing this with Miss Stern present. I am afraid it would shock her too much."

Grace's eyes widened. "I shall discuss it with Dotty when I return. She deserves to know. Look at all the lives she has changed today. Besides, it doesn't do any good to keep girls ignorant."

He groaned and his mother reached across and patted his hand. "Everything will be fine, Dominic. Dorothea is a sensible young lady. I only wish I'd had her courage and strength of mind when I was younger."

His mind rebelled. He couldn't stand the thought of her

knowing how ugly the world was. His uncle had always said he had to protect women. Keep them safe from things they couldn't understand. Dom didn't know how in the hell he was supposed to do that when she went willy-nilly throwing herself into the fray. He'd gladly donate whatever amount he had to in order to keep her from being involved in anything like this again. But how in damnation would he stop her without her hating him for it?

Dotty couldn't help grinning when Dom stood at the head of the stairs to the ballroom and searched through the crowd. He met her gaze and smiled.

Within a few moments, he was with her, kissing her fingers one by one. "Good evening."

Warm tingles skated up her arm. "My lord."

He raised his eyes to hers. His warmth and desire captured her as it had the first time. If only they weren't in public, he would kiss her on her lips.

A gentleman coughed. "Miss Stern, I believe you are promised to me for this set."

She glanced over at Mr. Garvey. "Yes, of course."

Dom held her hand fast. "Garvey, go away."

Louisa turned away with her hand over her mouth to hide her laughter.

"My lord, I did promise to stand up with Mr. Garvey."

Dom kissed her hand again. His tone was a low growl. "Have you agreed to dance with anyone else?"

Her heart flitted around making her breathless. Was it possible he was jealous? "No."

"Good. Don't." He relinquished her hand to her partner. "I shall expect Miss Stern back immediately after the set is over."

Mr. Garvey's eyes twinkled merrily. "Dash, if I don't believe I'll take Miss Stern for a stroll around the room afterward." Before Dom could answer, Mr. Garvey whisked her into the line forming for the quadrille. "Don't know what you've done with him, Miss Stern, but it's a vast improvement."

Dotty was tempted to protest, but both Charlotte and Louisa had said something similar at dinner. After hearing of Dom's part in Tom's rescue, even Theodora, Matt's youngest sister, had stopped calling Dom "his marquisship." "Have you known Lord Merton long?"

The pattern of the dance separated them, when they came together Mr. Garvey responded, "We should have known each other all our lives, but once his father died, his uncle kept him isolated from any of the other children in the area. I ran into him at Oxford, but we were never close."

"I can see why you would not be." Dotty couldn't imagine why a child would be kept secluded. Perhaps that was what caused Dom to be so stiff around most other people. "Can you tell me what he was like when you knew him?"

"He was a normal boy. His father was a great gun. When he was alive, Merton and I saw a great deal of one another and got into all the scrapes boys do. After old Lord Merton's death, my father and I stopped by to pay our respects and had the door shut in our faces."

She couldn't believe either Dom or his mother would have allowed such a thing. "But why?"

"The uncle didn't approve of us."

"Thank you for telling me." Today, Dom had been everything she could have hoped for, yet perhaps it was time for her to ask Lady Merton about Dom's guardian.

"Miss Stern, I see a great deal of Merton's father in him. It's a shame he didn't live."

She smiled. "I appreciate your honesty, Mr. Garvey."

When the dance ended, he placed her hand on his arm. "I was about to suggest a stroll, but I see Merton has other ideas."

Dom plucked her hand from her dance partner's arm and put it on his. "Come, my dear. You look thirsty."

Mr. Garvey chuckled as Dom led her away.

He grabbed two glasses of champagne from a footman's tray as they strolled to the terrace doors. "It's warm in here, don't you think?"

Her lips quivered as she tried to stop a giggle from bursting forth. "Indeed, quite uncomfortable."

Once on the terrace, he steered her toward the end where a large trellis supported a profusion of roses. She took one sip of wine before he set the glasses on the stone balustrade.

"Thea," he whispered as he caught her to him, his lips descending to hers. "I've wanted to do this all evening."

She wrapped her arms around his neck pulling him closer and opening her mouth to his. His hands ran possessively over her derrière and back up her sides to cup her breasts. Flames flickered under his touch. He brushed his thumb over her breasts; her nipples hardened and ached. She moaned as he kneaded them.

Sliding her fingers to his face, she tilted her head, melding her lips to his, deepening their kiss as his palms and fingers elicited a spiraling heat that struck her to her core. If only they could at least take their gloves off. She wanted to feel his bare hands on her.

When he broke the kiss, they were both panting. He feathered kisses along her jaw. "Dom, I want more."

His tongue teased a sensitive spot near her ear. "More what?"

She rubbed her hands over his chest. "I am not sure. I thought you might know."

He'd nudged her chin aside to nibble her neck, then stopped. "Good Lord, what am I doing? We still have two weeks until the wedding." He straightened. "I'm sorry. I should not have started this."

She searched his face, but could see nothing in the dark. "I wanted to kiss you."

He smoothed the fabric of his coat, before straightening her gown with quick efficient movements. "Remember who you are," he mumbled, more it seemed to himself than her. "Thea, you are the only woman who has ever tempted me so much. I shall try to restrain myself."

No, no, no. That is not what I want! "You don't have to."

"You are an innocent." He pitched his head back and blew out a breath. "You do not understand what this could lead to. I, on the other hand, do."

She lowered her lashes, but couldn't quite bring herself to play the coquette. Although the way he had suddenly cooled, she might have to work on that. "You like kissing me."

He glanced down, but instead of taking her back in his arms, he rubbed her shoulders. "*That* is part of the problem. We both like it. Yet I cannot have any hint of scandal attached to you."

When he took her arm and led her back toward the ballroom, Dotty could have stamped her foot with frustration. Why did he have to turn stuffy now after he had done so well all day? It was almost as if he couldn't allow himself to have fun. Well, he must learn. She would simply have to teach him.

Chapter Eighteen

Dotty sat on the small sofa in the Young Ladies' Parlor. The late-morning sun entered the room at an angle, creating a path in which the two gray kittens slept. A silver salver holding three stacks of neatly arranged missives lay on a low table before her. She picked up the ones addressed to her. Mama and Henny had written, as well as her brother Harry. Selecting her mother's letter first, Dotty slid the small knife under the seal, opening the sheet of neatly crossed lines.

Charlotte lifted her head from whatever she was writing. "Have you heard from your mother yet?"

Holding up the paper, Dotty nodded. "The doctor said she is not progressing as she should, and he won't allow her to travel for another week, but Grandmamma Bristol is coming."

Charlotte's smile turned quickly to a frown. "Will she want you to stay with her?"

"I doubt it." Shaking her head, Dotty grinned. "She won't want to chaperone me. She says Almack's is insipid and missish young ladies give her hives. My mother says Grandmamma will stay at the Pulteney where she can bully the staff."

"Who is bullying the staff?" Louisa asked from the door.

"My grandmamma. She doesn't really do it. Though she

is very particular and says the Pulteney is the only place that understands her. Even when my uncle Bristol is in Town, she stays at the hotel."

Charlotte's brows drew together. "I thought that was because she and your aunt do not get on."

"Oh yes." Dotty giggled. "They cordially dislike each other. If ever they are in the same room, it becomes so cold, one requires a shawl."

Louisa bent to pick up her missive and stopped. "Bristol? The Duke of Bristol?"

Turning her note sideways to read the crossed lines, Dotty replied, "Yes."

"I didn't know he was a relation."

"Papa says it is nothing to brag about. My uncle tried to stop my parents from marrying, which caused a schism in the family. It's a long, involved story, but suffice it to say my grandfather arranged my uncle's marriage, which my grandmother said ruined my uncle's happiness. So she opposed every match Grandfather tried to make for my mother, until she was of age and could marry Papa. She did the same for their other children as well."

Louisa tilted her head. "Are the rest of them happy?"

Dotty nodded. "Everyone except Uncle Bristol, so it must have worked. I do hope she approves of Merton. I would not like to be at loggerheads with her. She is my favorite relative."

"I hope she asks us to visit." Charlotte grinned. "She is such a grand old lady."

"I wonder when she'll arrive," Dotty mused. "We never have any prior warning."

Charlotte eyed the large stack of cards on the salver. "I suppose we should go through the invitations and choose the entertainments we wish to attend."

They each took several of the notes.

"Lady Bellamny is having a Venetian breakfast," Louisa said. "That should be fun."

"Here is one for a masque." Charlotte held up the card. "Do you think Grace will allow it?"

"Grace might." Louisa grimaced. "Matt won't."

"No." Charlotte sighed. "You are probably right."

"Here is one from Baroness Merton, who has that lovely bluebell wood. She's having a picnic next week," Louisa said. "It's such a shame she is not related to us. We'd be able to visit the garden at any time."

"Merton is her family name?" Dotty asked.

Charlotte and Louisa nodded.

"We should accept in any event. Bluebells are always delightful."

"I'll add that to the acceptances." Louisa placed the card on the appropriate stack.

Once they'd completed their task, they sent the list down to Grace for her approval.

A few minutes later, Dotty glanced at the clock and rose. "I'll see you later. Lady Merton's carriage will be here for me soon. We are going shopping."

"How busy you are. We hardly see you anymore." Charlotte hugged Dotty. "Are you happy?"

She wished she could confide her concerns to Charlotte, but it wasn't possible. She had been much better about not criticizing Dom, but with any provocation, she'd take Dotty's side against him. She gave her friend a smile. "Yes, I am. I think Lady Merton will be a wonderful mother-in-law, and I care for Merton a great deal."

"Then I am happy for you."

Dotty hugged her friend. "Perhaps you'll be here when I return."

She left the parlor quickly as tears pricked the back of her eyes. She was happy. Last evening, she had been sure that he was so close to telling her he loved her. If only Dom wouldn't hide himself in his shell, everything would be perfect. She would take the time she and Lady Merton had alone to ask about his upbringing.

Dotty was descending the stairs when one of the footmen came to fetch her. But once in the town coach, she was told Lady Merton would like her to come to Merton House first so that she could resume the tour.

Tom greeted her by throwing his arms around her legs again. "You'll never guess what I got today."

Hugging him back, she said, "You're right. I have no idea."

"My toys."

"Oh, Tom. That's wonderful." How kind of Mrs. Horton to send them over. "When I am finished with Mrs. Sorley, you shall have to show them to me."

Taking Dotty's hand, he led her toward the morning room. "And guess what else? Mrs. Sorley found Lord Merton's toys, and he said I could play with them as well."

Dotty's heart filled with joy. Dom had not allowed Tom to go to the Park as he didn't know if the scoundrels who had taken him might try to get the boy back. "That was very kind of him. Did you remember to thank Lord Merton?"

"Yes, miss, and he said I did a good job of it."

Mrs. Sorley was with Lady Merton when Dotty entered the morning room.

"Have a seat, my dear." Lady Merton indicated the chair next to her at a small table. "We are going over some of the household items that need to be replaced."

After she was settled, the housekeeper handed her one of the lists.

"Most of this one is just what you'd expect," Mrs. Sorley said. "Now the one her ladyship has is hangings and curtains."

Lady Merton gave Dotty the paper. "You will have a free hand in decorating. Do not think you will hurt my feelings if you want to make changes. Most of it hasn't been changed since my late mother-in-law's time. Dom's papa and I spent more time at Merton Hall than in Town."

It took much longer than Dotty had thought to inspect the large old town house. By the time they'd finished and discussed new fabrics, it was time for her to return to Stanwood

House. She hadn't had any time alone with Lady Merton to ask her questions.

Dom arrived home as Dotty waited for the coach to be brought round. He grinned and kissed her on the cheek. "I'm glad you're still here. Come with me." He ushered her into a rarely used front parlor and drew a small package from his waistcoat pocket. "This took longer than I expected, but it is finally ready."

Dotty waited until he opened the wrapping.

He took her right hand. "This was the one I thought you would like best." The ring he slipped on her finger was a wide gold band, set with a large square emerald in the center and studded with smaller emeralds on each side. "Tell me if I was right."

She held out her hand. The center stone caught a ray of afternoon light coming through the window and blazed. "You were exactly right. I love it."

He wrapped his arms around her, drawing her close to him. As she tilted her head back to gaze into his eyes, his lips covered hers. Their tongues danced and stroked, causing flames to flicker through her body. She worked her hand under his coat and caressed his strong back. If only there was a way for them to be alone together. Perhaps, when her parents arrived, she could convince him they need not wait for their wedding night.

That evening Dotty received a hand-delivered note from her grandmother.

My dearest Thea,
    I have arrived. I shall expect you tomorrow at
three o'clock at the Pulteney.

                    Much love,
                    Grandmamma

The Pulteney was every bit as opulent as Dotty had heard. She was escorted over thick Turkey carpets that muffled her steps to a room with royal blue velvet drapes pulled back with gold cords, allowing the afternoon sun to warm the chamber.

"Grandmamma!" Dotty rushed forward to hug the stately woman seated next to a gilt-trimmed fireplace. Though her grandmother's hair was pure silver, her eyebrows and lashes were still as black as her own.

"Thea!" Grandmamma gave Dotty a brisk kiss on each cheek before studying her. "You are the picture of a beautiful young woman. Tell me, have the gentlemen made up any silly names for you yet?"

Dotty grinned. "Louisa heard someone call us the Three Graces."

Nodding approvingly, Grandmamma pointed to the stool in front of her. "Very apt, I'm sure. I've not seen Lady Louisa, of course, but if she's got any of her mother's beauty, she'll do well indeed. I'm told Charlotte is even lovelier than she was as a girl."

Sinking onto the stool, Dotty took her grandmother's still-strong, capable hands. "Yes. They are both very beautiful and dear friends."

Grandmamma was quiet for a moment. "I received a letter from your mother that you are betrothed to Merton. She seems to think that there is a chance you will end up with a love match. I must say, the reports I have heard belie her opinion. However, you must tell me if it is true. Can you love him and more importantly, will he love you? No matter what has occurred, I refuse to allow you to wed a man who will not make you happy."

One of the best things about Grandmamma was one could tell her anything. Dotty related how Dom had helped her rescue the cats and Tom, about the brothel and, with a warm face, about the kisses.

At the end of her story, she frowned. "The only thing that

bothers me is the minute he realizes he's having fun, he stops. I truly do not know what to do. Until you came to Town, I've had no one to confide in."

Drawing her brows together, her grandmother looked thoughtful for several moments. "I'm glad to see he has something of his father in him. I did wonder if Lord Alasdair would drum it all out."

If her grandmother knew about the family, it would be much better than asking Lady Merton. "What can you tell me about what happened to Merton as a child?"

Grandmamma smiled wistfully. "Your Merton's father was a wild rogue. Up to every rig and row in Town. There wasn't much he wouldn't do for a lark, and he accomplished it all with such good-natured charm, everyone forgave him even his most outrageous stunts. Lord Alasdair was Merton's complete opposite. How the two of them became friends I'll never know. Their relations were stretched almost to the breaking point when Merton fell in love with Eunice, Dominic's mother."

A knock came on the door and a maid brought in tea. They moved to a table on the other side of the room. Once Dotty poured and added milk and sugar to the cups, she glanced at her grandmother. "What happened to cause the problems?"

Grandmamma took a sip then set down her cup. "Alasdair thought Merton would never be faithful to Eunice and didn't want to see her heart broken. Yet Merton surprised everyone. He immediately gave his mistresses their congé."

Dotty quickly swallowed tea. "He had more than one at a time?"

"Oh my, yes. I told you he was quite outré. Had a stable of them. Each with a different talent." Grandmamma took another sip. "I was there the first night Merton saw Eunice. She was in the center of her court, and he walked straight into the circle, went down on his knee, and proposed."

Dotty couldn't imagine anything so romantic. "What did she say?"

"She said it was the best proposal she'd had all Season and accepted. He never left her side after that night and remained faithful the rest of his life. He doted on her and Dominic. After his death, Eunice went into a decline. I heard she had lost the child she was carrying. All of that was bad enough, though in my opinion, Alasdair made it worse. He insisted she go to Bath and quack herself while he took over raising Dominic as he thought suited his station."

Dom's behavior made much more sense now, losing both his mother and father at once. She'd always thought he behaved as if he had two people in him fighting for control. "What can I do about it?"

"Be yourself, and do not allow him to be less than what he is." Grandmamma selected a biscuit from the plate. "Now, what do you have planned for the rest of this afternoon?"

"Lady Thornhill is having a drawing room." Dotty grinned. "Lady Merton will attend as well, *and* Merton always escorts her."

A twinkle entered Grandmamma's eyes. "Perfect. If you don't mind, I shall join you."

Dom put down his pen and leaned back in the leather chair. The other evening with Thea he'd been so close to losing control. Too close. He had wanted to drag her off somewhere and teach her more about the pleasure they would share. His fingers had itched to caress her perfect breasts. Taste her warm, fragrant white skin. The knowledge that she would have welcomed him had caused his shaft to harden painfully.

His uncle's words had broken through his miasma of desire in the nick of time.

Remember, Merton, you must always remain in control. Carnal cravings should not rule your head. Moderation is

*the key. Your future wife will thank you. No lady wants to be
mauled and treated like a whore.*

The need he had for Thea must be the cravings his uncle
warned him against. He'd heard of men being in battle and
wanting nothing more than a woman afterward. After being
at the whorehouse, that must have been what had occurred
to him. He had never desired a woman as much as he did
her. But that didn't explain his behavior yesterday. If his
footman hadn't knocked to tell them the coach was ready,
what would he have done?

His poor, darling Thea. She only thought of kisses. She
had no idea what the end result would be. Would she be hor-
rified when he wanted to see her naked? Would she hate
seeing him that way? Perhaps it would be better if they each
wore night clothing, but that wasn't how he wanted her. He
needed to see her skin flushed. Kiss and learn every inch of
her. He moaned as his shaft stiffened at the thought.

Despite him wanting her to live at Merton House, after
yesterday he should be thankful her parents would not arrive
for another several days. Having her here and not being able
to touch her was going to be torture. Yet at least he'd iden-
tified what it was he felt. It was merely lust, not love. Love
would be disastrous. It would make him neglect his duty.

Cyrille jumped up into Dom's lap, and, absently, he
stroked the cat. Every time Thea took it upon herself to save
something or someone, his life spiraled out of control. He
began wanting what he couldn't have, just as he'd done as
a child. He slammed his closed fist on the desk, unsettling
the cat for a moment. It would have to cease. She could not
continue taking in strays and risking her safety.

"My lord!" Tom burst through the door. "Look at what I
drew. Sally says it's my best one yet." The child crawled up
into Dom's lap, being careful not to disturb the cat, and
handed him the paper. "See?"

Dom stifled a groan. This vignette wanted only a three-
legged dog. But when he glanced down at the sketch, it

wasn't at all what he'd expected. The drawing was clearly Thea and even captured the twinkle in her eyes. The one he hoped he wouldn't snuff out when he told her she would have to cease her activities.

He tousled Tom's hair. "Very good."

At least the boy was doing well. Dom's attempts to track down Tom's grandfather, the Earl of Stratton, had so far been unsuccessful. The man wasn't in Town and the letters sent to his estate and man of business had not yet been answered. Major Horton agreed to inquire at the Horse Guards for the approximate date of Tom's father's return. Until a member of his family who was willing to take him could be located, it was up to Dom to care for the boy. He must find the time to hire a tutor, but who would work for an unspecified period of time?

After a few moments an idea struck him. Worthington and Grace might be willing to help Tom. With distaste, Dom remembered his unrelenting hours spent only with tutors. Even Garvey had stopped coming over to play. As much as it went against the grain to ask Worthington for anything, Dom would speak with his cousin. Sending Tom to study with other children would be good for him. Now the only detail left was finding a drawing master, but where the devil did one begin to search?

A knock sounded on the door, and his mother entered. Glancing at Dom, she smiled, no doubt seeing his future children on his lap. Would he have to keep his distance from them as well?

Tom jumped down, waving the drawing again. "My lady, look what I did."

Mama took the picture. "You have a great deal of talent."

She looked at Dom as if to ask what he planned to do.

"Do you have any idea where I can find a drawing master?"

Hesitating only for a moment, she replied. "I believe I do. I came to tell you Matilda and I are attending Lady

Thornhill's drawing room. She generally has a number of artists present. Why don't you join us?"

Long ago he had promised his uncle he'd never enter that den of iniquity. Most of her ladyship's guests made sport of the Prince Regent and discussed radical reform. Yet to be fair, Prinny did make himself a figure of fun. His difficulty was how to phrase his aversion so as to avoid hurting his mother's feelings. "I thought I would spend some time with Thea this afternoon."

His mother raised a brow. "Then you had best come with me as that is the only way you'll see her before this evening."

He stifled a groan. He'd forgotten. Grace frequently took the young ladies there. If he only went to find a teacher for Tom, what harm could there be? And he should see first-hand what Thea was exposed to in such company. "I shall be happy to escort you."

Attend the drawing room, find a drawing master, and remove his women, including Thea, from the Thornhills' influence. What could be so hard about that? In the meantime, he would take Tom over to Worthington's house.

Dom ordered a footman to make the child ready and called for his curricle.

He entered the hall, and Tom looked up with anxious eyes. "Are you going to give me to someone else?"

Dom took the boy's hand, leading him out to the pavement. "No, I am going to see about lessons for you with some other children. They are cousins of mine. I think you will like them."

The boy gave a little skip, but didn't reply.

He stopped at Stanwood House first, hoping to be able to discuss the matter with Grace.

The butler opened the door. "Good day, my lord."

Inclining his head slightly, Dom gave the man his hat, gloves, and cane. "Royston, is Lady Worthington at home to visitors?"

"Yes, my lord. If you will follow me?" He stopped before

a door at the end of the corridor and knocked, then opened it. "My lady, Lord Merton to see you."

Grace glanced up from the ledgers on her desk and rose. "This is a surprise." Dom's defenses started to rise, but she smiled. "A pleasant one. Royston, some tea please, and I believe Cook may have some jam tarts." She glanced at Tom, then walked to a small sofa. "This must be Tom. He cleaned up very well. Have a seat and tell me what I can do for you."

Dom sat in a large leather chair, and Tom climbed onto his lap. "If what I suggest is not possible, please feel free to tell me. I would like Tom to take lessons with your brood."

Grace gazed at the child as she considered his request. "I don't see why not, but I shall want to consult Miss Tallerton and Mr. Winters. They will wish to assess where Tom is in his studies, unless you happen to know?"

Dom shook his head. It hadn't even occurred to him to ask what the boy had been studying when his mother died. "No, please feel free to call them down."

Grace tugged the bell pull and a footman poked his head in. "I would like Miss Tallerton and Mr. Winters to attend me when it is convenient for them to make a pause."

"Yes, my lady."

That was not how to run a household. Anyone who worked for him was expected to come immediately upon his request. "I would have thought we could do this posthaste."

She regarded him calmly. "You have not had your tea yet."

"Yes, but—"

Then she gave him a look that would have done his old nurse credit. "I will not interrupt the children's studies. They have a strict schedule that must be maintained."

He grimaced. "I apologize. I should have realized that you must maintain order."

"Precisely. It would be utter chaos if I did not." She glanced at a large mahogany grandfather clock. "They will be down soon."

Shortly after tea arrived, he heard what sounded like a herd of horses stampeding through the house, accompanied by high-pitched squeals.

"Ah." Grace set her cup down. "Playtime."

How different this was to the way he'd been raised. After his father's death, he'd not been allowed to run in the house or yell. He knew he would sound stupid by asking, but couldn't help himself. "What will the children do now?"

"They will run about outside for the next ten minutes or so, then go into luncheon. After which they will have their individual studies."

Dom shook his head, not understanding.

"They each play a musical instrument and must be proficient enough not to embarrass themselves if called upon to perform. They also learn the rudiments of drawing, though I admit, the only one of us who can sketch with any skill is Matt. Then there are foreign languages. The older ones are taught Latin, Greek, advanced maths, and science. Then there is French and Italian. Additionally, the girls must practice their needlework."

Other than needlework, it was very much like what Dom had studied. What surprised him was that the boys and girls apparently had the same lessons. "Will you send them to school?"

"The boys, yes. Neither Matt nor I have a great opinion of girls' schools. Fortunately, there are enough of them that they will not be lonely."

As he had been.

A knock came on the door and a tall fair woman accompanied by an even taller gentleman with light brown hair entered the room.

"You wanted to see us, my lady?"

Grace waved at them to take seats. "Yes. Miss Tallerton, may I introduce my cousin, the Marquis of Merton. Merton, our governess, Miss Tallerton, and our tutor, Mr. Winters."

The two instructors took places on the sofa across from Grace and glanced curiously at Tom.

"I would like to know if adding one child more to the mix will disrupt your teaching schedule?"

They looked at each other and shook their heads.

"The only thing we must do," Mr. Winters said, "is ensure the boy is at the same academic level as at least one other child. Why don't you allow him to remain for luncheon and the rest of the day?"

Grace went to the door to the garden and called for Mary and Theodora, the two youngest children. They arrived at a full run, curls escaping from their braids.

"Yes, Grace?" Mary asked.

"This is Tom. He is visiting Lord Merton for a while and may join your lessons. I would appreciate it if you would take him out and introduce him to the others."

Theodora, the older of the two girls at eight years, grabbed Tom's hand. "Come with us and you can play until it's time to eat."

Dom's heart lurched as Tom grinned and smiled over his shoulder. "See you later, my lord."

"I'll send the coach for you." Dom watched as the children ran out the door. At some point, Tom would leave him forever.

"He'll be fine, my lord," Miss Tallerton said.

Dom cleared his suddenly thick throat. "Of course he will."

Two hours later, Dom entered Lady Thornhill's drawing room, but instead of feeling as if he had entered a lion's den, it was more akin to some sheik's abode and rather pleasant. He couldn't put his finger on just what was different about the room, yet it seemed to entice the senses. A tall slender woman in a brightly colored gown and turban greeted him, his mother, and cousin.

"Eunice, I'm so glad to see you here." The lady bussed Mama on the cheek.

"Silvia." Mama kissed her in return. "I daresay, you won't remember Dominic."

Lady Thornhill held out her hands. "You have indeed grown into a handsome young man. The last time I saw you, you were still in leading strings. My husband and I were on the diplomatic mission in Turkey after that."

He was so startled, he almost forgot to bow. "It is a pleasure to renew our acquaintance."

He'd not known his mother and Lady Thornhill were friends, or that her husband was in the diplomatic corps. With his mother's relationship to the lady, he would not be able to leave early. Mama probably wouldn't go.

Lady Thornhill laughed. "I doubt you believe that at the present, but perhaps you will find some of the conversation interesting to you." She gave him an arch look. "My husband and I are not as dreadful as some make us out to be."

Caught and very neatly as well. He grinned. "It appears I have much to learn. However, my first interest is in finding a drawing master for my temporary ward. He's quite talented."

The lady glanced around the room then stopped and squinted. "Aha." She pointed to the far corner by a window "That group over there should do. They are all young artists hoping to make a success of their endeavors. If one of them is not interested, they will know someone who is."

Dom bowed again. "If you will excuse me?"

"Of course. Best do it now. Your Miss Stern has not yet arrived."

Warmth crept up his neck. Lady Thornhill was nothing if not direct. "Thank you, ma'am."

She inclined her head and turned back to his mother as he made his way to the far end of the long drawing room.

A half an hour later, after questioning Dom closely about

the boy's abilities, an artist by the name of John Martin agreed to give Tom lessons. Having accomplished his purpose, Dom bid the men a good day and started back through the crowd of people. He caught sight of Thea entering behind a handsome older woman with silver hair.

He was within a few feet of his affianced-wife, when Lady Thornhill cried out, "Your Grace. It is about time you visited me."

Your Grace? What was Thea doing with a duchess? She must be one of Grace's acquaintances.

The duchess's eyes twinkled, but she replied sternly, "Silvia, I find your manners no better than before you put your hair up."

Lady Thornhill eyes misted as she grinned broadly. "I have missed you. We do not see nearly enough of you."

The woman hugged Lady Thornhill. "Still a baggage."

"Yes. Does it please you?"

"Indeed it does." Her Grace motioned for Thea to come up. "I believe you have already met my granddaughter, Dorothea?"

Dom stopped, dumbstruck.

Granddaughter? Thank God he had never suggested she needed to train as a marchioness. He would have looked a fool.

Lady Thornhill turned to Thea. "Yes. She is the image of you."

He studied the duchess then Thea. The resemblance was remarkable. Thea's features were a younger, more rounded version of her grandmother's, who was still an extremely good-looking woman.

Thea gave her grandmother a perplexed look. "I didn't realize you and Lady Thornhill were so close."

"Silvia is my goddaughter. After her mother died, I sponsored her for her first Season."

Dom stifled a groan and stepped forward. The pieces fell

into place like a puzzle he'd just solved. No wonder Thea was so self-possessed and appeared at ease in almost any situation. He caught her eye, motioning his head slightly toward her grandmother.

She held out her hand to him. "Grandmamma, may I introduce my betrothed, Lord Merton? My lord, my grandmother, the Dowager Duchess of Bristol."

The older woman regarded him with a gimlet eye. "Merton, I never thought to see you here, yet, I am delighted you are."

He could hardly believe this charming woman was the Duke of Bristol's mother. A more bitter man Dom had yet to meet.

He took the hand she offered and bowed over it. If that was a test, it appeared he had passed. "Thank you, Your Grace."

His plan to treat Thea's relations with the proper amount of well-bred condescension, thereby depressing any overly familiar behavior on their part, shattered. For a moment, he had trouble taking it all in. Her family connections could hardly be a secret, but no one had said a word to him. Even Alvanley hadn't known.

Her Grace regally inclined her head. "You two run along. I am sure you have more interesting conversations in which to take part."

Thea tucked her hand in his arm. "Thank you, Grandmamma."

His betrothed led him to a window seat on the other side of the room from the artists. "I'm glad to see you, but what brings you here?"

"My mother, and finding a drawing master for Tom."

Her brows drew together. "Still no word from his family?"

Dom shook his head. "Nothing and what is strange to me

is that Tom never asks. He takes it as a matter of course that his father will return whenever he arrives."

"He *is* in the army. Perhaps that is just the way of things for him. Grandmamma said Lord Stratton is an odd egg." Thea pulled her lush bottom lip between her teeth and Dom wanted to ravish her mouth. "You don't mind that Tom may be with you for a while yet?"

"You mean be with us if no one claims him before his father returns."

Her gentle smile tugged at his heart. "I am not bothered at all. The fact is that I'm growing quite attached to him."

"As am I." Which was part of the problem. "The longer Tom is with me, the harder it will be to give him up, and he would be better off with his family."

"Not if they do not want him."

Her tone was so fierce Dom ceased his casual perusal of the room and stared at her. "You think there is some sort of break with the family?"

"If not, then why were Tom and his mother not residing at Stanton House or at one of the estates?" She pinched the bridge of her nose. "The earl has a number of properties. Surely one of them could have been given over to her, particularly in her condition. Do you not remember that was one of Mrs. White's requirements? That there be no close family."

"I'd forgotten." Although how he could have was a mystery to him. He prided himself on his memory. Yet when he was with Thea, he had trouble thinking of anything but her. "It appears as you've done some research. What else did you find?"

"I had it all from my grandmother. She did not know much about Tom's parents' marriage. However, she did say his father is second in line to the earl, and, although the heir has been married for several years, they have no children."

Her eyes filled with concern. "Grandmamma also said Stanton is in poor health."

"Rather than continuing to attempt to contact the earl, perhaps I would be better served to find his heir. Do you have any idea what his name is?" Thea was right, something was seriously wrong and the sooner he discovered what it was, the better. The boy should be with his family.

She lifted her eyes briefly to the ceiling. "Were you not made to learn the peerage?"

"I always thought"—he gave her his most charming grin—"I would marry a woman who would know. Failing that, I have a copy of Debrett's around somewhere."

"He is Viscount Cavanaugh. His main estate is in Norfolk."

"In that case, I had better send a letter to him."

She tucked her small hand in his. "Thank you. I knew you'd take care of it." Sliding off the seat, she stood before him. "Come. Let's take a stroll to the picture gallery. I think there is a small portrait of Grandmamma."

As she led him away, he considered sending a missive to Tom's maternal grandfather as well. As soon as Thea or his secretary discovered who that gentleman was.

Once they'd left the drawing room, she turned the subject. "Have you found an appropriate house for the ladies yet?"

His mother, Thea, and he had agreed that a property close enough to London to be convenient, but far enough away so the ladies did not have a fear of discovery would be just the thing. "I have my secretary reviewing the listings. I had forgotten that I'd sent my steward away for a few weeks to Norfolk, or it would have already been done."

"Naturally, they would like to relocate as soon as possible. Most of them are afraid to go out, and the house holds bad memories for them."

They had reached the long gallery. With the number of

guests he'd seen, he was surprised to see it was devoid of people. Thank the Fates, they were finally alone.

Dom turned to take Thea in his arms, then stifled a groan. No matter how he felt, he must do everything in his power to keep his hands off her. He could not allow lust to control him.

Chapter Nineteen

Dotty hoped Dom would not notice or mind her slight stratagem. Grandmamma did say there was a painting of her and Lady Thornhill's mother somewhere in the house. Yet having already been in the gallery, Dotty knew it had a number of alcoves and was usually empty. Anticipating his touch, her body warmed.

After they'd traversed the wide corridor, she stopped at the far end near a niche wide enough to hold a full-sized statue. "It must be somewhere else." She faced him, and placed her palms on his broad shoulders. "Dom?"

He swooped down, capturing her lips.

"We shouldn't do this here." His voice was rough as granite.

Boldly, she stroked his tongue with hers. Her fingers dug into the silky waves of his hair. "Why?"

Dom's palm cupped her derrière, drawing her against him. "Anyone could come in."

Sighing, she allowed her body to melt into him. "We are betrothed. We will be married in another week."

"Would that we were married now, then I wouldn't be in a public place with you."

Dotty clung to him as his other hand caressed the side of her breast, causing her nipple to pucker. When he brushed his thumb over the tight nub, fire shot through her settling in the sensitive place between her legs and making it throb. She pressed against him, wanting something, relief of some sort.

Moaning, she tried to snake a leg around his, but was frustrated by her skirts. The sharp pulsations increased and a high sigh escaped her. "Dom, I need . . ."

"What, sweetheart? What is it you want?"

"I don't know. My body is aching."

"God, Thea." He sounded if he had trouble getting the words out. "You'll be the death of me."

He parted her legs with his and pressed his thigh against her mons. For a few moments the throbbing intensified. Just when she thought she couldn't stand anymore, she started to tremble, and her breathing hitched. Dom increased the pressure as wave upon wave of new sensations rolled through her. A moment later she flew apart.

Fusing his mouth on hers, he swallowed her scream with a kiss.

Dear Lord, what *was* that and when could they do it again? As he removed his leg, she slumped against him.

Dom held her. "We cannot do this anymore. Not until we're married."

That was not at all what she wanted to hear. She pressed soft kisses along his jaw. "But I liked it."

A deep chuckle rumbled in his chest. "That you did bodes well for our future. However, if we do not stop, I'll end up taking you before the wedding."

What was so bad about that? The idea of being able to make the choice appealed to her. Granted there were risks, but how likely was it that Dom would die before they married? She knew about the act itself from a discussion she'd had with the wife of one of her father's tenants.

Of course, the real question was how Dom would react when she told him she did not wish to wait. Then again, it might be better not to give him warning. There was enough time to convince him once her parents arrived and she moved into Merton House.

Holding his gaze, she reached up to smooth the back of his hair, and pressed her lips to his. Something lurked in the back of his eyes as he ran his tongue along the seam of her mouth, urging her to open.

Then his face shuttered, and he stepped back. "We must return to the drawing room, or someone will come looking for you."

Drat the man. This was going to be harder than she'd thought. She straightened her gown. "There. Now no one need know we did more than look at pictures."

When they returned to the drawing room a few minutes later, the crowd had almost doubled in size. She searched for her grandmother and finally found her with a group of older ladies, including Lady Merton and Lady Shirring. Which must mean Miss Turley was present.

After the morning visit she had made, Dotty had discussed the conversation she had overheard with Charlotte and Louisa. In the end, they decided that Lady Manners was the instigator and Miss Turley too easily led. She was certainly too biddable for Dom. Still, the reason Lady Manners had wanted her cousin to marry Dom remained a mystery.

The window seat was occupied, as were all the chairs and sofas. Large brightly colored pillows had been added to the seating, but even they were taken up by young men and some of the bolder ladies.

She led Dom to an empty corner. "I think Miss Turley is here."

His dark golden brows drew together. "What makes you say that?"

"Her aunt, the Countess of Shirring, is with my grandmother and your mother. She came to Town to take charge of Miss Turley."

"After the trick she tried to pull, it's about time someone did."

Dotty hadn't thought he would be happy, but she had never realized he would still be this upset. "I do not think it was Miss Turley's doing." Or perhaps he was being gruff because he had wished to marry Miss Turley. Was that the reason he'd pulled away in the gallery? If he truly did not want her, Dotty would release him.

Raising a brow, she lifted her chin. "In any case, if events hadn't turned out as they did, we would not be betrothed."

Dom had been studying the room, when the challenge in Thea's voice brought his gaze back to her. Damn. This was one of those moments other men complained about, that he had never thought to have. The problem was he had been listening to the music of her voice, and only half hearing her words. Was something wrong with their engagement? A martial light flared deep in her green eyes, and he instinctively knew there was only one response. "I want you."

Her countenance relaxed, and she smiled again. "I do wonder why Lady Manners wanted the match so badly."

He shrugged. He'd had all his prospective brides investigated. Their families were financially sound and there was no hint of impropriety concerning any of them. "Prestige. Her father is a viscount and the title isn't that old."

Thea's brow shot up again.

Good Lord, this . . . whatever they had was fraught with hidden pitfalls. He would not call it a love match—he had vowed he wouldn't fall in love—but it damn sure wasn't a marriage of convenience. There was nothing remotely convenient about his Thea. Brothels, kittens, lost children, and fallen women. He felt as if he were sinking into a bog. And who knew where it would end? Not he. Not only that, but after meeting her grandmother, he had given up any hope that he would be able to control her.

Before Thea could comment, he said, "Her family would naturally want to look as high as possible for a husband."

She mumbled something about her father and gave her head a little shake. "Not all ladies try to trap a gentleman."

Thank the Lord. He was on solid ground again. "True."

"There she is . . . with a young man."

"Her brother, Mr. Turley."

Her lush lips formed a slight moue. "Yes, I see the resemblance. I wonder if they will notice us."

"I hope not." Dom enjoyed having her to himself, even if it was in a salon crammed full of people. At least no one was asking her to dance or if she wanted refreshments.

Mr. Turley glanced in Dom and Thea's direction, then bent to his sister. She blushed and shook her head. He must have said something else as the next thing she did was nod, and they started straight for him.

Dom's jaw clenched.

"Be nice," Thea murmured. "After the rumors that have been started, the gossipmongers will watch how we behave."

What gossip? He'd not heard anything. Although he had not been around any of his friends lately, or at White's. He tightened his grip on her arm.

She smiled and held out her free hand. "Elizabeth, how good to see you."

Miss Turley shot him a frightened glance and focused on Thea. "Dotty, thank you. I know so few people here, but my aunt insisted we come."

He and Turley gave one another brief nods.

"Turley."

"My lord."

"Oh, Dotty." Miss Turley smiled brightly. "May I present my brother, Mr. Turley? Gavin, this is Miss Stern."

Had the brother been involved in the trap? Was that the reason Miss Turley had been arguing with him that evening?

As he bowed over Thea's hand, the man's smile seemed genuine enough. "My pleasure, Miss Stern. Allow me to wish you and Lord Merton happy on your betrothal."

Thea turned to Dom. The expression on her face was so

joyful his heart crashed around in his chest to know it was for him. And she was right. If it hadn't been for Lady Manners's machinations, he would have been back at Merton rather than marrying Thea. He grinned at Turley. "Thank you. We are extremely pleased."

He nodded and addressed Thea again. "Elizabeth told me how kind you've been to her."

"My dear sir, it is easy to be agreeable to someone as good-natured as your sister."

For a few minutes they discussed the weather and the number of Lady Thornhill's interesting guests.

Finally, Turley said, "Miss Stern, it was a pleasure meeting you. I can see why Lord Merton is so happy."

Miss Turley nodded as she took her brother's arm. "Yes. I think you have made the perfect match."

As Thea was thanking them and saying good-bye, it struck Dom that he was happy. Happier than he had been since before his father's death.

As the couple left, he murmured, "That went well and should put an end to any remaining talk. I might need to have my secretary send Lady Manners a thank-you note."

"My lord." Thea's eyes widened in mock horror. "Are you making a joke?"

He had to think for a moment, then he chuckled. "I guess I am."

Chapter Twenty

A few days after Lady Thornhill's drawing room, Major Horton had requested an urgent meeting with Dotty, Dom, and his mother.

The major leaned against the mantel in the study, his form tense. Lady Merton sat on the chair next to Dotty's in front of Dom's desk.

"How bad was it?" he asked the major who had arrived shortly after breakfast with the news that the ladies must be relocated sooner than planned.

"Woke the whole house up and scared the"—he glanced at her and Lady Merton—"scared everyone to death. Fortunately Mrs. Oyler was able to calm everyone, but it spooked the lot of them and had my wife nervous as well. The woman who screamed said she heard men talking outside her window."

Dom had an impatient look on his face. As if he truly did not understand the gravity of the problem. "They are well guarded, and we replaced all the locks. Simply tell them there is no reason to be frightened."

Dotty sucked in a sharp breath, then let it out. Mrs. White was in Newgate awaiting trial. Fortunately, the Runners had enough evidence against her that none of the ladies would need to testify. Miss Betsy, though, had somehow escaped, and no one knew who the scoundrels were who had helped Mrs. White.

Major Horton's posture hadn't changed, but he seemed even more rigid. "It's the second time in a week this has occurred. The women will never feel safe in that house."

He was right, and it probably wasn't safe. Even though Dom had stationed footmen in the house, who knew what type of violence the criminals were capable of? Housing remained a problem. Although Dom's steward had located a suitable-sized manor house near Richmond, it required renovations that were far from being complete. "We must move them."

Dom's gaze switched from the major to her. "With everyone in Town for the Season, there are no proper rentals to be had, and the landlords would be suspicious of a house full of young, comely, single ladies. They would have the exact impression we are trying to avoid."

"There must be something we can do," Lady Merton said. "Perhaps one of the country estates would do until the house is finished."

Dotty glanced at the major. "How soon do we lose you?"

"With Boney loose, my assignment's been put on hold, but chances are I shall be back on the Continent before too long. I don't want to leave my wife on St. George Street when I leave." He grinned suddenly. "A place in the country would suit me perfectly."

Raking a hand through his already disheveled hair, Dom leaned back in his chair. "Let me talk to my steward and see what the most viable option is. Have you had any word of Tom's father?"

"Nothing." The major shook his head. "As you know, his expected date of return is in December. I sent a letter with the official post, but it is too soon for him to have received it. How's the boy doing?"

That might be the only bright spot in this whole predicament. "Tom's well and happy. He is taking lessons at

Stanwood House and has a drawing master." Dotty smiled as she thought of his joy in being with Matt and Grace's brothers and sisters. "He has a great deal of talent."

"Unfortunately," Dom said, "we have had no luck contacting his grandfather, and when I drove by Viscount Cavanaugh's town house yesterday afternoon, the knocker was off the door. I sent a letter to his estate, but have not heard from him."

The major rubbed his chin thoughtfully. "Did you ever consider the lad might be better off remaining with you until his father returns?"

As if a candle had been snuffed out, Dom's face went from genial to scowling. "I have a duty to return the boy to his family."

The major folded his arms across his chest. "You still don't know the reason Cavanaugh left his wife in Town alone. What if they take the boy and mistreat him?"

Dotty thought the major had a very good point. In fact, Tom would be much better off living at Merton House until his father returned.

"He is a peer of the realm." Dom's jaw clenched. "He would not mistreat a child. Aside from that, he has a duty toward his grandson."

She stared at him, hardly able to believe what she had heard. This was not the man she was coming to love, but it was absolutely the one her friends disliked so much. Well, his mistaken beliefs could not go unchallenged. "Merton, you cannot seriously believe that? He has not done his duty thus far and, based on his past behavior, I do not trust him to do it now."

"Thea," he practically snapped, "you will leave Tom's welfare to me."

How could he be so pigheaded? And how dare he speak to her in that tone of voice and with the major present? Glaring at him, she rose. "Not if you plan to give him to people he does not know and who do not want him."

His face shuttered, and she no longer knew what he was thinking. "We will discuss this later."

He had never used that cold, hard tone with her before. Dotty's chest heaved, her temper held by a rapidly fraying thread. "Very well."

She turned and strode through the door.

"Thea, stop," Dom commanded.

She'd had enough of his high-handed ignorance. Whirling, she pointed her finger at him. "No, you wait. You seem to think a peer can do no wrong. Open your eyes and take a look around you. Peers are just as likely to mistreat their wives, and children, and dependents as anyone else. I have had enough."

"Remain where you are. I shall escort you to Berkeley Square."

"Do not bother. I need the walk." She bit her lip and left the study. Unable to get away from him fast enough, she strode rapidly down the corridor, stopping before entering the hall. She took a deep breath, assumed a polite smile, entered the hall, and called for her footman.

Fred arrived in just moments. "Is there anything wrong, miss? I thought you were staying for luncheon?"

"There has been a change of plans." She finished buttoning her spencer and addressed Paken. "Could you please have some of Master Tom's clothing sent to Stanwood House? He will be staying there for a few days."

The butler bowed. "Yes, miss. Would you like a carriage called?"

"No, thank you, Paken. The air will do me good." Lots of fresh air and a chance to work off her anger.

She walked quickly down Brook Street, turned on to Carlos Place, and from the corner of her eye, caught something move swiftly away. The back of her neck prickled, as if someone was watching her. Slowing, she turned, surveying the area, but no one was there. "Fred, did you see anything?"

"No, miss. Why?"

She was tempted to shake it off as a bird or squirrel, but it couldn't have been an animal. "I think someone may have been watching us."

He glanced around. "Let's get you home."

Dotty nodded and continued on, walking with the long strides she used in the country.

Not many minutes later they rounded the corner into Berkeley Square. "Come, I'll treat you to an ice."

Fred's face turned a deep red. "Miss, really I couldn't. It wouldn't be—"

"Keep an eye out for anyone following us."

"Ah, right, miss. I'm sorry, but why would anyone be following you?"

"When we went to Mrs. White's, Lord Merton used his name. I am not so naïve as to think there might not be repercussions. You must agree that it would not do to lead anyone to Stanwood House."

The footman tapped the side of his nose. "Very canny you are, miss."

She hoped Matt had hired the footmen for their brains as well as their brawn. Slowing to a stroll, she walked to the far end of the square and ordered ices.

"Miss Stern?" Miss Featherington waved at her from a table not far from the window. "Come join us, won't you?"

Dotty greeted the younger woman and her mother, Lady Featherington, who was busy going through a list. "Thank you. I am sorry, but I cannot stay long."

"I understand perfectly." Miss Featherington smiled. She was the opposite of her more taciturn older brother. "I just wanted to tell you that Mama received the invitation from your grandmother for her ball. I am so excited. I've never been to the Pulteney."

A ball? When had Grandmamma decided to host a ball?

In an attempt to cover her surprise, Dotty busied herself removing her gloves. "It is my grandmother's favorite place to stay when she's in Town."

"You appear very calm. I would be frantic if a ball was being held in my honor only two days before my wedding."

She took a spoonful of the ice. "Oh no," she said with perfect truthfulness now that she had gotten over the initial shock. "I'll have nothing to do with it you know. Grandmamma likes to take care of the details herself." Or rather, her companion and secretary would oversee all the preparations. Yet, just once Dotty wished her grandmother would consult the person involved before planning an event. She glanced at Fred who stood outside the door, his attention captured by something or someone, and took the last bite of the ice. "Thank you again for asking me to sit with you, but I really must be going. Lady Worthington will wonder where I've got to."

"Thank you for joining us," Miss Featherington enthused. "I so look forward to the ball."

Dotty rose and made her way to the door. Fred opened it for her. "Anything?"

"A young boy has been watching you from behind that big tree by the street. We might want to go to Worthington House first."

Until Worthington House, which was situated directly across the square from Stanwood House, was livable for the family, Matt kept his only office there. He would be able to advise her.

"An excellent idea." Pretending she had nowhere in particular to go, she weaved a path through the square, then to Worthington House.

The butler, Thornton, opened the door and escorted her to Matt's study.

He rose as she entered. "To what do I owe this pleasure?"

"Oh, Matt." Dotty sighed with relief. "I've gotten us all into a mess."

He signaled for her to take one of the chairs in front of

his massive partner's desk. "Has this anything to do with Merton?"

"Only a little." Sitting, she smoothed her skirts. "We had a disagreement and I left his house more than a little annoyed with him."

"Do you mean to tell me he did not offer his coach?" Matt's tone was dangerously calm, boding ill for his cousin.

"He did." She bit her lip. Perhaps she'd been a little too hasty. "But I was so angry, I decided to walk." She paused for a moment. "I was followed." She told him about the boy who had been watching her. "Fred suggested we come here first."

Matt tugged the bell pull; a few moments later Thornton answered. "My lord?"

"Have Fred go to the stables and describe the lad to the grooms. If they can get a hold of the child, I want him brought here." He looked at Dotty. "Go with Fred. I'll have you driven around to the back of Stanwood House. There will be no more walking between here and Merton House until we sort this all out."

At least she was not in trouble. "I understand. Thank you."

Matt's lips twisted into a wry smile. "Don't blame yourself too much. I expected something of the sort might occur. If we're lucky, we shall discover who wants what and with whom."

"If they are using a child, perhaps it's the same group who took Tom."

"That is possible, but many gangs use children for all sorts of things." Placing his elbows on the desk, he steepled his fingers. "Dotty, about you and Merton."

She pulled her bottom lip between her teeth. "Yes?"

"If you want to call it off . . ."

Tears gathered at the back of her eyes, and her throat

closed painfully. "And truly create the largest scandal of the Season?"

"We can delay the wedding. Your mother's health could be used as a reason."

After this morning, part of her wanted to grab at the chance of more time, yet her heart ached at the thought. Surely there was a way to make Dom see how wrong he was, and if she didn't do it, who would? "I'll give it some thought."

Dom stared after Thea as she strode down the corridor. He started after her, then felt his mother's hand on his arm.

"She is very angry right now, my dear. Give her time to calm herself."

He stabbed his fingers through his hair, again. He had never done that before he met Thea. Oh God. What if she jilted him? That didn't even bear thinking of. "If only she wasn't so stubborn."

"Dominic." His mother's brows drew together. "In my opinion, she was correct in her thinking. You shall have to apologize to her."

His jaw dropped. "Me? Apologize?"

"Indeed."

He turned to Horton still propped up against the mantel.

The major shook his head. "Don't look at me for help. I agree with her ladyship and Miss Stern." He straightened. "I must get back and assure the ladies you are searching for another house." As he passed by Dom on his way to the door, he grinned. "Don't worry too much about your betrothed. It's clear the two of you are in love. A little groveling on your part will help matters considerably and flowers wouldn't hurt as well."

Horton entered the corridor whistling.

"Very good advice," Mama said as she rose and followed the major.

"Hell and damnation!" Dom swore softly as he crossed to his steward's office. "Which of my estates would be an appropriate place for the ladies and Major Horton to reside until the renovations on the Richmond house are completed?"

Jacobs tapped his fingers on the desk for several moments. "There is the one near Oxford."

Dom shook his head. "Too near the university."

"St. Albans?"

"Find the information. It's been a long time since I've seen the property."

Dom took a seat as Jacobs set the file in front of him.

"Twenty bedchambers, my lord. Sufficient parlors. A nice park and gardens for them to walk in."

"Do you think it is far enough in the country to limit any talk?"

"My lord, we'll have to hire more servants than are there now. Before the ladies arrive, we could put it about that they are war widows and wives of deployed military officers." Jacobs gave one of his rare smiles. "I'll write the couple in charge of the house telling them of your new charitable endeavor."

"Charitable endeavors?" Uncle Alasdair sneered. "Strumpets. Do you really believe they'll change their ways? Those bits of muslin would have left if they hadn't wanted to be there."

For the first time, deep in Dom's heart, he knew his uncle was wrong. And if he was wrong about this, what else had he been mistaken about? "Yes, make sure they know the ladies are to be treated as such or they will answer to me."

"Yes, my lord," Jacob replied in a cheerful tone. "Shall I also ask Major Horton to provide some family history on the ladies? Just so there won't be so many questions?"

"Do that and find out how soon they can travel."

"My lord." Paken entered the room. "A message for you from Lord Worthington."

Bloody hell! That was it. Thea was leaving him. He took the missive. "I'll be in my study."

Dom sat behind his desk and stared at the letter in his hands. Well, putting off opening it wouldn't make the news any less palatable. He opened the seal, smoothing the paper out.

> *Merton,*
>   *I expect your presence at Worthington House within the half hour.*
>   *Depart from the mews. No one must know you have left your house.*
>
>   *Worthington*

Nothing about Thea ending their betrothal. Dom heaved a sigh of relief, then anger at his cousin's high-handedness sparked his ire. Was the man mad? How had it come to this? Merton skulking around in the alleyways. He'd half a notion to ignore Worthington's demands. But blast it all, what if he was right? "Paken, have a carriage ready at the garden gate in five minutes."

Less than a quarter hour later, Dom charged into Worthington's study and shoved the missive in front of him. "What the devil is the meaning of this?"

"Sit." His cousin's jaw clenched.

"You can't tell me to . . ." Dom dropped into the chair. What if Thea had been hurt or worse? "Is it Thea? Is she all right?"

"No thanks to you."

Merton ran a hand through his hair. His valet would leave him if Thea didn't. "What happened?"

"She was followed. I've got men looking for the boy now."

He groaned and dropped his face into his hands.

"I want an explanation as to why Dotty was allowed to leave Merton House on foot."

"We disagreed over Tom and the ladies."

"There had to be more than that." His cousin's eyes narrowed. "Dotty is one of the most level-headed young ladies I've ever met."

"I may have ordered her to leave Tom to me." He sucked in a breath. His words had sounded reasonable at the time. Now he wasn't quite as sure.

Leaning back in his chair, his cousin motioned with his hand. "Go on."

Dom relayed the meeting and what they'd discussed. By the time he'd finished, Worthington's face was flushed with anger.

He threw down the pen he'd been fiddling with. "Do you purposely go through life with blinders on? She might very well be right in her assessment."

Dom closed his eyes for a moment. "That is what the major and my mother said. I'm not used to all of this upheaval. I didn't know . . ." He rubbed his temple. "It's damned embarrassing to have a chit of a girl know more about the seedier part of the world than I do. What is worse, she never does what I tell her to."

"Your betrothed has a reputation for rescuing victims of that world." Dom's head whipped up. And he had prayed her behavior here was an aberration. "Not London, of course. She hasn't had time, yet. Still, the fact remains that you are correct. She probably does have a lot more knowledge than you. You may not like it, but you cannot continue to ignore it." Worthington poured brandy into two glasses, sliding one to Dom. "Before the incident in the brothel, I wondered if you had any Bradford blood in you at all. Your actions there gave me a ray of hope, but only you can open your eyes. There is more to life than White's, and your estates." He took a sip. "I'll tell you something else. When you get involved with the lower orders of society, being a peer will not always protect you."

Dom stared at his cousin. No one had ever spoken to him

like that before. Except Thea. Still, she would be his wife. He needed to have some control over her. "What about her not obeying me."

Worthington shrugged. "I can't help you with that. She has a mind of her own, as does Grace and, I might add, any other woman worth knowing."

That was not what Dom had wanted to hear. Which was occurring much too often recently. "I'll go talk with her."

An evil smile appeared on his cousin's face. "You want my advice? Grovel."

"Grovel?" Why the hell was everyone telling him that? "Merton does not grovel."

Matt stood, walked around his desk, and stuck out his hand. "Good luck. You'll need it."

Good Lord. The man was serious. Egad. "Where can I buy flowers?"

Chapter Twenty-One

Dotty sat on the small sofa beneath the window in the Young Ladies' Parlor and took a sip of her now-cold tea.

"We could send for a new pot," Charlotte suggested.

"Or a new betrothed," Louisa added archly.

Needing to unburden herself to sympathetic female ears, Dotty had given in to her urge to confide in her two friends. She would have been better off going to the Pulteney and crying in her grandmother's lap. Not that her friends weren't understanding. They had never been in love. Which for some strange reason seemed to make all the difference in the world.

Even she had trouble understanding her conflicting emotions. What made it worse was that Dom hadn't come after her. Even though she did not wish to see him and had given orders that she was not at home to him, he could have at least tried.

She placed her cup on the table in front of the couch. "No, thank you. I think I'll just lie down for a bit. Where are we going this evening?"

"You *are* blue-deviled," Charlotte exclaimed. "It's Miss Smyth's birthday ball."

"Oh yes." Dotty rose from the sofa. "How could I have forgotten?"

Charlotte gave Dotty a hug. "You will feel better with a rest. I just wish I knew how to help you."

Suddenly, the door crashed against the wall. Holding a bouquet of red roses, Dom strode into the room, grabbed her hand, and tugged her to him.

How dare he presume . . . "I told—"

His lips crushed hers as he wrapped one strong arm around her waist tugging her against him. His scent and the roses' mixed, overwhelming her senses. He slid his tongue over the seam of her lips and she opened, sinking into him. Giving her no chance to catch up, he drove his tongue into her mouth as if he'd claim her forever. Then she slid her hands over his shoulders and tilted her head, wanting more, wanting him.

After several long moments, when it felt as if they were breathing through one another, he lifted his head. "I'm sorry for my behavior." Backing up a little, but not releasing her, he handed her the bouquet. "These are for you."

Relief flooded her as she buried her nose in the flowers. "They are lovely. You've never given me flowers before."

"I shall have them delivered every day for the rest of your life if you wish."

She gave a wet chuckle. "Thank you, but if you did that, they would grow commonplace."

Placing one finger under her chin, he tilted her head up. "I should not have said what I did, and in the way I did. I should also have believed you about Tom and the ladies."

His deep blue eyes stirred like an ocean eddy. Warmth warring with fear. She cupped his cheek. "We will figure it out together."

A little puff of air escaped his lips, as if he'd been holding his breath. "Thank you." He kissed her once more lightly. "What were you about to say as I entered?"

Her cheeks warmed with a blush. "It doesn't matter anymore."

Smiling, he bent his head again and someone cleared her throat.

"Well. We are rather *de trop*." Louisa glanced at Charlotte. "I believe I remember that Grace wished to speak with us?"

"What? Oh yes." Charlotte grinned. "Dotty, we'll see you later. Merton, I shall tell the cook to expect you to join us for dinner."

"That will give them plenty of time," Louisa said as they closed the door. "I think I'm beginning to understand the attraction."

"That was certainly impressive," Charlotte mused.

Dotty lifted her eyes to the ceiling for a moment, then glanced at Dom who was staring at the door in horror. "My lord, I believe you are blushing."

"Flushed," he croaked. "It's warm in here."

"Is it?" She stroked his cheek. "I am rather chilly."

Dom lowered his head to hers and claimed her lips once more. "I shall see what I can do about that."

He kissed her so deeply, her toes curled and seemed to leave the floor. The next thing she knew, her back was against the wall.

His deep voice washed over her like a warm wave. "Thea, I want you."

Lord, yes. "I want you as well."

She reached up, pressing her lips to his. His fingers stroked her breasts and deep frissons of pleasure pierced her. The place between her thighs throbbed, and she moaned. Cool air wafted around her legs as Dom's hand caressed her calf, moving up to her garters, then to the bare skin of her thigh.

He broke their kiss. "Thea?"

"Yes." Her breath came so fast, she could scarcely breathe.

Dom's fingers stroked her mons, making it hot and wet. Her hips tilted toward him, urging him to deepen his caresses. Then his finger entered her. Oh God! Nothing, not even his previous caresses, had prepared her for this. This exquisite need and desire. The finger dipped in and out, then a second one was added. An excruciating tension grew and the throbbing increased. She tried to thrash her head, but he held her to the kiss. Finally, finally, it crested, making her tremble in relief, and she flew apart in his hands.

He picked her up as if she weighed no more than one of the kittens, cradling her to him as he sank down on the sofa. Holding her on his lap, he pressed soft kisses on her jaw and neck. When he reached the neckline of her bodice, his tongue traced the edge until he reached the crevice between her breasts. There his tongue licked lightly, just enough to give her a hint of the pleasure he'd give her later. Though not that much later if she had her way.

When he stopped, she stifled an unladylike urge to scream.

"I should tell you, I have found a place to move the ladies until the house in Richmond is ready."

She peered at him closely, only to ensure herself that he hadn't gone from kissing her to discussing their project without any ill effects. Fortunately for him, a shine of sweat covered his forehead and his breathing was labored.

"Dom."

He stared straight forward as if he was unable to look at her. "I should not have done what I did. I don't know what came over me."

She remembered what her grandmother had told her about Bradford and Vivers men. Was he fighting his natural tendencies? If so, was it because of his uncle? "Grandmamma told me about your father—"

"I am not my father," he growled, moving her from his lap to the sofa. "Please make my apologies about dinner. I must leave."

What in the name of Heaven had come over him? "I'll see you at the Smyth ball?"

"Yes, most likely."

He strode to the door and stopped. "I'm sorry."

Dom opened the door and closed it behind him.

"So am I." Searching for some clue as to his behavior, she leaned back against the cushions and tried to piece together everything she knew about both branches of the Bradford-Vivers family. Grandmamma had said they were passionate with the women they loved—so much so that the Bradford ancestor who had fallen in love with the Vivers lady who was a countess in her own right, had changed his last name—but there was always only one woman. Dotty's mother had once said that old Lord Worthington was never the same after his first wife's death because he had loved her so much. Matt and Grace were also very much in love and were not at all reticent about showing it. Had Dom's parents been the same? Dotty touched her lips. If he felt that way about her, why did he stop himself?

What did he have against his father, and who could tell her? Dom was clearly not going to. And why did he have to be so infuriating?

Dom dashed down the back stairs as quickly as he'd come up them. Something had to be wrong with him. Every time he was with Thea he lost all control of himself. The minute he had entered the parlor, he'd seen only her. What a spectacle he'd made of both of them. Yet, even that hadn't stopped him from ravishing her.

He was at the garden gate, before he slowed down. He would not be like his father. That kind of love brought too much sorrow. It was bad for his family and his estate. He prayed his mother had some other entertainment planned for this evening. He didn't want to see Thea. Or rather, he did wish to see her. Too much. For the first time he was glad her parents hadn't arrived. To have her in his house, so close, would be more temptation than he could bear.

When he reached the stables, he found his horses had been groomed and unhitched from the curricle.

"One minute, my lord," an elderly groom said. "We'll have them harnessed before you know it."

Dom nodded. Once he and Thea were married he would explain it to her. Maybe it would be better if he visited a mistress rather than risk . . . risk what? Experiencing passion with his wife? The thought of another woman disgusted him. Not only that, but it would hurt Thea. No. Better to deny himself. After he explained his family's history to her surely she would understand that they could not fall *in* love with one another. She had to. Love for one's family was well and good, but the unfettered passion of a love match—he shuddered—was dangerous.

A few moments later, he was in his curricle. He reached his stables sooner than he'd thought he would. Using the garden gate and the back door, he went directly to his study and poured a glass of brandy. It burned as it touched his tongue and made its way down his throat.

Refilling his glass, he tossed it off, giving a mirthless laugh. "Here's to you, Uncle Alasdair. To save my family, I will do exactly as you taught me."

"My lord, are you all right?"

Dom tried to open his eyes, but the flickering light blinded him and a sharp pain speared his head. "Get that damned thing away from me."

The footman, or at least that's who he thought it was, moved away.

Some time later, a hushed voice intruded on his sleep. "Boosey, he is."

"Nonsense, his lordship is never in his altitudes. He must be ill."

"If you say so, Mr. Paken, but that brandy decanter was full this afternoon."

"Good Lord."

The door closed quietly, and Dom was left by himself again. He really should go upstairs and dress. Kimbal would wonder where he'd got to. Mustn't upset one's valet. Although why Uncle Alasdair cared more for the valet than any other servant, Dom didn't know. Always had to tell Kimbal where he was going.

Dom must have drifted off again. When he awoke, the room was pitch dark. The door opened and he closed his eyes against the light, covering them with his arm.

Soft, firm footsteps approached him. "Oh my." *His mother.* "You will have to see if Cook remembers the remedy. He'll need it when he finally awakens. Get a couple of strong footmen and take him up to his chamber. They will probably have to help his valet undress him."

He didn't need help. He was perfectly capable of doing it himself. He tried to rise and rolled, landing on the floor, and hitting his head.

Ow. Damn, that hurt.

"Do you think he's going to cast up his accounts, my lady?"

"I certainly hope not. Bradford men can hold their brandy better than that. Just get him upstairs."

"Yes, my lady."

When Dom woke again, he was in his bed, sinking down into the soft mattress.

"I told Lord Alasdair when he hired me I could not work in a household where drunken licentiousness occurred." Kimbal's shrill tone made Dom wince.

He opened his mouth to protest and some vile liquid was poured down his throat. "What the hell are you doing?"

"Don't worry, my lord. It will make you feel better," his butler said calmly. What was Paken doing in Dom's chamber? He felt fine now and there was nothing dissolute about it. Although, he might like to be licentious with Thea.

Sniff.

"Then mayhap you'd like to find yourself a different employer," Paken replied.

"I do not work for you, Mr. Paken." *Sniff.* "I will discuss this with his lordship in the morning."

"You do that, Mr. Kimbal, and call for more of the remedy when his lordship wakes."

Blast it all, he was awake. The mattress refused to let him go. Maybe not for long.

"When Lord Alasdair was alive . . ."

"Well, he's not here any longer and even though I don't like to speak ill of the dead, we are well rid of him. Speaking badly of his lordship's father like he did and not allowing his name to be mentioned is something I don't hold with. A better master there never was."

Dom tried to sort out exactly what his butler meant, but his head throbbed as if he'd been kicked by a horse. Something warm curled up next to him and started to purr. That's right. Thanks to Thea he had a cat. All he wanted to do was sleep. He'd figure it out in the morning.

Chapter Twenty-Two

Dotty remained still as her maid wove the pearls through her locks. A light tapping sounded on the door and Grace entered, catching Dotty's gaze in the mirror.

"I've received word from Lady Merton that Merton will not attend the Smyth ball this evening." Grace paused. "He is . . . fuddled."

"Dom, drunk?" Dotty could hardly credit it.

"This is apparently the first occurrence."

She steadied her breathing and signaled for her maid to leave. "I believe that is correct."

A line formed between Grace's brows. "I understand from Matt that you and Merton had words today. Charlotte, who should not have left you alone with him as she did, said you made up."

The normal healthy pink of Dotty's complexion deepened. "Yes."

Grace sank onto a chair at the side of the dressing table. "Would you like to tell me what happened?"

No, but Dotty couldn't very well say that when Grace stood in *loco parentis* to her. "He apologized and we kissed. Then he apparently thought he should not have . . . kissed me and became distraught."

This time Grace's brows rose. "Kissed?"

Dotty cleared her throat, and her face felt as if it were on fire. "Perhaps a bit more."

Taking her hands, Grace said, "My dear, I am married and was betrothed. I do know how quickly passion can escalate. Did Merton do something you didn't like?"

"Oh no. Not at all. Quite the contrary. I was . . . um, very much enjoying it."

She smiled gently. "Well, that's good. You will take greater pleasure in your marriage if that is the case. Yet, what could have set him off?"

Dotty sighed. "I wish I knew. I mentioned something Grandmamma told me about his father, and he left. I spent the rest of the afternoon trying to understand what happened."

"Matt said something about Merton's Bradford nature being repressed by Lord Alasdair." Grace rose. "However, due to the fact that Matt does not like Merton's late guardian, I am afraid I did not pay much attention. Should we delay the wedding?"

Dotty shook her head. That was the last thing she wanted. "No. In fact, as happy as I've been here, I am anxious for Mama and Papa to arrive so that I may remove to Merton House."

"I'm very glad to hear that. I believe we shall see them in the next day or so." Grace's eyes sparkled with mischief. "Matt received a letter from Sir Henry stating your mother has declared the doctor was an old woman, and she was coming to Town, with or without his permission."

"Oh dear." Dotty grinned. "She sounds like my grandmother."

"In that case, I have no doubt your parents will arrive unannounced."

Pleased to have the discussion about Dom over, she laughed. "Yes, indeed."

Grace hugged her. "While you are here, I do not think it

wise for you and Merton to be alone for any length of time. The children do listen at the keyholes."

Oh no. The implications of that were too much to even think about. Having all the children know what Dotty and Dom had been doing did not bear thinking of. She said a quick prayer for her parents to arrive soon. "I see."

Perhaps it was fortunate he would not attend the ball this evening. She had questions for Lady Merton that would no longer wait.

An hour later, Dotty had no trouble locating her future mother-in-law. The problem was extracting her from Lady Bellamny.

"Good evening, Miss Stern," Lady Bellamny said. "I understand your betrothed is under the weather."

Dotty curtseyed and gave a polite smile. "So I've been told, my lady. I would like to hear how he goes on. May I borrow Lady Merton for a few minutes?"

"Of course."

"Let us stroll, my dear." She rose. "I'm sure we shall not be long." She linked arms with Dotty and once out of Lady Bellamny's hearing, asked, "Did Grace tell you?"

"Yes. What I do not understand is the reason." Dotty shook her head slightly. "Everything was going well, then I said something about his father, and he became upset."

Lady Merton maintained a smile as she nodded to other guests. "Act as if we are talking about nothing in particular."

Dotty assumed the polite expression expected as she waited for her ladyship to continue.

"I have been overhearing things that concern me greatly. It appears my brother did not honor my husband as he should have. I always wondered why Dominic was so different from David. For a very long time, I attributed it to grief. Unfortunately, I was seldom around him. I was quite ill for a long time after my husband died, and stayed in Bath for much too great a time. After that, when I was at Merton, Dom always seemed so . . . so capable, even when he was young. I longed to take him in my arms, but he never appeared to want me to." She took a shuddering breath. "Later, whenever I arrived, Alasdair always had him going this place or that." She glanced at Dotty. "It wasn't until this past year that I sensed something was wrong, and when I received his list of potential wives, I knew I had to become involved."

Dotty started to chew on her lip and stopped. If only they were not at a ball. "What do you think Lord Alasdair did?"

"I believe he tried to make my son—David's son—into the image of himself."

They had made a half circle of the ballroom and were near the open French doors. "I'm not sure I understand."

"Shall we go out onto the terrace? I find I am in need of some air." They strolled outside and away from the steps to the garden. "Alasdair and David were very close, but I'm not sure Alasdair ever approved of my husband. In having Dom to raise, perhaps my brother thought he could correct all the problems he perceived in David." She rubbed her forehead. "You see, my dear, I am almost as much in the dark as you. I've only recently begun to realize that my brother purposely kept Dominic away from me."

The emptiness in her voice tugged at Dotty's heart. How and why the uncle would have done such a thing, she didn't know. Yet, a great injustice had been done to both Dom and his mother. She wanted to hug her future mother-in-law and comfort her. If they'd been alone she would have. "But I know he loves you."

"I hope so. Still, there are times I wonder if attending to me is more of a duty that Alasdair instilled in Dominic than a desire on his part."

She pulled her lip between her teeth. Dom did mention duty quite a bit, yet he seemed sincerely attached to his mother. What would Lord Alasdair have stood to gain by taking Dom away from his mother?

"At least I know he loves you, Dorothea."

The statement startled her. "Does he? I sometimes think it, such as when he apologized today, but he has never told me."

Yet neither had she told him.

"It is in his eyes when he looks at you. The same as the way David looked at me, and Worthington gazes at Grace."

Dotty's heart swelled with joy, and, if she was honest, relief. "Thank you."

Lady Merton took her arm again and turned back toward the doors. "Come see me tomorrow and we shall talk some more."

They had almost reached the doors when a murmur rose inside the ballroom. Nothing loud, simply a general noticing of some occurrence. The circle of guests parted as they began to enter the ballroom. Dotty glanced up. Dom stood at the head of the stairs, searching, and though he was in evening dress and his cravat was beautifully tied, the rest of him was slightly rumpled. As if he'd slept in his clothes.

"Heavens," Lady Merton said. "I have never seen him look like that before."

He grinned and waved, then went down the stairs. When he reached the floor, Dotty could only see the top of his burnished hair as he made his way straight through the crowd toward her, just as he had done earlier today.

Lady Merton made a choking sound. "He is so like his father."

Dotty's heart skipped a beat. He had never appeared so devilish, or dangerous.

"After what you told me," Dotty said, "I will not repeat that to him."

She glanced at Lady Merton; her eyes were misty, and she had a small smile.

When he finally reached them, he took Dotty's hand and bowed over it. "Thea, I must apologize for arriving late."

The faint smell of brandy hung around him, and his eyes were overbright. He really had been in his cups and might still be affected. Well, this, as her grandmother would say, is the time to show what she was made of.

"My lord." Dotty curtseyed. "I had no expectation you would rise from your sick bed to attend me."

"I could not stay away." His well-molded lips tilted up. "Am I in time for a waltz?"

"Indeed you are." If she thought he actually knew what he was doing, she would have been more than gratified. Yet, he swayed a little as he stood before her. She suspected it was the brandy talking, and wanted to roll her eyes. She stepped back, further onto the terrace, and he followed.

At present, she must find a way of making him leave the ball before he caused a scandal. Otherwise, Miss Smyth would have the prestige of the Marquis of Merton making a figure of himself. Nothing was more likely to ensure the success of her ball.

She caught Lady Merton's eye. "One dance."

Her ladyship nodded. "I shall go back inside. Follow as soon as you are able."

"Find Grace," Dotty mouthed before bringing her attention back to Dom. With luck, the fresh air would do him good. "Let us stroll for a bit."

Tucking her hand in the crook of his arm, she kept him in the light of the ballroom and far away from any shadows. The Lord only knew what mischief he would get up to in his present state. In a few moments, he began slowing and leaning heavily on her.

"Dorothea?" His mother's steps grew near.

"I need some help."

"Here." Matt appeared, taking Dom's other arm. The silly man merely blinked and grinned.

Shaking his head, Matt guided them through a parlor, down a set of narrow stairs, then to the main hall.

"You must know the house well." She allowed the butler to place her cloak over her shoulders.

"I had to sneak out of it once upon a time."

A few minutes later, Dotty and Lady Merton sat facing the front of the coach with Matt and Dom across from them. The outer coach lanterns cast just enough light for her to be able to make out his features.

Lady Merton gave a small sniff.

Dom lurched forward and would have fallen if his cousin hadn't steadied him. "Mama, are you all right?"

She waved her hand a bit, but her voice wobbled. "Yes, dear, I'm fine."

He sat back, but a moment later mumbled, "Must take care of you."

Suddenly more alert, she stared at him. "What did you say?"

"Nothing. Mustn't bother you. I'm Merton now." Dom looked at his mother and frowned. "You don't want to go to Bath again, do you?"

Lady Merton's brows drew together. "No, dear. Why do you ask?"

"Uncle said it's better for you to be in Bath. No point in me crying. Don't cry now though."

"No, you do not." She glanced at Dotty. "What else did Uncle say?"

Dom swung his head toward his cousin. "Always wanted to go to school. Never had anyone to play with. Even Garvey stopped coming round."

"Who knew," Matt drawled, "that Merton would be an introspective drunk? This could prove interesting."

Dotty scowled at him. "Matt, shush." Reaching out, she covered Dom's hand, wrapping her fingers around it. "Garvey and his father came to see you. He said your uncle wouldn't allow him in."

Her betrothed's frown deepened. "Didn't approve of Garvey. Didn't approve of anyone." Dom glanced at her. "Wouldn't have approved of you."

She did not doubt that in the least.

He grinned boyishly, and said in a loud whisper, "But I'm going to marry you no matter what he says."

Matt groaned. A movement that appeared suspiciously like Lady Merton's leg striking out caught Dotty's eye.

Dom grabbed her hands and stared at her with an intensity she'd never seen in him before. "Thea, I want you."

Her cheeks began to burn. Thank God the light was dim. She took a moment to steady herself. "I want you, too."

"Well," Matt commented drily, "I'm glad we've settled that." He glanced out the window. "We have arrived."

The coach rolled to a smooth halt and a footman opened the door. Dotty withdrew her hands from Dom's. Once they were in the hall, it was clear his burst of energy had begun to fade.

"Dominic," Lady Merton said, "go on to bed."

He shook his head. "But Worthington and Thea."

Though Dotty could not approve of overindulging in drink, it certainly brought out another side of her betrothed. "We are leaving. I shall see you tomorrow."

He weaved just a bit. "If you're sure?"

Sleep would be the best thing for him. "I'm positive." She watched as a footman assisted him up the stairs. "Well, that was illuminating."

Lady Merton's countenance was awash with anger. "If Alasdair was still alive, I would kill him. Imagine telling a young child not to go to his mother, then keeping his friends away. No wonder Dominic was so lost when my brother died. He probably didn't feel as if he had anyone else."

"Well, he's defying his uncle by marrying Dotty," Matt said, apparently deciding levity was called for.

She fought down the blush as she remembered Dom's words in the carriage. "Very true."

"Merton's going to have a devil of a head in the morning." Matt turned to Lady Merton. "I can send over a recipe if you don't have one. It will make even a dead man feel better."

She pulled a face. "Please do. We have one. I gave it to him earlier. However, it does not seem to have worked very well. After seeing him earlier, I honestly do not know how he managed to get up."

"And dress," Dotty added. "He appeared as if he had done it without his valet. I wonder how that happened."

Dom was awake, but when he tried to open his eyes, the lids wouldn't cooperate. A bird made a loud racket outside his window, adding to his aching head, and his mouth felt like someone had stuffed dirty rags into it. He cast back in his mind for the reason he felt so badly. Ah, brandy. His uncle had warned him about it. Apparently, he'd not listened.

"Kimbal."

Long moments passed, and the man didn't answer. "Kimbal," he tried saying a little louder. His door opened. "I want Kimbal."

"I'll be right back, my lord." The door closed. He would have to speak to his butler about the footman slamming the door.

A few minutes later, Paken entered. "Yes, my lord."

Dom finally got his eyes open. Luckily the chamber was devoid of bright light. Although it must be late in the morning for that bird to be so cheery. "Where the devil is Kimbal?"

A smug expression briefly graced Paken's face.

Why was it he had servants that let you know what they were thinking, when Worthington's wouldn't crack a smile?

"You sacked him, my lord. Your new valet will arrive within the hour."

Fired Kimbal? What had Dom been thinking? Actually,

to be honest, he had wanted to get rid of the tyrant for a while, but his uncle refused to allow it.

A footman entered with a tray he set on the side table.

"My lord"—Paken picked up a large mug—"if you'll drink this first, you will begin feeling better."

At this point, Dom would try anything, especially with that damn bird outside. Having a vague recollection of how bad it tasted, he held his breath and downed it, but it wasn't as horrible as the stuff last night. "Coffee."

A cup was placed in his hands. "Thank you." He took a sip, savoring the heat and slight bitterness. He may as well know the worst. "Tell me what happened."

"You came through with flying colors, my lord. You even managed to attend the ball."

A memory stirred, but he had trouble bringing it into focus. "The Smyth ball?"

"Yes, my lord."

He stifled a groan.

"Her ladyship?"

"Brought you home with Lord Worthington and Miss Stern's help."

How much worse could this get? Being in ones altitudes in the company of one's betrothed. He would be fortunate if she didn't call off the wedding. He'd probably made a complete fool of himself. He tried to sit up and moaned as a pickax hit his head.

Paken took the empty coffee cup. "You're to stay in bed for the next hour. I shall send up a tray for you."

Dom glanced at the mantel but couldn't make out the numbers on the clock. "What time is it?"

"Close to two." Paken fluffed Dom's pillows. "The ladies will expect you for tea."

"Ladies?"

"Her ladyship and Miss Stern. Sir Henry and Lady Stern are due to arrive later this afternoon."

His mother and Thea probably planned to ring a peal over his head. "You said I had a new valet?"

Paken bowed. "Indeed, my lord. Mr. Wigman comes highly recommended."

Dom started to nod then stopped when his head started throbbing again. How anyone could live through this day after day, he would never know. "I believe I'll sleep some more."

"Yes, my lord." His butler left, closing the door softly behind him.

Two hours later, feeling much more the thing, he had eaten, bathed, met his new valet, and dressed. Wigman was a cheerful fellow who didn't argue about every detail of Dom's costume, and did not remind him of his importance with each breath. He had never known what a relief it would be particularly when his uncle's voice was constantly in his head.

He went to his mother's parlor, ready for the verbal flogging he was sure to receive. Merton or not, he was sure to have behaved badly last evening.

He knocked and entered the room. Thea glanced up. Her smile took his breath away, and she didn't appear at all angry; neither did his mother. "Good afternoon, Mama, Thea." He sat next to her on the sofa and took a cup of tea she handed him. "I'm here to apologize. I seem to be doing that quite a bit lately."

Thea raised a brow, but her eyes danced with laughter. "The first time my brother Harry came home in his cups, Papa woke him early the next morning and made him clean the stables."

Dom's stomach clenched. "I take it that was the last occurrence."

"To the best of my knowledge." She nodded thoughtfully. "Papa says all young men need to try it."

He had heard so many things about Sir Henry, Dom didn't

know if he was looking forward to meeting the gentleman or not.

She gave him a sympathetic look. "How are you feeling?"

"Paken tells me your parents arrive today."

"We received a messenger this morning. Mama is still using two canes, but she wouldn't remain at home any longer. She's very much like my grandmother in that respect."

He supposed he could veer the conversation to the duchess, but that wouldn't tell him what he needed to know. For some reason, he could not remember most of last evening. He closed his eyes for a moment. "Did I embarrass you last night?"

His mother brought her cup up to cover her lips, but she couldn't hide her chuckle.

Thea didn't even try to hide her mirth. She laughed. "In short, no. Though if Matt hadn't got us in the coach, there was ample room for the possibility. The only thing you did was appear in the ballroom and walk straight to me."

"After waving," his mother added.

Why would he . . . "Waving?"

"Yes." Thea grinned. "You stood on the steps to the ballroom, found me, and waved."

He dropped his face to his hands. "I'll never live this down."

"Come, dear," Mama said, "it is not so terrible. You merely looked like a young man in love."

Beside him, Thea's blush almost matched the bright pink of the trim on her gown. "'In love,'" he parroted. Yesterday, he'd come to the realization that he was in love with her. Thea stared at the tea service, and he knew he couldn't disappoint her. Taking her hand, he brought it to his lips. "Yes, very much in love."

She raised her head and the deep affection in her eyes shocked him.

"I as well," she said quietly.

Perfect. He wanted to groan. Now all he had to do was to keep their love from destroying everything. This was a disaster.

Chapter Twenty-Three

Try as she might, Dotty could not fall asleep. It must have been the excitement of seeing her parents again and moving to a new house. Her new home.

Mama and Papa arrived as expected, but Mama was in pain, though she tried to hide it. Grandmamma, who deigned to dine with them, joined forces with Dom and called a doctor who had trained in the newest methods in Austria. He said the leg had not healed and prescribed a tea with comfrey as well as some other herbs. He also gave Mama laudanum for the pain, then lectured her about using it only when she had to.

Dotty rose and searched through her books. Unfortunately, she'd finished reading her newest novel. Grabbing her wrapper, she shoved her feet into her slippers. Taking up the candle on the bedside table to illuminate the way, she went downstairs to the library. After quickly finding the right section on the shelves—Dom had a wonderful library—she perused the books and was surprised to find a good selection of novels. She reached for *Midnight Weddings,* a novel she hadn't yet read, when the silence was broken by a click.

Her heart leapt into her throat. *Get a hold of yourself. There is no reason to be frightened.* What, after all, could happen in the Merton library? Nevertheless, the boy that had been following her haunted Dotty. What if someone had broken into the house?

Hugging the book against her chest, she picked up the candlestick and swung it back and forth in the direction of the door to see what had made the noise. Well, she wasn't going to cower behind the shelves. "Who is there?"

"Thea, it's only me." Dom's deep voice reached her through the darkness on the other side of the room.

Thank the Lord. Her hand shook as she set the light back on a table. "Dom."

In less time than it took for her to draw another breath, his arms folded around her. "Did I frighten you?" He kissed her forehead. "I didn't mean to."

"I'm all right. I did not think anyone else would be up." Though she had stopped trembling with fear, her heart still pounded against her chest as he nudged her chin up and pressed soft kisses on her neck. Reaching up to wrap her arms around his neck, the book fell to the floor with a soft thump.

The palm of his hand moved down to cup her bottom, drawing her flush to him. "Thea, my darling Thea."

This time Dotty shivered for an entirely different reason. He had never called her his darling before. While one hand kneaded her bottom, creating a heat in the pit of her stomach, the other lightly rubbed a breast. His lips reached hers, and she opened her mouth, eager to feel his tongue against hers. The thin linen of her nightgown rasped her already-sensitive flesh. She moved her hand over the rough embroidery of his dressing gown. It opened slightly to her touch, allowing her to tangle her fingers in the soft hair covering his chest.

Dom groaned, pulling her closer. Although they were doing nothing they hadn't done before, somehow this was different. All the other times they'd been fully dressed. Now, only two fine layers of cloth stood between her and him. Did he have anything on under his dressing gown? A hard ridge rode against her stomach. The tingling that started when he'd touched her breasts and bottom met and coalesced before shooting down to the place between her legs. She needed him to take her. To make her his. If only she could be wanton enough, or brave enough to tell him.

His voice was a rough, anguished whisper. "Thea, please."

Joy filled her soul. "Yes. Oh yes."

Sweeping her up into his arms, he headed toward the fireplace, the opposite direction from the door. "Where are we going?"

"To my chambers. There's a secret passage."

He reached out and shifted one of the Greek maidens on the side of the mantel. A door swung open, revealing a narrow set of stairs.

Dotty giggled softly. "I've always wanted a house with secret passages."

"Hang on." Dom kissed her. "I'll have to carry you up sideways."

"I can walk."

"Dotty, are you in here?"

Lady Merton.

He said something under his breath that sounded like a curse, then gently slid her down until her feet touched the floor. "The candle."

Dotty bit her lip in frustration. If only she'd remembered to blow it out. "I'm here, my lady. I couldn't sleep, so I thought I would get a book."

The door clicked shut behind her, Dom was gone. She hurried to where she'd left the candle and picked the book up from where it had fallen.

"Neither could I." Carrying her own light, Lady Merton smiled. "It must have been the stuffed lobster."

Dotty considered walking toward the door to the corridor, then ducking around the shelves to the fireplace. If Dom was waiting, he could open the passage. "I'll bid you a good night."

Lady Merton reached out to the bookshelf. "Wait just a moment, and I shall accompany you to your room."

"Yes, my lady." Dotty clenched her hand. Her body was still alight with longing. All she wanted to do was find the passage and follow Dom. Once back in her chamber, she would either have to come back down here, or pass her parents' rooms and his mother's suite to reach his apartments. She cast a brief glance in the direction of the fireplace and stifled a sigh. It was probably too much to hope for another secret passage.

Lady Merton said good night to Dotty at her door. She entered the room, closed the door, and set her candle on the small side table. Her body still tingled and ached. If only there was some way to . . . The door leading to the next room opened, and Dom stepped through.

Swallowing a shriek, she flung herself into his arms. "How?"

His arms closed around her. "There's a short passage from my apartments to the end of this corridor. I think everyone's forgotten about it."

"We can't stay here," she whispered. "My parents are too close."

His palms skated up and down her body, heating her all over again.

"Thea, are you sure? I shouldn't even ask when you're under my roof. I should wait until—"

She cut him off with a kiss. "Yes. In three days we will be married. You are not seducing me. I want to be with you."

A low growl escaped him as his mouth covered hers. "I've wanted you since the first time I saw you."

Once they'd gained the corridor, he showed her a door set into the inner wall. It swung open silently. Someone must know about it. Otherwise the hinges would not have been oiled.

Dom held her hand as he walked ahead of her. In a few moments they reached his chamber. The bed, already turned down, appeared even larger now than it had during her house tour. Candles glowed from the candelabra on a round table, illuminating the snowy sheets. Tonight might be the first time she slept in it, but it would not be the last. She had declined the offer of her own bedchamber.

Dom wrapped his arms around her again. "Last chance."

She drew his head down, claiming his mouth as he had claimed hers earlier. "Never. I've had a lot of time to think about this."

"So have I. Too much."

Dom slid his hands under her nightclothes. The wrapper and gown slid off her shoulders landing in a soft plop on the floor. She glanced up at him as his gaze roved her body, and she started to cover herself.

He caught her hands. "No, let me look." He sucked in a breath. "You are even more beautiful than I had imagined."

Dotty's mouth dried, and her voice was thready. "Your turn."

She unbuttoned his banyan, pushing it off him, and stared. No statue could compare. Golden curls covered his muscular chest. His stomach was flat and strong, reminding her of the drawing of a discus thrower she had seen in one of her father's books. Dom's member jutted up between them. How large it was. She dragged her gaze back to his face. "You are perfect."

He drew her to him and laughed softly. "Not by any means, but thank you."

Just as she wondered what to do next, he picked her up and carried her to the bed, holding her to him as he climbed in.

"If I do anything you don't like, you must tell me."

She rubbed her hands over his chest, the hair soft and springy beneath her touch. "I shall."

Dom teased her mouth open, taking his time as he explored. She stroked her tongue against his, and he groaned. Her nipples ached and streaks of desire shot through her body, making her breasts tender and the place between her legs throb. He nibbled her jaw, fluttering kisses down her neck.

Dotty gasped when he drew a nipple into his mouth and pressed her legs together as the heat there grew.

"Are you all right?"

How could she not be? "Yes, oh yes."

He switched to her other breast, but rubbing the nipple he had been sucking between his fingers. Her whole body was on fire. Just when she thought she couldn't stand anymore, his lips and tongue moved over her stomach, down to her mons to a place she hadn't known existed, but was glad it did. "Oh God!"

"I appreciate your piety"—he chuckled—"but I would rather hear my name."

Dotty couldn't help but giggle. She couldn't believe the rogue, making her laugh at a time like this. "Dom. Do that again."

"What?" he teased, parting her legs with his shoulders. His tongue caressed her center. "This?"

"That's good, too." She panted and reached down, spearing her fingers through his hair.

Dom's low voice washed over her. "You taste better than any wine."

She raised her legs as his teeth lightly raked over her nub, then his tongue entered her, and she screamed. Her back arched as she shook with wave upon wave of pleasure. Nothing she'd heard had prepared her for this.

Dom lifted his head and inserted one then two fingers into her, prolonging Thea's climax. His shaft was harder than it had ever been, but if it was possible to make it good for her, he would. He covered her, positioning himself at her entrance, then thrust in, as her maidenhead gave way.

Thea gave a sharp gasp, and he waited. "My darling?"

Her face was pinched as if in pain. "I'll be fine. I knew it would hurt at least a bit."

She winced as he pushed in farther, and his heart twisted. If only he could keep from hurting her. "Try to relax. It will be easier for you."

Biting her lip, she nodded.

Damn him for a dolt. He trailed his tongue along the seam of her mouth. When she opened he captured her again. Stroking his tongue with hers and rubbing her breast with his chest. Finally her tension receded.

This time when he thrust she moved with him. "Put your legs around me."

Soon her heels pressed into his buttocks, urging him on. In a matter of moments, he thrust one last time, releasing his seed, swallowing both their cries with a kiss.

She was his. All of her. If only he didn't love her so much.

Rolling onto his back, he pulled her against him, stroking her as if he could make the pain she'd felt go away.

"How are you feeling?"

She was quiet for a few moments. "I'm fine."

She didn't sound as if she was fine. "Sleep. I shall wake you when it's time for you to go back to your room."

Yawning, she snuggled into him. "Good night, my love."

Dom blew out the candles, plunging the room into darkness even though the drapes were open. Thea's breathing evened out, and he held her boneless body tighter against him. He'd never spent the night with a woman before, but he did not want to and could not let Thea go.

Thoughts raced through his mind. *Uncle Alasdair*. Damn him for being in bed with them. How could he have told Dom to never fall in love? If he had not, he would have missed Thea's lovely face in the throes of passion. He would have proposed to someone entirely different and completely wrong for him. He gave up thinking and let Morpheus take him, knowing when he awakened his love would be in his arms.

He woke several hours later to a gray light inching its way through the window. Thea slept soundly next to him, her head on his chest, and his arm still wrapped around her. Her long black tresses wrapped around his fingers and spread over her, shielding much of her body from his gaze. This was how he wanted to waken every morning, though possibly a bit later. In fact, why the devil was he awake at this hour?

A scratching on the door to his dressing room roused him. Kimbal? Had they woken him when they'd made love? He certainly wouldn't approve. No, wait, Kimbal was gone. It had to be Wigman, but he didn't sleep in the dressing room. What was he doing up this early?

Dom glanced at the clock on the mantel. Five-thirty already. He had to get Thea back to her room before any of the servants saw her.

Unwilling to wake her, he carefully slipped out of bed, donned his dressing gown, wrapped her in her robe, grabbed her nightgown, then scooped her up in his arms and went through the door to the connecting corridor, entering her chamber as he had the night before.

She stirred as he drew the covers over her. "Dom?"

"You are in your own bed, sweetheart. Sleep for a while longer."

"Um."

The desire to climb in and hold her again was almost too strong. He made his way back to his own bed before the temptation overcame good sense.

For the first time since his father died, the bed was large and lonely. Unable to sleep, he tried to sort out what had happened between Thea and him. He'd never felt anything like this before. He needed Thea the same as he needed air

and water, and it scared him to death. How would he keep
his love for her from destroying everything they had?

Dom entered the breakfast room as Sir Henry accepted
a cup of tea from Paken. Dom's future father-in-law was like
no one he had ever met before, certainly not like the squire
near Merton who typified a country gentleman. Hunting
mad, a bit rough around the edges, and ever willing to curry
his attention. Sir Henry was cultured and serious, yet with
a wicked sense of humor that he did not mind wielding.
"Good morning, sir."

"Good morning to you as well, Dominic."

Any attempt at formality had quickly gone by the way
yesterday. Sir Henry treated Dom as if he were any young
man about to wed his daughter. And in spite of all his previous misgivings, it was a relief. He had never had a comfortable home life. Perhaps now he would. Of course, he
still had to pass muster with Thea's brothers and sisters.
What a strange thought that was. All of whom would descend upon them tomorrow.

Sir Henry finished his tea and stood. "Sorry to desert
you, but I've got business to see to while I'm in Town."

"Please feel free to do as you please. The only plans we
have today are the duchess's ball this evening."

"Won't do to forget that." He chuckled. "I'd never hear
the end of it."

Dom did not doubt that at all. Between the duchess and
Lady Stern, it was easy to see where Thea got her strength.

"Good morning, Papa." Thea entered the room, reached
up and gave her father a kiss on the cheek. "Are you off
already?"

"Good morning to you, my dear. I should be back by
tea." He gave Thea a quick hug.

She took her seat at the table, and Paken set a fresh pot

of tea before her. "Thank you, Paken." She turned to Dom and smiled. "Tell me how you like your tea."

After their lovemaking, he had been afraid she might remain in her chamber this morning, but she didn't appear to be at all embarrassed by last night. He sat next to her. Marriage with her would be very easy to get used to. "Strong with milk and two lumps of sugar."

She took a piece of toast. "We shall give it a few more minutes to brew."

"Have you seen the picture gallery yet?"

"No." She pulled the jam pot to her. "Your mother thought you would like to show it to me."

"Shall we do it after breakfast?"

She picked up the teapot and poured two cups, adding milk and sugar, then handed him one. "Try this."

He took a sip. "Perfect."

"Thank you. After breakfast will be fine. I am to tell you our mothers are breaking their fast together and that my mother is doing much better."

Afterward, he led her to the gallery. "The one at Merton is massive, but you'll get an idea. I think everyone has at least a miniature here."

"It is much the same at Bristol House."

He'd forgotten that she would be used to the duke's estates. "Here is the First Marquis of Merton. Before then we were viscounts."

"From the hair and dress, he looks to have lived in Charles the Second's time."

"Yes. That is who elevated the house."

She grinned. "What, no earls?"

He gave a mock scowl. "Only on Worthington's side. His title is actually much older, and inherited through"—he drew her to another portrait—"this fellow's wife during Queen Anne's time."

"It is amazing how the same color blue appear in the eyes of almost all the men."

He grinned. "The Bradford blue. It has been said that a Bradford man can tell if a child is his by the eyes. I suppose I should say the Bradford-Vivers blue. Until now, I never understood why a man would take his wife's name."

She moved down the wall. "Who is this?"

"My grandfather."

"Here is your mother." She glanced at him. "You were a beautiful baby. I did not realize your father had blond hair as well. You are very like him."

Dom gazed up at the painting of a young man, his father, holding a baby, his wife seated. A large hunting dog stood next to him. He did look just like his father. But he wasn't like him at all. He couldn't be.

He remembered the day his father had died and his uncle came. He had been six years old and had tried to hug his uncle Alasdair, needing the comfort, but after one brief embrace, his uncle set him aside. *"You are Merton now. You must behave as such. You cannot afford to indulge in maudlin emotions. Now, stop crying—you have duties to attend to."*

"I want Mama," the child had said.

"The doctor has given her something to make her sleep. This is what happens when one has such violent emotions for another. You may go to her after you've controlled yours." His uncle took his hand. *"For your own good and that of your dependents, I trust you will never form such a passionate attachment to a woman."*

"What was he like?"

Thea's question brought him out of his reveries. "He was passionate. About everything, but especially my mother."

He couldn't tear his gaze from the painting.

"And you too, it seems. Normally, the woman holds the baby, but he is holding you."

Dom's throat closed and his eyes grew moist. God, no, he couldn't cry. He hadn't cried since the day his father died. "Excuse me. I must go."

He took a step, and she grabbed his arm. "Dom, please tell me what is troubling you."

"I can't talk about it now." He glanced at her concerned face. "Thea, let me go."

She bit her bottom lip and released his arm. "Very well. For now. But you must tell me eventually."

Striding back down the gallery, he went to his study, but it wasn't the place he needed to be. This was where he performed his duties, where he wasn't allowed to feel anything. Where then? Leaving, he let his feet carry him to the schoolroom. Not the same one he had been in when his uncle had come to him, but close enough. Thankfully, it was empty. All the toys he'd had before his father's death were still there. The tin soldiers he and his father had played with, waging imaginary wars. The bat and ball his father had bought him to learn cricket. He had not touched a toy since that day. There was one adult-sized chair, and memories of his father rocking him in this same chair overwhelmed him. Sinking down onto it, he covered his face. Tears began leaking through his closed eyelids and down his cheeks. *"Papa, why did you leave us? Why did you leave me?"*

Sometime later, after the room had darkened, soft footsteps neared him. "Dominic," Mama asked, "are you all right?"

"I don't know. No. Everything I've believed in for years . . . is falling apart."

She sank down onto a stool and took one of his hands. "Tell me what it is."

He gazed at her, the need to unburden himself almost too much to bear. "I don't know if I can. Uncle Alasdair always told me not to bother you."

His mother's lips pressed together, forming a thin line. "If Alasdair was not already dead, I would murder him myself. What on earth was he thinking? Tell me now. *Everything* he said."

A short bark of laughter shot out from Dom, startling

him. He had never seen his mother behave so fiercely
before. "After Papa died, Uncle Alasdair told me I was now
Merton and it was my duty . . ."

As his mother listened, myriad emotions passed over her
face. At one point, she took out a lace-trimmed handkerchief and dabbed her tears. When he finished, she closed
her eyes for a moment and shook her head. "I never should
have listened to Alasdair. I should never have trusted him.
What he told you was not the truth."

Dom sat up. "What do you mean?"

His mother stared down at her hands for a few moments
as if gathering her thoughts. "It is not that he lied, precisely,
but he saw things only from his point of view. He and your
father were close friends, but disagreed on almost everything."

That was news. "Even politics?"

She nodded. "Especially politics and the duties of the
aristocracy. Your father believed that it was the duty of
the peerage to keep the king in check, and care for all the
people in the land, rich and poor." Her lips flattened into a
thin line. "Your uncle believed duty to the king took precedence over all else, and that a person's station in life was
ordained by God, and any evil that befell one was by that
person's choice. Yet, your father knew my brother loved you
and me."

His throat began to throb painfully and the fear that he
had not run out of tears rose in him. "Tell me what happened when Papa died."

Mama twisted the handkerchief in her hands. "He was
helping at the mill. They were installing a new type of wheel
when everything went horribly wrong, and Papa was crushed
by the wheel. We got him back to the Hall as soon as possible, but he was bleeding internally and passed shortly afterward. I was pregnant and lost the baby. At your uncle's
urging, I went to Bath for my health. By the time I had recovered, Alasdair was in place, and you seemed to be

doing well. I suppose I thought that because of your youth, Papa's death was easier for you. I did not know that Alasdair forced you to bury all your grief and tried to make you into a version of himself." She blinked several times before continuing. "He did not do as your father wanted."

Dom was having a hard time taking it all in. His father had died doing his duty. Something he would have done in the same circumstance. "But everything couldn't have been false. Uncle Alasdair said Grandpapa died young from loving his wife too much."

"If you can call five and sixty young,." Mama scoffed. "Dominic." She reached out, covering his hands with hers. "When the feelings are returned, there is no such thing as loving one's spouse too much. Your grandfather died from a chill he caught trying to get home. What Alasdair did not tell you, or perhaps did not know, is that your grandparents never spent more than one night apart the whole thirty-five years they were married." She smiled at him. "Bradford men love passionately, Dominic. Even you, if you will allow yourself to."

Rising, she left him alone with his thoughts. He had been trying to find a way not to love Thea as much as he did, and it was all for nothing. He scrubbed a hand over his face. She had looked so hurt earlier, when he wouldn't confide in her. Yet, maybe it wasn't too late. He would tell her everything. In any event, she deserved to know. He pushed himself out of the rocker and glanced around. One day he would be here playing with his child, but now it was time to find his wife.

Chapter Twenty-Four

Dotty walked slowly back down the gallery. She had to find a way to convince Dom to confide in her. What kind of marriage would they have if he did not?

"Dotty, Dotty." Tom's shrill voice echoed off the walls.

"I'm here, sweetie. What are you doing back so soon?"

"I missed his lordship and Cyrille."

She couldn't help but laugh. "What is it you need?"

"Sally is out." He placed one small hand confidingly in hers while he held his portfolio in his other. "Can you take me to the Park to draw? Mr. Martin gave me an assignment to complete before he comes again."

Part of her wanted to wait and speak with Dom. They must straighten out their differences before the wedding, yet perhaps a quiet place to think would be best now. "Of course. Let me get my spencer and bonnet. I shall meet you in the hall."

Tom skipped back down the gallery and disappeared. A few minutes later, Dotty joined him. The footman, Willy, who was assigned to Tom, was summoned. Dotty missed Fred, but had agreed with Dom that Matt's servants had no need to attend her at Merton House. After having been followed that day, some of Dom's grooms were always in the square, making sure no one watched the house.

The Park was largely deserted by the fashionable when they arrived. Avoiding the area where the other children were playing, Tom found a place with a bench where he could sketch. Although in very short order, he was ensconced on the grass at the base of a large elm tree.

She took out her pocketbook to review her list of projects. The attempt was unsuccessful as all she could think about was Dom and how distant he had been today. Perhaps she should ask for Lady Merton's help. Dotty would wager her last penny that most of her betrothed's problems stemmed from his uncle. It was probably a good thing the man was dead, otherwise she'd throttle him. Yet the fact that he was no longer with them might be worse. If Lord Alasdair was alive, it might be easier for Dom to rebel against the man. If only she knew what to do.

She closed her eyes and bit her lip hard as tears tried to escape.

"Hey, what you think you're doin'?" Willy shouted.

She jerked her head up as a large thug reached out and grabbed her arm, his fingers digging in painfully. His accomplice held Willy, twisting his arm behind his back. She glanced over at Tom who was not where he'd been five minutes before. Oh God. Please. It can't be the thieves trying to get him back. She prayed he'd got away. At least he knew how to return home.

Hoping someone would hear her, she screamed as loudly as she could until a meaty hand clamped over her mouth, dragging her to a black coach trimmed in gold. Not the robbers or the men who were kidnapping the women. Who then?

Dotty's bonnet tilted over her eyes as she landed on the seat and the coach took off with a jerk. Trying not to tremble, her stomach lurched and her hands grew clammy inside her gloves. Her heart crashed painfully against her chest. She'd never been so frightened in her life. Who would want *her*?

After taking a few deep breaths, she found the courage to straighten her hat, but hadn't raised her gaze. Then she saw them. Even in the dim light, her pale face was reflected back at her in a pair of black boots trimmed with gold tassels. *Fotherby?*

Anger and confusion raged as she raised her head to meet his smug countenance. He may be one of Dom's oldest friends, but her betrothed would kill him for this. Or would he? Perhaps that was what had been bothering him. He really did not wish to marry her.

She gave herself a tiny shake. *Stop being a wet goose.* Dom was much too honorable to have agreed to this, especially after making love to her. And he did love her. She knew it to the soles of her feet and deep in her bones.

If Fotherby thought he was going to scare her, he'd better think again. She lifted her chin. "What," she asked in a icy tone, "do you think you are doing, my lord?"

Elizabeth was in the morning room working on some very delicate white work for the handkerchief she was embroidering for her father's birthday, when Lavvie burst into the room smiling.

"I've solved all your problems," she announced, pulling off her gloves.

Elizabeth narrowed her eyes. She had the distinct feeling she wasn't going to like what Lavvie had to say. "What problems?"

"Why, Merton of course."

A chill ran up Elizabeth's spine. Her voice was much fainter than she'd meant it to be. "Merton?"

Her cousin removed her bonnet, sitting next to her on the chaise. "Yes. I would give it a few months, but he will be happy to marry a lady as steady as you."

Anger replacing astonishment, Elizabeth pushed her tambour aside. "Lavvie, what have you done?"

"I have just made sure Miss Stern would not be able to attend the wedding." When Elizabeth started to rise, Lavvie continued. "I've done nothing to harm her. I merely put it around that at the end of the day, marrying a marquis was too much for a country squire's daughter, and she ran home to her mother."

"Lavvie, have you lost your mind?"

Her cousin's eyes widened. "Miss Stern will be fine. She is housed not too far from Town, and in two days she will be released and provided a coach for her journey home. Naturally, she'll not want to show her face in Town again, at least not for a Season or two."

Elizabeth stared at her cousin, unable to understand how Lavvie could be so proud of essentially ruining another lady. This was undoubtedly the stupidest thing she could have done.

Elizabeth rose and struggled to keep from shouting. "*She will never be able to show her face anywhere*. After jilting Merton, what man would want her? And what will happen when it gets out that you orchestrated Miss Stern's disappearance?"

Lavvie paled just a little. "Oh, you've no need to worry about that. Fotherby was the one who actually abducted Miss Stern."

For a moment Elizabeth thought she would faint. "Why? Why did you do it?"

"To save you. If you do not marry Merton, who knows who your father will select next? He could be like . . ."

Her cousin fell silent.

"Manners? Is that what you were about to say? Lavvie, has he hurt you?"

Her voice was tight as she avoided Elizabeth's gaze. "He doesn't beat me."

She pulled her cousin into a hug. "Oh my dear. Papa would never make me marry someone I did not wish to."

Lavvie sobbed. "That's what I thought about my father as well."

Elizabeth thought back and realized she had not seen her cousin in private since that night Merton and Miss Stern became engaged. It was possible Lavvie didn't know Papa had lied. "I must tell you, we are not broke. It was all a hum. Papa told me that so I would marry Merton."

"Not broke?"

Elizabeth shook her head. "No, and I wouldn't marry him anyway. He is in love with Miss Stern." Elizabeth walked to the door to the terrace and back again, stopping in front of her cousin. She took Lavvie's hand. "As I have no need to marry for money, I want to marry for love. We need to tell Merton. When he finds her gone, he will be frantic with worry."

"It's too late." Tears filled Lavvie's eyes. "I received the message from Fotherby. She was taken this morning."

"Surely you know where."

"Well, sort of. Fotherby has a house near Richmond, but I don't know its exact location."

Elizabeth tugged the bell pull and a footman opened the door. "I need my bonnet, gloves, spencer, and my maid."

"Elizabeth!" Lavvie shrieked once the door closed. "What are you planning to do?"

"Tell Merton. He might know where Fotherby's house is." Lavvie's face lost all its color. "I will try not to mention your name, but is there a relative you can visit for a few weeks? You won't like missing the rest of the Season, but there will be less talk if you are not here."

She nodded. "I have already made plans to visit an aunt in the north, but why is it so important? I am sure Fotherby will not tell anyone."

Doing her best not to shout at her cousin, Elizabeth pressed her lips together. "You have picked the wrong country miss to play with. Her grandmother is the Duchess of Bristol. The betrothal ball is this evening."

For a few moments, Lavvie seemed frozen in place. Then she collapsed onto a chair. "Oh no. What have I done?"

Elizabeth donned her spencer and bonnet, which had arrived. It was time her cousin learned to cease meddling. "Add to that, her parents are in Town, and she has moved to Merton House."

Lavvie's already-pale complexion whitened even further. When she finally spoke, her voice was little more than a whisper. "How could I have been so stupid? I only meant to help you, and I've made such a mess of things."

"I shall take care of it," Elizabeth said, using a hard tone. "Pray God that no one finds out about your involvement. We would never survive the scandal." She embraced her cousin, brushing back one of Lavvie's curls. As much trouble as she had caused, she was still Elizabeth's closest friend. "I shall tell you how it goes."

For a moment her cousin clung to her. "I am leaving Town today."

Elizabeth nodded. "That is probably for the best. I shall miss you."

"And I you. It will probably be a while before I can write."

"I must go." She gave her cousin a quick kiss, leaving Lavvie to compose herself.

Tom, followed by his footman, Willy, who appeared much the worse for wear, dashed up the steps as Dom was about to descend them.

"My lord," Tom gasped. "Someone's 'ducted Dotty."

For a moment everything seemed to move more slowly than normal, and Dom's heart stopped beating. *No!* It was impossible. Nothing could happen to her. He addressed the footman, "Where is Miss Stern?"

"It's like Master Tom said, my lord. She's been taken.

Two big blackguards came at me. One held me in a lock and the other grabbed her. Master Tom hid behind the trees, but he drew a picture of the man in the coach."

Tom shoved the tablet up to Dom. "That's the gentleman that drove off with her."

He couldn't believe this was happening. It was all wrong. Images of Thea being taken to a brothel or to the docks assailed his mind. If she was harmed, it would be his fault. He should have never walked away from her this morning.

Tom shoved the drawing under Dom's nose, and his mind skittered to a halt. Fotherby? Why the devil would he take Thea? He didn't like her, but this was beyond the pale. Kidnapping an innocent, well not so innocent any longer, but bloody hell, the blackguard had abducted Dom's bride. Maybe Lady Fotherby was right. Her son was a loose fish. All he knew was that when he got his hands on the blackguard, he was going to kill him. He growled. "Paken, get a hackney."

Worthington entered the hall. "I've come to ask if Tom would like to play with my brood."

That was the other thing that wasn't right. "Wait just a moment. Isn't Tom supposed to *be* at your house?"

The child's face screwed up. "I missed you, so I came home."

"Take Tom with you." Dom raked a hand through his hair. "We'll sort this out later. I have to go."

Worthington lowered his brows. "What's going on?"

Tom jumped up and down waving the drawing. "Fotherby 'ducted Dotty and we're going to go save her."

Good God. Why did everyone in his house want to rush off rescuing everyone else? "*We* are not going anywhere. *You* are staying right here where you're safe. Paken, where's that hackney?"

"Merton, take a damper," Worthington barked. "We need more information before you go tearing off after Fotherby."

"I think I may be able to help."

Dom turned to the door and stared at Miss Turley. She swallowed. "I saw Lord Fotherby's coach on the Richmond Road early today."

Dom's fists clenched. The scoundrel. "Richmond?"

She appeared scared, but nodded. "Yes. I take it Miss Stern is not at home."

His temper rose and was hanging by a thread. Right now he wanted to throttle someone.

Paken bowed. "No, miss. Her mother arrived yesterday, and she is not at home to visitors."

Worthington rubbed his hand over his face. "What's in Richmond, or is he taking her farther west?"

To think Dom had called that curst rum touch his friend. "He has a house there. We stayed overnight at it after watching a fight."

"Do you remember the direction?"

Dom rolled his eyes. "Of course I do. Let's get going. We haven't a moment to lose if we're to get her back for the duchess's ball." He crossed to a small writing desk and scribbled a note then handed it to Paken. "Get the town coach ready. This is the direction."

"My lord, what shall I tell their ladyships and Sir Henry?"

Despite everything, Dom grinned. "Tell them we've gone to Richmond." Dom glanced at Miss Turley still standing in the doorway. "Miss Turley, thank you for your help. I'd appreciate it if you did not repeat anything you heard."

"You may be sure I shall not." She descended the steps quickly.

"Paken, horses, now."

His butler sent one of the footmen running.

"Mine's in your stable," Worthington said as they made their way to the back of the house.

By the time Dom and Worthington reached the stables, their horses had been saddled. They rode as swiftly as possible through the busy afternoon traffic. It would take at least an hour for them to arrive and close to two hours before the coach reached Fotherby's manor house. The dinner prior to the ball started at nine o'clock. It was almost one o'clock now.

He scowled. "I'm going to murder Fotherby."

"So you've said. I don't blame you at all. Take my advice, and do it straight out and not in a duel. The ladies don't like them."

They reached the first toll and had to wait for the gate-keeper for so long, Dom was tempted to jump it. Finally, an old man came out and collected their money. They rode as fast as they could, slowing only to rest their horses at intervals, until the village of Richmond came into view.

Dom reined in. "It's not far now. About a mile past the village." For the first time he was a little lost as to how to proceed. "Do we just ride up the drive or go around to the back?"

"I would rather not be shot as a thief," Worthington replied drily. "We shall approach from the front." His lips twitched. "You may announce you are a marquis."

Dom tossed his head back and laughed. Since being around Thea, the only time his rank had mattered was when his uncle's voice had crept unbidden into his mind. "As I'm the one Fotherby's trying to hide her from, I do not think that will work. We'll pretend we're lost. If he has anyone other than the old couple who care for the house there, I'm more than happy to take them on."

And if anyone hurt Thea, Dom would not be responsible for his actions. It was time he behaved more like his father than his uncle.

Dotty waited impatiently for Fotherby to answer her. She drummed her fingers on the seat until finally he said, "I mean you no harm, but Merton deserves a suitable bride, and I intend to see he finds one."

Trying to control her temper, she bit the inside of her lip. "What do you plan to do?"

"I have an old manor house not far from Town. I'll hold you there until after the wedding. Once you leave Merton at the altar, he'll forget about you and find someone else to marry." Fotherby leaned back against the squabs. "Don't worry, your virtue is safe. We'll send you home to your parents in a couple of days."

Obviously, the saphead had not done his research and was unaware her parents had arrived at Merton House yesterday. "And who will want to marry me after I jilt Merton?"

Fotherby's jaw opened and closed like a fish. "Hadn't thought of that, but the scandal will blow over in no time. They always do."

Dotty held back a snort. He was an idiot. Mayhap they would stop and she could jump out of the carriage, but then what? With the shades down, she didn't even know where he was taking her. Did she even have enough money to travel back to London? Surely Dom would discover her missing and search for her. Yet, would he even think of Fotherby? No. Somehow she must rescue herself.

Closing her eyes, she tried to rest. Something would come to her. She was nothing if not resourceful.

When the coach stopped, she sneaked a peek at her pin watch. They'd been traveling close to two hours. Well, if they had gone north, she should recognize something; if not . . . Fotherby unlocked one of the doors and it opened. The footman standing next to it helped her down. An old couple stood in the doorway. Obviously the caretakers. They might help her.

"Well, here she is," Fotherby said as if they'd been expected. "I sent a message to her parents, and they will arrive in a few days."

The old lady glanced at Dotty and gave her a severe look.

"Don't try none of your tricks with us, miss. There will be no more running off with fortune hunters."

Obviously, there would be no help from the servants. If she thought she could get away with it, she would hit Fotherby. Instead, she assumed her most demure expression. "Indeed, Mrs . . . ?"

"Whitaker," the woman said, seeming surprised to be asked.

"Mrs. Whitaker"—Dotty added an injured tone to her voice—"truly, I thought he loved me, not my money. I never meant to do anything too wicked, and I would never dream of causing my parents any more distress."

Mrs. Whitaker seemed to thaw just a little bit. "You will be treated well here as befits your station, miss. But I'm sorry to say, you'll have to stay in your room."

"Of course, ma'am." Dotty lowered her lashes in a show of contrition. "I shall do as you say."

"Follow me then."

The coach drove off and, obediently, Dotty followed her gaoler. As the woman led her through the house, she took notice of every detail until they reached a large chamber on the first floor. "What a lovely home. How old is it?"

"Built during Jacobean times." Mrs. Whitaker bobbed a curtsey. "I'll bring you a nuncheon and tea."

"Thank you." Dotty gave a grateful smile. "That would be lovely."

The door closed and the lock clicked. She removed her bonnet and gloves. The first thing she must do was convince the housekeeper she was resigned to her fate.

A porcelain pitcher decorated with roses filled with warm water stood on a stand next to a matching bowl. Aside from the bathing stand, the room held an old oak wardrobe, bed, sofa, screen with a chamber pot behind it, and a dressing table with a chair. Dotty tested the window, but it wouldn't budge. A door to what looked like a dressing room was next to the fireplace. She lifted the latch, and it opened with ease.

When steps sounded outside the door to the corridor, Dotty rushed back into the bedchamber, taking a seat on the sofa. The housekeeper and her husband entered. He carried a tray filled with tea, sandwiches, and fruit. It was enough to feed three people, but if she could find a way to escape, the extra sustenance would come in handy.

Mr. Whitaker set the tray down on the table in front of the sofa. "Here you go, miss. Don't say we tried to starve ye."

Dotty smiled. "No, indeed. Thank you very much. I am extremely peckish."

Mrs. Whitaker pointed to the bell pull. "Ye just call if ye need anything. I put a nightgown and wrapper in the wardrobe for ye. Dinner is at five," she said defensively. "We keep country hours here."

"Truth be told," Dotty replied sincerely, "I prefer country hours."

Mrs. Whitaker nodded, her lips softening just a little. Given time, Dotty knew she could win the woman over, but time was one thing she did not have. She must not miss her betrothal ball this evening.

As she ate, she considered her options. If this house was truly as old as the housekeeper said, it might have a secret passageway. Most houses of that age did. No, they would never have put her in a room with an easy way to flee. Unless they thought she could not find it or . . . or if it was as in Merton House, mostly forgotten.

She spent the next hour knocking, poking, and pulling anything that could possibly be a hidden lever. Picking up another sandwich, she pulled the chair over in front of the fireplace and studied it. Yet, nothing popped out at her as being in any way different. Rising, she went back into the dressing room and knocked on the walls. Finally, she opened the wardrobe and ran her fingers over the seams. A few moments later, she hit a bump. It was in the shape of a rectangle. Could it possibly be a small lever? If so, it had been cleverly recessed into a corner. If she hadn't been searching so thoroughly, or if her fingers had been larger, she wouldn't have found it. Saying a brief prayer, she pushed it up and waited as a panel in the back slid open.

From somewhere in the house a door crashed open and shouting erupted.

"Where is she?" Dom's hard voice reached her.

Thank God he'd come for her! Her heart raced, making it hard to breathe.

Boots pounded up the stairs. She poked her head out of the dressing room at the same time the chamber door slammed open. Time seemed to slow for a moment, then she was in his arms, and shots were fired below.

Dom glanced at the door. "We need to get out of here."

"This way." She seized his hand, pulling him into the dressing room. "There is a tunnel."

Dom peered into the darkness and gave her a quick kiss. "How clever of you."

"I pray it leads to the outside."

"Even if it doesn't, it will give us time to elude your captors."

"Who is with you?"

"Worthington."

"I hope he hasn't been hurt."

"That would definitely complicate things. Let's go."

Holding one hand to the wall for balance, she followed him as they made their way down the old stone stairs. There was a dank smell to the air, and she grimaced at the thought of all the dirt. Her gloves would never be the same. Then she ran smack into Dom's broad back.

"A door," he whispered. "I hope it's not rusted shut." Releasing her hand, he tugged on the door. Moments later, with a loud screech, it flew back, and a wall of ivy greeted them. "You wait here. I must ensure Worthington is all right."

"No, I'm coming with you." Dom narrowed his eyes at

her, and she huffed. "What if the caretaker finds the tunnel? I am much safer with you."

"Very well," he said, not at all happy. "But if there is trouble, stay out of the way."

She nodded as he took her hand. Keeping close to the house, they rounded a corner and found themselves facing the drive. Matt stood on the steps, his pistol pointed toward the open door. Two horses waited patiently off to the side nearest her and Dom.

He whistled softly, and a neatish gray swung his head around and walked to them. After lifting her onto the horse, in one elegant movement, Dom mounted behind her, and barked, "Worthington, it's time to depart."

Matt reached in, slammed the door shut, and in a matter of seconds was on his horse, galloping down the drive. Dom and Dotty followed, not slowing until several minutes later.

Finally she breathed a sigh of relief. "I'm so glad you came when you did. I found the tunnel but had been trying to figure out how much money I would need for transportation back to London. I did not know if I had enough."

"I'm thankful you're not injured." Dom looked at her as if bemused. "Had you really been thinking of money for a coach?"

"Naturally, I had. I did not want you to—"

"You are remarkable." His lips took hers, and she threw her arms around his neck.

After a few moments, Matt coughed. "If the two of you wouldn't mind, we must decide what we're going to do while we wait for the coach. Is there an inn nearby?"

Dotty glanced at her gloves and the arm of her spencer. "Not one I would go to at present. Look how dirty I am."

For the first time Dom seemed to notice the state of her wardrobe. "It was rather filthy in there."

"How did you escape?" Matt asked.

She grinned. "There was a secret staircase."

"Thea had found it by the time I arrived." Dom tightened his grip on her. "My clever love."

She was pleased with herself as well, but it was time to decide how to return home. "We can't ride through Town like this."

"Quite true." Dom said, looking up the road. "The coach should be here soon."

"If nothing else," Matt added, "we can find a coaching inn and hire a carriage to take Dotty back to Town. We'll say she had an accident, which will account for her soiled garments."

"What an excellent idea." That would solve the problem. "It's always best to have an alternate plan."

Dom groaned. "Why do I feel as if I have a lot of catching up to do when it comes to subterfuge?"

She straightened her skirts as best she could, but there was still too much leg showing. "If we stop at an inn, I would like to send the Whitakers a note."

"The Whitakers?" Matt asked.

"The couple at the house. Although they would not have allowed me to go, they were very kind."

"That *kind* old man shot at me, and his wife tried to bash my head with a pan," Matt snapped. "The only reason I was still at the door was I knew he was out of bullets."

"Oh." Naturally, she'd remembered the shots, but then Matt had been unharmed. "It truly wasn't their fault. Fotherby told them I had eloped with a fortune hunter, and my parents would arrive in two days to take me home."

"Then let Fotherby tell them the truth," Matt growled.

"Did that bounder touch you at all?" Dom's voice was sharp as a blade and black with rage.

She shook her head. "No, no. He abducted me so we would not marry. He said he would send me home after I had missed the wedding."

"Merton," Matt said with a scowl, "if you don't end his worthless life, I'm sure the ladies will be happy to."

She twisted her head around in an attempt to see Dom's face, but he now held her so tightly, she couldn't see much of him. On the other hand, it was very pleasant, perhaps more than just pleasant being crushed against his hard body. Still, she would have liked to see his expression. He sounded thunderous. "I think we should tell his mother."

Both men seemed to be struck dumb, then Matt started to laugh, big belly laughs, and Dom joined in.

Finally, when it seemed they would never stop, Dom nuzzled the back of her neck. "You may not know it, my love, but that is a far worse punishment than I could ever mete out."

For the first time in her life Dotty wanted to preen. "He has a very nice house that is going to waste. I do not see why he cannot house war widows or orphans."

Dom kissed her ear. "You are diabolical, but will she go along with it?"

"I believe she will," Dotty smiled "I met her at Lady Thornhill's, and she is extremely interested in our cause. Now about the Whitakers . . ."

"No!" Dom and Matt said in unison.

"Ask my mother or better yet, yours, to write them when we return." He pulled her even more snugly against him, as if he would never let her go. "Speaking of dinner. We're never going to get anywhere plodding along at this pace."

Matt glanced over at them. "I seem to recall a coaching inn not far from here. If you'd like, I can go ahead and make the arrangements."

Just then, she glanced up the road to see a coach bearing down on them. "Move to the side!"

To her surprise the coachman pulled up the carriage and hailed them. "My lords."

"We didn't expect to see you for at least another half an hour," Dom called out.

"Mr. Paken told me to get to you as soon as I could."

The coachman tapped his nose. "I know every toll keeper around."

She breathed a sigh of relief. "Well, thank Heaven. Sweetheart, let me down."

Once she was in the carriage, he made to climb in after her. "Tie my horse on the back."

"Oh no, you don't," Matt said. "You're not married yet. Get back on your horse."

Dom swore under his breath. "But we're betrothed. It is perfectly acceptable."

"I don't care."

She put her hand over her mouth to keep from laughing. "Dom, just get on your horse, so we can go home."

"Two days."

"Yes." She nodded. "Then you may ride in the coach with me all you wish."

He gave her a swift kiss and remounted his horse. "There is no point in arguing. We have a betrothal ball to attend this evening."

"Now, ye just wait a minute there."

Dotty's eyes widened. Oh no! It was Mr. Whitaker. She would not go back to that house. "I did not expect to see you again. I wanted to say that I am—"

"No doubt about that, Missy. He pointed his rifle at the coachman. Ye just get down from there. I'm taking you back until your father comes for you."

"Look here." Dom's tone was haughtier than she had ever heard it. "Miss Stern told me what Fotherby said. It is a lie. I am the Marquis of Merton, and she is betrothed to me. Her parents are at my house in Town."

Mr. Whitaker scowled. "I know all about you lords. You can be anything you say you are and still be a fortune hunter."

"Here is my card." Dom reached into his pocket, and flushed. "I must have forgotten them, but this gentleman is the Earl of Worthington." Dom glanced at Matt. "Give him your card."

"I don't think I have them with me either."

Mr. Whitaker smirked. "Marquis this and Earl that. Sounds like a Banbury story to me. I'll just take the lady with me, and she'll be safe with my wife until it's sorted out."

For Heaven's sake! At this rate, she would miss her grandmother's ball. "Mr. Whitaker. If you do not believe them, come with us. I assure you, my mother and father, Sir Henry and Lady Stern, as well as Lord Merton's mother will swear to you that I did not run off. Our betrothal ball is this evening. My grandmother, the Duchess of Bristol is giving it and we must not be late." She paused for a moment and frowned at the older man. "And no shooting anyone."

Mr. Whitaker scowled, clearly undecided as to what to do when the coachman said, "Whitaker, is it?"

He nodded.

"I can vouch for their lordships and the lady. As they said, she was snatched from the Park this morning. But there is no need to take my word for it. You come up here and ride with me. Wouldn't want you to think you hadn't done your duty."

"Thank ye." Mr. Whitaker lowered his rifle. "I'll do that."

Dotty breathed another sigh of relief. "Take me home."

Chapter Twenty-Five

Dom rode next to his cousin in front of the coach. "I've decided being a marquis is not such a great thing after all."

"It's all what you do with it," Worthington said. "I wouldn't give up being an earl. I'm not ashamed to admit I like the privilege that comes with the title. But there are responsibilities as well, not only to my estates and dependents, but to society at large. It's something your father knew that your uncle never understood."

Dom mulled the thought over for a few moments. His cousin was five years older than he. "You knew my father?"

"Our fathers were friends."

That was a surprise. There were so many things he was just discovering. "I never knew."

"No. My father was another person of whom Lord Alasdair didn't approve."

They fell silent for several minutes, giving Dom a chance to think. How much had he missed? How much did he have to make up for? If Thea hadn't come into his life, he might never have found love, Tom would probably have been transported, and Cyrille would be dead. Not to mention the women they had saved. "I'd like to talk to you about legislation to help the poor."

His cousin gave a slow smile. "I'd like that as well. What do you have in mind?"

They turned into Grosvenor Square and pulled up to Merton House. Footmen ran out to attend to them. Whitaker was ushered in through the front door. Dom started to have Sir Henry or his mother called down, but after meeting Paken, Whitaker quickly decided Fotherby had lied.

Once Dotty disappeared to her chamber to see their mothers and ready herself for the ball, Dom led Worthington to the study and called for wine.

"What, no brandy?" Worthington joked.

The mere thought made him ill. "Not this early, at any rate." Dom wasn't used to this type of bonhomie with his cousin but decided he enjoyed it. "Worthington, I don't know how to thank you for accompanying me today."

"You can start by calling me Matt. We are family."

"Yes—yes, we are. A fact I will not forget."

Matt raised a brow. "You'll probably not get a chance. Remember, Dotty is best friends with Charlotte and Louisa."

"How could I forget?" Dom grimaced. "I trust Louisa will eventually forgive me for marrying Thea."

"I believe she already has." Matt cleared his throat. "I am almost sure I heard something about a kiss."

Dom blushed. There was no other word for it. "Um, yes. I have a hard time seeing anyone else when Thea's in a room."

"So I've noticed. I have a similar failing with Grace. It must be a Vivers fault."

"Originally, a Bradford fault if I remember correctly." Dom grinned

"Indeed." Matt set his glass down and stood. "I must go home. Tom has probably told everyone that Dotty was taken, and they'll be worried. However, I'll see you tonight." He shook Dom's hand and clapped him on the back. "I haven't said it before, but congratulations on your marriage.

Whether we call ourselves Vivers or Bradford, Dotty will make a good addition to the family."

"I agree, wholeheartedly. Thank you, again."

Dom sat twirling his wine for a few minutes after his cousin left, mulling over all that had happened in the past few days. He still hadn't had a chance to speak with Thea alone. Tonight, after the ball, he would tell her everything. Most importantly, that he would never shut her out of his life again.

Chapter Twenty-Six

"Miss," Polly mumbled, "stop your fidgeting while I get this last comb in place."

Dotty ceased trying to see how her hair was coming along and sat still until her maid stepped back.

"There now." Polly canted a second mirror. "Look all you like."

Finally, Dotty was able to make out the elaborate knot of coils and braids. "It is lovely. Where did you learn to do that?"

Polly grinned widely. "We looked at one of those magazines. May didn't think I could do it. My only regret is that she won't ever see it."

"Well"—Dotty barely kept herself from laughing—"my hair has never looked so elegant."

Her maid handed Dotty a flat square case. "This is from his lordship. He asked if you'd do him the honor of wearing it."

"Did Lady Merton leave something? She said she was going to."

"Yes, miss. A pair of earbobs. I'll get them next."

Dotty took the case, opened it, and blinked at the delicate gold necklace set with diamonds. "Oh dear. I have never seen anything so exquisite."

Polly handed her the earrings, also diamonds.

"How perfect they are with this gown." Dotty fixed them to her ears.

She drew her gloves on, while Polly placed a spangled shawl over her shoulders, then handed her a painted fan and a reticule in the same fabric as her gown.

Polly nodded with approval. "That ought to knock his lordship out of his shoes. You'll be the prettiest lady there."

Dotty did wonder what Dom would think. She descended the first level of stairs to the landing overlooking the large hall. He stood at the bottom, impressively dressed in black evening clothes. His cravat was perfectly tied. His only ornaments a pocket watch, quizzing glass, and a heavy gold signet ring.

He glanced up at her and his jaw dropped. "You are enchanting. Exquisite."

"Thank you, my lord." Dom's intense blue gaze warmed her, reminding her of last night when they had made love. Goodness, if his thoughts matched hers, they would be lucky to make it through the evening. She reached the bottom tread, and he took her hand. "The necklace is perfect. How did you know?"

"The image of you in diamonds"—Dom raised her fingers to his lips—"has teased me for a while now." He leaned closer and spoke in a deep, soft tone. "Though in my mind, they were the only thing you wore."

This was definitely an improvement. Perhaps being abducted hadn't been such a bad thing after all. "Perhaps"—heat rose in her cheeks—"your dreams can become reality."

His grip on her hand tightened. "Allow me"—his voice was a low growl—"to undress you tonight."

If only she could. "Soon we'll be married and you may do so every night."

She thought he would step back as he'd done previously when he allowed himself to desire her. Instead, he brushed his lips across hers. "That is a promise I will make sure you keep."

"Dominic?" Lady Merton said from the door to the drawing room. "Bring Dorothea and come in here. Sir Henry wishes to discuss what occurred today."

"Oh dear." Dotty glanced at Dom. "We forgot to consult Papa before sending the note to Grandmamma."

Dom rolled his eyes to the ceiling. "That was an oversight. I hope he agrees with us. Something tells me I don't want to be on your father's bad side."

Papa stood next to the sideboard pouring a glass of wine as she and Dom entered the drawing room. Her father held up the decanter, and she and Dom nodded. Once they were all seated, Dotty told them how the abduction had taken place and who had done it, as well as their decision to inform Fotherby's mother.

"Only because we don't wish to flee the country, sir," Dom said. "My first instinct was to kill the blackguard, but Thea came up with this idea."

Lady Merton nodded thoughtfully. "I agree with your plan. There is no one better to deal with Fotherby than his mother." She lifted her wineglass. "I doubt you will see him again until he can behave."

Suddenly, Dom had a wicked look on his face. "That's right. Lady Fotherby holds the purse strings."

What they were saying didn't make sense. "I do not understand," Dotty said. "Fotherby is of age and a peer."

If anything, his smile broadened. "Yes, but until Fotherby is forty or married to a lady his mother approves of, all the funds are in trust. He's on an allowance and a pretty small one if he's to be believed. All she has to do is demand he rusticate."

"Well, then," Mama said, "when do you wish to approach Lady Fotherby?"

Dotty smiled ruefully. "I sent a note to Grandmamma asking her to do it. With the rest of the family arriving tomorrow, and the wedding the next day, I decided that was the best way to handle it."

Papa leaned back against the chair cushions and chuckled. "You're a devious puss, I'll give you that. It'll be interesting to hear the result."

"I think," Dom said, "I'll take a look in at White's tomorrow."

Papa slapped his thigh and stood. "I think I'll go with you, my boy." He turned to Dom and lowered his brows. "Then we'll stop in at Brooks's and start your membership process."

Silence fell and Dotty tightened her fingers around Dom's hand.

He squeezed them in return. "Whatever you say, sir."

When they arrived at the Pulteney, Dom was still a little dazed at Sir Henry's proposal he join Brooks's. There was a good chance he'd be rejected. Yet, while he and Matt had ridden back to Town, they'd begun working on legislation to help the poor. A matter that would not endear him to his own party in the least. It might be time for more changes. Still, he could worry about that when he returned from his wedding trip. Speaking of his honeymoon, he'd not had any time alone with Thea since he helped her into the carriage earlier that day. The moment they'd arrived home, she'd been spirited away to dress. He'd not even been allowed a kiss, and he wanted much more than that.

However, the Pulteney, which was the former home of the Marquis of Bath, was very large. Surely there must be somewhere he could be alone with her. And Dom didn't care what anyone said. He had every intention of remaining next to her all evening.

His party was the first to arrive at the large salon set up as a drawing room. He glanced through the double doors leading to the dining room. A waiter handed them glasses of champagne as the duchess waved them over to a grouping of chairs and sofas. Matt and Grace accompanied by Charlotte, Louisa, and the Dowager Lady Worthington were announced not a quarter hour later. Lady Bellamny arrived with the ever elusive Lord Bellamny, a tall raw-boned man with red hair and a large smile. They were accompanied by a well turned out gentleman who looked to be in his mid-forties.

"I wonder how the devil he does it," Dom said to Matt in a low voice as Lord Bellamny greeted the duchess.

"Does what?"

"Keeps his wife in line."

Matt choked on his champagne. "He probably gave up the fight years ago."

They were called over to greet the new arrivals, and Dom noticed that Lord Bellamny looked at his wife like the sun wouldn't shine without her. Did Dom have the same expression on his face with Thea?

"And this is Viscount Wolverton." Lady Bellamny smiled as she introduced the gentleman to the other ladies. "He's been a friend for a long time, though he hardly ever comes to Town."

"Well, my dear," Lord Bellamny said, "you couldn't be here so often if it wasn't for his help."

Dom, his attention caught by the quick, intense glances exchanged between the Dowager Lady Worthington and Lord Wolverton, missed Lady Bellamny's repost, though it made everyone else chuckle.

The next to arrive were Lord and Lady Thornhill.

Frowning at her guests, the duchess announced, "The numbers are not even. Some of you gentlemen will have to escort two of the ladies." She turned to Charlotte and Louisa. "I didn't wish to give any of the young gentlemen the idea they were being singled out for you."

Charlotte turned a becoming shade of red, while Louisa thanked the older woman.

Dom made his way back over to Thea. Each time he'd attempted to keep her by his side, someone drew her away. Soon the men were in one group and the women in another. Across the room, Dotty blushed charmingly. "What can they be discussing?"

"The ladies?" Lord Bellamny asked, then continued before Dom could answer. "You're better off not knowing. It might embarrass you."

"Indeed, my boy." Sir Henry cracked a laugh. "There are some things about which we should not inquire."

Dom glanced at Matt to find him staring at Wolverton who seemed to have a hard time tearing his gaze from Matt's stepmother. "I wonder what that's about."

"I don't know, but I'll find out."

When the duchess's personal butler called them for dinner, Matt strode to Grace and was about to offer his stepmother his other arm when Wolverton beat him to it.

As the highest ranking man, Dom made his way to the duchess, but she waved him away. "Go find Thea. We are sitting informally this evening."

That was a welcome surprise. He bowed. "Thank you, Your Grace."

"You'd better start calling me Grandmamma."

It had been a long time since he'd had a grandmother and he grinned. "Thank you, ma'am."

Thea found him first and twined her arm in his. "Well, this is turning out to be an interesting evening."

They took their place behind the duchess. "Wolverton?"

She slid him a look. "Indeed. I'll tell you what I've learned later."

Covering her hand with his, he bent his head so no one could hear him. "I'm fairly certain that is not what I will wish to discuss."

Her breasts rose more rapidly, and her lips formed an "O." "No, perhaps not."

"Thea, I need to be alone with you."

Dotty's heart thudded harder. She wanted that as well.

"Merton," Lady Worthington said, "have you decided where you are going on your wedding trip?"

"Yes, ma'am. We shall spend a fortnight or so at a small estate I have near Penzance."

"After which," Dotty added, "we shall tour each estate. The trip could take several weeks."

Lady Bellamny glanced at the clock. "Do you plan to return for any of the Season?"

"Not if I can manage it," Dom muttered under his breath.

Dotty schooled her countenance to keep from laughing. "We don't know yet. It will depend on how the estate visits go."

Thankfully, the conversation turned from her and Dom to politics and philosophy. Grandmamma had the centerpieces removed to encourage talk across the table. Dom seemed a bit startled at first, but soon fell into the way of things. It seemed like no time at all before the butler announced that Grandmamma must prepare for the ball guests.

The group rose, and Dom took Dotty's hand. "Come with me. We should have a good half hour before the dancing begins."

"Dorothea, Dominic."

She turned to face her grandmother. "Yes, ma'am?"

"You two will join me in the receiving line."

He let out a low groan.

She tugged his arm. "Have you ever done it before?"

"No, Mama doesn't give large entertainments."

"Then it will be a good experience for you."

His breath and possibly his lips as well brushed past her ear, causing a shiver to streak through her.

"I'd rather practice something else." His voice was a deep whisper.

She beat down the heat rising in her breast. Not a week ago, Dom would have stiffly agreed to do his duty, instead of making suggestive remarks to her. His fingers caressed the back of her neck, and she swallowed. "Nevertheless."

"Come, you two." Grandmamma stood with one dark brow raised, but a small smile hovered on her lips.

"There really isn't any way out of this, is there?"

Dom took Dotty's arm and accompanied her into the corridor where the butler stood ready to announce the first names.

As they reached Grandmamma, she leaned slightly toward Dom. "You're becoming more like your father every day."

Dotty held her breath, but for the first time, Dom responded easily, "Yes. Yes, I am."

Not a quarter hour later, Lady Fotherby was announced. She curtseyed, then held her hands out to Grandmamma. "It's so good to see you again, Your Grace."

"You, as well, Catherine. I trust our little problem has been dealt with?"

"Yes, indeed." Lady Fotherby's eyes narrowed slightly. "Thank you for allowing me to handle it. You may rest assured my son will not be allowed off the estate until he has learned his duties."

Grandmamma bussed her ladyship's cheek. "I knew it was the right decision when my granddaughter suggested it." She motioned to Dotty. "This is my granddaughter, Miss Dorothea Stern. I believe you are already acquainted with Lord Merton."

"You will make a fine marchioness." Lady Fotherby smiled at Dotty. "My lord, congratulations on your good fortune."

Dom bowed, then placed his hand on the small of her back. "Thank you. I certainly have good fortune on my side."

An inward glow started in her stomach and spread

through her body, and she could not wait to begin their married lives.

Dom led Thea out for the first dance, which was fortunately a waltz. From the start, he held her closer than he ever had before. Years of worry over how he should behave fell away as he gazed into her brilliant green eyes. It was all he could do not to drag her off and find someplace to be alone with her. Fortunately, the ball was a crush, and there were so many couples on the dance floor that, during the turn, he was able to draw her against him. She moaned lightly as his leg moved between hers. "I need you."

Desire lurked in her eyes as she gazed up at him. "Yes."

That one word almost sent him over the edge. His member was harder than it had ever been. If he didn't make love to her soon, he'd go out of his mind. Why the hell hadn't he thought to reserve a chamber? Still, there must be somewhere they could go.

The set ended, and no sooner had they reached the side of the ballroom, Louisa, Charlotte, Miss Featherington, and another young lady descended upon them.

"Dotty." Charlotte took her arm. "You must come with us for a moment."

She cast him a chagrined look. "I won't be long."

His cousin and Miss Featherington giggled as they spirited her away from him. They must have planned it. He leaned against a pillar. If this was how the evening was to go, he may as well not even be here. A glass of champagne was pressed into his hand.

"Hide behind the plant." Matt took a sip of wine. "If you're caught not doing the pretty, one of the ladies will put you to work."

Dom gulped half his drink. "What about you?"

His cousin gave a sly smile. "I'm married and a chaperone."

"I'm betrothed. That ought to count for something."

"Only if you keep your lady next to you."

From the corner of his eye, he caught the sight of Lady Bellamny coming like a galleon in full sail toward him. "Damn. Which way did Thea go?"

"Across the room where the tall redhead is. I'll try to detain Lady Bellamny until you're away."

Nodding, Dom slipped behind the large potted palm. He circumnavigated the room until he stood behind Thea. He didn't know how she knew he was there, but she glanced over her shoulder and her face lit up.

"My lord, you are just in time to take a promenade with me."

He bowed. "My pleasure, Miss Stern." The other ladies giggled as they strolled off. "That is the last time I am letting you out of my sight this evening."

Her eyes widened. "Why? What happened?"

He steered them slowly but purposefully toward the terrace doors. "I made my escape as Lady Bellamny was bearing down upon me."

"Oh that"—her voice trembled suspiciously, as if she was trying not to laugh—"must have been dreadful."

Dom slid a glance at her. "Well, it was. Matt practically shoved me behind a plant. As it was, I had to cling to the edge of the room to get to you."

She drew her lush bottom lip between her teeth for a moment. "You are safe now."

The open doors beckoned not only him. Other guests stood taking a breath of the cooler air. "The ballroom is warm."

Thea leaned into him a bit. "It is rather cooler out here."

Dom looked around for some nook or place in the shadows where he could have her to himself, but at least half of the guests were out here. Damn. He escorted Thea to the end of the terrace, and still had no luck. Lanterns lit the gardens, which were also full of people.

He tested the latch on one of the parlor doors leading out

to the terrace. Finally. Yet when he pushed it open, he heard a muffled scream and closed it again. Everyone was conspiring against him.

Next to him Thea's shoulders shook with laughter. "I do not think we are meant to be alone at present." She stood on the tips of her toes, cupping his ear. "Do not forget, we have all night."

Clasping his arm around her waist, he held her against him and willed himself to relax. "You're right. I don't know why I'm so agitated."

"I do. You got to play knight in shining armor today and didn't even receive a proper kiss for your trouble." She placed her hand on his face, turning it toward her.

As he bent his head, the sounds of light giggles and a lower voice chuckling reached him. Damnation, more people.

Thea turned in Dom's arms. "Harry?"

A tall young man with black hair approached. Louisa on one arm and Charlotte on the other. "In the flesh." He grinned. "The ladies thought I'd find you out here somewhere."

"As well as most of the other guests," Thea replied tartly. "Dom, this is my scapegrace brother, Harry."

Dom held out his hand, which Harry grasped in a strong grip. "Pleasure to meet you. I thought you weren't due in until tomorrow sometime."

"After a couple of hours in the coach with the children"— he gave them a rueful look—"I hired a horse and decided to press on."

Thea stilled. "You didn't leave them, did you?"

"Good God, no. Mama would have had my head. I just couldn't stand the racket anymore. Not to mention Stephen insisting he be allowed to sit up with the coachman."

Charlotte laughed. "When my brothers and sisters were traveling to Town, Daisy, our Great Dane you know, tried to make friends with a pair of horses. Their tutor decided they would not spend the night on the road."

Harry laughed with her, then glanced at Thea. "I say, Dotty, is it really the thing for Dom to have his arm around you like that?"

"No," Thea said grudgingly, "I suppose not."

Recalled to the proprieties, Dom placed her hand on his arm instead.

Louisa gave Thea a sympathetic look. "We've come to fetch you. Your mothers are ready to leave."

Dom stifled his sigh of relief. That was the best news he'd had all night.

Chapter Twenty-Seven

Dotty sat on a chair as Polly unpinned her hair, before combing it. A prickling sensation ran across her shoulders. *Dom.* Lately she always knew when he was near. "Thank you. You may go to bed. It's late."

Her maid yawned. "I'll bid you good night then."

"Pleasant dreams."

The moment the door closed behind Polly, Dotty was in Dom's arms.

"Thea." His tongue traced her outer ear. "I've been waiting all day for this."

She slid her arms around his shoulders. "As have I."

"I need to tell you something." Dom's lips covered hers, kissing her as if he couldn't get enough. "I will never hide or run from you again. Ask me anything you wish. I love you with all my heart."

This was everything she had wanted with him and had been afraid she might not have. "I love you, too."

"I must tell you what I discovered today. . . ."

At the end of his tale about what his uncle had done, Dotty could have screamed with rage and sorrow for him. How much Dom had missed, not being allowed to be a child, or to have any of the adventures other young men had.

She couldn't give that back to him, but she would ensure he knew how much she loved him. "Let us go to bed."

He scooped her up into his arms. When they reached the corridor, he had to turn sideways. "I can walk."

"No, I've wanted to do this since this afternoon." He kicked open the door to his chamber. "There. Not so difficult."

Dotty winced at the noise it made bouncing against the wall. "Someone is bound to have heard that."

Dom set her down next to the bed, then shrugged. "What if they do? It's my room." He grinned wickedly. "Soon to be ours."

He untied her wrapper, pushing it over her shoulders. It fell silently to the floor.

"Somehow I do not think that reasoning will persuade our parents." She slid her hands under his banyan, spreading the halves apart. The heavy, embroidered silk made a whooshing sound as it joined her wrapper on the thick Turkey rug.

She caught her breath as Dom's lips covered hers. When he probed with his tongue, she opened to him, tasting him as he tasted her. Heat roiled within her as he fluttered kisses down to her breasts. Taking one tight bud into his mouth as he played with the other. Streaks of pleasure shot through her, coalescing in the apex of the thighs. She spread her legs, encouraging him, wanting him.

"I love you." His voice was deeper and huskier than ever before as he kissed his way down her body.

When he licked the pearl nestled in her mons, Dotty almost came off the bed. "Oh, Dom, I love you, too."

He entered her slowly, and though she willed herself not to tense, she was unable to stop.

"It won't hurt this time, sweetheart. I promise."

He took her in a searing kiss and the only thing she was aware of was their joining. No pain; only him moving slowly, stoking her to even higher levels of bliss. Her nipples rubbed against his chest, increasing her desire and need with each stroke. She wrapped her legs around him, urging him on. Then the pressure spiraled, like spun glass, and she gasped for air. "Dom, please, please."

His breath rasped as he chuckled. "Soon, my love."

"Ah, there." Her legs trembled as she flew apart into a thousand pieces, and he plunged so deeply into her, she could feel his release.

Dom rolled off her, pulling her with him, stroking her hair, raining soft kisses on her head and neck. Her heart pounded against her chest. This was how it would always be with them.

A cool night breeze blew over Dotty, chilling her.

Dom dug his way under the bedcover, pulling it back, and somehow maneuvering her underneath it.

Once he had tucked the sheets around her, he rose. "I had wine and food prepared for us this evening."

She raised a brow. "You were quite sure of yourself."

Leaning over, he gave her a swift kiss. "No. I was sure of us. It wasn't until today that I realized the depth of feeling I had for you and you had for me." He lifted a domed cover from a large tray that had been placed on his writing desk. "I'll have to give my new valet a raise."

He handed her one of the glasses of wine that had already been prepared.

"I agree." Warm now, she sat up against the pillows. "What else did he bring us?"

"A little of everything." Dom placed the tray on the bed before climbing carefully in on his side.

There were regular-sized sandwiches as well as smaller pieces of bread, some topped with ham, or beef, or cheese. "This is wonderful. You should indeed keep him." She took a bite of one of the small squares covered with beef, horseradish, and some sort of green. "This is delicious. What is his name?"

He devoured a ham sandwich. "Wigman. Paken found him."

"I like your butler as well."

Dom's hand stopped as he raised his glass. "We are going to be happy."

His voice wavered a bit, as if he needed reassurance, and she smiled, touching her glass to his. "We are going to be exceedingly happy."

Hours later, the early morning light filtered through a slit in the curtains, waking Dom. Thea's inky, black curls splayed over the pillows and down her body and his. He carefully moved her heavy locks aside to run his tongue over the edges of her ear. He was rewarded by a soft moan. They had made love deep into the night, but he was hard again. He'd never known a woman like his Thea. He hovered between waking her and allowing her to sleep a bit longer. Too soon, though, he would have to take her back to her room.

He lightly stroked her breasts before moving slowly down to the apex of the thighs.

"Yes." She sighed softly.

Thea arched up as he stroked her core. He understood now why his grandfather had refused to spend a night away from his grandmother. To think that he had almost resigned himself to a life without love.

"Now, Dom. I want you now."

A life without her. He plunged into her soft, wet heat.

Moments later, she cried out, and her convulsions gripped him. One last thrust and he joined her in paradise.

Dom knew he should take Thea back now, but he couldn't bring himself to release her. She was so snug and warm in his arms. Just a few more minutes and he would carry her to her chamber.

A light thump disrupted his thoughts, and a moment later Cyrille patted Dom's shoulder. If there was anything the cat was good at, it was finding him. "How did you get in here?" He glanced to the hidden door. "I must not have closed it all the way."

"Closed what?" Thea turned in his arms and smiled, her brilliant emerald green eyes still glazed with sleep. "Good morning."

Cyrille climbed over Dom, settling between him and Thea.

She stroked the cat from his head to the tip of his tail. How pitiful that Dom wished it was him she was petting.

"Good morning to you as well. I don't remember him being in here last night."

"He wasn't. I must have left the door open."

Thea's eyes widened. "Which means the other door is open as well." She sat up and rubbed her face. "I must go back to my chamber. If anyone sees . . ."

"Sorry, Cyrille." He dislodged the cat. "Let me get my dressing gown and your wrapper."

"Where do you think this leads?" a high girlish voice asked.

"Probably to a hidden room," a second voice answered. "To think Dotty gets to live in a house with secret passages."

"Henny is going to be green with envy that we found it."

"I wonder if anyone else knows it's here."

"As dirty as it is, I doubt it."

Dom could almost see a small nose wrinkle in disgust. He quickly donned his banyan, and leaned over to whisper to Thea, "Your brother and sister, I take it?"

"Naturally, who else? It's a good thing they cannot see me here."

"I'll take them out to the corridor and promise to show them the secret stairs in the library. That will give you time to go back to your room." He tossed Thea's wrapper to her and closed the bed hangings. "I'll see you at breakfast."

He turned toward the door just as it swung open and two

dark-haired children emerged. He put his hands on his hips. A little stern intimidation should set them right. "Good morning. Do you always make a point of searching the houses you're visiting?"

The girl glanced up at him and beamed. "You must be Lord Merton."

Whatever response he had been expecting, it wasn't that. "I am."

"I like your house."

The boy smiled and stuck out his hand. "I'm Stephen, this is Martha, and I do, too. Like your house I mean. Do you have any other hidden passages?"

That hadn't gone as planned. He heard a sound that reminded him of someone laughing.

Stephen's eyes grew round. "What was that?"

Deuce take it, Thea was going to give herself away. "The cat."

As if he'd been shoved from behind, Cyrille suddenly appeared from the bed hangings. Dom caught Martha as she stepped forward. "He can go into the corridor with you." He picked up Cyrille before opening the main door to his chamber. "What are you two doing up and around?"

"We were looking for Dotty," Stephen replied.

Martha nodded. "She's always up early, but her maid said she'd see us at breakfast."

Casting a glance back to the bed, Dom stepped out of his room and closed the door. "Go find your nursemaids." He escorted the pair to the stairs leading to the schoolroom floor. "If you wish to break your fast in the breakfast room with your sister, you must be properly dressed."

The children scampered up the stairs, and he turned back to his dressing room. Fortunately, Wigman was ready for him.

Less than a half hour later, he walked into the breakfast room to find Thea with the children. She was cutting a piece of ham into pieces for her sister.

Pausing at the door, he took in the scene, and decided he liked it. Although in his vision Thea was helping their child.

She glanced at him and grinned. "Good morning. Did you sleep well?"

Minx. Two could play this game. "I did. Very well, indeed. There is something about having company that causes me to get more rest."

Her eyes danced wickedly. "Ah, I take it Cyrille spent the night with you?"

Martha looked up. "He's a pretty cat, but he makes strange noises."

Thea widened her eyes at her sister. "Does he indeed? What sort of noises?"

"This morning he laughed."

Struggling to keep a straight face, Dom glanced at Thea. "If you think that is odd, you should have heard him moan—"

"If that is the case," she said primly, "you might wish to call the doctor."

"Hmm." He filled his plate. "I think you may be right. If things keep on the way they are, a doctor will most definitely be required for a consultation." He took the seat on the other side of her. "I do not believe I have ever been so hungry."

"That is what Dotty said before you came in." Martha helped herself to a piece of ham. "I think you are both being silly."

He and Thea exchanged a glance. "There is nothing wrong with being silly."

Or happy, or in love.

Not long after the rest of Dotty's family joined them for breakfast, Paken entered the room. "My lord, miss. There is a gentleman here to see you."

Dom raised a brow.

"About Master Tom."

She started to scoot her chair back when a footman sprang to assist her. "Show him into the study, Paken. His lordship and I will be there directly."

Dom rose and joined her. "Who do you think it could be?"

"I don't know." She shook her head. Who indeed? "It was very strange of Paken not to have mentioned his name."

Another footman hurried up to them holding a calling card. "Mr. Paken said you'd want this, my lord."

Dom took it, holding it so she could see as well. "Major Robert Cavanaugh. Tom's father. I thought he wasn't due back for months."

"Bring tea and toast, please," she said to the footman. "I don't know if he's broken his fast yet." Once the footman had gone, she turned to Dom. "He must be worried sick."

They arrived to find a tall man dressed in the distinctive green uniform of the 95th Rifles pacing the room. When he saw them he bowed. "Lord Merton?"

Dom held out his hand. "Yes, this is Miss Stern, soon to be Lady Merton. You must be Major Cavanaugh. Let me assure you that Tom is fine. He is at my cousin's house on Berkeley Square for the moment."

"Thank God." Major Cavanaugh ran his hands over his face. "Thank God he's safe. I had a message that my wife was murdered, but that you'd found my son. But how?"

"Major"—Dotty sank onto the small sofa near the fireplace—"please have a seat. Tea will be here in just a moment."

He perched on the edge of the sofa opposite her. Dom stood behind her, his hands on her shoulders.

"We are extremely happy to see you," Dom said. "Apparently, your wife made Tom memorize your family details. I've attempted, without luck, to contact your family."

"Yes." His voice broke, and he stopped for a moment. "With all the traveling we did, she was convinced he might someday . . . That is the reason I was called back from my mission. My older brother died, and my father is not in good health. He wasn't well before I left, and the death has taken its toll. I must post to Lincolnshire as soon as may be, but first"—he sucked in a breath—"can you tell me what happened to my wife?"

Dotty told him about meeting Tom and what they discovered afterward. When the tea arrived, she poured a cup and added a little extra sugar.

The major took it from her. "Thank you." He took a sip, then set it down. "We go off and fight for our country"—his voice cracked—"expecting our families to be safe. I never even suspected . . ."

He appeared as if he needed time alone. "Major, Lord Merton and I have a few things to attend to. If you'd like, you may remain here for a while. When we are finished, we shall take you to see Tom."

"Thank you. You're very kind."

Dotty rose, signaling him to remain seated. Once they were out of the study and had closed the door, tears sprang to her eyes. "I need some fresh air. Walk with me?"

Dom held her in his arms. "Whatever you want, my love." He took her to a parlor in the back of the house that led to the terrace. "I can't imagine what he's going through. Losing his wife like that."

"Senseless greed on the part of Mrs. White and the others." She forced her thoughts from the major to the gardens. Anything to keep her mind busy. "I think I would like new plantings for next year."

Dom was quiet for a moment. "It could probably use some refurbishing. Perhaps some statuary as well."

She nodded briskly, glad he was not making her discuss Tom's situation. "Yes, maybe an arbor or two." She wiped a lone tear that had leaked out. "Oh, this isn't working very well at all."

"No, I didn't suppose it would. Shall I just hold you?"

"Yes, I think that would be best."

They stood in full view of the house while Dotty hugged him as hard as she could. All the time they'd dealt with the ladies and Tom, she had concentrated on making it all better. Now with the major's grief so new and raw, she had trouble holding back her own tears. Thank the Lord she had Dom and he understood. Long moments later, she said, "I'm all right now. We should send a note to Matt and Grace. Tom will be excited to see his father again."

At least she could give the major his son.

Chapter Twenty-Eight

During the walk to Stanwood House, Thea and Dom focused their conversation on what Tom had been doing since coming to live at Merton House. She seemed to need to emphasize the happier news, and he hoped the major would agree.

"It was his drawing that enabled me to find Miss Stern when she'd been abducted." Dom placed his hand over hers. "That information must, of course, be kept among ourselves."

"Naturally," Major Cavanaugh responded. "I can't tell you how thankful I am that you agreed to take him in, my lord."

"Your gratitude should be directed to Miss Stern. She saw immediately what needed to be done." Dom suppressed the sick feeling in the pit of his stomach. If he'd had his way, the result didn't bear thinking of.

The major glanced at Thea. "Thank you. My lord, I'll be happy to repay you for the expenses you've incurred."

"Don't think of it. I've liked having the boy around." Dom waited for his uncle's voice to invade his thoughts, but it didn't happen. Relief filled him. Perhaps he would finally be able to live his own life.

The door to Stanwood House opened as they climbed the stairs.

"My lord, miss," Grace's butler, Royston, bowed regally. "Lord and Lady Worthington are in her ladyship's study. If you will follow me."

Dom bent to whisper in Thea's ear, "It's deuced aggravating when an earl's butler is more stately than a marquis's."

The corner of her lips canted up. "You were high enough in the instep without Paken being so as well."

"Well, you might have a point there."

The door to the study opened and Royston announced them. Matt and Grace came forward to greet them. "Please have a seat." She motioned to the sofas next to the fireplace. We wanted to speak to you before calling Tom down."

The ladies gracefully sank onto the larger sofa. Dom sat in the leather chair closest to Thea, and Matt took the place on the other side of Grace. The major sat opposite them. Tea arrived almost immediately.

Before long, Grace said, "I have been informed that you have recently arrived back in the country. What are your plans, Major?"

Major Cavanaugh took a sip of tea. "My kit and batman are at the Horse Guards. It is not possible for me to have Tom there, and I must post to Lincolnshire as soon as possible."

Grace nodded. "We heard of your brother's death. You have my sympathies."

Thea leaned forward slightly. "Would you consider staying at Merton House until you depart and allowing Tom to remain with us until your business is finished?"

Cavanaugh blinked as if he couldn't believe what he was hearing. "I suppose that would be better then dragging Tom around until I'm settled," he said slowly. "However, I don't like to impose."

"No imposition at all." Dom grinned. The day after tomorrow, he and Thea would begin their wedding trip. "My in-laws are remaining in Town for another week or more so that my brothers- and sisters-in-law can see the sights. The two youngest are close to Tom's age."

"Our brothers and sisters," Grace said, "will take a short holiday from classes to go around with them."

Dom was sure he'd paled at the thought of all those children loose in London together.

Matt's lips twisted into a wry smile as he glanced at Dom. "My thoughts exactly. I'll have every footman in my service out with them."

After glancing from one to the other, Major Cavanaugh asked, "If there is a problem, perhaps I should take Tom with me."

"Oh, there is no problem," Grace assured him. "Worthington is simply not yet used to the logistics involved. Between us we have eleven children. Although two are making their come out and one is at Eton."

The color seeped from the major's tanned face.

"Don't worry," Thea said. "They'll be fine. Lady Worthington is used to it all. It will be much more fun for Tom than being dragged around the countryside without even a nursemaid."

Grace rose, walked to the bell pull, and tugged. A footman stuck his head around the door. "My lady?"

"Please have the children as well as Miss Tallerton and Mr. Winters attend me. We have a visitor to see Master Tom."

"Yes, my lady."

Not long afterward, the sound of stampeding horses could be heard throughout the house.

"What the dev . . . I mean," Cavanaugh said, "what is that noise?"

Worthington chuckled as the door burst open, and eight children all under the age of fifteen piled into the study.

"Papa!" Tom launched himself at his father.

"Tom, Tom, my boy." Cavanaugh caught the child to him. "By God, I've missed you."

"I've missed you, too."

Mary, the youngest, tugged on the major's jacket. "Are you going to take Tom away from us?"

Cavanaugh looked at the children, then down at Mary and smiled for the first time that day. "Not quite yet I think."

"That's good." Mary nodded seriously. "We have become quite fond of him and should like to keep him for a while longer."

"Papa, Papa." Tom leaned back in his father's arms. "I've got so much to tell you."

Grace rose. "When you are ready, Major Cavanaugh, we will meet you in the morning room. Tom knows the way."

She hustled everyone out the door and into the main hall. "That went well, don't you think?"

"I do." Thea slid her arm around Dom. "Why did you have all the children and their teachers come in?"

"I wanted them to see Tom's reaction to his father. As Mary said, they have become quite fond of him, and it was necessary for them to see he would be happy with his father."

"That makes sense." Thea nodded thoughtfully. "Now we just have the wedding to get through."

Dom put his arm around Thea, tugging her closer. The wedding, the wedding night, the honeymoon, and the rest of their lives.

Before dawn the next morning, Dotty woke in Dom's arms. This would be the last time she had to sneak from his chamber back to her own. In only a few hours, this would be where she legally belonged. She moved carefully to slide out of his arms and not wake him, when one of them clamped down on her.

"Where are you going?" He fluttered kisses on her neck.

"I must go to my room." She tilted it to give him better

access, then sighed. "Unless I miss my guess, it is already after six o'clock and our wedding is at nine."

"Who was the idiot," he growled, "that set the time so early?"

"You were, my love. In one of your lord of the manor moments."

He flopped back against the pillows. "Go then. Before I start something that will make you late."

She turned to him. "Not long now." Dom drew her down for a kiss. "No, no, no. I must leave."

Flinging his hands up, he scowled. "Soon."

"Yes, soon."

Dotty made it back to her chamber just as her maid entered. "Good thing you're back, miss. Her ladyship's already up and asking for you. The tub will be here in a few moments."

She sat at the dressing table for Polly to comb out her hair. "Why is she awake so early?"

"Don't know. Excited about the ceremony, I guess."

A knock came on the door and two footmen carried in a copper tub. "The water's coming now," one of them said.

Once her bath was ready, Dotty sank into the hot water, wanting nothing more than to stay there for a while. Once she had washed, breakfast was delivered on a tray and set up in the small adjoining parlor. "This is too much for me."

"Your mother is joining you."

As if she'd heard her name, Mama entered the chamber. "Good morning, my dear. I feel as if we have not had any time together at all. Though I am very glad you and Dominic are getting along so well, and I have greatly enjoyed the time I've spent with Eunice."

Dotty poured tea, handed one cup to her mother, before fixing her own. She took a sip, savoring the smooth taste. One of the first things she'd done was to order her own blend. "She is everything I could want in a mother in-law."

Mama took a bite of toast and chewed, while Dotty sliced a piece of beef. She was so hungry.

"Dorothea, since we haven't had a chance to talk before now"—Mama turned bright red—"I . . . well, I suppose I should"—she swallowed—"speak to you about what goes on between a man and a woman."

Oh dear. Poor Mama was going to have apoplexy before she got it all out.

Suddenly she brightened and asked almost hopefully, "You haven't anticipated your vows, have you?"

Dotty sputtered, grabbing the serviette to cover her mouth. "Mama!"

Her face fell. "No, I didn't suppose you'd have had an opportunity. Not with all of us between your chamber and his." She sighed. "I better get on with this—"

"There is no need," Dotty interrupted. Better to stop this conversation now before her mother expired of embarrassment. "If you remember last year when Papa told Mr. Brown he had to marry?" Mama nodded. "I'd wondered how anyone could get in such a fix, so I asked his wife and she told me everything."

"Oh good." Mama breathed a sigh of relief. "It is not that it isn't nice, I just do not like to discuss such personal things. Perhaps when your sisters are ready to come out, you could . . ."

"Yes, I'll be happy to. Now, let us enjoy our breakfast."

They'd just finished, when Dotty glanced at the mantel clock. "Stay here if you wish, I must dress."

Mama rose. "I brought you something that has been passed down through the family. I'll fetch it now."

"Thank you, Mama." Dotty bussed her mother's cheek, then went back into her room.

"I was just going to get you." Polly's arms were full as she stepped out of the dressing room.

By the time her maid was done, Dotty's hair was styled in an elaborate arrangement of curls and braids.

Mama brought a package of sapphire and pearl hairpins. "These will work perfectly. It might be a bit early in the day, but it is your wedding."

Polly held the gown of deep turquoise with silver netting over Dotty's head. "Oh dear, maybe I should have put this on you first. Let's not muss your hair."

Once the gown was in place and fastened, Lady Merton knocked on the door. "I had the rest of the Vivers jewels sent to your dressing room, but I thought this"—she held up a simple necklace made of sapphires—"would be perfect with your gown."

Tears pricked Dotty's eyes. "It's perfect, thank you."

"Hmm," Mama mused. "We have old, blue, and borrowed, but we're missing new."

"My lady," Polly called from the door. "I think we've got it! This is from his lordship."

Dotty took the rectangular box, opened it, and almost laughed. "More sapphires. A bracelet." She took the jewelry out and held it up. "It's beautiful, but how did he know?"

"Your coloring is perfect for them," Lady Merton responded.

"Yes, but he could have given them to me anytime."

"Well"—Polly smiled sheepishly—"it could be because when Mr. Wigman asked the color of your gown, I told him."

Dotty grinned. "I hope you made him work for the information."

"Oh I did, miss." Her maid blushed. "You can be sure of that."

Another knock came on the door. Polly opened it and Papa strolled in. "I've been told it's time to get you to the church, missy. Worthington took your bridegroom off about a quarter hour ago. I just got a message telling me to hurry."

Polly placed a small bonnet made mostly of ribbons and netting on Dotty's head. "There you are, miss. While you're gone, I'll get the rest of your things and take them to the other chamber."

Tears misted Dotty's eyes. By the time she returned she'd be Dom's wife. She'd never been happier.

"Where is she?" Dom paced on the pavement in front of the side door to St. George's. The church was already full. He had picked nine o'clock so that they would not have everyone and their brother here gawking at them. Wasn't it enough that they would all be at the wedding breakfast?

Matt raised a brow. "Thinking she's jilted you?"

Less than three weeks ago, Dom wouldn't have understood his cousin's joke. Then he remembered Fotherby. "No. Thea is safe. She'll be here. It is not like her to be late."

Matt shoved his pocket watch under Dom's nose. "It's not nine o'clock yet."

"Have you looked in there?" He pointed to the church. "Why the devil are there so many people?"

Matt cracked a laugh. "They are not so many. It's mostly the children."

Heaving a sigh, Dom stopped pacing. It had seemed like more than that. "Did you go through this?"

"No, we had a small wedding." His cousin smiled. "Just the children, a cousin or two, and sundry other relatives."

In other words, half of London. "Men should be warned." Good Lord. Was he actually growling, "This must be the most nerve-wracking thing I've ever gone through."

"At least you have a honeymoon to look forward to."

Dom glanced away from the street to his cousin. He'd forgotten Matt had not had any time alone at all with Grace, and he was stuck chaperoning for the Season. "I'll tell you what. After Thea and I return to Merton, send the children to us."

Matt was silent for a few moments. "You're serious?"

"Yes, of course I am. We've plenty to keep them busy.

I'm sure Thea will enjoy being with Charlotte and Louisa, if they're not married by then." Dom smiled. "It's the least I can do. After all, if you hadn't been so dead set against me marrying Thea, I might have let her cry off."

"I don't believe it. Once a woman gets to you, it's impossible to let go."

"That was part of the problem. Thea scared me to death. She was exactly what I wasn't looking for." Yet she was everything he needed.

"You can stop worrying. They have arrived."

His large dark green lacquered landau pulled to a stop. Sir Henry alighted before handing Thea down.

The wind rushed out of Dom as if he'd been punched in the stomach. How did she become more beautiful every time he saw her? His valet had been right. The sapphires were perfect. He reached out, took her hand, and stared.

A light blush rose in Thea's cheeks as she smiled at him.

"Come on now." The duchess's voice ripped him out of his daydream. "You gentlemen are all the same. Can't wait for your bride to arrive, then you do nothing to the point. We've got a wedding to make happen, guests arriving in less than an hour, and you're standing here mooning." She prodded him on his back with her cane. "Let's go."

"Yes, Grandmamma."

"Impertinent jackanapes."

He resisted when her father took Thea's hand from his.

"Don't worry," Sir Henry joked. "I'm going to give it right back. Have to do this properly or I'll never hear the end of it." He lowered his brows. "She'll be yours in a few minutes, young man. Take care of her or you'll answer to me."

The tension he'd felt since she'd left him this morning faded away. "I will." Dom grinned. "And I am positive she'll tell me if I make a mistake."

Sir Henry placed Thea's hand on his arm. "Welcome to the family, son."

Dom tried to swallow past the lump in his throat as they

walked into the church. Matt had been right; only their families and a few friends were present.

Several minutes later, Sir Henry placed Thea's hand in Dom's. He captured her gaze when he said his vows to her. Thea's calm never seemed to waiver. In a clear, strong voice she promised to take him as her husband.

The vicar, a younger man, grinned as he pronounced them man and wife. "I wish you both a long and happy life together."

As soon as they signed the register, it was as if some spell had been broken. The children's voices rose and they were engulfed in hugs and kisses.

"Well, Vicar," Matt said, "you're getting better at this."

The man flushed. "I've had some practice now."

Dom glanced at his cousin. "He's the same one who married you?"

"Yes, Grace and I were his first. By the time he's done with all of us, he'll be the most experienced clergyman in London."

"My lord, I think we should go home." Thea smiled up at him.

"As you wish, my lady."

When they got to the carriage, he handed her up. "Are the rest of them coming?"

"No, Matt arranged for other coaches. We have a few moments to ourselves."

"In that case"—he nuzzled her ear, and was gratified when her pulse quickened—"I shall tell you how I plan to remove this delightful gown from your equally delightful body."

Her smile lit her face, and her voice was a siren's call. "You perceive me all ears, my lord."

Still gowned in their new clothing, Tom, along with Mary, Theo, and Philip crowded at the schoolroom window of Merton House overlooking Grosvenor Square. Two rough-looking men stood watching the house. It was the first time Tom had seen them since Dotty and Lord Merton had saved him. At first he'd been afraid, but now, with his father, and Matt, and his lordship, he knew no one could hurt him again.

"Are you sure that's them?" Theo asked.

"Yes." Tom nodded. "I'll never forget."

Philip, the oldest at eight years, narrowed his eyes. "We'd better tell someone. You stay here and watch. I'll send for help."

Tom's nursemaid, Sally, joined them. "Keep back a ways from the window so they can't see you."

Not long afterward, some of the grooms entered the square one and two at a time, talking and walking slowly as if they had nothing else to do. His father and Matt were with them. Soon the two men were surrounded, but they hadn't seemed to notice. Matt gave a signal and the grooms grabbed one of the men and Papa smashed his fist into the other man's face.

"That was a perfect flush hit," Philip exclaimed. "Your father has good science."

"Come on with you now." Sally hustled them away from the window after the grooms took the men away. "There's nothing more to see here, and Cook's got treats for you in the breakfast room."

Mary took Tom's hand in hers, squeezing it. "Do you feel better now?"

"Yes. I feel a lot better. Thank you."

Dotty strolled out to the terrace with Dom. Louisa, Charlotte, Meg Featherington, and Elizabeth Turley sat around a table.

"Sweetheart." He brushed his lips across hers. "Don't be too long, will you?"

"No. I'm as anxious to leave as you are."

Saying if they remained at Merton House, they'd never get away in good time in the morning, Grandmamma had reserved a suite of rooms for them this evening at the Pulteney.

A footman brought a chair and a fresh bottle of champagne to the table. Once he'd finished pouring, he bowed to Dotty. "My lady. May I say we are all very happy to have you here."

"Thank you, George. I am glad as well." Ever since she returned from church this morning the servants had made a point of welcoming her as their new mistress.

Her friends smiled as she took her seat.

"Who would have guessed," Meg said, grinning, "that Lord Merton would turn out so well?"

"Not me." Louisa took a sip of champagne. "Even *I* like him now."

"How do you like being married?" Charlotte asked.

"It has only been a few hours, but so far, it's everything I thought it would be."

Elizabeth sighed.

"Don't tell me you still wish you'd married him?" Meg asked.

"No, not at all." Elizabeth stopped playing with her glass and took a drink. "It wouldn't have done. Dotty is perfect for him. I would merely like to be married."

Suddenly, Dotty felt much older than the other ladies. Could being wed do that to one? "You will be. The right gentleman will come along."

"At the beginning of the Season," Charlotte said, "Lady Evesham told me to wait for the right gentleman."

"True." Louisa tilted her head to one side. "Lady Rutherford said the same to me, and look at Grace. Matt was the only one she ever loved."

Charlotte raised her glass. "Here is to all of us marrying our heart's desire."

Meg poked Elizabeth. "And no settling for anything less."

"Very well." She joined the toast. "To our heart's desire, wherever or whomever he may be."

Beautiful, innocent, and managing,
Lady Louisa Vivers is halfway through her first Season,
and she still has not met the gentleman she wishes to wed,
until Gideon, Duke of Rothwell shows up in her brother's
study that is. Morning rides, and evening waltzes
have her convinced he is the one. After their first kiss,
when another lady claims the duke is going to marry her,
Louisa immediately announces they are betrothed.
What she doesn't know is that he can't afford
to wed anyone at the moment . . .

Please turn the page for an exciting sneak peek of
Ella Quinn's next Worthington historical romance,

IT STARTED WITH A KISS,

coming in April 2017
wherever print and eBooks are sold!

Early morning, Hyde Park, May 1815

Dawn had broken only a few minutes before, but a light fog clouded the air making the sun look like a small yellow ball. Gideon, Duke of Rothwell was certain he was the only rider at this hour of the morning. Needing the calm a hard ride gave him, he thundered down the empty carriage way. Suddenly, from out of nowhere, a dark bay burst through the mist disturbing his solitude. Yet it was the massive dog, almost the size of a pony, keeping pace with the horse that caught his notice.

What the devil?

Faisu, his black Murgese stallion, pranced nervously as Gideon brought him to a halt. "Easy, boy. We don't need that beast tangling with you. He could sever your hamstrings in an instant."

A moment later, a twist of long, dark hair pulled loose from under the rider's hat, riveting his attention on the woman. By the time she was even with him, he'd taken in the neat figure incased in a dark blue riding habit, and her excellent seat.

She glanced over, slowing her horse for a bare moment

as she passed him. Her cheeks were pink from the cool air and a smile graced her lush rose lips. Their gazes collided and held. As if they were the only two people on earth. In that second, Gideon felt as if he would tumble into the vivid blue of the rider's eyes.

She cannot be real.

He blinked and she was gone. He might have dreamed her except that a few seconds later, a groom raced by, clearly attempting to catch up with his mistress.

For a moment he was tempted to follow as well. He wanted to follow her, but it wouldn't do him any good. She was obviously a lady, and even if he could obtain an introduction, and their relations proceeded satisfactorily, he was not yet in a position to wed.

It was pure fantasy to think of marriage in conjunction with a woman he'd seen in passing. Still, he would have liked to have been able to dream.

Blast Father! If he was still alive, I'd shake some sense back into him.

But the old duke had been in the ground for over three months when Gideon had returned from Canada. Now all he could do was pick up the pieces his father had left behind.

"Come on, boy." Shaking the blue-eyed image from his mind he urged Faisu to a trot. "It's time to go back. As long as I am here, I may as well gather information, and settle some accounts."

He should never have left. The waste was his fault. Had he stayed home, none of the damage would have occurred. What was the old saying about reaping what one sowed? Well, it was now his job, his alone, to restore the dukedom's holdings to what they had been only a few years ago, before he'd left for the colonies and played at being a backwoods man. Unfortunately, those experiences would not help him bring back and modernize his holdings.

Fifteen minutes later, as he rode up to the stables in the

mews behind his town house, he surveyed the building, searching for any signs that it would soon need to be repaired. When he'd returned from Canada, his first shock was discovering his father had died. A letter had been sent, but not arrived before he left the colonies. The second shock was the poor condition of the estates. It baffled him that the once prosperous properties could fall into such disrepair in such a short period of time. If only he knew what had occurred to make his father neglect his holdings when he'd prided himself on them in the past. To make it more baffling, no one at Rothwell Abbey could explain, to Gideon's satisfaction, what had occurred to change his father.

If only he had remained at home where he belonged instead of hieing off across the ocean. This was a lesson not to allow others to tend to his responsibilities.

He really did not have time for this bolt to Town, but his cousin, the Marquis of Bentley had written begging for Gideon's help, and here he was.

"Yr Grace." Barnes, his stable master, strode quickly to Faisu's head taking hold of the harness. "I've got him now."

"How is the roof?" Gideon asked as he swung off the horse. In the short time he'd been home, he had learned to ask. No one, it seemed, wanted to volunteer information. "I want the truth. It is much easier to fix a small leak than the damage it can do."

"Dry so far, Yr Grace. I'll keep an eye out. The glazing's comin' off from around some of the windows."

If that was the worst of it, Gideon would count himself lucky. It would take time and patience to make the repairs on the buildings that had been neglected, but he'd be damned if he'd allow anything else to fall into disorder. "Make arrangements to have them repaired."

"Yes, Yr Grace. Going to be here long?" the man asked, a hopeful look on his weather-beaten face.

"A few weeks, perhaps less. There is a deal to do at Rothwell and some of the other estates."

"Bad doings all of this." The older man tapped the side of his nose. "I'll make sure the town coach is in good order then. Won't do to have it break down when you need it. Or lookin' shabby."

"If it's the same one I remember, it probably needs to be replaced." Gideon's tone was even grimmer than he felt which was quite grim enough.

"It's got another couple o' years yet." The stable master started to lead Faisu into his stall and stopped. "Leave it to old Barnes."

"Thank you." Gideon hoped he'd conveyed the gratitude he had for his old retainers. They truly were gems. Without their loyalty and patience, his life and the lives of his family would be much more difficult.

"Now that yer here, what you planning on doing with the new carriages the old duke ordered from Hatchett's?"

"New carriages?" He fought to keep his jaw from dropping. What the deuce had his father been thinking? Although, that bit of unnecessary extravagance went along with the other information he was slowly piecing together about the old duke's recent behavior. Spending that left little with which to maintain the estates.

"Got a landau and a high perched phaeton—"

"The devil you say." His father wouldn't have seen seventy again. "What was he going to do with a phaeton?"

Barnes flushed. "I think it was fer that high-flyer he took up with."

Gideon's breath stopped. His parents had been the most devoted couple he knew. What had happened to make his father change so drastically? And why in God's name had no one written to Gideon asking him to return home?

Damn his eyes! It needed only that.

Frustration coursed through him. He raked his fingers

through his hair, knocking off his hat in the process. Yet, somehow, this fit the fractured story he'd heard, or rather had not heard, about Father's death. It was probably the reason Mama had been so tight lipped. No one had or would explain what exactly had happened to make the duke ignore his holdings as he had. Thank God, most of the assets were entailed or Gideon might have found them mortgaged to the hilt at best or sold. "Do you happen to know who this barque of frailty was?"

"Her maid called her Mrs. Rosemund Petrie." Barnes spit as he said the name. "Like she was royalty and should be treated as such. Nothin' more than a whore, if you ask me."

His stable master might not know much about the woman, but Gideon would make sure he found out not only exactly who the female was, but what, if anything, he could recover from her. Then a thought he did not want to consider occurred to him. "I was told he died in Town."

Barnes, picked up Gideon's hat where it had fallen, running his hand around the brim, for a moment before saying, "Died in bed, he did. With her."

"Here?" He eyed the older man sharply. "At Rothwell House?"

Not looking up, the stable master nodded slowly.

"For the love of Jove! What had Father been thinking?"

"Don't no one know that, Yr Grace," Barnes said quickly, as if he would be blamed for the old duke's indiscretions. "I got her out of there with no one the wiser . . . except'n fer two of the grooms and Mr. Fredricks. Those that works here know which side their bread is buttered on. Won't no one be carrying tales." He made an "X" over his heart. "Strike my name from my ma's Bible if they do. Mrs. Boyle even had the mattress changed out. Said it was full of wickedness."

Gideon didn't think that a mattress could have a wicked nature, but he was just as glad for the new one. He would likewise swear that his mother had a good idea where her husband had been when he'd gone to his Maker. "I am sure you did everything necessary."

"Yes, Yer Grace. I'll get them windows fixed. What about that Mrs. Petrie's horses and carriage she's got here?"

He speared Barnes with a hard look. "I would greatly appreciate it if you would tell me everything at one time. How many horses, carriages, and whatnot? Did my father buy them, or were they hers before he became involved with her? Please feel free to add any other information you believe necessary as well."

The stable master rubbed his nose, as he thought. Finally, Barnes replied, "The old duke bought her a nice Arabian hack, and two dark bay high-steppers for the phaeton he bought her a couple o' years ago—"

"Matched?" Gideon could barely spit out the word.

The servant looked at him as if he'd gone mad. "Wouldn't have expected anything else from His Grace, would you? Now if I can finish, Yer Grace?"

Clenching his jaw, he gave a curt nod. Not that it mattered how much more there was. It would all be sold as soon as possible. He calculated the costs of the cattle alone to be at least three thousand pounds. Father had never stinted on horseflesh. Gideon turned his attention back to Barnes who was still reciting his father's purchases over the past three years.

"Sell it all."

"I was about to get to the saddles and other tack," the older man said in an aggrieved tone.

"Keep the horses I brought with me and whatever you think best for the town coach. The rest goes."

"What about the curricle. Won't get much fer it, and you might need it."

He could use a sporting carriage. It would certainly save money in hackneys. "Very well. I'll keep it, but contact Tattersalls and whoever else you need to about the carriages and other items." Barnes opened his mouth again. "Keep anything you think I shall require."

"Thank ye, Yer Grace."

Stanwood House, Mayfair

"Measles?" Lady Louisa Vivers exclaimed. "All three of them?"

Excited to tell someone about the gentleman she'd seen in the Park, she had gone directly to the parlor she shared with her friend and new sister, Lady Charlotte Carpenter.

Just before the Season began in earnest, Matt Worthington, Louisa's brother had married Lady Grace Carpenter. Grace had guardianship of her seven brothers and sisters. The marriage had given Louisa a total of ten brothers and sisters, including her own three sisters. Sometime this coming winter, the number of children would increase to twelve with the arrival of Matt and Grace's first child. The girls were ecstatic to be aunts. Even the boys were excited.

However, as Louisa opened her mouth to speak, Charlotte told her of the doctor's diagnosis. Obviously, that news took precedence over Louisa's.

"Yes," Charlotte replied. "Theo, Mary, and Philip. According to Cousin Jane and the information your mama left for Grace, the others, including Grace and Matt have already had them."

"Will that put off Grace and Matt's trip to Worthington?" The addition of so many family members meant that not only Worthington House, but the Worthington main estate must undergo extensive renovations in order to accommodate everyone. In fact, the only one of her brothers and sisters not residing at present in the Carpenter town home, Stanwood House, was Charlie, Earl of Stanwood, who was at Eton. Even Louisa's mother and her new husband, Richard, Viscount Wolverton, would stay at Stanwood

House for the rest of the Season while Worthington House was being renovated. Well, after they returned from their wedding trip to Richard's estate in Kent, of course. Fortunately, the two houses were directly across Berkeley Square from each other.

"I think they must go." Charlotte said. Sitting at the desk, she tapped the feather end of the quill against her cheek. "Renovations must be started in the schoolroom there if we are all going to reside at your family's estate after the Season."

Louisa and her sister were almost half-way through their first Season. This new development certainly complicated things.

Chewing her bottom lip she began to mentally adjust her plans to account for the new development. "Hmm, I suppose we should write notes excusing ourselves from the entertainments we had planned to attend." She glanced at the writing table. "What a bother. Why did the children have to choose now to fall ill?"

Charlotte let out a peal of laughter, lightening the mood. "That is almost exactly what Matt said."

Louisa grinned. "What did Grace say?"

"She told him, he should ask and see what the children said. Grace is making arrangements for our chaperonage in the event he still wishes to make the trip." Charlotte heaved a sigh. "The poor things. I remember having the measles. The worst part was when I began to feel well again and was still not allowed to leave the sick room. I wish Charlie was here to help entertain them. I shall, of course, help with nursing."

"As shall I." Louisa picked up her pocketbook from the desk. "We should make a schedule that will allow us to attend our entertainments and help care for the children."

She ducked as Charlotte threw a small embroidered pillow at her. "You and your schedules."

"How else do you plan to accomplish our marriages? By the by, how is it going with Harrington?"

Charlotte's lips formed a moue. "Not as I wish it to. He appears to think he has jumped all his hurdles. Consequently, he has gone off to his estates for a week." She raised a brow. "I can only imagine he thinks me a sure thing."

"That won't do at all." Louisa frowned. Charlotte deserved to be treated better. "If he ignores you now, imagine what he would be like as a husband."

"My thoughts exactly." Charlotte agreed. "I do like him, yet I shall not be taken for granted. I think I must strike him as a potential husband."

"I cannot say that I blame you." Louisa wandered to the table next to one of the sofas and placed her hand on the cold teapot. "Will you ring for another pot while I change?" Charlotte nodded absently. "I have finally decided what to do about Bentley"—Louisa gave her friend a wicked grin—"You must help me find a match for him."

Edmond, Marquis of Bentley heir to the Duke of Covington had been one of the first gentlemen Louisa had met this Season, and despite the hints she had dropped, her most persistent suitor. Nothing she had done thus far had convinced him that they were not suited.

Her sister went off into whoops. Several moments later she pulled out her handkerchief and wiped her eyes. "That is the best idea you have had yet. If he transfers his affections to another lady, you will have managed to rid yourself of him without hurting his feelings."

"Indeed. The only problem is who. She must be intelligent enough to be a duchess, managing enough to ensure Bentley performs his duties, and possess a great deal of patience in order to deal with his dithering." Louisa could not help but to grimace. "Something I do not have in abundance."

"More patience than you?" Charlotte's tone was serious,

but the corners of her lips twitched. "That does sound like an almost impossible combination. She would have to be a perfect paragon."

Ignoring her sister's facetious comment, Louisa said, "If we are still attending the ball this evening, we can begin searching for her." She paused for a moment, her fingers on the door latch. "It will not be an easy task, yet I am sure we will succeed. I'll see you in a few minutes."

"We are going to the ball," Charlotte called after Louisa. "Will you do me a favor and tell Matt? I was about to change my shoes, but you are already dressed."

Their brother continued to use his study at Worthington House, saying that even with the construction it was quieter than Stanwood House.

"And smelling of the stables. Hold off on the tea, and I shall go straightaway." Making her way down the stairs, Louisa strode out of the house, and crossed Berkeley Square.